# JAKE THE HORSE THIEF

A Story of the Jews Who Were Left Behind

ROBERT STEINBERG

Copyright © 2017 Robert Steinberg
All rights reserved
First Edition

Fulton Books, Inc.
Meadville, PA

First originally published by Fulton Books 2017

ISBN 978-1-63338-354-8 (Paperback)
ISBN 978-1-63338-355-5 (Digital)

Printed in the United States of America

# ACKNOWLEDGMENTS

When *Jake the Horse Thief* began percolating and spewing wisps of caffeine, Janice—the queen of our castle—began slashing verbal forehands at my "Billie Jean King's forehand volleys" in endless profusion. For the last three years, thankfully, she hasn't ceased. Without her presence, *Jake* would have never been completed. At least, I discovered that there are "rules for punctuation."

Cousin Arthur Romm was nearby for the entire three years and assured me that Latvia, Belarus, and Lithuania were slices of the European continent at the time of *Jake*. Also, his criticism of my excess verbosity was well placed.

I didn't hesitate to call on my professional friends for advice and confirmation to increase the accuracy and meaning of the story. My personal physician, Dr. Lawrence Solomon, was in great assistance in seeing that I was able to continue writing during a trying time of these last three years. His corrections and advice on *Jake* was invaluable. My lawyer friend, Ben Bronstein, kept me on the straight path on some vital passage. Marvin Solomon, a captain of a US Minesweeper in World War II at VE Day, gave me correct advice on naval matters and from floundering in Nazi-infested seas in my story.

During the last three years, the members of the Chatham Club had to be regaled with the birth pains of *Jake* and listened with great forbearances. Atty. Mark Coplin struggled quietly through several stumbling versions of *Jake* and just smiled and continued reading.

Last, but certainly not least, I must remember cousin Herbie Glaser, for it was he who asked me if we had a *Jake the Horse Thief* in the family, and that started the juices flowing.

I finally realized that my son David's background was the very best for editing my novel. Much of the story's earliest segments are his creation. He has been the editor of *Jake the Horse Thief*. There is more family that edited and proofread *Jake*. My daughter, Ronda Cooperstein, is an award-winning playwright and offered important suggestions in the overall concept of the book. In the earliest struggles of *Jake*, Mark Squirek, an accomplished playwright, added several ideas to the plot in general.

# PROLOGUE

"You're still looking for Jake the Horse Thief! You're one crazy sonavabitch. You may not run outta money, but you're gonna lose your fuckin' mind!" With that, the door slammed behind her.

Mae had stayed with me longer than most women. Denver had been fun—at least, she thought so. For me, it had been work. But when we got to Santa Fe, she balked. And as far as she was concerned, Arizona wasn't on the map.

She won't be missed for very long. None of them have lasted.

My quest to find the most interesting man that I have ever known means that I must follow any clue or any lead. Mae didn't see things the way that I did. That's fine with me.

This long, torturous, blood-splattered trail that I was following now pointed westward from the courthouse in Phoenix. Yes, I've led myself into blind alleys before, but this one had the ring of truth.

Tonopah isn't much of a town, even by Arizona standards. It sits along Route 10, nestled in the White Tank Mountains. The wilderness and canyons shadowed by those brown hills have a history of hiding men who were escaping their past—men who were looking for a quiet, safe, and new beginning. The last I heard, someone who bore at the very least a vague resemblance to Jake had petered out just about there.

The White Tank Mountains was said to hold a small-time silver mining operation that, in its time, was known to operate under less-than-legal circumstances. Fire, bandits, the occasional collapse of its poorly supported walls—all manner of trouble had led to a closing of the mine. For a while, local authorities had been able to look the other way. It took the deaths of more than dozen men in a violent explosion and the resulting fire for the mine to finally be closed down by the federal authorities.

With Mae gone, I was now free without distraction to take a long, hard look at this almost-forgotten site in the White Tank Mountains. There was a slight wind that day, and around me, the sand and dust rose to fill my nostrils as I stood at what was once the entrance to the mine.

The space was locked and blocked by huge rocks and timbers, bolted across the once-open way. To the left, there was evidence of something that was not exactly a cemetery but more of a quickly dug burial ground where the fire had flamed and died. The names of the men who were buried there were scrawled on wooden planks, each one sticking above the ground at various odd angles. It was a haphazard, unorganized arrangement for men that had led haphazard, unorganized lives.

Frustrated by the lack of any real detail, I stood, wiping the dust from my forehead. Looking down to my right as I put the handkerchief in my back pocket, my eye caught something familiar. To my amazement, on one wooden plank, I saw what I knew could only be a hastily scraped Jewish star!

Stepping over the plank, I dropped to one knee. My heart began to beat rapidly. This had to be the ring of truth that I had felt when Mae had left. I wiped over the star with my hand, eventually drawing the cuff of my sleeve up to remove more dirt. As I did, my knuckles brushed against the cut outline of the star. A small splinter broke away, slipped under the middle part of my middle finger, and stuck. As much as it stung, I didn't care. Wiping away all the accumulated debris and dirt with a vengeance, I knew that this board simply had to bear the name of the man I was looking for. Otherwise, my entire journey would be for naught—ending in this desolate range of hills, slight patches of grass, and barren land.

Seven, eight, ten quick strokes removed years of dirt and rock and deterioration. Finally, a name emerged. I fell back when it became clear to me who was under the ground on which I was kneeling. The worn board bore a single name: Jesse Horton.

I was at the grave of Jake the Horse Thief. My course, the journey that had engulfed me for ages, was almost done. A mixture of sadness, relief, and joy filled my heart as I realized what I had discovered.

With nothing else to go by other than this crooked marker, I jumped up, returned to my jeep, and hastily started the engine. The next step meant my return to the nearby town of Tonopah to find if there was anyone left who could provide detailed records of the mine or the men who perished there.

As I laid into the gas of my rented jeep, tearing down Route 10, my mind raced as I went over what I knew.

"With the severity of the fire and fear of lawsuits, the locals don't even have records of who owned the mine. This means city hall is out. The feds clammed up when I asked about the place at the state capitol, so that's out."

I went over in my mind anyone that I thought could be connected to the mine. No matter what I came up with, I was drawing a blank.

Years of investigations had taught me to not panic, for that only clouds the brain. To solve a problem, your mind must be open to hearing the answer. This is where intuition and fate met me at the side of the road. Coming up on my right, just a few miles—before I would hit the one-horse town known as Tonopah—I saw a black dot growing larger and larger as I approached.

It rose quickly before me, eventually revealing itself to be an old general store that I now remembered passing on the way out to the mine. In front, there were two battered gas pumps that had probably not seen a refill since Jimmy Carter was president. The red paint on each of the pumps, once so bright and shiny in the unrelenting Arizona sun, was now chipped away and faded. On the other side of the pumps was an old Mobil gas sign, its wooden board suspended twelve feet in the air by two creaking chains. The word *MOBIL* and the red-winged Pegasus were as faded as the pumps.

The store itself was as beat down as the land from which it rose. There was a rail on each side of the screen door, each one again as red and faded as the rest of the surroundings. As I pulled up in front of the left one and turned off the engine, I noticed that there was a banged-up little house behind the store. Both buildings were painted white with green trim around, and each had been whipped and scoured bone-dry by the rough sand that was constantly being fed by the incessant wind. There were areas on the outside walls that were scraped down to bare wood.

Slipping out of the jeep, I dusted myself off and walked up to the front of the store. Pulling at the screen door, I saw that right above the handle was a metal sign, advertising a local bread called Aunt Billie's Fresh Loaves. Judging from the age of the sign and the quiet inside, Aunt Billie's hadn't made a delivery to the store in quite a while.

Stepping in, I saw a store with not much more to offer anyone other than canned goods and boxes of rice on two rows of half-filled metal shelves. To the left was an old wooden cabinet with some candy bars in boxes behind glass. On the right was what I believed to be a freezer—its massive wooden doors surrounding thick opaque glass placed in another time, another world.

Leaning over the counter was a thin teenaged boy with uncombed brown hair sitting atop a deeply tanned head.

The boy looked up from a gossip magazine and spoke, "Gas been empty for years, but something tells me that you ain't stopping for gas. What with the town about five miles up the road and a brand-new Shell station ready to take your money. We used to serve the mine, so all's we got is supplies now. And with the mine long gone, as you can see, we ain't got much of that either." He smiled and went on, "So whadya need there, pal?"

Despite the desolate nature of his surroundings, the kid seemed happy to be there. I doubt he sees many people during the course of a day—which, lucky for me, makes him a talker.

I went over to the freezer, pulled open the wooden door, and grabbed a bottle of beer that sat on a shelf.

"Don't see many freezers like this anymore. Jeez, looks like a classic." I walked to the counter, set the bottle down, and pulled out my wallet. "Looking for someone who can answer some questions about the mine. You know anyone who can help a guy out?"

The kid stood up straight and said, "Two bucks for the bottle."

I pulled out a ten and handed it to him. He took it and began to make change as he spoke, "My Grampa is in the house out back. His name is Ike Parker. Go knock on the door. He loves to talk about the mining days. Grampa Ike used to run this store, when the miners were coming in thick as thieves. Made a good buck in the day. But he's too stubborn to shut the place now. Believes someone is going to buy the land and open the mine again or build houses for a suburb of Tonopah. Then he'll be sitting in tall cotton again. So he pays me to sit here and read all day."

He leaned into me, laughing as he handed me the change, "You see suburbs in this dirt farmland?" Once I had my eight bucks, the kid pulled back, picked up his magazine, and put it in his back pocket. "Let me take you to Grampa and make an introduction."

The kid walked out from behind the counter and went to the front of the store. His good nature brought out the best in me as I followed him outside. Once we were back in the sun, I put on my sunglasses and said, "Can't say I see suburbs anywhere around this land."

"Don't get fooled by Grampa Ike. He has a memory like a trap. Knows if I short him ten cents on a day's take. Sharp as a tack, that old man. If he tries to sell you something, 'cause he's got a lot of stuff that miners left behind and stuff from cars that got left here and he had towed away, be careful. He will get your last nickel."

Walking to the back of the store near to where the other house sat, my intuition suddenly caught on fire. There was a familiar tingling at the base of my skull, one that I only get when I am 100 percent sure that something is going to be important and will help me with a case.

Gretchen, a girlfriend from two girlfriends ago or so, once told me that, "I am sure this is the same feeling that gamblers get when they risk it all on a fifty-to-one pony that they just know is going to hit. And then…they lose it all!"

She had told me that three days before she slammed a door behind her, cussing me just like Mae had not a week ago.

No matter what I felt, right or wrong, I knew that the answer was close by. The kid chatted as we walked to the house.

"Me? My Ma is in Phoenix. She's a nurse. She wants me out here watching Grampa so that no one comes along and tries to get him to sell the land around here. Grampa Ike owns about two hundred acres of this nothing. But two hundred acres is still money, even here. So she wants me…"

I wasn't listening to the kid. I was looking at everything around me. There were old bicycles, tires, and rusted nails sticking out of badly repaired window frames. Burlap sacks were piled up along one side with a big pile of bricks, half of them broken. Right next to it, a beat-up Chevy pickup was off to the left. The place was nearly dead.

So was the man who came to the door.

The kid stopped in front of the house as the door opened. "Grampa Ike, man here wants to know about the mines. Got a minute?"

## JAKE THE HORSE THIEF

Sticking out a wrinkled, spotted hand that slipped out from the cuff of a thick plaid shirt, he said, "Got nothing but minutes, maybe hours. For God's sake, Timmy, I am knocking on the door of ninety. Got nothing but all the time in the world." Turning to me, he said, "Now, shake my hand so we can make a proper introduction and come on in."

I took his hand, told him my name, and the three of us walked into the house, Timmy following behind.

Once we were inside, I was surprised. The interior was cleaner than I had thought it would be. There was plenty of light that came in through the picture window. A blanket with the design of a snowman sewn into its center hung over the back of a beat-up rust-colored couch. Across the coffee table in front of the couch were a few medicine bottles, several old-fashioned magazines, an ashtray, a coffee cup, and a half-eaten bag of Halls Mentho-Lyptus drops. A TV sat at an angle in the corner, and about eight feet in front of it, there was a chair with a folding tray next to it that served as a side table.

"Sit on the couch, the chair's mine." The back of the old man was so hunched that it left him at nearly a forty-five-degree angle to the floor. His trousers—as they do on almost all the old men I have ever seen—were pulled up high along his waist, and the flannel shirt hung out over the back until it reached past his bottom. He walked on brand-new Nikes.

"The boy orders them online for me. Comfortable as shit. Made by poor little kids over in China."

This guy was on top of everything, but thoughts of finally finding Jake the Horse Thief were all that filled my head. I was sure that years of searching were about to pay off. What Grampa Ike had said caught me off guard.

I said, "What?"

"You're surprised that an old man has such comfortable shoes. You were looking at my feet so you wouldn't stare at my screwed-up back. All those years in mines when I was a kid, until I saved the money to buy this land and open the store, they have all caught up with me. I need comfortable shoes, and Timmy orders them from a store that ships right to my door. I lived long enough to see the future!"

The kid was right; the old man was sharp.

He laughed at what he said in such a way that I could hear echoes of it in the way his grandson had laughed when we were back in the store.

Timmy dropped into the couch and spoke, "Grampa Ike, he's looking for info about the mines."

The old man stopped where he stood and turned to me, "You want stories, or you want to look through things them poor dead bastards left behind? We can do both if you're in a hurry."

I nodded yes and said, "I appreciate your understanding, Ike."

"Follow me while you ask your questions." Gesturing that I should accompany him, he began to walk to the back of the house.

As we moved into another room, Ike said, "I figured that one day someone would come along and ask about some of this junk. Most of the others who stop here are just looking for their dead father or some uncle. They mostly just ask questions and look through these boxes we still have. If I have something they want, they are always willing to pay ten or twenty bucks for it."

Turning back to me, he laughed again. "Storage costs. After all, a man's got to eat."

As we passed the kitchen and walked into the main body of the house, I thought for the briefest of seconds that I might be heading for an ambush. After all, I had been asking all over the state for info—who knows what was actually going on. Maybe somebody had something to cover up and was willing to pay to stop someone as nosy as I had been.

## JAKE THE HORSE THIEF

Any fear that I had built up disappeared as quickly as it had come. The kid was a lightweight who couldn't stop talking, and Grampa Ike was a walking question mark with expensive tennis shoes. I had nothing to worry about.

With windows that spread across the entire back of the house, the porch was as bright as if it was out of doors. Off to the left, there was a washer, dryer, and a couple of shelving units that looked as if they had been pulled from the store. Ike stopped by a chair that was beside the back door and sat himself down.

"Timmy, get him the boxes, will ya', boy?" He looked over to me and went on, "We don't have much left."

The boy moved to the shelves and knelt down. First he pulled one box, then another from the bottom of the unit. As he did, the clothes, soaps, and shoes that sat on other shelves shook.

"Don't drag the got-damn thing down on top of your ass, boy! Show some patience. Our guest isn't going anywhere." He smiled at me, as if it he was ribbing the boy instead of chastising him. For his part, Timmy slid the first box across to where I stood.

Grampa Ike looked at me, "Go on, that's why you're here."

I knelt down on one knee in front of the box and opened it. Inside I found magazines, hats, shoes, shirts, what looked to be a couple of wallets and other accumulations from the lives of forgotten men.

Ike spoke as I rifled through the junk, "Now, let me tell you about the mines. They were hell for most of the men—dirty, shit-filled conditions. The men who worked there didn't have the dignity of a pack mule. But most of them had no choice. They wanted to disappear, and they came to the right place. Word was that they had escaped convicts working underground, rooting about for silver…"

I paid scant attention to what the old man said as I dug. The first box held nothing, nothing at all. My intuition began to disappear, and I heard the sound of Gretchen and several others who have been at my side, laughing at me from far away.

Still, I had the mind to set aside a wallet in case the second box held something that I might want. I also pulled some old magazines and a comic book and put it in a pile on the side. This would give me a distraction, a bargaining chip, if something valuable was there. But with nothing worth my time inside this box, I began to feel as if my chase for information on the life of Jake the Horse Thief might have reached an end.

Sliding the first box back to Timmy, Ike slid the second, smaller box in front of me. My hope had just about run out as I began to open the container. I began digging through much of the same rubble that filled the first container: shoes, hats, magazines, a stray wallet, handkerchiefs, just crap. Pure crap.

Then I noticed a small dark book with a leather cover. It spoke of ages and miles traveled along a long, long road. My heart skipped a beat. I could recognize the *siddur* (prayer book) of a Russian Jew from a mile away. Not wanting to give anything away, I passed it and went for another magazine and pulled two of the wallets as well, setting them in the pile I had begun earlier.

Timmy pulled the book from the box. He looked at Ike and spoke, "This is the one with the Jew stuff in it, isn't it?"

Ike replied, "Yeah, about five years ago, I had Lester out here from the courthouse, he wanted to look through this stuff. I thought it was Chinese writing in it. But Lester said it was Jew stuff, so I guess one of the miners was a Yid on the run from somewhere."

For the second time in three minutes, my heart stopped for the briefest of moments—not from the anti-Semitic language, I am too old and have too many miles on me to be shocked or hurt by ignorance, but from what I realized when I saw the book.

The book had belonged to Jake the Horse Thief.

## JAKE THE HORSE THIEF

I put another issue of *Field & Stream* on the pile I had built. Timmy reached into the box and pulled out the little leather-covered book.

"You want the Jew book with all that magazines you got there?" he said.

I shrugged my shoulders, "Don't care, but it might be worth something, who knows. I mostly want to see if any of the wallets have IDs in them, or if the magazines have a subscription label on them so I can trace them back to where they came from. Looking for a man who owed a friend of mine money."

The kid put the book on my pile, and I reached for a wallet. Opening it up, I noticed that there was a paper ID, an old Social Security card, and nothing more. I tossed it back into the box.

Ike chimed in, "If it's out of the box, you should buy it, fella. You took it out, it should be yours."

I replied to the old man's request, "It's worthless, Ike. No disrespect meant, but the money's long gone, and the paper is worthless." I moved on to another wallet.

Timmy grabbed my hand. "I told you, Grampa Ike's a hard man to deal with. How much for the whole lot? Just take it all."

I looked the kid straight in the eye, and he quickly moved his hand off my arm.

Seeing my discomfort, Ike spoke up, "Sorry 'bout the kid. He don't mean nothing. 'Pologize to our guest, Timmy."

Timmy pulled back and was quick to speak. "Sorry, man, I don't get many people around here, and when they do show up, I get jumpy." He smiled at me and tilted his head in a form of apology.

Smiling, I looked at Ike, "Good thing he has you around to watch over him."

The old man smiled and went on, "Thirty bucks, and everything you piled up is yours. I would have said forty, but I figure we owe you something because the boy jumped the gun." He shot a look over at Timmy, and the boy looked away.

Hesitating with an answer, I looked back at Timmy. He was still smiling. I looked over at Ike. He sat motionless, waiting for me to speak.

Reaching for my wallet, I said, "I got a twenty and the eight bucks Timmy here gave me as change for the beer I bought." The old man didn't move. Instead, he looked over at Timmy.

"He bought a beer?"

"Yeah, Grampa, he got a Coors," came the reply.

Ike put his hand out for my money. "Might as well take his twenty-eight. That beer has been in there so long it might be skunk beer. You like skunk beer, mister?"

"I like beer in all forms, Ike."

The money changed hands, and Timmy got up, went to the shelves, and pulled a small brown paper bag off the second one from the top. He tossed it over to where I had piled up the magazines, cracked wallets, and the little leather-covered book that I had been searching for since I-forgot-when.

Gathering everything up, I placed it in the bag and got up. Timmy came over and slid the box back under the shelf from where he had pulled it.

Ike said, "I'm gonna sit here in the sun for a few minutes, boys. Timmy, you walk him back out to his car, truck, or whatever." He put his hand out for me to shake. "Deal ain't ever over till two men have shaken on it. We good?"

Taking his hand, I shook it and said, "We're fine. Thanks for your time, Ike."

With business done, I walked past the old man with Timmy following my shadow. I stepped aside so that the kid could walk in front of me. We passed through the house and went left through the front door. Walking around the back of the store, Timmy began to talk again.

"Grampa wasn't really mad. He just likes a reason to knock down a price these days 'cause, as he says, 'I ain't got much haggle left in me, boy,' so he just spits out a price and lets whoever visits take what they want. Still, I got to say I like that you took out the price of the beer. That was funny. I know he liked that."

By now, we had reached the front of the store, and I walked in first. Picking up my beer off the counter, I tucked it under the arm that was holding the bag with the book and put my other hand out for Timmy. He shook it like a gentleman.

"Remember, don't get pissed if that is skunk beer, Grampa warned you." He shook my hand and walked behind the counter and bent over to pick up the magazine that still lay open on the counter.

Walking out to the jeep, I hopped in, put the bag behind the seat where it wouldn't fly away, and placed the beer on the passenger seat. The radio crackled as I started the engine, and the sounds of Debussy filled the Arizona desert. I backed out and headed straight back to the mine.

Once there, I grabbed the bag from behind the seat. Casting the rest of what I had bought aside, I took out the little book. It didn't take five minutes for me to find the grave that bore the Jewish Star. The name "Jesse Horton" was still visible.

Sitting down, I opened the beer, and once I was sure that the beer hadn't gone "skunk," I took a long, long swig. Capping the bottle, I sat it in the dirt behind me. It was only then that I picked up the book.

Opening the cover, I knew beyond a shadow of a doubt that this was what I had sought for so long. Inside the book was the notification that it was *Nusach Polin*, which told me from the outset that it had to have come from the same region as Jake. For Polish was, indeed, his first language.

What I saw next confirmed everything. In the margins, faded as to be almost indecipherable, were pencil marks made by what could only be Jake's own hand. Squinting hard, I could make out swirls and straight lines—writing that I had seen the man make in my presence on numerous occasions before he disappeared.

I let the book fall gently to my lap. It was over. Mae had run, Gretchen had stormed out, and almost everyone had told me that I was insane to devote all the time and money that I had spent in order to find Jake's story. But now, at last, through a combination of divine providence, fate, luck, and sheer mule-headed stubbornness—I held his story in my hand.

Reaching again for the beer, I uncapped the bottle and took another long swallow. Setting it aside, I opened the book for a second time. The truth was before me.

There, in the prayer book's page margin, was the first and most important scribbling clearly written in Jake's own hand: "Pinsk to Minsk."

A year later, after what I held in my hands that day was translated and deciphered, the entire story would be written. It was a year that had seen the *Little Jew Book* be magnified and x-rayed and gone over with a thoroughness reserved for the most scholarly of documents, by the most learned of men and women. Empty spaces between words and letters would give rise to speculation. Meanings would be debated until everything was verified as true. Eventually, a cohesive and stunning narrative would evolve. His story was a story of loss, horror, adventure, brutality, danger, and love. This is what I am about to tell you.

But you and I know that all stories must have a real starting place—a secret place where the scholars and the press and the lazy and the uncaring and the selfish would never think to look.

## JAKE THE HORSE THIEF

This story begins that day in the hot, near-boiling sun as it shone down across the Arizona desert. It starts with me sitting on a pile of dirt that was the grave of one of the most heroic and unselfish men I have ever met.

That story began after I took a second swig of beer and then cracked open the yellowed, thin, and aged pages of the *Little Jew Book*. For much of what I read that day, he had already told me himself.

Here begins the true and amazing story of Jake the Horse Thief.

# Jake the Horse Thief

# A BRIDGE NEAR PINSK

The rain was now coming down so hard that it stung his face as it fell. In minutes, his hands had grown cold. Looking to rub them together for warmth, he loosened his grip on the reigns for just a second.

Not a second later, lightning burst across the sky. It filled the heavens above him with arcs of brilliant light that spread in every direction that Avram could see. Turning his head to the left, he watched as the strike made contact with the ground less than a mile away.

At the moment that he had chosen to loosen his grip, the sound of thunder filled the sky around him. It created such force across the plain that Avram could feel the bridge below him shake.

Before he had a chance to tighten his grip on the reigns, a second burst of silver-and-yellow light born of electricity was followed by another wave of thunder.

Echoes from the deafening outburst rolled across the open fields and drenched marshes. The combination of noise and lightning in the two quick outbursts tore through the air and lit the horizon in a spectacular glow that caused Avram's steed to rear back in cold panic.

Staring wide-eyed at the outline of his horse against the sky, Avram felt the bridge swing to the left and then over to the right in quick, sudden movements. He wasn't sure, but he thought that he heard a sharp crack behind him on his right.

*It has to be the post. Nothing else could be that loud over this thunder,* he thought.

On the bridge, Avram watched as the full weight of the horse came down upon the now-fragile crossing with so much force that he could feel the wagon leave the ground. Before the wheels could return to the ground, the horse bolted for the rails that served as a slim guard against the raging stream below.

The noise he had heard was, indeed, the post behind him. It was supposed to anchor the right wall of the bridge, but the constant downpour of the last few days had weakened its place in the ground. The weight of the horse dropping on the planks of the bridge had caused the entire center to snap in two. This left the entire right side of the bridge vulnerable.

The unexpected force of the action tore the reigns from Avram's cold, tired hands. No longer in control of the wagon, he watched as the animal fell before him. The animal's great bulk shattered the meager protection of the rails completely. Large timbers of wood smashed and began flying everywhere. The horse screamed as it began to fall, but Avram could hear none of it, as once again thunder raged across the world.

None of the previous three bursts would prove to be brighter than this last explosion.

His horse was now moving into open space while the structure that had supported them was collapsing below him. Avram, understanding his fate lay in the water and rocks beneath him, sighed and thought of his children. He felt nothing for himself, for he had long understood that death comes to us all. In the eternity that seemed to pass as he fell to his death, he knew that his children were to become orphans.

# ON THE FARM DURING THE STORM

Less than a mile away and not two minutes earlier, when the lightning had first burst above them and filled their house with an otherworldly brightness, Leah and Jacob instinctively turned to look at each other. From the time their mother had died, they had become so close that there were times when Leah felt she could hear Jacob's thoughts. The boy had shown no signs of panic, but she knew that his heart had begun to beat faster.

The two had heard many, many storms in their life. But the unnatural nature of the light around them coupled with the relentless assault and sheer volume of the thunder produced by this storm confused them. The rapid flurry of activity had caught them by surprise. Before the first crack had faded, Leah looked to her brother for guidance.

Jacob took his sister gently by her arm and led her to the foot of their father's bed. Together they knelt and crawled under the space. They had done this before, when their father was late returning from town, when darkness had fallen too quickly. As the storm began to rage, they lay side by side, Leah's arms tightly around her brother's shoulders and he returned her embrace.

With the thunder no longer ringing and the lightning no longer illuminating the interior of the house, Jacob and Leah slowly emerged from the safety under the bed. The young boy lit a candle, and together the brother and sister sat by the fire that had somehow miraculously lasted throughout the storm. For the next hour or so, they remained silent—each knowing that they could only pray that their father would return.

When they heard a knock at the door, they looked at each other with smiles of joy. Jumping up, they ran to the door, screaming, "Poppa! Poppa!"

Leah got there first and threw the door open, expecting to see her father.

Instead, she found their friend and neighbor Naftali Krakolawski and his wife, Tzofiya, standing there soaking in the light drizzle that was falling.

The boy said nothing as his sister began to ask and then scream, "Where is Poppa, Mr. K.? Where is our Poppa, please tell us that he is well, that he…"

It was only as she stopped yelling and saw that the Krakolawskis could say nothing that the awful truth dawned on her.

Her father was gone.

Tzofiya Krakolawski stepped into the house. As she did, she took the young girl into her arms. Leah hung on the woman's soaked apron tightly, while her body was wracked with deep, unrelenting sobs.

Comforting the girl as best she could, the wife looked to her husband, only to see a blank expression of grief. Looking back to Leah, she placed her arm around the girl's heaving shoulder and walked over to the fireplace. Together the two sat as one in sorrow.

Naftali looked at Jacob. In the rain that was blowing through the door, the boy's red hair appeared to be even wilder than he remembered. It had been over a month since he had last seen him, and he was surprised at how tall he looked for his age. The slight frame of the child was rigid, unbending, and his eyes burned with questions.

Naftali spoke first, "In the fury of the storm, the horse bolted and left the bridge. Your father followed him with no choice."

"He died in the stream?" said Jacob in perfectly calm tones.

"Yes," came the reply. "But it was the rocks that took him as he lay there…" Naftali found himself unable to go on. Avram had been his friend as well, and only now was the loss catching up to him. For Jacob's sake, he struggled to hold back tears or even the slightest hint of emotion.

Jacob looked at the man before him. He saw a full grown man, cold, shivering, and now quiet. He could feel the man's pain. For a second, he was unsure of himself. He had never even begun to think of what life would be like without Poppa.

Over the next minute or so, the realization that he and Leah were now orphans settled in. In response, he did what any six-year-old would do. He began to cry, and putting his arms out in front of him, he reached out for the friend he knew.

Naftali took the boy into his arms and hugged him as hard as he had ever hugged any of his own four children.

Together Naftali and the orphans sat and wept until the rain ceased to fall.

# THE TOWN AND THE ORPHANS

The comfort that Leah and Jacob had found in the arms of Naftali and his wife that horrible night was only temporary. It was clear that, as close as they had been to Avram and as open as their hearts were, the family could not take either Leah or Jacob under their roof. With four children of their own and a fifth on the way, the couple could not possibly care for two more children. They could barely feed themselves.

However, the couple was able to arrange for the funeral. When Miriam had passed away, Avram had bought two small burial plots in the tiny Jewish cemetery, in the town of Pinsk. It was there that he was buried next to his late loving wife. Other than that, he had owned only the house he had built by his own labor. The land it sat on was rented, and the sale of the small house barely paid for the expense of Avram's funeral and burial.

Living such an isolated existence, Avram Horvicz had known few people in the town. Aside from Naftali's family, there were only three other Jewish mourners accompanying Rabbi Vilnish and the two weeping orphans as the wooden casket slid into the ground. In contrast to the darkened skies that had held the town captive over the last few days, at the burial of Avram Horvicz, the sun shone brightly.

The mourners who did attend were heard to ask each other in low tones, "But what about the children?" and, "Who is thinking of them?"

These concerns did not escape the ears of Rabbi Vilnish.

As the Naftalis rode homeward that day, the orphans, Leah and Jacob, were taken from the cemetery straight to the center of the town of Pinsk. Neither their mother, Miriam, nor their father, Avram, had relatives in Pinsk. Nor were there any known family members in any other part of Belarus. The few relatives that Leah and Jacob knew were scattered throughout Europe or had left for America.

There was no one to take care of the Horvicz children's welfare. Rabbit Vilnish considered such a concern to be the responsibility of the town. He hoped that someone would step forward to at least offer shelter until something more permanent could be arranged.

Most of Pinsk's inhabitants had gathered at the town center. No one wanted to see the two children starve and become little beggars in their small Jewish community. While Leah and Jacob stood terrified by the side of the aged rabbi, the townspeople began clamoring for someone to step forward to take responsibility.

No one wanted to see two little Jewish orphans becoming beggars or, even worse, thieves, in their town.

An hour after he had presided over the burial of their father, Rabbi Menachem Vilnish stood by Leah and Jacob, looking over the faces of the crowd.

Already over sixty, Rabbi Vilnish wore his years in wrinkles that made their way across his face in deep, cracking lines. Years of study over books had left his back curved, which caused his head to look as if it were hanging low from his shoulders. When he became exhausted, his hands would shake. Never a vain man, he understood how his years looked to others.

Leah and Jacob stood to the side of Rabbi Vilnish. Her eyes red from several days of crying in quiet, Leah looked exhausted as she clung to the rabbi's robe. He had taken care to dress them both in the best clothes possible. She was in the same dark dress that she had worn to her father's funeral—only now, as she walked into the center of town, it had become coated along the edges with mud.

However, Jake neither held the rabbi nor bore an expression of any sort. His oversized coat hung loosely from his shoulders and created the effect that he was smaller than he actually was. Standing perfectly still, his red hair peeking out from under his small cap, he looked straight ahead at no one in particular.

Later, after the meeting had ended and the fate of the children had been sealed, a few townspeople would quietly say that they were spooked by the way that the young boy appeared. Many had found his stoic and nonexpressive demeanor threatening.

Jake had just lost his father and was wearing a very uncomfortable coat. He had other things on his mind than his appearance. He was praying that he could stay with his sister.

Stepping away from his charges, the rabbi looked out to the faces of those he knew. Silently, their eyes met his. One elderly couple raised their eyebrows as if they wanted to take the children, but then they put their hands up, as if to say they were sorry. Another, a farmer and his wife that the rabbi had counseled about marriage not three months earlier shook their heads no with a firm look that told the rabbi to not even ask.

Looking around at the people he knew from synagogue and services and the street, he could not find a single family willing to take both the boy and girl. Mumbling gave way to yelling as the crowd became unsettled with the way that the rabbi was handling the problem.

A woman over in the corner raised her head above the others and said loudly, "This is free labor for someone! All the kids need is a blanket and one potato a day!"

The crowd laughed, and the rabbi noticed a few of the men smirking while looking at Leah. Despite his age, he knew what their hearts held. Tired from the funeral as well as his duties over the last weeks, the rabbi began to ask men that he had always counted on if they could take the orphaned pair.

One by one, all family heads had the same excuse: "We are so poor that we won't be able to feed two more mouths." This was a fact the rabbi could not deny, for food was a major concern in the town of Pinsk.

The crowd began to start talking again, which forced the rabbi to make two impulsive decisions that would have far-reaching consequences for Leah and Jacob.

The first was to approach the one man he felt should have stepped up immediately, Mayer Malkin. Malkin was a butcher and farmer who served not just the Jewish community but the entire town. He was also the leader of a large family.

Rabbi Vilnish knew that none of this would make Malkin an ideal candidate to take the two children. But he did have the economic and social wealth to at least help for a while.

Taking a deep breath and looking into the black eyes of the butcher, the rabbi spoke, "Please, please have pity and do not separate the children! With the gifts that you have been given, two more mouths could not be much of a burden…"

The butcher gritted his teeth, looked menacingly at the rabbi, and tilted his head sideways, as if to say, "Why are you bothering me?"

Behind him, a voice rang out loudly, "Why should we take both?"

Mayer's wife, Dora Malkin, was a large woman who, to her husband's delight, had already bore him five sons and no daughters. Among the Jewish community she had a reputation as a chronic complainer, whose voice was seldom stilled. By her own diagnosis, she had been ill for many years. With a husband and so many boys in her house, there was a glaring need for someone to cook, clean, and wash clothes for the large household.

Pushing her way forward until she came within inches of the rabbi's face, she continued, "Nobody else could take both brats! However, we could use the girl in the kitchen. She can do all the cooking and clean the downstairs. We have a small room off of the kitchen for her."

Crossing her arms, she pulled back from the rabbi as if she was doing him a favor by even speaking. The Butcher Malkin, accustomed to his wife's outbursts, could only sigh. He knew that Dora had more on her mind.

Turning away from the rabbi, she looked back to her husband and whispered loudly, "Now we can let the shiksa go and save the fifty kopecks."

She made no effort to mask her delight at the possibility of gaining free labor. As to taking income away from a deserving woman, who had served her well, she could care little.

"Fifty kopecks was fifty kopecks," she would say when the years passed, often adding with a laugh as she pointed to Leah, "and I still think I got cheated!"

Her husband looked over to Leah and gave the once-over as if she were a horse in his corral. A sly smile crossed his lips, and his eyes began to narrow as he thought of the future. Looking back at his wife, he said, "If you think that is best. I could care less one way or another."

Then taking care to make eye contact with Jacob, he pointed to Jacob, "Take off your hat, boy," he commanded as if he might consider taking Leah's brother.

The six-year-old did as he was asked. His red hair tumbled out from under his cap as he pulled it down. His eyes never left the gaze of Mayer Malkin. Several in the crowd began to giggle. A redheaded Jew was something that many in the crowd had never seen before.

Mayer Malkin began to laugh. "I have a house of roosters and another in the coop already. I don't need any more of them." With that, he turned around and declared, "Take the girl, Dora, but leave the boy!" Still smiling at his own joke, he began to walk back to his shop.

The crowd roared with delight at his behavior, while the rabbi sadly dwelled on the moral state of his diminished Jewish community. A sense of rage began to fill his heart.

The rabbi now stood at the center of town, in front of a good many of its citizens who had just heard others say no to taking care of the orphans. Pushing the issue, he implored Mayer Malkin loudly to take both Leah and Jacob as a unit. For as he said loudly, for all to hear, "I fear that to break up the sister and brother would do irreparable harm to both."

A small rush of vocal disbelief spread throughout the crowd. For many knew that to confront Malkin directly about some issues, especially in front of others, could lead to serious problems. Many felt he would "rip the head off the poor hapless rabbi" as one was overheard to say. Others imply said, "Uh-oh…uh-oh."

To his eternal credit, the Butcher Malkin stopped in his steps, turned back to the rabbi, and told the crowd in a sincere and warm voice, "I do understand, my dear rabbi. Your request is, indeed, noble and righteous, for to break up the two would be unfair in the eyes of us all. But I have now five sons, all still growing, and a large business that contributes much to the community, I am already overburdened."

Once he had made his statement, he then wiped his hands on his apron. Many who knew him took the gesture as a sign that the matter was settled. For they had also asked for favors of Malkin, just as the rabbi had done. But unlike the rabbi, they understood that when Malkin wiped his hands, he expected what he said to be understood and not questioned. If someone did dare to question his decision, he would then show them the force of his temper and cruelty.

The rabbi, unaware of any special significance to the gesture, took Malkin's calm refusal as simply the opening salvo in a discussion. So once again he presented his request to the massive butcher.

"Certainly, I do respect what you have built and what you mean to this community, Mr. Malkin. Your five sons are strong, and each one is healthy as a result of your labor and generosity. But that success is also due to gifts we are given by our Creator. Because your heart is so open to so many of us in this town, I believe there is a corner of your house that can house two such small field mice until better arrangements can be made. Please, have pity and do not force circumstances to separate the children!"

With that, the rabbi placed his arm around Leah and his hand on the top of Jacob's red hair. For her part, Leah did her best to smile as the rabbi talked. There were others who felt that they had seen Jacob wince in disgust at what transpired.

None in the Jewish community stepped forward to answer the rabbi's plea.

One said out loud, "We have trouble feeding our own kids!"

Malkin balked for a moment at what had been said. Those who knew him could see that he was controlling his temper out of respect for the rabbi's position. It was his wife, Dora, who was the first to break the silence.

"Why should we take both?" she loudly exclaimed. "Nobody else would take both brats!" Her exclamation and name-calling confirmed what many had said about her in whispers—that she was, indeed, petty and shrewish.

As was her way, she added on final observation, "The boy is, indeed, worthless to us, Mayer."

Sensing that he may jeopardize their offer to take Leah, the rabbi backed away and exclaimed,

"As your wife has said, the girl is nine years old and already big enough to take care of everything."

Leah had inherited her late mother's, Miriam's, long dark hair and was beginning at age nine to show a hint of the fulsome figure that her mother had possessed. This had not escaped the eye of Malkin, nor others in the crowd, for a young wife will always valuable to someone. Down the line, there might be money to be made from a "donation" made by a prospective husband for a guardian's consent…So the butcher was seeing gold coins, and his wife could envision a complete housekeeper in Leah.

Meanwhile, sensing where the conversation was going, Leah had a faint recollection of her mother working in the kitchen. There was one very distinct incident that stood out after all these years. Her mother had made a doll for her out of scraps of cloth from worn and discarded clothing. That was Leah's "trousseau."

That doll was now hiding inside of her jacket, held in place by the pressure of her arm against the sleeve. It sat only inches from the black-and-white portrait of her mother and father that was hidden also in an inside pocket.

After Dora's outburst was met without argument, the rabbi knew that he would have to, indeed, break up the children.

It was a solution that the rabbi had hoped to avoid. His wife had perished in the same flu epidemic that killed the children's mother, and as much as he had hated to admit it, he had grown accustomed to his privacy since her passing.

A short bald man who wore glasses that always seemed to lie crooked across the bridge of his nose, the rabbi valued his time. His days were spent alone in study, reading of God's Word and deeds and administering to the religious needs of the Jewish community of Pinsk. The world found at the center of Pinsk, as small as the city actually was, held no interest for him.

Jake, as strong as he looked, was only six and would not be of much use to a farmer or shopkeeper for at least another two years, if not longer. The silence that Rabbi Vilnish had enjoyed for so long was about to become something else.

One thing that the rabbi did understand was that in times of need, it was his unspoken job to stand and help those that needed it.

Not wishing to diminish either himself or what the town felt about his fellow Jews, the rabbi said, "I will gladly offer the boy what I can under my roof."

With the problem at hand now solved, the crowd began to break up. Some walked away, congratulating themselves for living in a town that took care of problems in such a kind and understanding fashion. Others made plans to bring by the rabbi's house that old shirt they no longer wore or a small bit of tomatoes and noodles as soon as they could. They wanted to help the boy if they could.

Their fate decided for them, Leah turned to Jake and gave him a long, long hug. With that, she turned and found Dora Malkin waiting for her. The old lady took the girl by her shoulders and looked over her head.

"You don't have lice, do you, girl?" she asked without a care for who heard the answer.

"No, Mrs. Malkin," came the reply from the terrified child.

"You'd better not! I run a clean house, girl!" exclaimed Mrs. Malkin.

She then turned and walked away while snapping her fingers at one of her sons. It was Leon, Malkin's fourth son, who came up to Leah next.

Speaking to the girl, he said, "It will be okay, she is just having a day. Let's get you home and give you something to eat."

At fourteen, he was a full five years older than Leah. Those who knew him in the village considered him the nicest and most civil of Malkin's sons. Malkin and the other four boys were already at the door of the butcher shop, anxious to reopen after having closed for the town meeting.

The rabbi took Jake by the hand and bent down to whisper in his ear, "We will see your dear sister every day, son. We will be okay. I promise you that I will do my best for you as long as I am able."

It was a lie—not an intentional one, but a lie. The rabbi couldn't have known that the Butcher Malkin and his wife, Dora, would grow to consider Leah their legal property and forbid Jacob from seeing his sister without supervision.

Jake looked up to the rabbi and said, "I am fine, Reb Vilnish. We will be okay."

The rabbi found himself oddly reassured by the boy's confidence in the situation. He and his new charge began walking toward his house. Given the circumstances, the rabbi felt that he had done at the very least a credible job of solving the problems that day.

There was only one thing that really troubled the rabbi, and it wasn't the responsibility of his new charge. He knew full well that Jacob Horvicz was a strong boy with an independent soul (anyone could see that, even a man as oblivious to so much as he was). Together the two of them would find a way to live together for a few years.

What troubled him was that, for a brief second, he allowed himself to feel a small bit of pride at what had transpired in the town square that afternoon. When he examined what had taken place that day in the bigger picture of God and teachings he studied so carefully, he felt his momentary burst of pride fall away. What he had done was done in order to cover for the lack of responsibility in his community. Any pride that he had was quickly replaced by shame at how little moral influence he had over those he served.

The rabbi showed Jacob his new bed in the alcove at the rear of the small house. As he prepared their first meal together and as he finally set the boy to sleep on his first night in a new home, the rabbi found himself unable to think of anything else other than the diminished sense of moral obligation to others he had found in his Jewish community.

It would not be the first time that the residents of Pinsk would damage his heart.

# The Years Pass...

# LEAH

Dora Malkin wasted no time in firing Tzviya Stolarz, her current housekeeper, without notice. As she reasoned it, she owed the housekeeper nothing. In her mind, she rationalized, *The woman had been working for the family for the last eight years as a favor to her husband who had, when he was alive, owed the butcher money. I owe the bitch zero.*

Besides, Mrs. Malkin had never been completely happy with the woman's work.

The sheets were never as white as she would have liked them. In the kitchen, Tzviya's way with a chicken was, according to Dora Malkin, "just lazy." As a cook, it was claimed, she would overuse paprika as a rule—no matter how many times she was told to use less. No matter what her husband said ("the man would eat anything"), Tzviya's brisket was continually being served dried out and burned. The boys would devour it, and her husband never complained, but Mrs. Malkin thought it had been a disaster for years.

On the other hand, the orphaned girl standing next to the rabbi at the town meeting looked to be strong, willing, and best of all, desperation filled her face.

*When someone is desperate, they will work harder*, thought Mrs. Malkin.

This is the idea that caused the butcher's wife to speak up so loudly and risk embarrassing her husband. One look had told her that this girl was willing to do anything she could to stay alive. Seeing an opportunity to have someone who feared her in the house, Mrs. Malkin couldn't let this opportunity pass. All she would have to do would be to give the girl a cot in the closet off the kitchen.

With the death of her father, Avram, and now the separation from her brother, Jacob, Leah knew that she was alone. Despite living in a packed house, one filled to the roof with all sorts of people, there was no companionship. There was no affection, and there was no one with whom to share her fears. There was no letup for even a single minute in a day for the demands of meals and scrubbing and dishes and sweeping. Even worse were the harsh comments she endured from nearly all the members of the household.

The older Malkin barely acknowledged her, and when he did, it was with a guttural grunt.

When Leah sobbed or complained, Mayer Malkin had—on more than one occasion—roared at her, "You shouldn't complain! I've given you a roof over your head and plenty to eat!"

Four of the five boys regarded her as little more than a nuisance. Even the fourth son, Leon, who initially had appeared to be friendly to her, had eventually drifted from her life. She couldn't have known this, but their indifference toward her came about for a single reason.

Before she had even made it to her room on that first day, the Butcher Malkin had gathered all his boys in one room that was out of sight of Leah. In his most threatening and abusive manner, he told them each face-to-face that if they laid a hand on the girl, behaved in an untoward way, or even made a joke about her—the beating they would receive, as a result, would cripple them for life. The boys had all experienced a beating at the hands of their father, many of them more than once, for he would often beat them without warning. Any temptation they felt toward Leah would be tempered by the memory of all previous beatings.

In truth, the Malkins considered her no better than a servant. Worried that she might run off, they afforded her no time to herself. For the first few months, until they were comfortable with Leah's generally meek and reserved manner, one of them was always around.

Dora Malkin was constantly hovering over Leah's shoulder. Despite her close proximity, she offered nothing in the way of friendship or even a moment of kindness. Her only comments were on the quality of Leah's work, and somehow, no matter how hard the girl tried, her work was never up to the older woman's satisfaction.

As an example for the young girl to follow and learn, Mrs. Malkin was an unworthy example of a grown woman, much less an example of motherhood. Any redeeming qualities that she had once possessed as a woman or a friend to anyone had disappeared some years ago. She was cruel and demanding to her sons, cruel and demanding to her husband, and especially, cruel and demanding to her new servant.

All that remained of the young girl known as Dora Malkin was a hulk of a woman who craved cheese and sweets and lived to harass or complain to anyone within earshot.

When her work was done, and the noise of the house fell to almost nothing, Leah would retire at night to her small corner cupboard near the kitchen. There she would quietly pull her doll from under the straw mattress and clutch it to her chest as tightly as she could. In the darkness (Dora Malkin felt that if she allowed the girl a candle, she risked burning the house and shop to the ground), Leah would sometimes trace the outline of her mother's face from memory, using the moonlight that slipped through the curtains and across her bed.

For the first few months, there was hardly a night when she didn't cry as she fell asleep. The love that she had once known from her parents and brother, Jacob, was absent in this household. There was no warmth and barely even any kindness. Each night she fell asleep dreaming of someone who would rescue her from this hell.

It didn't take long for Leah's loneliness to turn into resignation and then occasional bitterness. But through it all, she somehow held on to a sense that life would improve. There was the dream that in the future, she and Jacob would be reunited in a grand adventure and then settle down to a house of their own—that he would farm, and her husband would work by the side of her brother. Then she would have handsome and smart children, and then, on holidays, she would have a daughter to help her cook.

# JACOB

A few streets from where Leah slept, Jacob's situation was different and, in its own way, just as difficult.

After the town meeting had ended, the rabbi remained in the square for a few minutes to shake hands and talk to anyone who needed his time. As to his new charge, the rabbi had merely looked down to him and nodded his head. Jacob understood this to mean, "Stand here, and I will be right back."

Jacob stood by quietly as he watched the man, who would now be responsible for his life, nod to each person that he met. He watched as the rabbi shook their hands vigorously and looked at each of them straight in the eye as they spoke. Some offered good wishes, thankful that they hadn't been forced to take in another mouth to feed "in such difficult times."

Others asked him to stop by their house, for they thought that they might have an extra shirt or a maybe a pair of pants that could be altered to fit his new charge. Some extended the invitation of a dinner. All of which found the rabbi nodding gratefully in response.

Eventually, the crowd thinned out, leaving only the rabbi and six-year-old Jacob alone in the square. Extending his hand down to the young boy, the rabbi felt shocked when his offer was accepted. The boy himself did not notice any reaction.

Jacob was hungry. He was also thinking of how to find out where Leah had been taken.

The rabbi was surprised at exactly how small the boy's hand felt in his own. Panic filled his heart. He may not be the farmer or have the ability to barter in the way that the boy's father had been able to do so, but it was at this moment that he decided that he could only give the boy what he knew: the love of the Word of God and the teachings that accompany it.

As they reached the front door of the rabbi's house, he stopped and said to Jacob, "This is where you will live for a while. Please look around the street, and remember exactly where we are."

With that, he turned the boy away from the door and pointed out to him several landmarks.

"We are five streets from the river moving north. That is why we smell fish so often. Do you like the smell, Jacob?"

The boy stood still, looking ahead of himself. He saw the dirt roads and looked to see where they turned to other streets. He wanted to know one thing and one thing only.

"Where is the street where Leah lives?"

The rabbi replied, "We will visit your sister when we can. But for now, I do not want a young man like yourself to ever get lost, do you understand me? I cannot have it said that Rabbi Vilnish cannot keep track of his charge."

It was then that Jacob surprised the rabbi in a way that the man of God would have never imagined.

"Rabbi," began Jacob in the voice of a child, but speaking as if he were a full grown man, "we walked three streets from the square and took a left. Now we have walked to the end of the lane where your free-standing house is butted up against a small wooded area. Almost all the buildings were of stone and concrete. If we were to stand back from your door and look back to the town proper, we would see the outline of the cathedral in the distance to the right and the larger buildings of the town's business district getting smaller as we looked out to the horizon."

The rabbi took the boy's hand and knelt before him so that they could look each other eye to eye.

As he did, Jacob went on, "My father taught me to know where I am at all times. I would ride in his wagon with him on the way into town and make note of special trees or landmarks. Then when we would ride, he would point to certain trees and ask me questions about them."

"Why would he do that?" asked the rabbi.

"He did not want me to be afraid in the woods. He did not want me to be afraid in the town. He wanted me to know where I am at all times. He said a man must see with his eyes, hear with his ears, and make them all work with his mind. 'Only when everything works together will a man survive in the world,' he would say."

Leaning into the boy, the rabbi said, "And where is God in this world, young Mr. Jacob?"

"He is in the trees and in the sky and in earth and in the town and in the people we love so that we must never get lost in this life. That is what holds us to this earth."

The rabbi thought that Jacob was talking about the Word of God and hugged him tightly.

The boy had been talking about the geography of the world he lived in. His father had never mentioned the Word of God, only that "he had created the land and sky in order to guide us to market and back."

The rabbi stood and put his hand out in front of him for Jacob to shake. The boy did as the rabbi asked.

As they shook, the rabbi said, "I will always trust you, Jacob."

Jacob nodded his head and broke the handshake by asking, "When can I see Leah?"

Turning to unlock his door, the rabbi said, "I cannot promise you much other than at some point, we will see your sister." He held the door open for the boy to pass through as he went on, "I fear

Mrs. Malkin has plans for the girl, and for now, we must make our own plans to set up our house. In time we will have a moment for the girl."

Then he walked over to the small table near the fireplace. "We have half a pot of stew to heat." Pointing to the wall, he said, "Hang your coat on the small hook. Later we will fix it so it is easier for you to reach."

With that, the life of Jacob began to take shape.

Later in that first day, one of the townsfolk stopped by with a small cot for the boy. Together the two men set it up in the far corner of the house. The back room would remain the rabbi's to sleep in. For now, and until his bar mitzvah seven years later, Jacob would sleep on the cot in the corner of the front room.

To whatever a degree a boy who has lost both parents and been separated from his sister can feel secure, Jacob felt secure in the rabbi's house.

The days began to pass. The memory of his father's death began to take up less and less of his time as his life grew. Jacob did his chores, and when the time came for him to start school, he started school.

Though the town of Pinsk did have schools for the very young, the rabbi taught Jacob at home. He gave him instructions on the Torah and did what he could to be a friend to the boy. But as much as he might wish that he could, it was not in the rabbi's personality to extend much warmth or understanding to someone so young.

Jacob could sense that the rabbi was uncomfortable with a young boy under his feet. As with anyone at his young age, he was quite restless and spent a good amount of time outdoors. This was agreeable to both of them, as it left the rabbi alone to study his books and write commentaries on what he had read.

It was at their second meal on the second day that they lived together that Jacob asked the rabbi about his wife, "Did you have a wife like my Momma?"

When he heard the question, the rabbi sat back, put down his spoon, and rested both hands on the table. Together they sat in silence for a minute. The rabbi thought about how to properly respond to the boy's question.

Reb Vilnish then answered, "My wife died in the same flu epidemic that took your Momma, my son."

"Did lots of people die in this flu epidemic?" Jacob queried. "And will it come again?"

"Only God can truly answer that question, young Jacob," the old man answered, "but that sickness seems to have departed. Let us try to forget those terrible days of the flu and find comfort in our holy books, like the Talmud."

Sadly, the widowed rabbi was never meant to be a homemaker. After her passing, he had become careless in the way he took care of both himself and his house. With the absence of a woman in his life, his small home had grown dingy and fallen into disrepair. It was poorly heated and had cracks in the walls. The impoverished Jewish community of Pinsk could only furnish the rabbi with the barest of necessities. Barely comfortable himself in such a small space, he wondered out loud how he was going to take care of the boy.

The house had two simple rooms. The front held a small kitchen with a single burner stove that served to heat the house. There was a dining table that could, in a pinch, seat four. This is where the rabbi and his wife had learned to talk to each other. He loved their meals together and hoped that the boy would grow to become someone that he could discuss both the Talmud and the price of a half-pound of good brisket.

The back room was the rabbi's study and also held his bed. A window in one wall was permanently closed by a wooden shutter that, due to excessive moisture, had expanded past its frame. There was a rickety old bookcase with three shelves next to a small desk that held a candle stuck on the top of an old bottle.

Even though he had not wanted to raise the boy by himself, once he accepted that the boy's life had become his responsibility, he held on to a secret hope that the boy would bring some light and life to his dark surroundings.

In the first few weeks, the rabbi did try as hard as he could to relate to the boy. When they ate, he asked Jacob questions, "Jacob, my child, do you like living here?"

"It's okay," the boy quickly grew into a pattern of one- or two-word answers. He would be respectful but remain distant and unknown to the rabbi.

When they were studying, the rabbi could feel that the boy was somewhere else.

"You understood what I just read from the Talmud, didn't you?"

From a place that the rabbi would never know, Jacob answered in a monotone, "Yes, Rabbi."

A smarter man might have realized that the boy was in shock, just as the rabbi had been when his own beloved wife passed away. But the rabbi's intelligence lay in books, not in the experiences of life. The sadness in the heart of Jacob eluded the rabbi, for though he knew that Jacob was only six, he couldn't help but to think of him as just another man.

In time the initial energy that he had found in focusing on the boy's presence in his home began to dissipate. During the times he was there for meals and to study with the rabbi, Jacob realized that he was free to run around outside as long as he returned to the small house in a timely fashion.

"Jacob, my son, you were late for dinnertime, so you must clean out all the dinner pots."

"I am sorry, Reb Vilnish, I will not be late in the future."

While he was allowed great leeway in his time outdoors, the rabbi had warned him not to venture into the woods. It was a legitimate request, as an occasional wolf was known to prowl along the far edges of Pinsk. But Jacob was young, inquisitive, and restless. He had been born to a desolate and rural surrounding. Within a few weeks, he knew every inch of the world around him.

As the rabbi went about his work in town, he was primarily paid with work done in kind. Sometimes it was carpentry; sometimes it was plumbing. Sometimes he was paid in candles to light on Friday in order to bless the Sabbath meal. On the best of occasions, there was a chicken to prepare for a Friday night meal as well.

One thing that he had never considered was that the house was in no way equipped to house a small boy. There were no toys or sporting equipment. The house was simply not the proper environment for a six-year-old boy. Instead of providing games, friends, action, and activity for the child, Reb Vilnish decided to inculcate Jacob into the mysteries of the Talmud and Torah.

Staying still and learning was not part of Jacob's plan. He longed for the outdoors and the sounds and smell of the river and farm land around the town of Pinsk. However, he knew that the rabbi meant well, and he could see that the rabbi was trying as hard as he could. So he would sometimes pinch his own thigh to stay awake when the rabbi spoke of Rashi and Tosafos, and he would sometimes give a longer answer than the question required just to show the rabbi that he was engaged.

Regardless, most of Jacob's life was filled with loneliness. The rabbi would often instruct him for two or three hours and then leave him alone while he went off into his own study and shut the door. As he was being schooled at home, the boy failed to build any real friendships with others his own age.

During mealtime, the rabbi would speak of the books of the Bible, while Jacob could hear the sounds of other boys running and laughing. Jacob would wash the dishes and then retire to his own end of the house where, through his own studies, he was expected to build his own future.

At a dinner, the rabbi said, "Jacob, my son, you must study and study hard, for in only a few years, it will be your bar mitzvah. You will appear before the entire congregation and will prove that you are worthy of being called a man."

Understanding that he was lucky to have a roof over his head and that he, almost always, found a good meal on a plate before him—at least once a day—the boy would argue no further. In order to keep the rabbi happy, Jacob would often read Exodus. He read this book because he found hope in the idea of escape.

If school seemed to be boring his young charge, the rabbi was not above bringing the memory of Jacob's father into the picture when he needed to. He would incorporate passages in the Torah for emphasis.

"Your father, of blessed memory, would be proud to see you someday stand before the congregation in Shul and recite the prayers of a bar mitzvah."

The image of his father, though growing confused in his mind as the years passed, would never leave his heart. When the rabbi mentioned Avram's name, Jacob would straighten up and work twice as hard. Gifted with determination and a fine sense of discipline, Jacob made a successful bar mitzvah his goal.

In a long moment of introspection, he said to himself, "When I become bar mitzvahed, I will then be a man, and I will rescue Leah from servitude, and we will leave Pinsk forever."

Neither the butcher nor the rabbi ever thought it was important for the brother and sister to maintain contact. Both men had experienced loss or loneliness in their own childhoods. The butcher had lost siblings to flu, war, and ignorance. The rabbi had grown up alone under his mother's care, and his father left when he was too young to remember him. In adulthood, both men were also preoccupied with their own lives, leaving little understanding for how deep the bond between Leah and Jacob had been. To them, loss was a part of daily life.

It was Jacob's separation from Leah that stoked his desire to explore. A year after moving into the rabbi's house, he developed the habit of slipping out at night. He held his journeys on nights where the limited shine of a quarter moon was high above the streets of Pinsk. It would be just enough light for him to slip along the walls and the trees of the village nearly unseen. A full moon would make it too easy for a townsperson to see him as he quietly drifted among the streets.

Two or three times a month (and only after he had stood by the door to the rabbi's room and listened to him snore for at least ten minutes), he would slowly open the latch to the front door of the rabbi's house and sneak into the night. That the house he lived in was at the end of the road helped him stay unnoticed. Behind the house were dense, thick woods that often served as cover if he felt he was about to be discovered.

Over the next few years, he would sneak out when he could. During winters, he seldom ventured out for fear that footprints in a recent snowfall would betray his journeys. Regardless of the season, he chose the nights that he slipped out cautiously. Jacob knew that to be caught would mean that he would probably be sent away to a home for orphans. This would be a fate far worse than sitting for a few hours while the rabbi discussed the Talmud.

Alone, he would travel clad in dark pants, dark coat, and his heavy black shoes, while wearing a dark cap over his easily recognizable red hair. Despite the occasional joke at his expense, he had never felt bad about being a redheaded boy. In fact, he found it kind of special to be the only one in the village, as if he was singled out for glory. But he realized that if someone did see him at night, it was his hair that would give him away. So he took special care to conceal as much of it as he could. Feeling his way carefully along buildings, counting random bricks in each as he walked, Jacob grew to know every inch of the City of Pinsk.

During the day, he could openly explore the woods and beyond, for the rabbi was often too distracted to know where he was going. The rabbi enjoyed the quiet he found when the boy left after his lessons.

Jacob loved the woods almost as much as he enjoyed traveling at night. The first few times he explored the wooded areas, he would use large buttons or, if it was close to sunset, a small bit of colored yarn as markers so he could return easily. As he went out into the unknown land, he made sure to pick the markers up when he traveled home.

As the years went by, Jacob had only one goal in life: escape—escape with his sister from the Malkins and escape from the confines of Pinsk. He plotted promising paths leading out from Pinsk. He absorbed the wooded areas in and around Pinsk so that they became like a coat of his own skin. He discovered the possible advantages of the nearby Pripet Marshes as a means to evade pursuers.

Most of all, he had to know how he would have to extricate Leah from the Malkins' compound. Jacob studied—usually at night—the ill-kept stable area, the old guard dog's habits, and the presence of the horses. Jacob, working at night, learned the feeding habits of the horses. The guard dog was old, and table scraps could easily quiet him. The crude wire lock on the stable could be easily circumvented.

Harnesses were clean and well kept, but once inside the stable, they were there for the taking.

Over the period of two years, Jacob constructed a plan to rescue Leah and leave Pinsk forever!

# LEAH AT SIXTEEN

Leah's life had taken a different shape than Jake's. From the time she had arrived at the home of Mayer Malkin almost seven years earlier, Leah had not once found companionship among the boys. In time they had come to regard Leah as nothing more than the housekeeper. With the exception of Leon, they spoke to her in dismissive tones, seldom showing her much more concern than they showed to an animal on their farm.

There was no one with whom to share her fears and no companion with whom to confide. Certainly, no one in her life showed her the slightest affection. From the first day in the house, there was no letup all day in the cooking and cleaning and washing.

"You dumb bitch, you left streaks on the dining room table. Get it clean before we eat!" cried Dora Malkin, was not an unfamiliar imprecation.

In addition there were the harsh comments continually thrown at her by all the members of the household. But none were more hurtful and dismissive than those uttered by Dora Malkin.

After her first month at the house, the woman had thrown the laundry down the steps to where Leah was standing.

"My boys deserve clean shirts! Their shirts were never clean enough, you stupid girl."

After each meal, the criticism came before the second bite was taken.

"The food was too salty…" "The bread was uneven…" "The greens were overcooked…" The complaints were endless. Dora Malkin was never satisfied with anything that Leah did.

The love that she had once known from her parents was absent in this household. There was not a shred of kindness. For most of the first year, she fell asleep each night crying for someone to rescue her from this hell.

After a while, as time passed, Leah started to come into her own. Her nemesis, Dora Malkin, eventually tired of berating the girl and, over the years, found better distractions in her imagined ills and her evolving status in the town.

This provided the girl with time to develop her own manner as she conducted her duties. In time it was Leah who was running the house from the top floor to the bottom. She eventually grew to oversee the kitchen and cooking as well. The butcher shop would employ part-time cooks to help with preparation for holidays and certain catered occasions, such as weddings. In this, Leah proved to be extremely skilled and was spoken of by those who came to work on those days as a kind boss. Mayer Malkin, upon learning that Leon was teaching her to read and write, had her start scheduling the shifts of the workers in the store.

As she had grown, Leah had developed the same roundness in her hips that her mother had. With a basic understanding of the idea of chastity, and unwilling to give any of the Malkin boys even the slightest idea toward an advance of any sort, she wore her top high to cover her growing breasts. Her hair was now long, and she styled it in the same way that she remembered her mother's hair: a curl over a curl followed by a small twist and final curl—all held in place by a discreet pin.

To uphold his standing as the butcher of the Jewish community, Leah was allowed to attend Sabbath services in the small synagogue of Pinsk. She was delighted to see Jacob assisting Rabbi Vilnish in the services. Though she had to sit in the women's section, she was able to view much of the entire congregation. Leah became aware of many of the male congregants casting long glances as she took her seat. She wondered if, among the young men, there would be a prospective husband for her.

Leah had never been made aware of the full responsibilities of marriage. Dora Malkin, a selfish woman, had never once thought to sit the girl down and explain the ways of the world to her. A year or so earlier, she had begun to notice several of the boys and even one or two men pausing to watch her as she went about her way.

In every instance, either Dora or her husband, the butcher, would yell at the culprit.

"If you keep staring at her, I'll give you a black eye!" Mayer Malkin roared, sending them on the way with a warning to never return.

Neither of the Malkins ever felt they should sit down and explain to Leah why the boys were starting to smile at her.

There were precious moments that Leah and Jacob were able to steal from their strict duties.

No matter how often they did this, in every meeting, Leah would tell him, "I'm amazed at how thick your red hair has become and how tall you've grown in such a short time since I last saw you. I'm proud of you for staying in school with the rabbi while other boys played until it became dark."

Looking at Leah, Jacob knew that she was growing in ways that he had begun to notice on other women that he had seen. She was now becoming curvy where she had once been as straight and thin as a pencil. Her chest, even though she made an effort to hide it, was growing in ways he didn't understand yet. Her hair, even when she wore it in a tight bun as she did almost every day, had become dark, dark black.

"Your hair looks as if it is made from the finest of rare silk," her brother said.

Once, when she had noticed him looking at her, she said, "At night I brush it one hundred times before I go to bed. You don't remember much, but Momma would brush mine just like that when I was a little girl, back when you were still in the cradle, and then I would do hers."

"I kind of remember," said Jacob between bites of his sandwich. "Momma sat there, and you would circle around the back of her chair. Poppa read something, maybe a newspaper, and I was sitting on the ground, in front of the coal stove. Sometimes it seems as if I make this stuff up, but I swear that it seems true to me."

# LEAH'S PROBLEM

A few months before Jacob's bar mitzvah, Leah mentioned to Jacob that she had always been deeply uncomfortable around Mayer Malkin and that while her discomfort had always been there, it had suddenly grown especially troublesome.

She began speaking nervously, "He starts to pass me in the close hallway, in the back, where he never used to go. I don't like it. He grabs my arm and holds it for a minute when he talks to me, and he puts his face so close that when he does…" Leah recoiled as if his very face was now inches away from her and then continued.

"The man smells horrible, as if he has been eating pickles all day, which I know he does because I see him eat at least three…" Seeing the look of concern in Jacob's eye, she caught herself and tried to pull back on what she felt. "Yes, I did mention it to Leon. He is the only one I can really talk to. But he told me the old man is harmless!"

As Leah laughed and smoothed out the bottom part of her dress, Jacob felt a sickness in his stomach. He knew something very bad was being described, but he didn't understand it.

"You tell me if he goes too far," he said. "He is your boss, you are not a slave. You just hang on, and I will get us out of here."

"How?" his sister asked.

"I am not sure. There has to be a way. When the moment is right, we will be free! I think about it all the time! Right now is not our time. Our childhood will end shortly," came his reply.

Leah gasped at what she heard. This wasn't the little fuzzy red-headed boy that she had grown to love so dearly. This was a forceful, determined young man sitting next to her.

It was then that Leon Malkin walked up to them and said, "Momma is coming back in a few minutes. In fact, she's late already."

Jacob looked up. "Thanks, Leon. We are always thankful that you look out for us."

Leon Malkin replied, "You're a good guy, Jake. I don't want you to catch any shit from the old lady." He paused and smiled, "Remember me if you get to Minsk. I am going to move to Minsk to live with my uncle next year, so keep your eye peeled."

"Who knows, it may be sooner than you think." Jake smiled and thought that he should keep his mouth shut before he said anything about his plans for escaping Pinsk.

"Look, Momma is coming back any second, and she won't want to see you here near the pen. She thinks that you're going to take Leah from her in the middle of the night." When he saw that they weren't jumping when he spoke, he went on, "You hear me, you two? Get out of our yard, and get to work." Leon began to talk louder and added a bit more authority in his voice, "Maybe you had better stay away for a week or so, Jake."

Jake did, indeed, stay away for more than a week. Leah had made him more than aware of the vindictive nature inside the heart of Dora Malkin. The last thing he wanted to do was to cause more trouble for his poor sister. He hated that, except for Leon—who, at best, spoke to her sparingly—she had no one in that house who really respected or valued her as a human being. She was their servant, a half step above slave.

That night he knew that it wasn't a matter of *if* he was going to leave Pinsk with Leah but a matter of *when*. In his nighttime solitary forays, Jake planned the fastest and the safest way to exit Pinsk and the Malkins. He observed the likes and dislikes of Mayer

Malkin's animals. He scouted out the forest and swamplands of the Pripet Marsh.

None of this occurred overnight. He slowly and carefully, over several years, planned the escape with his sister.

# THE BAR MITZVAH

In the weeks leading up to Jacob's bar mitzvah, Leah did what she could to help with the plans for the celebration. In the few moments that the two siblings were able to find together, she did her best to keep Jake the center of all they discussed. She quizzed him on his studies, especially what verse he would read from the Torah and what he would do to prove himself in the eyes of the community.

Despite the brightness of her smile, the winning way she spoke of what lay in store for him, and the animated stories that she told of customers who passed through the door of the butcher's store—he felt that she was masking something. The connection between the two, spoken or unspoken, was too deep for him to not know that something was wrong. He thought that she covering up a darkness that had developed in her life.

He was right. In the past year, Leah had seen a change in the way that the butcher and others had begun to treat her. In many ways, she and Jake shared a similar problem. For all the people they had met in the years following their father's passing, they were still alone. Despite being surrounded by others—many of whom were much older than they were—neither one had acquired a mentor, someone to help them answer questions and offer honest advice.

The rabbi was simply too distracted by his studies to help Jake with any of life's more awkward questions.

In the house of the Butcher Malkin, Leah was almost an outcast. Of the brothers, only Leon had shown any real concern for her on any level, and even that was fleeting. She had discovered that he was a moody boy, who only spoke when he felt like it. His four other brothers regarded her as little more than a slave.

The abusive nature of Dora Malkin was well known. At times, it seemed that nothing could ever stop the woman's attacks on the poor girl. The butcher was a foul man, who cursed and drank when he worked and brooded when he was alone.

In Jacob's eyes, they both had been held captive for almost eight years. While other boys in the town played raucously, Jacob kept to himself, planning an escape with his sister from Pinsk and everything that the town meant to them.

Leah had never attended a proper school. Every moment she lived was spent under the constant and watchful eye of Mrs. Malkin. Her opportunities for friendship with someone her own age were limited. She had seen her body change, and as it had, she learned to rely on the hand-me-downs of Dora Malkin. There were skirts that were too long or too big, shirts and blouses that were faded and worn, shoes and undergarments that were too tight or too loose.

The girl had questions about her body, but when she raised them to the only real woman in her life, they were met with laughter and disdain. She was called "stupid!" and told "to stop being a complainer."

"All women suffer, read your Bible, it is our payment for sin!"

Jake learned what he could about women from the farmhands and from observing the cattle that they brought with them at fair days. He understood what was necessary for his job and little more.

As his bar mitzvah drew near, he was sure of one thing: Leah was troubled, and she was doing what she could to cover it up.

The problem had begun almost three years earlier when she was fourteen.

One day, while she was sweeping the shop near closing time, she noticed Mayer Malkin standing at his cutting table holding a large knife. A hint of vodka hung in the room. As she looked around, she saw the bottle sitting on a far shelf. When she caught his eye, her stomach grew queasy and she felt a bit dizzy. She stopped sweeping, and a wave of embarrassment raced across her body, until she could feel a blush in her cheeks.

Involuntarily, her hand covered her mouth, and as it did, the butcher brought his knife down on the table with a loud *whack*! She saw evil in the brief smile that crossed his face before he started laughing. Smiling weakly, she finished her job and ran from the room. Leaning against a wall in the hallway leading back to the family kitchen, she found herself breathing quickly, as if in a panic.

When she fell against the wall, distraught and confused, Dora Malkin walked by and yelled to her, "Lazy stupid girl, get in here and finish sweeping before you mop this kitchen."

Leah, fearing even harsher comments or possibly reprisals for something she didn't fully understand, immediately did as she was told.

From that night almost three years earlier, the butcher had gotten in the habit of passing her in close quarters and rubbing against her. Sometimes, when she bent down to sweep up the dirt in her dustpan, she felt his eyes on her. Once in a while, he would make a movement toward her, making her jump involuntarily. Everything he did began to take on new meanings. Not six months ago, when she found the feeling of being watched overwhelming, she looked up to find the Butcher Malkin standing three feet away and towering over her menacingly while she knelt to do her job.

After every encounter with him, she felt unclean. In time she had found ways to avoid him, especially in close quarters. When she did see him, he would sometimes say, "I know what you're doing, little girl," or, "You know whom you belong to, don't you?"

## JAKE THE HORSE THIEF

She hated the idea that she belonged to anyone.

Leah understood that she was growing and that men were starting to look at her differently. There were customers who lingered in the store too long, only to find themselves chased away by the butcher or his overweight wife.

Those feelings came to an end near her birthday in January. Coming around the corner with a package of some cheese that had been dropped off at the wrong door, she saw a young man in the corner of the shop. Immediately, her heart began to race. She was surprised to see anyone staring at her. As she responded to his gaze, she saw that he was staring at something she couldn't see.

Another step revealed what he saw. Mayer Malkin, the butcher all six feet of him, clad in a bloody apron and holding a knife—was standing before the young man. The look on his face was the same one that she had seen when he discovered someone cheating him or unable to make a payment on the money that he loaned. The boy looked over at her, then looked back at the butcher, and raced out the door. She froze where she stood.

The butcher, upon seeing her, took two steps toward her. "He needs to understand the difference between someone's property and a real woman."

As he had the first time that he looked at her in a disturbing way, he laughed. This time he added a wink as he walked back to the counter of his shop.

Meanwhile, Jake's life was expanding. His thirteenth birthday was approaching and, with it, his bar mitzvah. Jake's bar mitzvah meant that in the eyes of the Jewish people, he would become a man. Over many years, the rabbi had prepared him for this day. For years, he had studied the Torah with the idea that he would select the perfect verse to reflect his new life. For years, he and the rabbi had studied and spoken in Hebrew (a language that complemented his understanding of Yiddish). For years he had attended Shabbat services at the synagogue in order to be ready.

Granted, he did live with a rabbi, so attendance at any religious service would have been essentially compulsory. But as the years passed, he had grown to love his faith as well as the history of his people. He saw them as part of who he was.

A quiet boy, he kept his counsel during discussions. His constant devotion to the rabbi had gained him a reputation as a good boy. On the coming Shabbat, he was now going to become a trusted young man.

A strong boy, some residents of Pinsk had occasionally asked for his help over the years. This is how the day before his bar mitzvah, Jake found himself standing in front of a mirror at the home of the Widow Reis. She had asked him to assist her with packages that had come in on the train that afternoon. After placing the packages in her front room, he was waiting for her to return from the kitchen. When he had helped her in the past, she had gotten in the habit of giving him a small baked treat before he left.

Looking in the mirror, he said the name out loud to himself: "Jake."

Looking back at him through the smudges of dirt on a cloudy background that was the Widow Reis's mirror, he saw an unfamiliar face dotted with green eyes and slight freckles and what he felt were ears that may be too large. On top of it all was a shock of tangled red hair that, from a distance, could only serve as a calling card.

He said his name again: "Jake."

The rabbi had a small mirror that he used for shaving—a habit Jake had yet to acquire. This was the first time that he had ever really taken a second to evaluate his own appearance, to see who he was to other people.

Once she had returned with three large cookies, he said, "Thank you."

As she handed him the cookies, she paused for a minute.

Jake said, "Yes, Mrs. Reis?"

Moving her slim arm out from the sleeve of her dark shirt, she touched him on his arm and said, "Thank you for taking the chair out of the back shed and moving it into the front room last week."

There was something odd about the way her touch felt. He looked up and noticed, for the first time, that her eyes were almost blue and that her hair was lighter than most of the other women's in the city. She had always been so kind to him. And Jake found himself lingering on the idea that he should hug her good-bye.

She went on, "You take care of so many of us, Jake. I can only offer you these small cookies right now, but I will see you at your bar mitzvah in a few days."

She then squeezed his arm, and Jacob found himself almost overwhelmed with the feeling that he was about to cry. It had been so long since he had thought of his mother that as she looked at him now, he felt as if he wanted to cry.

Swallowing hard and biting his tongue at the tip she proffered, he straightened his back and replied, "No need, Mrs. Reis, I am always glad to do anything for you."

For the first time ever, he responded to her touch and patted the top of her hand.

She looked him straight in the eye. "You would have been a good son for my husband and me. He wanted a boy, but it was not what was planned for us."

Jake saw that her eyes were now growing misty, and he became confused. He felt that he had to leave as fast as he could.

Slipping out from her hand, he put a hand up to wave good-bye. "Your husband and you would have had many good sons, Mrs. Reis. And I know that you would have treated them all well. And the rabbi is going to spend time with me on some questions after dinner."

She began to blush and quickly pulled back away from him, as she spoke, "Of course, Jake. Excuse me, but it does get lonely sometimes. I do miss my husband…" she trailed off as if caught by embarrassment and didn't know how to end the thought.

He bowed a bit as he left and walked out. Once in the sunlight, he felt confused while at the same time as strong and as sure of himself as any boy a few days away from thirteen-year-old ever could.

There were those who asked for his help and did nothing, not even utter a simple "Thank you." The eldest son of the butcher was one of them. Jake had accompanied him to the station one day to drop off a trunk for shipping, and when they were done, the Malkin boy had simply walked away, leaving Jake on the platform alone.

In time he had grown to understand that what he was doing for others was part of the mitzvoth, for he considered his kindness just a human thing to do.

"You must help others as they needed it," was something the rabbi had said every time he was called upon to do something for a member of the synagogue.

The bar mitzvah of Jacob Horvicz was a cause for celebration for many. Over the last eight years, Jake hadn't realized it, but he had grown to be a part of the town of Pinsk. The number of people who turned out to see him at the ceremony surprised him. He had been so busy studying for the big day that he had never thought to ask the rabbi exactly who would be there.

Standing in front of many of the people in his life, waiting his turn to speak in front of a large group, Jake found that there are different sets of nerves for different occasions. Speaking in front of people was a lot more difficult than sneaking out at night to feed a horse some carrots.

The night before the "big day," Jacob tossed and tuned in his small bed. That he was an orphan with only his sister and the aged

## JAKE THE HORSE THIEF

Rabbi Vilnish that exhibited love for him was a reality. He didn't expect from others and was determined to make his life with nothing else to depend on other than his sister, Leah. He faced the congregation for his bar mitzvah with a calm demeanor that amazed everyone, including Reb Vilnish!

Others, such as the Widow Reiss and the Station Attendant Havel, looked on with smiles.

Jake had never really developed friendships with boys his own age. Having been schooled at home by the rabbi, he had missed out on a lot of the activities and friendships that a school setting would have provided.

No matter whom he looked at, his eyes always came back to his sister. The Malkins had allowed Leah to attend with the understanding that when she returned home, she was expected to take off the fancy dress that Mrs. Malkin had lent her and finish her work as usual.

She had arrived trailing the Malkin clan, just as she had grown accustomed to doing over the years. Removing her coat, she placed it with the others. For a reason that Leah couldn't understand, she had been allowed to dress in one of Mrs. Malkin's oldest and finest dresses.

When she had first tried it on, it fit her so tightly that it emphasized her growing curves, as if it had been made especially for her. Her modesty had made her take the dress out a bit so it wouldn't fit so tightly. Even hanging loosely, it still flattered her enough that Jake saw several of the men there that night staring at her with smiles.

Her hair, covered as it should be for temple, still shone in the light that fell through the windows. Parted down the middle, it had grown down past the center of her back and fell in such a natural way that it looked as if she had never combed it once in her life. To Jake she looked radiant, filled with the true spirit of beauty. He was proud to have a sister who, despite the harshness of her life, carried herself with such grace and dignity.

Leaving her coat, she turned around to see several of the men attending looking at her with smiles. She nodded slightly and ran to the side of Dora Malkin.

Dora Malkin was there in her best dress and with her husband. Jake looked at the butcher in his starched collar and his shiny suit and wanted to laugh. He looked like a cow squeezed into a pen that was half of its size. Leon and one of his brothers also attended. The other three couldn't be bothered.

The service went according to plans. When called to speak, Jake spoke in calm, somber tones and with a sense of authority. He chose passages from Exodus and read from the book of Prophets, as custom dictated. Jake performed well and took pride in seeing smiles on faces of the rabbi and Leah as they looked up at him.

After the service had finished, the celebrants moved into the hall for a small gathering. A feeling of shared warmth and joy permeated the event. Many had donated food or a small plate of baked goods. Everyone was happy for the boy, who many had thought would either run away or perish after being left an orphan. There was wine and good water for all.

Jacob met his well-wishers with a smile and a handshake. He watched as the rabbi beamed with pride while those around him complimented him on the job he had done with the boy. The rabbi's reply was always the same: "He was good boy to start with. I did nothing."

It didn't escape Jake's eye that men, both single and married, all managed to find time to stop by Leah's table. Dora Malkin stayed close to the girl and spoke to all the men as they drifted by. Some she met with a steely glance, as if to say, "Don't waste your time." Others, if they met her unspoken qualifications, were allowed to approach and say a few words to the girl.

At first Jacob was uncomfortable with what was happening. At the back of his mind, it was always there that one day he planned to remove her from the slavery that the Malkins had created for his sister. He knew they had come to view her as servant, one who owed them something, that they believed that she should be grateful for what they had done.

He despised them but kept such feelings to himself.

It was only when Mr. Littman pulled him aside and let him know that this kind of attention toward his sister was to be expected, that he needed to find a way to be comfortable with it.

He went on to tell Jake that, "Beauty was a gift from God, and it was also natural for a man to admire such a gift." He also pointed out that, "It was what a woman did with such a gift that made her what she was." Lowering his voice, he leaned in and told Jake in a very matter-of-fact manner, "The fat old hag is looking to cash in on your sister. Some of these men have money, and money is just as attractive to an old woman as a young girl is to a man of any age."

The two men, for this was the day that Jake was now a man, stood silent for a few minutes. Jake fumed as he knew that what Mr. L. had said was true. Dora Malkin saw money in the eyes of those who passed by her charge. As she ran interference with possible suitors, she also made it clear that she viewed "young Leah as the daughter I have always wanted."

When Jacob overheard this, he could only think of the soiled clothes, the worn shoes, the broken cracks in his sister's hands from too much dishwater, and the never-ending stream of insults that Dora Malkin had spewed at the girl over the years.

Customs of the time and place dictated that Leah was not much more than property. With the Malkins responsible for her keep and her well-being, Jake realized that they had also assumed control of her destiny as well.

Two other men, one of whom Jake recognized as the ticket master at the railway station, clustered around the widow whom he had just helped a few days earlier, Mrs. Reiss. She looked profoundly unhappy, bearing a false smile as the two men refused to allow her to leave the corner in which they had trapped her.

When someone started playing an accordion and another broke out in song on a violin, each of them demanded that she dance with him. She looked at Jake as if to say, "Please, take me out of here."

He felt helpless—a feeling he seldom had experienced before—as he watched the ticket master put his arm around the Widow Reiss and move her into the open space for a dance.

The boys who had known Jacob all shook his hand and asked him if he would come to their bar mitzvah. Even though he knew it was a lie, he told them, "Yes, of course." More than one of their parents had taken a few slices of brisket home in their pocket or purse.

As he left, the butcher needed to be supported by one of his boys. The wine that he had so graciously supplied had done its job on his aging legs. This left only Dora Malkin to walk her "daughter" home. As they were getting ready to leave, Dora Malkin came over and asked for a few moments alone with the rabbi. This was the first time in the evening that he and Leah would be able to be alone.

While the two adults stood off to the side, Leah and Jacob caught up with each other. She spoke of the attention of the men, and then she began to talk to Jacob about their plans.

"This is home," she said as she brushed her hair under her hat. "I hate the Malkins as much as you, but until tonight, I never thought that I was an option. No matter what you think you saw, my only real option in this life to find a way to be with you."

Outside the rain had begun to fall. She looked at her brother and took his hand. She spoke quickly with panic in her eyes and more than a hint of it in her voice.

"When the time comes, we must leave. This is not our lives. Our lives will start elsewhere. Will you find a way for us to leave here? Please don't let me marry a man that she chooses. I will marry a man in accordance with our faith and our tradition, but not a man whom she sees fit for his fat wallet or the property he owns. Please save me."

Returning her gaze, he answered her question with one word, "Yes."

She knew that today her brother was, indeed, a man, for she could never doubt him after such a sure and confident answer. They didn't have to say another word.

The rabbi and Mrs. Malkin came over and stood by their respective charges—she, by the side of Leah, and the rabbi, by the side of Jacob.

Mrs. Malkin put out her hand to Jacob, and he took it.

"The rabbi and I agree that the food we supplied should be more than enough of a gift for you today, Jacob." Dora Malkin looked over to the rabbi and said, "I know that he can't have been as much help as Leah has been to us, but still we are glad that you took him when you did. We couldn't hold another boy in that house."

Smiling, Rabbi Vilnish said, "We are all grateful for the good that God puts in our life, Mrs. Malkin. And I know that Jacob is grateful as well."

Realizing what the rabbi meant, Jacob spoke up, "Of course, I am appreciative, ma'am. The food was something everyone here valued and appreciated."

Dora Malkin looked at the rabbi and sneered, "I notice there wasn't a 'thank you' in that noble little speech."

Jacob stepped up to meet her at eye level. For today he felt taller than he ever had before. "I am most thankful for what you have done today, Mrs. Malkin. It makes the future so bright."

The wife of Butcher Malkin stepped back and sneered, "You don't fool me, little Orphan Boy Horvicz. I know what you are."

Leah stood behind the woman, and her eyes grew large. She was afraid that anything that Jake said would come back to her.

Jake looked at the woman as warmly as he could, "Mrs. Malkin, my sister and I thank you for everything that you have done for us. Please be assured that what you have done for us is a debt we will have a hard time repaying," he swallowed and added, "if we ever really can."

Mrs. Malkin looked at him up and down. Smelling of wine and bread and sweet cake, she exhaled, leaned in, and kissed Jacob on the cheek. "I know you do, dear boy. Sometimes I grow a little testy. And it has been a long day."

Turning to Leah, she said, "Do you have my shawl, girl?"

Leah produced the woman's wrap from around her arm and placed it about the woman's shoulder. Nodding good-bye to the rabbi, Mrs. Malkin turned and began to walk out of the building, taking the arm of Leah as she did. All Leah could do was wave good-bye to her brother.

It was now that only the rabbi and Jacob remained in the hall. They looked around and saw the mess they had been left to clean. The rabbi moved to a chair and sat down. He pulled something from his packet and beckoned for Jacob to sit down next to him.

Alone, the two men looked at each other and said nothing. The rabbi placed a small wrapped package on the table and motioned for Jacob to open it.

He did as he was asked and discovered a beautiful leather-bound prayer book that could easily fit in any man's pocket. It not only held prayers but the entire Book of Exodus as well. Jacob looked up to meet the rabbi's eyes and said nothing. He was afraid that he would start to cry.

The rabbi said, "We can write your name in it tomorrow morning. If you look along the edges, there is room to make notes as you study and learn."

With that, he took a second gift from another pocket and placed an envelope on the table.

Jacob hesitated before reaching for it. The rabbi nodded that he should. After a minute, he picked it up, opened it, and found that it held eighteen kopecks.

"Do you know why it holds eighteen, Jacob?"

"Yes, Rabbi Vilnish, I do."

With that, the old man got up and stood over the boy. "Good, I thought you would." Before he went on, he sighed deeply and looked at his young charge. "It has been good for us both to live as we have, Jacob. Now, let us enter into a new stage, a friendship based on respect."

Jacob stood up and hugged the man, who for the last eight years had helped him get to this point in life, "We have always been friends, Rabbi."

"Yes, I know. Now, be a good friend and clean this up while my old bones find comfort in sleep." Laughing as he walked out, he added, "Just get the big stuff, the rest we will get together tomorrow. This is your hall as much as it is mine."

"Actually, Rabbi," said Jacob, "it belongs to us all."

The rabbi smiled to himself as he left the building. He had done something he had never thought he ever would have. He had raised a man.

# THE KITCHEN OF BUTCHER MALKIN

Walking through the darkness on the way back to the Malkin's house, holding the arm of Mrs. Malkin as they moved through the night, Leah let herself dream for just a minute that she was walking with her real mother.

It was, for a few moments, a beautiful and comfortable dream, until it was shattered by the sound of Mrs. Malkin coughing and then spitting on the cobblestone path that led back to their shared house.

Then the woman spoke, "Look, girl, when we get back, I want you to take off that dress and clean it before you go to bed. Iron it, and make sure that tomorrow morning, it is returned to my closet. I don't want the smell of kitchen and stench of failure to get caught in the weave of the fabric."

They reached the house in silence and went in through the front door. Standing by a chest kept near the front of the house, Dora Malkin removed her shawl and handed it to Leah.

"Take care of this. I am going upstairs to change. I may find it in myself to come down and check on how you are taking care of my dress…"

With that, she took a small part of the garment's cuff between her fingers and began to rub it back and forth. Leah watched as her eyes began to grow moist. Looking up from the girl's sleeve, the older woman went on.

"I met Mayer Malkin at my youngest brother's bar mitzvah." Sighing at the memory, she continued, "I fit in this as well as you did tonight." Suddenly, the nostalgia seemed to fall from her eyes as she looked up at Leah. "But don't you get no ideas! I should not have married the man my mother chose. I could have found a young, good-looking young man! Instead, I got this disgusting old farmer because I couldn't have a choice. So rest assured, I won't let the same thing happen to you!" Dropping the fabric, she stood and started up the stairs, leaving Leah alone and deeply concerned about her future.

Once safely in her room off the side of the kitchen, she lit the small lamp that Mrs. Malkin had given her just months earlier. Without looking back, she began to remove the dress as quickly as she could. Smoothing it on the bed, she took a second to examine it for stains and damage.

Some may find the blackness of the dress and its simple design plain. But in the eyes of the girl who worked eighteen hours a day, nearly seven days a week, in the house of Mayer Malkin, it still looked beautiful. In her eyes, it was a gloriously perfect garment with the exact color she needed to bring out the shine in her hair and to contrast the red in her cheeks.

Standing back, she felt pride at having ever worn such a garment for even only a few hours. As to the slight alteration she had made earlier in the day, she knew that there was little chance of discovery as the current incarnation of Dora Malkin had little chance of ever fitting into such a perfect dress ever again.

Smiling to herself at the memory of the evening—the men, the food, and the look of pride on her brother's face as he read each and every passage perfectly—she thought that, at this moment, it may never be a better time to be Leah Horvicz.

Thinking of how Jacob was going to someday spirit her away from the torture and slavery of the Malkin household filled her with hope.

"Tonight we made a commitment to each other," she believed. "Jake will take care of me. I have a strong, able brother and don't need a husband picked out for me by horrible Dora Malkin."

Dora Malkin was not always a "horrible woman."
Dora Saltzer and Mayer Malkin was an "arranged marriage." The Saltzer family regarded Dora as one less hungry mouth to feed, and the butcher paid off the mortgage on the small Saltzer home as a major factor in the "deal." Dora was less than sixteen years old, and by the time she was seventeen years old, she was pregnant with what was to be four more births for the Malkin household—all boys.

After the birth of their fifth child, Dora rebelled. No more sex with the sweaty, foul-smelling Mayer, the butcher of Pinsk. She engaged in sexual foreplay for a short period with him before cutting off sex entirely, with the butcher's frustration simmered barely under the surface for several years for Mayer Malkin.

With the advent of a young female, Leah Horvicz, in the Malkin household, the butcher went to bed every night with the thought of a young female body and the pleasure that he could envision. As Leah reached her teens and her breasts began to strain against the thin garments that Dora supplied, Mayer's sexual thoughts increased whenever he came in close contact with the young woman. The thought of her breasts and buttocks in his hands became almost a constant condition when she brushed by him. Mayer was going crazy with desire!

Unaware of what she was to face, a tired Leah slowly returned to her very sparse quarters. For the second time that night, the smell of sweat and working and dancing and wine filled her nostrils. As it filled her senses, she stood straight up, as a jungle cat would do when it sensed danger. While she wanted to believe it was just a faint whiff of what she had smelled a few minutes earlier, she knew in her heart that it wasn't.

The light in the room shifted, and a thin shadow fell across her body. Turning slowly, she saw the heaving bulk of the Butcher Malkin standing in her door. Sweat was dripping from his brow, and his eyes held what she could only believe was evil. A small bit of spittle fell from the corner of his mouth.

"How could I have not heard him open it?" she said to herself. "How could I have been so careless and stupid to not lock it? I knew he was drunk…"

Taking a step toward Leah, the butcher was a towering, imposing figure. To Leah, he presented a frightening apparition, who had become an ugly reality. Mayer Malkin pulled at the buckle of his belt and slid it from the loops of his pants. He slowly wrapped it twice around his hand, leaving a good bit of leather dangling from his fist. Leah shrank fearfully from what she saw!

Standing as he was, in the flickering light of her small lamp, Mayer Malkin looked to Leah as if the devil incarnate had come into her life. Shadows bounced against the wall, growing large and small as he moved closer to her.

She said the first thing that came to her mind, "Mr. Malkin, are you worried about your wife's dress?"

The belt in his hand was now raised over his head, and in the light, she could see that he had left about eight or nine inches of the belt hanging. As the meaty hand of the drunken giant brought the belt across her stomach, it snapped loudly as it stung her flesh.

Leah remembered that she was in a slip that reached past her knees. Her undergarments had done little to protect her from the blow. She had heard the short, sharp crack of the leather before the pain had made it to her brain. Leah instantly doubled over and clutched at the air.

"I'll clean the dress before I go to bed!" she cried out. "I will clean the mess in the other room…"

Before she could finish her thought, a second crack split the air, and she felt a wild, stinging sensation rip across her arms when she tried to fend off the blow.

When she slumped, the enraged butcher grabbed her hand and wrenched her from the floor. In one swift motion, he picked her up from the floor, spun her around, and pushed the front of her body against the wall.

She felt his breath against her neck and began to struggle, while trying to turn herself around. She beat her fist against the wall. Reaching out with his right hand, he grabbed her wrists and forced them to the top of the wall.

His lips were now brushing against the softness of her neck. It felt as if hot water tainted with lye was burning her skin. Spit from his lips started to drip down her neck as he began to grunt. One of her hands broke free from his grasp, and she vainly tried to hit him.

Once again, he used his body to slam her flat against the wall. He used one of his legs to push her legs aside. When she tried to bring her together, his knee rose against her bottom. In the process, he whispered in her right ear, "If you stand still, it won't take so long, and there won't be a problem."

With that, he laughed and stepped about a half a foot away from her, kicking her legs apart. She wasn't sure what his intentions were, for she had never heard or dreamed of what was happening to her.

Then the butcher's left hand pushed her face against the wall, until her skin was sliding across his palm.

Leaning against her face, he mumbled, "I told you to stand still!"

She felt his knee push her thighs apart. The sound of the keys and change in his pockets hitting against the floor told her that his pants had fallen off.

## JAKE THE HORSE THIEF

Leah Horvicz had never had the details of men and women explained to her. She still thought that he was going to beat her for not cleaning up the mess he had made in the other room.

Suddenly, she felt him tear at her slip and then her undergarment. He had never beat her bottom without clothes on before.

The coldness of the breeze that always floated across the kitchen slipped through her door, finding its way across her exposed flesh. She grew cold.

Leah began to cry, and as she did, his hand found its way over her mouth and her nose. It was suddenly hard for her to breath.

Behind her, the drunken farmer stabbed away at her with what he could manage of his manhood, while she was still wiggling and moving. On his third attempt, he found what he was looking for, and Leah screamed into his face! Pain raced across her stomach as she felt his hips stab at her. The pain didn't let up when he moved backward.

He thrust himself down upon her forcefully three more times before he loosened his grip and stumbled backward.

Finally able to breathe, Leah drew a series of quick, short breaths as she tried to fathom the horror of what had happened to her!

Realizing that her slip, after having been pushed up the small of her back, was hanging from her shoulders, she pulled it down to cover her bottom. Her undergarments hung to her side, and she felt unclean and filthy in her most private area.

Slowly, she turned around and saw that the butcher wasn't even looking at her. He was fumbling with his pants, attempting to fix the clasp at the top of his fly. Looking up as he fumbled with the clasp, he saw that she was crying and trembling from the trauma she had just endured at his hands.

He felt powerful and laughed when he saw her holding her slip over the nude parts of her body. Bleeding between her legs, Leah sank to her knees and collapsed on the floor.

"Stupid little bitch! I have owed you that for at least five years. Don't think that I haven't seen you looking at me the way you do." With that, the Butcher Malkin finally finished buckling his pants and walked out of her room.

Behind him, he left a quaking, quivering woman, who at first hadn't really understood what had happened. It was only now, after he had left her bleeding between her legs, that she full grasped what had occurred. While no one had ever explained to her how nature and the world works, she wasn't stupid either.

Leah Horvicz now knew that she was unclean. She believed that no man would want her and that the butcher had destroyed her life.

Trying to stand, she felt her knees give way. Falling across the bed, she grabbed at Dora Malkin's dress that she had worn that night. She crushed it between her fingers. Sitting up, she tore it into fragments. When she had finally rendered it unrecognizable, she stood up and smoothed out the folds of her slip.

Her chest was still heaving, and her eyes were burning from her tears. The smell left behind by the Butcher Malkin would not leave her room. Looking around, she grabbed her work dress and threw it over her shoulders. Her slip nearly destroyed by the encounter, the harshness of the fabric now tore at her skin.

Bending down to look under the bed, she found her work boots. It was then that she realized that she hadn't removed her dress shoes. Sitting on the edge of the bed, she removed them and flung each shoe into a corner. She found comfort in the familiar feel of the boots and laced them as quickly as she could.

It was her intention to sneak out into the night and run to the house of the rabbi, hoping he would offer her safety. Composing herself as best she could, she stifled the urge to cry out, for it was possible that Dora Malkin would hear her cries from the second floor.

Once her work shoes were tied, she reached over and grabbed a few things from the top of her dresser. Gathering what she could, she slipped out of the door and into the kitchen. Her next step was to make it to the hallway and grab her coat from the front hall.

Stepping through the doorway of her room, into the kitchen, she saw Dora Malkin sitting at the kitchen table. The woman was in her nightclothes and sitting quietly. She looked up to where Leah stood and rose from her chair. Her gaze never left Leah's.

For a second, the two stood in front of each other. Still quaking from her encounter of the past three horrific minutes, Leah wasn't sure what her future was.

She screamed, "I want to leave now!" and tried to walk past Mrs. Malkin.

The older woman grabbed the girl by the arm, swung her around, and slapped her across the face. Leah, stunned by the action, recoiled in terror. For the second time in as many minutes, she was being beaten by a Malkin.

"How dare you tease my husband like that!" yelled the butcher's wife. "I knew that dress was too much for a stupid little bitch like you!"

With that, she slapped Leah a second time. The blow fell across the girl's arm. A third blow from the woman fell across Leah's face, this time leaving a brilliant red mark.

The force of the blow caused Leah to fall to the floor. She began to scream!

Dora Malkin began kicking the girl. Once, twice, three times, Leah felt the woman's foot slam into her midsection.

By now, the house was awake. Leon was the first to arrive in the kitchen. He grabbed his mother around her waist and moved her to the corner. Once this was done, he picked up Leah and attempted to straighten her clothes.

Leah, now in shock, ran toward the back door and took off into the night. Tearing through the early fall evening, she ran down one street and then another. At one point, her boot fell off, and she left it where it stood. It felt like forever to reach the small house of Rabbi Vilnish and her brother.

Once in front of the door, she began banging on it with all her might. Then she screamed Jacob's name over and over, "Jacob! Jacob, save me from this woman!"

Hearing the screams of his sister, Jacob bolted from his bed and raced to the door. Throwing it open, he saw her standing there, clutching at her dress and crying uncontrollably.

Reaching out into the darkness, he grabbed her as she fell into his arms and whispered into her ear, "I'm here, my darling,"

Behind Jacob, the rabbi came running in, clutching his nightshirt. "What is happening here? Why is there screaming?"

Leah bolted through the door. As she did, Jacob kicked it shut. He pulled his sister close and began to stroke her hair. She looked up at him, and he saw red marks across her cheek that bore the imprint of a man's hand.

Still holding her close, he asked her quietly, "What happened, my sister? What happened, Leah?"

Another knock came to the door. Jacob turned to the rabbi and shook his head no. The old man stood still.

The next knock seemed to shake the foundation of their house. A voice came out of the night. It was that of Dora Malkin.

"We saw her come in here, Jacob. She had a small episode when we told her to do some cleaning, and we are here to take the girl home," Dora Malkin muttered.

Leah struggled to control herself, but she was crying so hard that all she could say between sobs was, "She…knew what he…was…doing. She didn't stop…him…"

A third knock rang out as hard as the second. Jacob recognized the voice of Leon.

"Come on, Jake, things got a little out of control back at the house. Just open the door. This will be fixed quickly."

Behind the boy's plea, his mother added, "Why are you kissing their ass? We are the ones who had to come out in the middle of the night after this crazy girl. She has been nothing but trouble, since day one!"

The rabbi stepped to the side of Jacob and touched him lightly on the shoulder. "We must answer the door, Jacob." He then moved to touch Leah's arm and spoke very quietly to the two, "No matter what has happened, we will make sure that…"

Before he could finish speaking, the house began to shake from another powerful knock at the door.

Dora Malkin yelled out, "Open the door, Rabbi, this is a family matter, and you know that the law is on our side!"

The rabbi grabbed the doorknob and flung the door open. With every bit of force and conviction that he could muster, he said, "This is *my* house, Mrs. Malkin, and if you try and…"

While he was at least as tall as the woman, he was still an aged and slight man. At nearly twice his weight, she easily pushed the rabbi aside.

Before he could finish his threat, Dora Malkin entered the room, yelling, "You get that crazy girl to come back to my house, right now!"

Jacob took Leah gently by the shoulders and moved her behind him. Once she was there, he stood as tall as he could and looked the old lady straight in the eye. He said nothing. Everyone in the room followed suit, and for a second, the only sound heard was the muted sobs of Leah as she tried to suppress her fear.

Leon had followed his mother into the house and saw that the rabbi was now leaning against the wall, rubbing his elbow. There was a small bit of blood flowing from a new cut at the top of his head.

Stepping in front of his mother, Leon met Jacob's defiant gaze and said, "Momma, let me talk to Jake about this."

Jake, just thirteen earlier that month, lowered his head. Clenching his fists, he looked at Leon with eyes blazing, but he said nothing.

Dora Malkin yelled again, "Leon, stop kissing their ass!" Reaching toward Leah, she continued, "She has problems, and we all know that. Right now, we will take…"

As she tried to reach around Jacob, Jacob slapped at her arm and then put the other arm across Leah's stomach. His sister felt odd to his touch. She was shaking, and he got the distinct impression that she was bleeding internally.

Mrs. Malkin took a step back and screamed, "The little shit is as bad as the girl! He hit me, Leon! He HIT me!"

For his part, Leon remained calm. Taking his mother by the shoulder, he said, "Momma, let me just fix this." He moved her to the side and stepped into Jacob.

"Jake, come on, you don't know what is going on, but no matter what, you can't hit people."

Off to his side, his mother yelled again, "That's right, you little shit! You hit me! I paid for your food at the party this evening, you ungrateful little shit! That's right, you little shit…"

"Momma, stop it now!" said Leon forcefully. "This doesn't get fixed if people are yelling, so be quiet."

Mrs. Malkin drew her robe around her waist, looked over to the rabbi, and said sarcastically, "Fine little man you have raised, Rabbi."

Leon chastised his mother a second time, "I said, stop it, Mother." He shot her a look that held enough menace to keep her quiet for a moment. Returning his attention to Jacob, he went on, "Now, look, Jake, we know each other. You know how I feel, but the girl has to come home with us. You know that."

Jacob turned to the rabbi and kept silent. Instead, he cocked his head to the side as if to ask, "Is this right?"

Touching the top of his head where the blood was dripping, the rabbi stepped to the side of Jacob and said quietly, "The law is the law, Jacob, and she is bound to the Malkins. No matter…"

The rabbi, for all the goodness in his heart and all the spirit he held in his soul, knew that in the town of Pinsk in the year 1934, he was no match for the economic might and political influence of the Butcher Malkin. There was no way to resolve the issue other than to let the girl return to the house where she lived.

Jacob never took his eyes off of Leon. The fourth of Butcher Malkin's boys had inherited his height but not his bulk. Jacob was trying to decide whether to hit the man and run away with his sister now or let a day or two pass and then leave in the middle of the night.

It was Leon who broke the quiet in the room again, "Jake, we know each other. The old man was drunk and pissed about something. He took it out on Leah. I am sorry."

Dora Malkin started yelling again, "Why are you apologizing to this little shit again, boy? Did I raise a coward? Take the girl, and we will go home." In two steps, she had moved across the small house and over to where Jacob and Leah were standing. The rabbi stepped between the two.

He tried to speak, "Mrs. Malkin, you are…"

With her disgust raging across her face, she once again pushed the rabbi to the side and advanced toward the brother and sister.

It was Leon who now yelled, "Momma! Stop this right now, and go outside!" Everyone stood still.

Looking to the rabbi, he said, "Take my mother outside." The rabbi hesitated, and Leon asked a second time, this time nearly yelling as he did, "Go, take her now!" Looking to his mother, he went on, "You are not solving the problem. Just go with the rabbi, and wait for me outdoors!"

The woman looked around at everyone indignantly and then spoke as if she was doing everyone a favor, "Rabbi, come with me. My boy will fix this quickly." She started to walk to the door.

The rabbi stayed where he was and said, "I will not be forced from my own house. It isn't much, but it is mine."

It was then that Jacob finally spoke for the first time that evening. In a calm and measured tone, he said, "Rabbi, if you will take Mrs. Malkin outside, I would appreciate it."

Mrs. Malkin opened the door, and Jacob saw that a small group of neighbors had gathered around the house.

Jacob spoke again, "Rabbi, our friends are concerned. Can you counsel them while we talk inside?"

Leah hid her face from the growing crowd outside. She moved over to the chair, next to the small table, near the stove. It was the first time that she had ever been inside the rabbi's house. In all her years of living with the Malkins, it had never occurred to her to think of how Jacob had lived, or in what conditions.

She was surprised at how small the place was, how sparse the accommodations were, at how little the space was that the boy had as he grew up. Looking over to the corner, she saw a small cot that she knew had to be too short for his growing legs. Above the cot, she saw two hand-drawn pictures of horse and thought of her brother lying on his bed in the night-light and holding the pencil as he drew them.

The rabbi nodded and walked past Mrs. Malkin. As he did, he said, "Please come with me, Mrs. Malkin."

Looking to her son, she saw him nod. With that, she walked to the door, with her face deep red with equal parts anger and hate and frustration.

When she reached the doorway, she turned to look at Jacob, and with all the menace that she could muster she said, "You hit me, you disgusting little redheaded shit. You will pay for that." Moving her gaze to Leon, she continued, "If you haven't got the girl on the road to our house in one minute, I will go for the sheriff."

With that, she closed the door behind her. Leon, Jacob, and Leah were alone in the house.

Leon spoke softly, "Jake, this is ugly, I know it. But we know how it ends."

Leah moved swiftly from the corner of the room to where Jacob was standing and clutched at his coat. She was still panicked, but when she spoke, it was with a sense of defiance and determination, "I am not going back."

It was Leon who replied, "Leah, I don't know exactly what happened, but I do know this is ugly." Leah tightened her grip on Jacob's shirt as Leon went on, "But it only ends one way, so let's clean it up before Momma gets the sheriff."

Jake's response was curt, "No."

"Why, Jake? Why make this hard? Come on, man."

"Something is wrong, Leon, and…"

As he was finishing his thought, the door flung open, and Mrs. Malkin came bursting through for the second time that night. Moving straight for Leah, surprise was on her side. Slapping the girl on the back of her head, she was spitting as she spoke, "I am sick of this nonsense." She grabbed the girl by the arm and began to shake her as she continued, "We feed you, give you a roof over your head, and you humiliate us in front of our friends and neighbors. Now, move, you stupid ass, and stop embarrassing me in front of everyone." With that, she began pulling on Leah to leave.

Looking to the door, Jacob saw that a good crowd of almost twenty was now looking in through the door. If he hit the woman, he would go to jail. He looked over to Leah and lowered his head, holding eye contact as tightly as he could.

She returned his gaze and knew what she should do. Shaking free of Mrs. Malkin's grasp, she straightened her shirt, ran her hands through her hair, and tried to clean it up as best as she could. With that, she moved toward the front door, walking past Leon as she did.

Mrs. Malkin spit on the floor of the house of the rabbi and Jacob. "What an ungrateful little bitch." Looking to Jacob, she shook her finger at him and continued, "You will pay for what you did, you little redheaded shit." Moving her gaze over to Leon, she finished by saying, "You come home now, and don't think I won't forget how you represented this family so poorly, you disloyal jackass."

Without so much as attempting to straighten herself, she walked out the front door with her robe hanging open. As she did, she began addressing the people who were now standing outside the house, "So sorry that you had to see my family like this, but that little girl tried to assault my family."

This left Leon, the rabbi, and Jacob still inside the house.

"I wouldn't come around for a long time, Jake. Right now she is pissed, but she will calm down. There probably won't be repercussions, but there is no reason to risk pushing her. You're a good kid, Jake, let's just…" said Leon.

Jacob cut him off in midsentence, "What happened?"

Leon seemed to be taken back by the question. He looked at the boy where he stood.

Jacob repeated his question, "What happened?"

The rabbi stepped in and put his arm around Jacob. "Look, Jacob, it is over, let's go to bed and see what tomorrow holds."

The boy shook off the rabbi's arm and took a step into where Leon was standing. The older Malkin boy stood almost five inches taller than Jacob and while thin, still had at least thirty pounds on him as well.

Despite the clear physical advantage that he had, it was the look in Jacob's eyes that made him answer, "It is something that I can't say, Jake."

Jacob stood silent.

Leon began to grow nervous and went on, "I don't know. I just heard the girl race out, and then Momma started running out after her."

The voices rose into a cacophony in his own head. Jacob froze where he stood. It was only the touch of the rabbi on his shoulder that brought him back to his senses. When he turned to look at the man, he saw how old he had grown over the years, how his beard had become gray, how his glasses were dirty, and how his slippers were worn and in desperate need of stitching.

"Jacob, my son," he said as he looked up into the boy's eyes, "shut the door. We need the quiet."

Slowly, Jacob shut the door. As he did, he said to the rabbi, "Thank you for so much, Rabbi."

"Thank God, Jacob, not me. He provides for us in all our times, good and bad." Moving into the kitchen, he sat down and made a motion for the boy to follow suit.

He cocked his ear to the door to make sure that the crowd was leaving. When the sound outside their door had disappeared, the rabbi started to speak, "Listen to me for a second, Jacob, and then we will retire."

Jacob moved restlessly in his chair. He wanted the lights to go out so he could sit in the darkness.

Thinking that he knew what the rabbi was going to say, he spoke quickly, "I will not visit their store or farm for a long, long time, Rabbi. Do not worry about revenge or anything like that..." his voice trailed off as the rabbi reached across the table to cover his hand.

"Today you are a man. If I haven't done my job properly, there is nothing I can do now." He looked across the table into Jacob's eyes and went on, "I know you are good and honorable. I am not worried about the Malkins. You understand their economic power and that any battle you wage against them will be lost."

"Then what is it you want to say, Rabbi?"

Standing up, he kept a hand on the table for support as he stood. "I am, indeed, old. And time has taught me that there are things you can fight and things you can't. The butcher is a powerful, powerful man with friends and allies that you can't imagine. They reach to Minsk and beyond."

He sighed, and Jake noticed the weight of his years coming through as he spoke.

"I do not want to lose you to an orphanage, or a work farm, or even the army. For you are big, and they could take you, Jake. Think carefully of every move you make."

Across from him, not two feet away, the rabbi extended his arms. Without a word, Jacob walked into the man's embrace, and for the first time in the eight years they lived together, the two men hugged.

"Good night, Jacob," said the rabbi.

"Good night, Rabbi Vilnish," said Jacob.

Without a word, the rabbi turned and slipped into his bedroom, shutting the door behind him as he did.

The light from the lamp flickered cross the kitchen wall as Jacob sat down. The crowd was gone, and for what seemed to be the first time in an eternity, silence filled the air around Jacob.

After a few minutes, he stood, blew out the lamp, and walked over to his cot, thinking of the day when he could ride a horse out of Pinsk with his sister in the saddle behind him.

The next day, the rabbi and Jacob rose to clean up the remaining mess in the hall. Afterward, the rabbi held instruction for Jacob in math and, as he did during every lesson, the Torah. When it was over, he left Jacob to return to his own studies. Not once did either of them discuss the events of the previous night.

Jacob's brain had only one thought: he and Leah must escape from Pinsk and what it represented.

It would be all he thought of for the next four years.

# QUIET YEARS OF PATIENCE

So it was in the City of Pinsk. People continued to shop at the Butcher Malkin's store, and people continued to borrow money. When they saw Leah at the store, almost everyone who knew what happened that night several weeks ago smiled with kindness in their hearts and nodded. After the first two or three times, Leah found herself nodding back—but only after she was sure that Dora Malkin or the butcher wasn't looking.

She was unaware that two days after the incident, Leon had cornered his father in the back of the store. The fourth son of Mayer Malkin was well aware that the girl was in great distress physically, and her mind seemed to be elsewhere. She seemed to be unable to prepare the meals as well as she had before the incident. Her other onerous chores were falling by the wayside. Just last night, Leon had heard his mother threaten to beat her if she didn't stop her moaning.

Whether from sympathy or an intellect that examined the aftermath of his father's rape of the young girl, he upbraided the unconcerned old man and boldly stated, "Do you realize what you've done to her?"

"I'll do whatever I damn please. I'm giving her a home where there is no other for her!" the old man screamed.

"But damn it, Poppa, you're ruining a valuable asset. Have some sense!" Leon continued, "Get some help for her. Momma runs her into the ground with her demands. Goodness, Poppa, the girl wasn't that sharp to begin with, and now she is a sick, scared girl!"

"What the hell do you mean she's a valuable asset?" Mayer grumbled.

"Leah does all the cooking and most of the cleaning. She can't easily be replaced. She's worth more than one of your prize horses!"

"My ass, she is! No woman in the town of Pinsk is worth a good horse, boy. And besides, Momma tells me that she has to redo almost all the chores, that the girl does and that…"

Waving his hand in disagreement, Leon cut his father off in midsentence, "You know that Momma loves to exaggerate. Until you did what you did to her, Leah did a fine job. At best, Momma would refold a napkin just to belittle the girl."

The old man looked at his son and almost spit out his answer, "She is an animal to me, and I will treat her as such." Pausing, he then added, "But maybe you are right, for even an animal has value. Okay, I will not touch her again."

"And you have to tell Momma to not mess with her brother either. She was out of control that night, and she hit him several times." He stretched the truth to cover for Jake.

"Oh, screw the little bastard!" With that, he left the room and walked back into the store.

For the next four years, the house of the Butcher Malkin would function in the life it had known before Jake's bar mitzvah. Leah went back to work. Mrs. Malkin continued to be controlling, bullying, and dishonest. The butcher went on with his business and ate pickles and sold meat and horses. Every once in a while, when he passed the girl or found her alone in a room, he would stop and stare, smirking as he did.

Every time he did, Leah continued with her task as if he didn't exist. She seldom met his eye and would ignore him when he talked. The first few times that she did this, the butcher took issue.

Braying like a mule, he roared, "I'm responsible for her and feed her," and so on. After a while, he just laughed and said, "She's a stupid girl, always was, always will be."

Scrubbing, washing, cleaning, cooking—Leah now kept to herself as she went about her day. Few noticed, but after that day, she stopped talking to almost anyone. When someone would start a conversation, she would smile and nod—just smile and nod.

She and Jake were no longer able to enjoy their few stolen moments together. Mrs. Malkin had made it clear that "if she saw that horrible little redheaded orphan," on her property, she would shoot him.

Birthday after birthday came and went for Leah and Jake. Not once were they allowed to spend a minute together. He saw his sister only at the synagogue, which the Malkins felt obligated to attend after, as Dora Malkin said, "Our money practically built that little hovel. Why should we be forced to leave because of this stupid misunderstanding?"

This was the only time that Leah and Jake could be together. A smile would pass, a nod, a wave. For four years, this is all the conversation the two could ever enjoy—small, quick gestures that kept a slight ember of connectivity burning; silent acknowledgments in small rooms that reminded them that they, and only they, were all each other had.

Then, one rainy night in the fall of 1939, everything changed.

# THE RACE FROM PINSK

He was too nervous to eat much this evening. Besides, there wasn't that much soup left in the pot, and he felt the rabbi needed it more than he did.

"My goodness, Jacob," said the rabbi as Jake set the bowl down in front of him, "is there enough for you?"

Food had always been a problem at their house. Of late, it seemed to have become an even bigger one.

Together the men sat silently in prayer.

Then, as he began to dip his spoon into the soup, the rabbi spoke, "You are worried about my appearance."

It was true, for over the last few months, Jake noticed how the rabbi seemed to be growing smaller, eating less.

The learned man went on, "As to my age, I can only say that gray hair is a crown of splendor. It is obtained by a righteous life."

He smiled at his joke as Jake watched a small bit of soup fall from the bread that he was holding. It landed on the table, creating small puddle. The rabbi was oblivious to what had happened. The boy knew that the rabbi's eyes had been failing him as well.

"*Mish lei*. I am not sure exactly where it is mentioned, Rabbi. But I know that you are speaking of what others call Proverbs," replied his charge.

As they spoke, Jake watched for more signs of the rabbi's vision failing. The fact that he hadn't wiped up the soup that he had dropped was one of them. Just a month ago, he would have used the bread to soak up the few spilled drops. Today he just let them lay there as he spoke.

"That is good, Jacob. I can live with that. I will never stump you on the story of Exodus. So it is nice when you step outside of the familiar and refer to Proverbs, proving to me that my years of instruction haven't been wasted."

Pushing the remaining slice of bread toward the old man, Jake said, "Exodus has been my guiding light, Rabbi. But it is only one story out of many."

The rabbi didn't answer. He ignored the bread and continued to stare into his soup. Jake looked on in silence. Finally, after taking several more spoonful of soup, the rabbi looked up to his charge with only sadness in his aged eyes.

"Your birthday has come and gone with no acknowledgment. Forgive me, but I forget the days as they pass, Jacob…" He looked across the table to where Jake sat.

Jake slid the small plate with a single slice of bread on it closer to the rabbi. "Have some more bread with that soup," he said and watched to see if the man would either push the bread away or take another piece.

The rabbi did neither, choosing to stare out in front of him with a blank look across his face.

Jake said nothing about the forgotten birthday. Looking into the rabbi's eyes, he saw that the milky-type substance coating that had been growing daily in the right eye had gotten worse. The left one was clear, but the old man would squint in bright light, as if he was either trying to focus on what was in front of him or thinking of something in the past.

Putting down his spoon, the rabbi said, "Dear Jacob, you are now seventeen. We should have done something on that day…when was it?"

"Rabbi, my birthday was a week ago, and you gave me a piece of bread with honey. It was nice."

Pulling back in his chair, the rabbi said, "Yes, *yes*! Now I remember. The sun was bright, and yet fall was in the air. I could feel the cold. Then the rains came."

While he had proved to be forgetful on occasion, Jake was happy to hear that the rabbi, when prompted, did remember details.

"Yes, the rains started three days ago. It is good for the farmers and good for the town."

For the first time in ages, Jake thought back to the storm that took his father. That one had lasted over three days as well. As he did so often, when memories of the past came to him, he shoved them deep into somewhere hidden inside of himself.

Standing, Jake took his empty dish with him. Though it had never held food, he had set it on the table out of habit. Reaching down to pick up the rabbi's dish, he asked, "Are you done with your soup?"

"Yes...yes, boy. Take it away."

As he did what was asked, Jake saw that the rabbi's eyes never left their focus on the chair where he had just been sitting.

Moving three steps back to the table, Jacob sat down and told the rabbi, "I want to have Dr. Nussbaum look at your eyes again. I don't like the way you can't seem to focus when we talk. Why don't you visit him when the rains stop, Rabbi?"

"I never fight your suggestions, Jacob, but I will see him in my own time. Tomorrow I need to read a new chapter that I found on..." he trailed off as he spoke and sat silently at the table as if he was catching his breath. A second later, he picked himself up and started again, "I must feel better if I can still read, for that is what I was supposed to do in this life, son."

They sat in silence until the rabbi sighed, looked up to Jake, and spoke again, "Have you heard the latest news from Germany?"

"I know they are threatening to invade our land, Rabbi," he said.

Jake had followed the rise of the Nazis closely over the last few years, through stories in the local paper. Naturally, he had heard farmers and shopkeepers talk about the danger that their neighbor Germany posed to Poland. The topic came up nearly every day. Fear of what seemed imminent spread over the village and nearby farms, gripping Pinsk in a great unknown.

The rabbi had trained Jacob to be aware of the world around him, to know what lay outside the artificial boundaries that defined Pinsk. He had made sure that his young charge kept an open mind and taught him to be as fair as possible when judging a man. But that did not mean that Jacob was naive about the idea of anti-Semitism. From everything he had read and heard, it was becoming a national idea in Poland's neighbor to the west.

Jake was reluctant to discuss any harsh news with the rabbi. With the sudden deterioration of the rabbi's health, he looked to avoid upsetting his teacher and friend. So he would only ask questions in way of a reply.

"Why do you ask, Rabbi?"

"The papers have been saying for months, maybe even as long as a year now, that the Germans will cross the border any day. They may already be on their way."

Jake knew this to be true, for he had read it as well. Over the last year, he had followed the rise of the Nazis and their little corporal. Still, as relative as it was to their lives, the rabbi was ill. Jake wanted him to stay calm.

But that was beyond his control, for the rabbi was growing anxious as he spoke, "Anti-Semitism is a strong driving force for these men. They look to find a reason for their economic problems and blame the problem on the easy few who cannot protect themselves, those they believe to be different than they are."

Pausing for a second to think, the rabbi went on, "The paper tells me that if they do, they will most assuredly take over the town we live in. It could be weeks. It could be days. Jake, my day is coming soon, but you are young. You have a life in front of you. Just be prepared, that is all I ask. The hatemongers can have these old bones. I am done with them. They have served me well."

Standing, he crossed over to Jake and put his hand on the young man's shoulder as he spoke, "Can you clean up tonight for us? I am more than tired. I spent an hour with Mr. Klimkowicz. As you know, he is a hard man who thinks he can bully God with demands. The God I love and study and worship does not magically give a man a good horse because that man screams and bellows like a child."

Jake watched as his teacher smiled at the memory of Klimkowicz growing red in the face as he had this afternoon in the temple. The two old friends laughed together at the idea.

The rabbi patted Jake on his shoulder and said, "Tonight you and I will skip study in favor of rest. The rains have been hard on all of us. If the Nazis come this evening, tell them I am sleeping and to come back tomorrow when I can serve them a good kugel."

Leaning down, he kissed Jake on the top of his head. "Your hair has always made me smile, Jacob. Even if my eyes fail, I will always be able to see this lighthouse of fire. When I have seen it coming down the street, it makes my heart smile. I do not long for the day when I will not see it again. But I am not as old and so vain as to think that that day isn't soon. Good night, son."

Without another word, he went into his room and closed the door.

If the rabbi had been able to see everything before him, he would have seen that his charge was now just over six feet tall. Years of work in the sun and wind and rain had darkened his still-youthful light skin. The freckles that once showed across his nose and cheeks now blended together, leaving his face a more even tone than he had as a child. His jaw now looked as if it was set in stone, carved at a specific sharp angle. The farmwork, as well as his own natural lack of appetite, had given him a body that was lean and muscular and taut.

This turn of the weather gave Jake the perfect window of opportunity. His original plan was to take Leah and leave the following week once he was sure that the rabbi's immediate needs were assured. But the shift in weather coupled with the threat of a German incursion into Poland created a sense of urgency in the young man's heart and mind.

Any doubt that he may have ever had about the trip was settled. He was certain that he was ready to leave the only world he had ever known. The conditions were perfect. The noise of the rain would cover the sounds he'd make as he made his way out of Pinsk. It would also mask his trail. The moon, while generally obscured by the constant downfall, would provide just enough light to guide him and Leah as they rode toward the Pripet Marshes in the north.

For the last four years, he had thought of nothing else but leaving since the night that Leah ran to the house of the rabbi screaming for his help. Jake had looked for this—this perfect time to leave Pinsk.

Every time that Jake had made secret, solitary ventures north, he made a special effort to learn as much as he could of the details and passageways that lay inside the Pripet Marshes, for he knew that these wetlands would be his best path to freedom. Measuring over a hundred thousand acres, the Marsh was packed with twists and turns, rivers and large bodies of water. All of which were barely navigable by the most experienced of travelers.

He could go northwest or even straight north to the Baltic Sea. But that way lay Germany and the rising Nazi Party. With his knowledge and understanding of the Pripet Marshes, he felt that northeast was the direction to go. Anyone who would follow him through the Marshes with mechanized, heavy equipment could soon find themselves sunk in the quicksand-like mud. In the past, many have found themselves tangled and lost in the ever-changing roads and waterways that comprised this massive region.

In the past few years, Jake had been able to travel through a good part of Poland's beautiful country. Standard, well-traveled roads, regular paths, and normal routes of transport would create too easy a trail for anyone to pick up. Footprints could be followed; wagon wheels could be analyzed; and the marks left by any horse would be easily identified by most simple trackers.

However, his plan was to have the Pripet Marshes confuse those who might follow him and his sister when they rode away from Pinsk. He planned to stop in Minsk for a few months and start building a new life. When the time was right, they may even book passage overseas. All he knew was that he wanted to rescue his sister from the hell that was her life among the Malkins.

Rain was an important part of his plan. It would provide the perfect cover. When the rains came to Pinsk, as they did every fall, the storms were usually so strong that the town would effectively be shut down for a few days. This meant that if he and Leah were discovered leaving in the middle of the night, not too many would be anxious to pursue them under the adverse conditions. No one would dare risk looking a horse or a loved one in the middle of the night with such driving rain during their search.

Despite the separation that had been forced upon them, Jake and Leah had found a way to pass short notes to each other. Using a small piece of paper torn from a printed page, they would pass short messages when there were silent opportunities.

It was Leah who had taken the initiative. One day, two months ago in late July, as he left the synagogue, Jake had reached into his coat pocket looking for some change, only to find a folded piece of paper.

When he unfolded it, he saw that it simply said, "I miss my brother."

Given the strict way that the Malkins kept tabs on Leah, it was a miracle that she had been able to pass the note. For years, Dora Malkin and her boys had kept a watchful eye on their fractious charge.

Three weeks later, Jake had returned the gesture. He managed to slip a note into Leah's coat pocket that said, "Late in the fall."

When the fall rains came ten days later, she found another note. It simply said, "Listen for a whistle at night. Be ready."

Leah knew exactly what Jake meant. As small children, in the time before their separation, they had developed a high-pitched whistle so they could find each other across the expanse of their father's farm. Every night she listened for that familiar whistle.

After that, they never risked sending another message.

While she had grown used to the demands placed on her by Dora Malkin and the rest of the family, Leah could never understand why she couldn't leave if she wanted. From the first days that she had been taken in to live with them, it seemed as if she was considered the property of the Malkins.

About eight months ago, shortly after her twentieth birthday—a day that came and went with no song, no cake, no good wishes—Leon had explained to her that she was considered an indentured servant and the work she did was considered as exchange for room and board. To run off would mean that she owed the Malkins for what they spent on her to keep her alive. He concluded that they could legally chase her down and add penalties for what it cost them to find her.

The girl laughed in his face. "I am now twenty, and I have never signed such a contract. How can you tell me such a foolish thing?"

Normally, she had been respectful to Leon, but today she was speaking in a mocking tone, and it hit a nerve with the young man.

His anger showed as he spoke, "My father took you in and gave you everything to make you comfortable. Today you sound ungrateful!" Continuing, he said, "Do you see many women attending school? I taught you to read! That cost time, and time is money."

She was confused by the idea that though she worked from sunup to sundown, she would still owe them money. Leery of finding Mrs. Malkin lurking around the corner, she asked him in a much more mannered way to explain to her how such a thing could happen.

Snapping at her again, Leon said, "Our ways are the ways of our fathers and their fathers. A woman has different rights from a man, and that is how it always has been. The fact that you can even read is a miracle."

Not once in all her years did she ever think in terms of a woman's place inside the small part of the Jewish community that she lived in. Her years were spent behind closed doors. When she had gone outdoors, it was only to synagogue or when Dora Malkin told her to go to the bakery.

It never occurred to her to ask for money for what she was doing. The idea that she owed money to the Malkins struck her as wrong. But she did nothing to move the idea any further.

Sadly, years of belittling, harsh treatment, and endlessly cruel words had crushed much of her spirit. She accepted what she had been told as fact.

"Thank you, Leon, I guess it all makes sense now." Without another word, she turned to the kitchen and began thinking of how to contact Jake.

It was time to leave.

It was after the first of September, and the third night of the rains brought lightning and thunder. Jake lay in his bed, unable to sleep. It wasn't the storm that bothered him. What bothered him was something else.

## JAKE THE HORSE THIEF

This was the night that he was going to steal a horse from the butcher, pick up Leah, and ride past the Pripet Marsh to a new life.

Restless, but knowing that it was too early for him to sneak out just yet, he reached over to the small wooden crate that served as a table beside his cot. Picking up the prayer book that the rabbi had given him for his bar mitzvah, he opened it to a random page and began to read. Then he read another page. And another.

Every word he read seemed to speak of freedom and how God will guide his people in their lives. As he sat there, nervous and worried over what he was about to do, what he found in the little book inspired him. As he read over every prayer, every passage, every invocation, and every plea, his conviction to move forward grew.

Jake pulled a small pencil from his pocket and began to make notes in the margins. He made lists and annotated passages that inspired him. An hour passed, then half of another. Looking up to the small window in the wall across the room, he saw that it was now time to put it all his planning into action. Closing the book, he stood and put the pencil in his pocket. Reaching under his bed, he brought out a small pouch that held what money he had saved.

Opening the bag, he spread the coins out across the flat cover of his cot. He saw the eighteen kopecks that the rabbi had given him on his bar mitzvah. While he had given almost all his salary to the rabbi (and the rabbi had in turn used the money for the synagogue), he had been able to hold on to some extra money for himself.

But the man that Jake had become wasn't one to be fooled by appearances.

"This is not something I will ever allow," he whispered. "I will never see beauty of gold or the value of money as anything other than a tool to help my goals."

Making two piles for the coins—one with gold, the other with kopecks—Jake walked to the front door. He looked at the two coats that he owned as they hung from a nail off to the side.

Knowing that the ride would be long and that he would sweat and be tired, he selected the lighter of his two coats. The storm would pass, and the late fall certainly held warm days afterward. He felt that there was no reason to burden himself with something heavy. Protecting himself from rain was the most important thing to consider. He thought, *This was a coat that will dry out quickly.*

From the small set of drawers near the sink, he pulled out three candles, a box of matches, and then wrapped them both tightly inside a thick handkerchief. Feeling along the left side of his coat, he made sure that the inside pocket still contained a second box of matches. He smiled at the memory of that warm spring day so long ago when Mr. L. had taught him to always keep matches in two different places in case one accidently got wet.

Picking up the pile of cold coins, he hid two of them in the same pocket as the extra box of matches. The third, he left on the bed. The kopecks, he placed in a more accessible pocket, one on the outside coat. These were for food and shelter. Or if the worst was to happen and he and Leah came across bandits, he could appease them with the kopecks and pray that they wouldn't search him for more treasure.

Standing at the table, he went over his list one last time—candles, matches, dry shirt, some food, gloves…Each item that he thought of was now either in his pocket or in the small leather bag that he had packed the day before. Over the last few days, he had bought a small bit of meat and bread that was now in the pouch as well. After a minute, he could think of nothing else that he would need.

There was only one more thing to do before he left. Moving back to his cot, he picked up the remaining gold coin and then placed it on the table. Pulling the pencil from his pocket, he tore a small piece of paper from a bag that sat off to the side.

On it he wrote, "Thank you."

He then slid it to the side of the table where he had watched the rabbi eat his meals so many times over the last eleven years. Placing the gold coin on top of the note, he went to the door, opened it, and without looking back, walked out into the night.

The moonlight was just managing to sneak through the rain clouds overhead. It was still bright enough for him to find his way along the streets. After all these years of racing out at night, he could have found his way to the Malkin farm in total darkness. The rain was falling lightly, but Jake knew that it would soon gain strength and speed, for off to the west, he could see the dark, dark heavy clouds coming their way.

As he dashed over cobblestone and pavement and dirt, the ground was covered with so many puddles of standing water that it was almost impossible to try and avoid them. Years of experience had taught him where the big ones would be, and as he made his way to the house of Butcher Malkin, he did his best to avoid them. He had miles to go that night and had no desire to travel for hours in wet and soaked shoes.

He knew the town so well that he could have moved through its streets blindfolded. One house slipped past another. The roads went by in a series of lefts and rights and curves as he moved across each one. Every step he took was executed with caution and restraint and patience.

The house and farm of the Butcher Malkin was normally a ten-minute walk from the rabbi's front door. As he crossed toward it in the darkness, he took care to watch for a lit candle in any windows of the houses. Moving swiftly across alleys and down slim passageways that opened up shortcuts between houses, he listened intently for any movement or sounds made along the roads.

Years of sneaking out late at night had tuned his ears to the world in the dark. In the distance, to the south, there was the dim rushing of the river. When he was just a few blocks away from the Malkin farm, he thought that he heard the Rapp family arguing. Focusing on the noise, he wrote off what he heard as the wind in trees.

Overhead, he heard a small pack of birds as they flew over Pinsk in the dead of night. He smiled at the idea that he was doing the same—simply flying from life in one place to better conditions elsewhere.

To be out and open in the night air brought back memories of how timid, scared, and worried he had been that first night he had snuck out nearly eleven years ago. Jake enjoyed the idea that on this evening, he found himself filled with confidence, experience, and was today sure of himself in a way that seemed right.

In no time, he found himself at the farm of Mayer Malkin. It sat on the northeastern corner of the town of Pinsk. One of the largest lots that were considered to be part of the town itself, it gave way to acres of farmable land behind it. An open field took up an acre to the left of the house.

At the center sat the worn two-story main house. On the right, connected to the house by a poorly built passageway, stood the butcher shop. Behind the shop stood the corral and then the barn.

If Jake was going to get out of Pinsk in fastest way possible, he would need to double back through town and grab the main road about a half a mile away. Then he could turn north toward the Pripet Marsh.

Sneaking up the path to the back of the house, he knew that a large German Shepherd slept near the back door of the shop. The poor old, filthy, and uncared for dog had lain there in rain, sleet, and snow every night for as many years as Jake could remember. Jake knew that the dog was old enough to have lost his bite. But his bite wasn't what worried Jake; it was his bark.

Jake had noticed that a good-sized chunk of beef would keep old Scrappo busy and quiet for more than a few moments. Once the dog was content, Jake could hurry on to free his sister!

## JAKE THE HORSE THIEF

Jake crept along the side of the house until he reached Leah's window. As he stood, the rain began to fall again. Reaching up as far as he could, Jake knocked gently at Leah's window. Then he whistled, just as he had when he was six and she was nine.

There was no response. He knocked again, whistled, and then crouched low against the side of the building, hiding in the darkness of the shadows.

After a minute, he stood for a third time, knocked at the window, and whistled again. As before, he heard nothing in response, and his stomach dropped.

The rain was now picking up its pace. In the distance, Jake saw lightning flash in the west. A second later, there was the rumbling of rolling thunder. Frustrated and starting to grow cold, Jake rose quickly, wondering what he could do to avoid detection yet still able to contact his sister. It was then that he heard the sound of a door open at the back of the house.

A shadow grew out of the light that spread cross the back of the house. The shadow spread across the ground until it seemed to extend in front of him forever.

Jake decided to take the offensive. Quietly, he crept long the edge of the building, shielded by the darkness. One short step followed by another. He watched as the shadow come to a standstill. All he could see was a shapeless form, silhouetted in the moonlight.

A tiny, shrill voice filled with nervousness came calling through the confusion of rain, fear, and thunder, "Jake…? Jake…?"

The voice called out again, "Jake…Jake?"

Now just a foot from the corner of the house, Jake stood ready to leap. The figure turned the corner, and as it did, he grabbed whoever it was by the shoulder, spun them around, and threw their body against the side of the house. Putting one hand over their mouth, he brought his hand up to their throat in one swift motion!

He had never confronted someone in such a calculated and dangerous manner ever before. Ready to break the figure's throat, it took all the concentration he could muster to stay focused and not slip in the mud.

As his eyes met theirs, he saw panic and fear looking straight back at him.

Jake also saw dark hair spill out from under a hat. As he pushed the person against the wall, he realized that he was pressing against someone in a long skirt.

It was Leah.

Pressed against the wall on top of her, he could feel his sister shaking in confusion. Together they stood in half light, half shadow.

"Shhhhh..." he whispered. "I am going to remove my hand, Leah. But not until you can let me know that you are calm."

Her eyes were as wide as a full moon. Paralyzed by fear, she was shaking involuntarily.

His hand began to loosen, and as he pulled away, she continued to shake. It took a half minute or so for her to calm down to the point where he was able to pull away completely. Leah raised her hands to her chest and drew her shirt up in knots. Her shoulders moved up and down rapidly as she grabbed for a breath. Even over the noise of the rain, Jake could hear her gasping.

Taking her free hand, he spoke, "We will stand here for a minute. Everything is good so far. No one has heard us, so we have all the time we need." He looked at her and continued, "Shake your head if you understand me."

It was when she pulled her other hand to her chest and began clutching at her blouse that Jake saw she was carrying a small cloth bag.

"Good. Now, we are going to leave tonight. I need you to go inside and only take a few things. I have food and money. If you have any, bring it with you."

She shook her head no.

"What?" he said in surprise. "You don't want to go?"

She shook her head no again. Jake couldn't figure out that the problem was.

He asked her again, "Don't you want to go?"

Now she shook her head yes.

"Well, what is it?" he added in frustration.

Leah finally spoke, "I have no money," was her reply.

"Oh…" said Jake, "I didn't understand."

Leah held up the small cloth bag and said nothing.

"What is that?"

"A shirt and a pair of pants, and one or two small things."

The one or two things were the doll that her mother had made her as well as her mother's brush.

"Good," said Jake. "Let's head up to the barn. You all right?"

Leah dropped her hand from her shirt and took his sleeve. "I am good…"

They crossed from the dark side of the house and moved into the moonlight. He remembered that rain was falling as he moved to cover Leah's head. She took her hand from his sleeve, brushed him away, and then grabbed the sleeve a second time.

In silence they moved across the yard. In a minute, they stood in front of the large twin barn doors. Leah released her grip, and with a knowing touch, she slid the bolt locking the doors together out of its sleeve.

Pulling at the door on the right, she spoke quietly as she waved Jake inside, "There is a dark saddle in the corner, on the far rail against the wall. That's the best one. The others are in horrible condition. That Arabian you loved is long gone, so put it on the brown horse in the second stall on the right. Not sure if he is the fastest, but he is the smartest and won't make any noise as we leave."

Jake looked at her with surprise. She waved for him to walk pass her, and with that, he stepped into the darkened barn. Slipping in behind him, she drew the door shut and pointed to the back corner.

With the storm outside, his eyes were already adjusted to the darkness. Moving quickly, he found the dark saddle exactly where she had said it would be. Pulling it from the rail, he felt the leather straps brush against his legs as he turned to find the stall she had mentioned. He then reached for a blanket hanging on the wall and threw it over his shoulder.

Looking back to the door, he saw Leah standing there, peering through the cracks in the wood, checking to see if anyone had lit a candle in a window.

It had never occurred to him that she would have her own set of skills, her own plans in the whole affair. While he hurried to grab the saddle, he felt ashamed for not thinking that his sister would have those skills. That feeling quickly became pride. Never in a million years had he thought she would be as able as she was.

Jake recognized the horse she had suggested. She was right. He had seen it on the roads with one of the Malkin boys and knew it to be a good, sturdy horse. Covering it with the blanket, he then threw the saddle over the animal's back, pulled a strap from underneath, and tied it off. He then took the reins.

Standing in front of the animal, he pulled a carrot from his pocket, held it out so that it lay flat against his palm, and placed it under the long snout of the horse. The animal sniffed along the edges first, then he grabbed it between his teeth, throwing his head back as he began to eat. Jake placed his hand across the long neck of the animal and began to pet him softly.

He whispered, "We are going on a trip, a good long trip, and I trust you…You are a strong one, and we will be good friends when it is over."

Leading the horse out of the stall, they moved together to the front of the barn. Leah opened the door a crack and looked out. Ducking back inside, she pushed the door open just enough for the three of them to pass through. Once Jake and the horse had passed, she closed the large half of the door with no problem, latched it as she had found it, and stepped out into the rain.

The corral was a sea of mud and soaked ground. On her second step, she felt the softening earth starting to grab hold of her foot. Struggling to make it through the muck and mess, Leah waved for Jake to follow her. Moving past him, she went to the far side and opened the gate to the corral. The rain picked up speed as Jake and his new friend moved through the opening into the yard.

Lightning that was cracking in the distance was growing closer with every burst. When the thunder broke so quickly after that last strike, it sounded to Jake's ears as if the storm was moving toward Pinsk a lot faster than he had counted on.

Leah touched him on the shoulder, and he looked over to see that she was standing next to the horse, waiting for him to act.

She whispered, "It's a small saddle, so get on, and then pull me up. I'll ride behind you."

"You're a strong girl, you shouldn't have trouble holding on!" Jake assured her.

Once he was in place, he wiped the rain from his face and put his arm out for Leah to grab. Mimicking what she had just seen him do, she put her left foot in the stirrup and, after bouncing once or twice, hopped up behind her brother. Once she was settled, she dropped her arms around his waist, locked her hands, and said, "Let's go."

Picking up the reins, Jake made a low clicking sound and dug his heels into the side of the horse. Together the three of them began to move slowly through the muck and the filth of the Malkin farm. They moved toward the side of the house, where the kitchen and

Leah's room were. The darkness on that side would give them cover as they rode on to the village street.

Looking over in the direction of the dog, Jake saw that despite the noise and the rain, Scrappo now lay sleeping, his head down atop his crossed paws and lost in dreams.

When they neared the corner, Jake leaned over to ride as low as possible. Leah matched his every move. Looking to his left, he saw no lights in the house and heard nothing other than the rain.

They were less than two strides away from the barn when the largest crack of lightning he had seen hit in the rear of the Malkin farm. The electricity was so bright that the world looked as if a white sun had risen, and it was suddenly high noon. Behind him, he felt Leah sit straight up and hit him on his left arm. She was pointing to the house, and from there, he heard a muffled scream.

There, standing on the porch that led to the kitchen door, was the butcher's dreaded wife, Dora Malkin!

The rain pelting her large body had caused her nightshirt to cling to every fold and crevice.

That frighteningly unappealing image wasn't what scared Jake.

It was the pistol in her right hand.

At the top of her voice, she yelled, "GET OFF OF MY HUSBAND'S HORSE, YOU RANCID LITTLE SHIT!"

Pointing the weapon toward the sky, she fired a shot. Jake watched as she lowered the firearm and pointed it straight at his head.

At that moment, he realized that she was aiming to kill him!

The supernatural light faded, and darkness fell. Turning his shoulder to Leah, he yelled, "Hold on!"

Jake slapped the side of the horse with his reins. Feeling the sting of the leash, the animal bolted from where he stood and took off as fast as he could through the mud.

The sudden movement threw Leah backward, but somehow, she managed to stay on. Behind him, she tilted to her right side to avoid a second shot by Dora Malkin. Together Leah and Jake raced for the street.

In all the confusion, Jake was never sure if Dora did fire a second time, but he was certain that he heard a sharp crack rip through the night as they galloped away!

It wasn't until he was on relatively steady ground that Jake could look behind him. When he did, he found that almost every window in the Malkin household was now blazing with candlelight. This meant that in the next few minutes, Mayer Malkin was surely raising a fast posse of skilled riders to catch the two runaways. Jake figured that he had, at best, a five-minute head start.

# THE MALKINS REACT

Inside the Malkin house, Dora Malkin was now running from room to room, yelling at the top of her lungs, "The damn girl is running away! The damn girl is running away!"

At every room, she kicked at the door and howled, "The little bitch is running away! The little bitch is running away!"

Reaching the room she shared with her husband, Dora found him already awake and putting on his pants. As he stood, she saw that he was missing a shoe and had a suspender half hanging over his side. He started to yell as he pulled a rifle that was standing in the corner of the room.

"Goddamn him, goddamn him! He stole a horse! I knew that he was going to do this to us!"

Realizing that he was missing a boot, he dropped the rifle on the bed and began to look around the room. His wife pointed to where it lay to his left, and he bent over to pick it up.

As he did, his youngest son, Gill, ran into the room.

Tying the lace around his boot, his father spit out directions, "Go next door, and get Klimkowicz and his boys. Tell them it is a gold piece each if they come with us. Then saddle as many horses as you can so we can leave in two minutes."

The boy raced out of the room while his father finished dressing. Skipping over three steps at a time, he was near the bottom when saw a fully dressed Leon tucking a pistol in his belt.

Looking up at his younger brother, he said, "*Gill!* You get three horses ready. I will go get Klimkowicz and whoever else I can." With that, he ran out of the front door.

Still tucking in his shirt as he moved, Gill grabbed a coat out off of a hook near the back door and threw the back door open. The ferocity of the rainfall surprised him. For a second, he thought that he should go back and get a heavier coat. Mindful of his father's wrath, he continued on his path to the barn. Once there, he slammed the latch open, threw open the double doors as far as he could, and ran inside.

A quick look around the barn showed Gill that Jake had taken the brown stallion that his father had bought late last year.

"Little bastard took the fastest horse," he said aloud to no one. "She must have been watching us."

Pulling a saddle from the rail in the back of the barn, he didn't stop to cover the back of the horse with a blanket. Throwing the saddle over his father's favorite steed, a strong and fast black Arabian, Gill saddled the animal.

Repeating the process two more times with different horses—the first for Leon, and the last for himself—he began to lead the three animals out of the barn. As he did, he heard several riders approaching the front door of the wide-open barn. One of them was carrying a torch that caused light to flicker about with wild abandon in the rain.

Gill paused for a second as he reached the front door, wrapping the reins around a wooden plank when he was outside. Next he picked up a long stick covered with rags that was sitting in an old open barrel next to the doors. Then he took the lid off the barrel that sat next to it and pushed the stick to the bottom. The thick, pungent odor of tar filled the air as he slowly removed it.

With the black goo dripping from the end, he then removed the lid from a metal canister that someone had forgotten to cover. It was filled with oil. He knew that the tar would burn for a long time.

Adding oil would give the torch a brighter flame. Knowing he had no time left, he rolled it around in the liquid for a second and looked up to see it was well lit.

Mayer Malkin cried out, "Where did they go, boy?"

Gill pulled on his reins and turned his horse toward the street. "North, Papa! They were going out through the north road!"

With a direction established, Leon moved toward the road in front of the house so that a torch could lead the way. The other four men followed.

It had taken roughly six minutes from the time that Mayer Malkin had heard the gunshot fired by his wife! He knew that the boy and his sister had a good lead. But he also knew that there were now five of Pinsk's best horsemen chasing Jake and his sister. The posse led by Mayer Malkin was fueled by righteousness and vengeance. They rode solo, and each one of them knew the outlying regions well. He was positive that he would hang a man that night before returning home.

Factoring in that Jake was burdened by an inexperienced girl hanging on the back of his saddle, he believed that they would catch him in about ten minutes, if that long.

# THE CHASE

Jake and Leah, riding hell-bent, strained to distance themselves from the Malkin's posse that they knew were on their trail. Passing the town's borders, they looked back and saw lightning striking the ground and jumping off in all directions. Booming thunder momentarily upset their horse and frightened Leah. Jake looked over his shoulder to catch a glimpse of Leah. All he could see were her shoulders hunched over and her head buried into his back. He was unable to see her face. But he knew that she had to be terrified.

With nothing but flatness and mud and road in front of them for another few miles, Jacob took a look behind, just as another wave of lightning washed over the land. It was then that he saw the posse. Looking back a second time, he counted two torches behind him. There were at least four, possibly five, riders. He couldn't make out if there were more, for the clouds had covered virtually all the moonlight.

Over his shoulder, he heard Leah yelling. What she was saying got lost in the wind and the rain, but he did hear the name "Malkin" repeated several times. Reaching behind him, he grabbed one of her arms and squeezed it. As he did, she pushed the top of her head into his back as a way of saying, "All right."

Pulling his hand from Leah's arm, he reached up and pulled his cap back down on his head. It didn't seem that the storm was going to end anytime soon, and he couldn't afford to lose their momentum.

All he could do was maintain a steady pace and move in as straight a line as possible, toward the Pripet Marsh. Once inside the wetlands, he knew that he could lose the posse.

To meet them on the open plains would be a different story. They were undoubtedly carrying pistols. The storm gave him a certain advantage, but a single shot could change everything. He didn't fear his own death. Since his earliest days with the rabbi, he understood death as a part of life. While he wasn't looking forward to his own death anytime soon, he didn't want his own reckless nature to be the cause of Leah's passing.

Looking back again as a bolt of lightning hit behind him, he was able to see that there were, indeed, five riders. Counting off between the frequent strikes of lightning as they landed across the flatlands, he was able to determine that they were gaining on him. But not by much.

Behind Jake, the Butcher Malkin drove his own horse relentlessly. Fearful of the whip, the animal moved as fast as it possibly could. Unable to understand that every living thing has its limits, Malkin used the open space between him and his gang as a test of endurance.

Mayer Malkin hated thieves, but the idea that he would lose both a horse and a servant in one swift act burned at his very soul. If a horse lived or died, it mattered little to him. It was the man who stole his belongings that he wanted.

"Catch that little thief!" he yelled out over the commotion of the storm and racing horses that was around him. "I will kill Jake the Horse Thief!"

His son Gill picked up on the cry, "Kill Jake the Horse Thief!"

The elder Klimkowicz then added to the noise as both father and son echoed the cry, until all but Leon were screaming for Jake's red head to swing from a tree, as they moved through the night.

Led by the unrelenting mania of the outraged butcher, the five men rode as hard as they could. Their heads down against the rain, their collars pulled tight, each one of them whipped their horses relentlessly. Around them the storm raged on, as they each bent over in their saddles, riding almost parallel to their mounts.

Half an hour passed as the chase went on. The weather began to calm down as the worst of the storm passed. Slowly, the moon began to emerge from behind the darkness of the clouds, until it cast an eerie glow over the land. Looking backward occasionally, Jake always saw the torches, each still burning bright despite a nighttime filled with an onslaught of wind and rain. He knew that his horse was becoming exhausted, and as a result, the posse was now less than half a mile behind him. The only solace in this thought was that they were tiring also.

Leah's grip around his waist had grown loose. Several times, he found himself reaching back to pull her hands and arms tight around him. He himself was so numb from the punishing pace that he could feel nothing in his hands or arms.

An hour earlier, the butcher had determined that Jake was leading them into the Pripet Marsh. He didn't care, for he felt that once the boy entered the quagmire, he would be lost, finally giving Mayer Malkin a chance to bring vengeance on the boy.

Klimkowicz had realized as much when they left the farm. But knowing the rage that fueled his employer, he had kept his mouth shut. He wasn't driven by anything other than a paycheck and figured that the butcher could easily buy ten horses better than the one he had just lost. As to the girl, he was only concerned with the horse. Servant girls were a dime a dozen in Pinsk.

Looking ahead, Jake kept his eyes peeled for an entrance to the Marsh. On his many visits, he knew that there was a path through the Marsh that even in the best weather was hazardous.

Undeterred, the posse drew closer and closer until Jake could almost feel the heat of their torches on his back. With the rain almost gone, he heard what they were now calling him.

"Jake the Horse Thief! We will hang you tonight!"

Undeterred, Jake rode on. Though her form felt lifeless behind him, Leah somehow managed to hang on to him. He worried for her safety, but as long as she was able to maintain a hold, he had to keep moving. To stop meant a far worse fate for her than if she were to fall as they rode on…

Before him the Pripet Marsh grew in shape as a vast, overwhelming waste. Many riders with far more experience than Jake had tried their luck and never come out of its deep waters and potential quicksand.

Inside there stood broken trees with their hanging branches swaying low as they swept across the top of the million ponds. There were miles of swaying reeds that came up from nowhere, without warning, each one dancing in the wind in a thousand directions. There were large areas of land-, water-, and fine-textured dirt that was one step removed from quicksand. That land looked solid to the eye, but one wrong step, and that seemingly beautiful land could easily swallow both man and horse.

A rider could be stepping slowly through what they thought was a low, shallow body of water and, with a single step, find themselves falling into a hole deeper than the horse and man were tall. In some instances, a horse had encountered a range of weeds that slowly tangled their legs without the rider seeing what was happening below the cloudy water. On the very next step, they would fall headfirst into the water with the inevitable struggle, drowning both man and horse.

Minutes before he started to enter the wetlands, Jake saw the sun begin to inch its way up in the east. Exhausted from the ride, he welcomed the idea that he wouldn't have to navigate the marsh in darkness.

The butcher and his gang were now only a few hundred yards behind him.

Hitting his nearly wasted steed softly in the animal's side, he said loudly, "Only a few more miles until we rest. We have the strength to make it. We can't have come this far to lose now, you wonderful friend of mine." With that, he bent down and hugged the neck of the horse.

The shift into marshland happened gradually. First Jake saw the flatlands start to disappear around him. Then he saw a tangled brush of bushes and reeds off to the far left. In front of him, he saw the worn path that he had traveled often in his many explorations. All he had to do was keep the posse at bay for another mile or so, then he could take an unknown side path that would allow him to watch them all race past him.

Patting him on his side as he spoke, he told the horse, "Good boy. That's a good boy…" The animal's heart was beating so fast that it felt to Jake as if it was ready to burst through its hide. "We'll get you a rest soon, real soon. Just stay with me for another mile or two. I promise."

It was a promise that he hoped he could keep. Once they hit the Marsh, Jake was counting on the butcher and his gang dropping out quickly. It was a calculated risk—one he hoped that he would win.

Thinking of Leah, he yelled out, "How are you doing back there?"

The wind was still so strong that all she could do was to push her head into his back as an answer.

Mustering all the encouragement he could, he went on, "We will be done in less than half an hour. Hold tight, Leah, hold tight!"

The sun was starting to rise. The light meant that he could now see that the posse was roughly a hundred yards behind him. Looking back for the hundredth time, Jake saw that both of their torches had been discarded into the small puddles of water that dotted the land around them. All five riders were galloping as hard as they could. Jake began to worry that the next time he looked behind him, he would see a raised rifle pointing at his back.

A minute later, he saw that he was right.

Behind him, Shimson Klimkowicz had been the first to discard his torch. He was now riding with the reins to his horse between his teeth. Looking forward, Jake saw what he considered to be a possible entrance to the Marsh—one commonly used as a shortcut to Minsk. The opening was now less than one hundred yards away. He knew that the cover provided by the Marsh would make it hard for Shimson to take an accurate shot, so he moved to ride as low in the saddle as he could.

Screaming at the top of his lungs as he rode toward the entrance, he yelled, "LEAH! Duck down as far as you can go...HURRY UP!"

There was no response from his sister. He yelled again, and then a third time, but still there was no response. He felt her grip around his waist loosen, while at the same time her head began to bounce against his back. He prayed with all his might that she hadn't passed out. But he knew that she was, at the very least, close to losing consciousness.

In an attempt to get her attention, Jake slapped her leg as hard as he could. She continued to fall to the right, so he hit her a second, and then a third. Each blow fell in rapid succession.

Despite his best efforts, Leah showed no response. She was now starting to fall out of her place behind him. The speed at which they were riding made it impossible for him to consider slowing down to help her.

Grabbing at Leah below her upper right thigh, he managed to stabilize his sister for just a second. In front of them, the entry to the Marsh was approaching fast. The path to the entryway was worn and clear. The horse was having no problem holding his footing. But there were signs that this was going to change quickly.

The land around him was starting to show signs of the wetland. To the left, they were whipped by small clusters of reeds waving in the night wind. Around them there were clumps of bushes taking shape, their numbers growing larger with every step the horse took. Jake knew that if he took his eyes off of the actual entrance to the main body of the Marsh for just one second, they could hit a tree or stumble into a rain-filled ditch that they couldn't see.

He also knew that it was important to slow his horse down as he entered the Marsh. The growing overhang kept the ground softer than it had been on the flatlands. This meant there were more pockets of water and more places where the horse could trip. Any sudden shift in the surface of the land could easily trip the steed.

Behind him, he could feel Leah continuing to fall. While he had a firm grip on her right leg, her left leg now started to shift on the other side of the horse. The weight of the girl was pulling her to the right as it shifted, pulling him to the right as it did!

A loud crack rang out and broke the quiet of the night. Jake felt something, a small tear across his left shoulder!

He felt nothing and assumed that he was either in shock from being hit or that the round had at the very least ripped his coat. It dawned on Jake that if Leah hadn't been falling to his right, she would have been right in the path of the bullet!

Leaning down further down to his right, he managed to maneuver Leah's arm under his own right arm while he slipped his hand under her thigh. This helped even out the distribution of her weight a bit more evenly and helped him to pull her halfway back into place. Even with this adjustment, she was still swaying behind him.

A second shot rang out, and he heard the snap of a branch in front of him and to his left. For the second time in as many minutes, he felt lucky.

Leah's falling had taken up so much of his attention that he failed to slow down as he entered the Marsh. It was only when he heard that second shot that he noticed the larger trees flashing past him on each side. With the sun just starting to break over the horizon, their upper branches were creating patterns of diffused, broken shafts of light around him.

He was now inside the Marsh, and he had not even realized it!

Then he heard the cries of, "Kill Jake the Horse Thief!" and "Kill the little bastard!" now ringing out behind him.

Without needing to look backward, he knew that the posse was coming too close for comfort. Barely able to hold Leah in place at the dangerous speed with which they were traveling, there was no choice but to keep riding at a breakneck pace! To slow down would mean immediate capture!

The perils of the Marsh that he had so rightly feared suddenly revealed themselves. Not twenty yards in front of him was a massive hole, which held a body of rain and marsh water that stretched out across the width of the road. It covered the dirt road ahead for at least ten feet. There was only one real choice before him as they were riding much too fast to stop. The only real solution was to trust the horse's instinct.

The minute the horse realized that there was a hole in front of him, it was either going to come to a complete stop, causing Jake and Leah to fly off in front of him, or it would try to jump over the approaching crevice. Either way, the outcome didn't look good!

A sudden stop would definitely throw them both to the ground, or a badly timed jump could cause them to tumble with the horse ultimately falling on top of them.

Jake made the only choice he could. The posse was too close, and they were moving too fast. He started to drive the horse as hard as he could.

"Come on, boy, come on!" he screamed. "You have it in you, it's there…"

With one hand holding the reins and the other holding Leah's leg tightly and clutching at the fabric of her skirt, he started to hit the side of the horse with his heels, holding on for life.

As they came to the rain-soaked abyss, it now looked to be the size of a lake. Jake found himself unable to breathe as he knew that he had misjudged its size! As to the horse, it seemed to be blind to what lay before him.

With one step until they collapsed, Jake pulled on the reins, wrapped his legs tightly around the animal's midsection, and yelled, "Jump, you son of a bitch!"

Providence took hold as, to his amazement, the horse leaped forward, completely leaving the ground!

For just a second, the two passengers and their four-legged host found themselves weightless as they hung in the air. Jake could only feel the trees rush by and the wind fly across his face, for his eyes were nearly shut. Leah's head fell into his shoulder, and he began to feel himself lose his grip on her.

Just then, in the second before they were to either land or fall to earth, he felt her reach out for his waist with both of her arms. At the exact moment they fell to earth, she clasped her hands tightly about him.

The roughness of the landing nearly took them out of their seats. Jake counted at least three bounces in the saddle before, somehow, they managed to work together through it all. This instinctual, natural-born teamwork between all three had allowed them to stay upright!

Once on the ground, the horse rode on without missing a step. Gasping for breath, Jake looked back and saw that they had cleared the puddle, with over a foot to spare!

Taking a series of deep breaths, Jake pulled on the reins and slowed down the pace. If the posse could make it across that pond, then there was no point on moving forward. He would just have to deal with them somehow.

He heard Leah mutter, "What happened?"

"Hold on, Leah, just hold on to me, we are almost free!"

She let out a breath, and Jake could feel her struggle to take another. When she finally had control of her breathing, she sighed loudly and tightened her grasp. It was good that she was conscious once again. But he could feel that the long ride and the constant jostling had taken a great toll on Leah. She had already passed out once, and Jake was sure that it would happen again very soon.

It went without saying that they couldn't risk another jump. The horse had performed one miracle, and Jake knew that he had no right to expect a second. It was imperative that he get a grasp on where he was in the Marsh, even if it meant that the posse would gain on them.

He pulled on the reins, bringing the horse down to a trot.

"Thank you..." muttered Leah as they turned to watch for the posse of Butcher Malkin.

They were now about seventy yards behind him. At the speed with which they were riding, it became apparent to Jake that they had yet to see the massive puddle that he had just miraculously flown across. It was then that Jake got an idea.

The boys, Leon Malkin and Shimson Klimkowicz, were in the lead. Each of them were riding so hard that they were now, that Jake could figure, about thirty yards in front of the others.

Riding at full gallop and tightly focused on Jake, it was clear that they were unaware of the low-lying water that lay before them. Neither of them had the experience to read the Marsh like Jake did. In addition, they weren't looking where they should. Instead of watching the ground, their concentration was completely on Jake. He knew that if he could see them so clearly, they could see him just as well.

## JAKE THE HORSE THIEF

Jake knew that his options were limited. His horse was exhausted, and he had been lucky to not lose Leah in this long flight from Pinsk. There were not only five men chasing them, but at least two of them also had guns.

But Jake knew the Marsh and the land he rode on. They didn't. This is where his long, sleepless nights of preparation were going to pay off.

Bringing his horse to a complete standstill, he turned completely around to face them as they rode. Leon was lying low in his saddle. His shoulders hunched, Jake could see his ankles dug into the side of his horse, pushing him harder with each kick.

Shimson was holding the rifle in one hand and sitting upright. Both riders were side by side, each one staring at Jake with a hate that burned a hole through his skull.

Waiting until he estimated that they were just about twenty feet from where he had first seen the watery quagmire, he put his plan into action. He only needed to get the full attention of one rider for his idea to work. If it didn't, he and his sister were as good as dead.

Standing in his saddle, Jake looked Shimson in the eye and simply smiled. This seemed to enrage the man who, still clutching his rifle, stood in his seat to meet his gaze. Jake watched as Leon took a quick glance to his left to see what Shimson was doing.

Neither one of them was paying attention to the road in front of them. At the exact same moment, they both hit the edge of the swamp water. Leon's horse stopped at the edge, rearing back in terror! The action sent the fourth son of the Butcher Malkin far into the air. When he came to land about ten feet away, he hit the ground so hard that Jake flinched as the man rolled on through the muck for another five or six feet. He only came to a stop as he fell into a smaller pond that bordered the path on their right. There he lay motionless.

Seeing the water before him, Shimshon's steed had done the opposite and tried to run straight through the large puddle. The minute that he hit the edge, the horse started to fall forward. His momentum was so great that the animal began to roll over headfirst into the mess before him. His rider, paralyzed by fear, found himself unable to let go of the reins.

Together both man and horse began to tumble over each other. The first roll happened so fast that Shimson had escaped unhurt. Being considerably lighter than the horse, the boy's momentum carried him further and further out in front of the beast. This meant that as they rolled a second time, the weight of the horse dropped straight on him as they spilled into a nosedive.

Jake saw Shimson disappear completely under the mud as the horse fell on top of him. When the horse kept moving, he involuntarily jerked the reins so that the poor man was now being pulled out of the mud.

Jake was sure that he saw one of the long legs of the horse crack as it hit the ground at the end of that second roll.

It wasn't until the end of the third roll that they finally stopped moving forward. Shimson was trapped in the mud directly in front of the beast. He cried out loudly as the full weight of the animal's body rolled across his legs. The animal finally came to rest a few feet from the boy, his body half in the mud and the other half on more solid ground. In panic, the animal writhed in pain as he found it impossible to rise out of the mud.

Shimson, unaware of how serious his injuries were, pushed against the quagmire and tried to stand. Screaming in pain, the poor boy collapsed into the water, his arms waving wildly behind him. He cried out for his father.

The horse, its front leg broken in the fall, continued to cry out in pain as well. It struggled against the combination of loose dirt, sand, mud, and standing water. As it fought against it, Jake could see that the mixture had trapped the animal so that it couldn't free itself without help.

Each of the other three riders—Gill, Klimkowicz, and the Butcher Malkin—had managed to slow to almost a standstill when they saw what was happening in front of them. The other three riders in the posse could only watch on helplessly as the tragedy unfolded. In shock they watched, unable to help.

Before them, Leon's horse, which had stopped at the edge of the massive hole, was now rearing back on his hind legs while shrieking in terror and confusion. Seeing the riders at his side, the animal then started jumping up and down, kicking wildly with his back legs on every leap. With every jump, he was turning to his right, and then to his left, making it impossible for anyone left standing to pass.

Still standing in his saddle, Jake looked out at the scene before him. Two of the horses that had been chasing him were down—one trapped in the muck, the other out of control as it marched back and forth, threatening anyone who approached it. Each of two fallen riders was laid out in mud and dirt, screaming in unimaginable pain.

Trapped behind the raging horse at the edge of the swamp, Mayer Malkin noticed Jake standing about fifty yards in front of the mess.

Shaking his fist in the air, he screamed, "GODDAMN YOU, JAKE, YOU HORSE THIEF!"

Jake did nothing but stare out blankly. He had never seen such a horrible accident in his life. Seeing the boys, as well as the animals, in such pain tore at his heart. Knowing that he had caused it drove the dagger home even more.

But the man that Jake had become also knew that he had no real choice in the matter. If the posse had caught him, they would have hung him on the spot. After all, he was now a horse thief! God only knows what they would have done to Leah. No matter what had happened, Jake had acted in the only way that he could have to protect himself and his sister.

The butcher looked out across it all and brought his animal up on its hind legs, yelling at the others.

He ordered them, "Go around this shit! Go around this mess! Both of you, go get that little bastard!"

Gill rode up to his father's side and saw the destruction before him. No matter what his father was screaming, trying to cross the disaster before them was not going to happen until they could get control over the horse screaming before them.

Ignoring his father, he jumped off of his horse. It took a minute, but he was finally able to slip past Leon's screaming horse. His only concern was to get across the water and help his brother. Moving as close to the edge of the immense puddle as he could get, he slipped down the side along the brush, doing his best to avoid being dragged into the horrible mess.

He looked to the sides for dry land and saw nothing but water and reeds and trees and mud that went on forever. Leon was now about five feet away from where he was. From the way he was clutching at his head and screaming, Gill assumed that the fall had cracked his skull.

Hearing his father yell out, "Get the little shit, Gill! I'll get the other boy," he looked away from where Leon lay and saw Jake down the road with his red hair blazing in the early morning sun.

Seeing him standing in his saddle, the youngest Malkin couldn't understand why the horse thief wasn't using the time to ride as far away from them as he could. He then looked back to where Leon was lying and ran through the mess to his brother's side.

For all the pain that he was in, Leon was still aware of what needed to be done. He too was facing Jake and saw that the boy wasn't moving. He saw that Leah was slumped over, hanging nearly lifeless behind her brother.

Unable to stop pressing at the side of his skull, he yelled, "Gilly! Get the pistol out of my belt. Shoot the prick! Shoot him, Gilly!"

Jake heard what had been said but still found himself unable to move. He felt as if he was in the calm at the middle of the storm. To move would only put him in danger. He saw Gill and Leon, but what really caught his eye was what was going on behind the brothers.

The elder Klimkowicz had moved his mount until he was now right next to the Butcher Malkin. The two horses were bumping against each other.

Adding his voice to the turbulent condition, he was crying, "Dammit, Malkin. My boy is down, and now we'll have to shoot my horse!"

The butcher ignored Klimkowicz and yelled to his sons who lay fifteen feet away, "Shoot the little bastard! Gilly, get that fucking pistol!"

Klimkowicz grabbed the butcher by the arm and screamed, "We will get him later. I ain't losing my boy or another fucking horse, you pig bastard!"

The butcher shook off the farmhand and kept yelling at Gill, "Do it, boy, DO IT!"

The horse that had been jumping around the road had finally tired himself and was now standing off to the side, looking out into space blankly.

Jumping off of his mount, Klimkowicz ran straight into the muck. He moved past the damaged horse and went straight into the deepest part of the water. With every step, he sank deeper and deeper into the mire. Moving past the trapped horse, he went to his son's side. The boy was coughing up blood and mud and water.

Mayer Malkin yelled for Klimkowicz to shoot Jake.

The reply came quickly, "FUCK THE HORSE THIEF, MAYER!" yelled Klimkowicz as he tried to pull his son from the slime.

Digging in, he found that he was unable to move the boy. As he struggled with his broken son, he looked to the butcher and went on.

"I need help! Get off that horse, Mayer! Help me! I can't pick the boy out of the mud." He moved his arms under his son's back and tried with all his might to lift him out of the mud.

The boy was in too deep, but the Butcher Malkin was too consumed by rage to think rationally.

Looking at Jake in the distance, he yelled, "Your day will come. You will die at the hand of a Malkin, Jake! I promise you that!" Dropping into the dirt and water and gunk, he repeated his threat.

Behind this scene, Leah said quietly to Jake, "Leave now."

Jake had become so engrossed by the wreckage before him that he had forgotten that she was there! Touching her arm, he turned his horse around and began to make his way down the path.

The sound of Mayer Malkin screaming began to fall away as he and the horse regained their breath. In a minute, they were moving through the Marsh, picking up speed with every careful step.

Jake patted his steed on the neck and said quietly, "Thank you."

# JAKE AND LEAH IN THE MARSH

The accident had served its purpose. It had delayed the posse while giving him and Leah a chance to catch their breath. Now they stood a good chance of gaining some ground on those who had been chasing them.

As much as he would like to believe that the posse had turned around, he knew that he had to keep moving forward, lest they were still coming after him. There was also the possibility of a far greater danger lurking close by—one that he would undoubtedly have to face at some point as they approached Minsk.

Less than twelve hours ago, he and the rabbi had spoken of the threat that modern Germany posed to their country. Not wanting to upset the old man, Jake had kept his opinions and feelings on the subject to himself.

Now, riding into the densest part of the Pripet Marshes, he had to move those concerns at the front of his mind. The most recent newspaper he had read told him that at this very moment, German tanks and troops were crossing into Poland. He just didn't know where they were. But at some point, either they or the Russians were going move into Minsk. He needed to get to the city before any of them did.

Jake lost track of time as he and Leah rode on for mile after mile. After days of rain, the sun now beat down on their necks and faces. He wanted to remove his jacket, shake off the mud, and let his clothes dry out. Finally, with the sun straight overhead, Jake spotted a deep alcove covered by vines and weeds.

They could hide in there and take a break.

He took the horse as far in the brush as it could go. As it was throughout the Marsh, even alert experienced riders found it difficult to tell how much of the ground was covered with water and what was actually dry land. Luckily, the alcove held dry land.

Hopping off the horse, Jake's legs nearly buckled when they hit the ground. He had been riding for at least ten hours, and they were wobbly.

Without his support, Leah was now falling off the back of the horse. Catching herself on the edge of the saddle, she said weakly, "Jake?"

"Right here, Leah. It's over, the posse is gone."

He stood strong and let her fall into his arms. She couldn't stand on her own, so he walked her slowly over to a shady spot. When she came to a stop, a cloth-covered bag fell from her coat. Jake sat her down and leaned her against a tree. She was exhausted and could barely hold her head up.

He went back to tie up the horse. Next he took off the saddle and laid it across a long bent tree that stood a few feet away. He then removed the blanket. It was soaking from sweat. Wringing it out, Jake then laid it across another branch to let it dry.

From the side of the horse, he removed the small leather bag that he had filled with fresh water before he had left the rabbi's house.

Brushing the animal with his hand, he said, "Good boy… Good boy…"

Jake made sure that he was close to a healthy stretch of grass as well as a small pond of water. Bending down to a small puddle, he touched its contents with his fingertips. He drew a few drops to his lips. It was, indeed, fresh.

Turning to his sister, he said, "Leah, we need to drink some water."

"Give me my bag," she whispered.

Jake walked back to her and bent over to where she had dropped it. He raised it as she asked and handed it to her. Taking it from his outstretched hand, she opened the clasp slowly, removing what looked to Jake to be a raggedy pile of old cloth.

Placing the bag to her side, she fluffed up the pile of rags. Jake realized that it wasn't a pile of rags at all. It was the doll that their mother had made for her, twenty long years ago.

Lying down on her side, Leah kicked out her legs and let her head fall on the cloth bag. Pulling the doll to her chest, she mumbled, "Good night."

Jake sat down next to her with his back against a thick tree trunk that formed the base of the alcove. Looking up, he saw that a delicate weave of vines and brush and thorns and leaves had formed a small natural roof. It blocked the bright light of the late-day sun, so they were now in shade.

A few feet away, the horse started lapping at a small puddle of fresh water from a hole in the ground. Once he was sure that the horse was taken care of and that Leah was safe at his side, Jake was asleep in less than a minute.

# OUT OF THE PRIPET MARSH

Torn and tired from the chase, Jake slept more than he ever had in a single day of his seventeen years. After witnessing the debacle that had lain the posse to waste, he and Leah had continued on for what seemed to be an eternity. Hour after hour, they rode their exhausted steed through the wetlands of the Marsh. By the time they had finally stopped, the sun was beginning to set—which meant that they had been riding for, by Jake's account, over twenty hours. He had been awake for over thirty-five hours.

He wasn't so much worried for himself as he was for his sister. Looking to where she lay, he saw that she was asleep. The temperature had fallen drastically during the night. When he had awakened shivering, he took the horse's blanket from the branch where it had been hung to dry and covered them with it. Together the two lay side by side through the night, occasionally embracing each other for warmth.

Sleeping as much as he just had was unusual for him. Normally, Jake was capable of functioning on just a few hours of sleep, sometimes as little as three or four. This is one of the reasons that he was able to sneak out at night and explore the town of Pinsk so much when he was younger. With daylight and renewed energy, Jake dared to set a small fire. There was always the danger of detection by the Malkins; however, he believed they had put enough miles between them for the dare of a fire.

## JAKE THE HORSE THIEF

Looking ahead, he believed that he needed at least three, maybe as many as five, more days in order to get out of the Marsh. It has been his original plan to go straight through and ride into Minsk. But if the butcher was on his trail, it might be best to head in the direction of the City of Slutsk, which was located further to the west. It was far enough off of the beaten path that they would be able to sell the horse and avoid detection.

Another advantage that Slutsk had was that it was located in a rural area. The surrounding lands held farms where he could barter labor for food or, if needed, spend some of the kopecks that he had hidden.

He then wrote some brief notes concerning the last evening in the margins of the prayer book. As he had done since he had first received the book, he jotted down words and ideas that jumped out to him. One day, not long before they had left Pinsk, he noticed that almost all the words that he singled out were about freedom and family.

"Not a bad thing," he said to himself while the fire warmed his legs.

Off to his side, he could hear Leah starting to rumble around. Jumping up, he felt his shirt and socks and found that they were dry enough for his tastes. Dressing quickly, he went over to Leah and shook her gently.

"Good morning." Taking the stick from her, Jake adopted a serious tone as he spoke, "The Malkins are over. Forbid that we should never see another Malkin in our life."

He handed her the stick and, for the first time in years, found himself only a foot away from his sister. He had never seen her this close-up before.

The work, both mental and physical, that the Malkin family had given her had taken a toll. Where he remembered a girl with curves and rosy cheeks, he now saw a woman with pale skin that, even in the morning sun, seemed to hold hints of gray. Her long black hair, now hanging down past the center of her back, looked frazzled and dry—its once-glorious luster dimmed by age and soap and heat. Her eyes, once so bright and wide, now looked tired, smaller, and each one held a twinge of fear.

Leah had always been a good worker, strong. But Jake knew that she was a worrier as well. Her nerves could be tender.

He watched as Leah moved and started pulling her hair behind her, running her hands across it, and making a ponytail as she spoke, "I don't mean to talk about the Malkins, but that is all I can remember. It is all that I know." She hesitated and then went on, "Sometimes I forget what Momma looked like." She shook her head. "When I lived there, even after the…Well, the boys left me alone. But it was always her that I was afraid of. She was horrible, fat, smelly, and mean, always had…" Her voice trailed off as she thought of her life.

Jake reached over and touched her. With a tenderness that he didn't know that he had, he said, "She is gone. Right now you are fifty miles away from where she sits. The truth is, you will probably never see her again."

Jake then relaxed and gave his sister the largest smile she would ever know.

As the brother and sister looked at each other, they began to laugh. Jake couldn't remember the last time that he felt so good.

With no warning, Leah yelled out, "We did it, Jake! We did it!"

As she spoke, she leaned over and squeezed him with all her strength. Jake was surprised at the muscle on the girl. On the outside, she looked so frail.

Leah continued to hold on to him as she spoke, "You are the smartest and strongest man… and risked so much for me…You never quit, do you?"

Her kind words caught him off guard. Suddenly, he felt nervous and unsure of himself. He wasn't prone to analyzing himself or thinking about himself in such a way. To him, it was simple: you took care of your family. In the end, they are all that you have.

"I am your brother, I am supposed to help and take care of you."

He watched as she went from overjoyed to sad in the space of a second. Looking at him, she had begun to cry.

Trying to comfort her, he went on, "We need to make as much time as we can. The horse looks good. So with some luck, we will be out of here in three or four days. I plan on heading east toward Slutsk. You have to know that this is going to be tough."

Leah answered him quickly, "I can handle this. Every night for the last four years, I have dreamed of this moment. Nothing will stop us."

"Good," said Jake, "because we need to make some hard choices."

"I can ride at night, if that is what you are worried about."

"I can see that. You haven't complained once about yesterday and the long ride."

"I am just sorry that I passed out, but I was exhausted and sore. And today my butt does hurt." She laughed and then went on, "I am naked under a blanket by a campfire and just had a potato for breakfast. I think I can deal with anything!"

Just the same, he needed to tell her something that was bound to upset her.

Taking a deep breath, he began by saying, "Look, Leah, we have to make some choices. One of them is what we look like, how we appear to others. Having a girl with me complicates things."

"What do you mean?" she said innocently.

"Girls are few and far between on the road we are traveling." He tilted his head, hoping that she would understand.

"So? I am big. I am strong. I can fight if I have to," came the reply.

"That's true, but if you lose…" he became nervous, hoping that he wouldn't have to spell the idea out for her, "there are other complications. We need to cut your hair so we don't attract attention to the fact that you are a girl."

She ran her fingers across her hair. Panic began to grow in her voice as she spoke, "But I have always had long hair. Momma and I...I mean, I can't remember much about her...but she always brushed my hair. It is one of my only memories...one of my earliest..."

She jumped up and ran over to her own bag. Opening it, she pulled out a brush and held it up for Jake to see. Clutching the blanket tightly, she sat back down.

"This is all I have," she said, shaking the brush at Jake while she spoke. "Every night I did one hundred strokes with this very brush. It was Momma's...hair that I was brushing.... She would then do mine." She looked at him with disbelief. "I can't cut my hair...It is part of me. It is part of my life. I won't know who I am..."

Jake walked over to the branches where her clothes hung and checked to see if they were dry. "About five more minutes, Leah."

Walking back to the fire, he saw that it was starting to die down. Time was of the essence. He didn't want to waste another minute. They had already been sitting for too long.

As he moved to sit down next to her, she moved away from him.

He sighed and said quietly, "Leah, we have to plan for the future. But in order to get there, we have to live for today, right now. If a bandit sees you are a girl, he will take you at gunpoint. You might even be sold into slavery. We need to cut your hair as short as possible. We have to at least try and make people think that you are a young boy."

Terror filled her eyes as it dawned on her what Jake was trying to tell her. Immediately, she thought back to that dark night of Jake's bar mitzvah—how sweaty the hands of Butcher Malkin were, how his breath stank of beer and wine, how she had run through the night after the horrible incident...

As a result of that night, she feared that no man would take her for his wife because she was unclean. She had been violated in the most horrific way imaginable, leaving her undesirable… doomed to spend life alone, for no man would have her.

Determination filled her eyes as she looked at her brother. No matter what had happened in the past, nothing should stop them from moving forward.

Taking the brush in her hand she said, "Let me brush it out and get the tangles out. It will make it easier to cut."

With that, she adjusted herself so that her back was to Jake. After a few quick strokes through the thickness of her hair, it all evened in front of him. It now lay there flat, ready to be cut.

Using just a finger and a thumb, she grabbed it as close to the top of her skull as she could. "Go ahead, one quick cut. Let's not waste any more time."

Behind her, Jake had already taken out his knife, opening it quietly while she was talking. He saw where she had grabbed her hair and said, "Move your grip about an inch or so down. If we cut it that high, you will look bald."

"Can't have that now, can we?" said Leah.

He moved his hands to where she was holding her hair, gently placing his free hand over hers. Slowly, he began to move the knife back and forth near the back of her skull. Moving the knife slowly, he thought for a second that he heard her whimper just a bit. He was so deep into the cut that even if she had, it was too late to turn back.

It took less than a minute to cut through the thickness that she wore so proudly. Looking down to his hands, he saw that his right hand held a knife, and in his left hand, he now held the last ten years of their life in the town of Pinsk. For a second, he was speechless. Those ten years had all gone by so fast, yet every minute had seemed to be so long.

Leah's voice brought him back to the job at hand. There was focus, a determination in her voice as she spoke, "Throw it far away. I don't want to see it. Make sure that you throw it behind us. I don't want to go past it as we ride."

He shook his head as if roused from a slumber. "I will bury it when I bury the fire and all our waste."

"Good. Let me go get dressed."

With that, Leah stood up and ran her hands across the back of her head where Jake had made the cut. Without looking back, she walked over to her clothes and picked them up from where they lay across the rocks next to the fire.

Seeing that the flame had almost run its course, she said to Jake, "I could have used another potato…"

Jake watched her walk into the bushes as she kept talking, "And a couple of eggs, maybe some bread." He could hear her laugh as she changed. "And some juice or some tea." She now sounded wistful, as if the memory of a certain morning was carrying her through the difficulty. "Some tea would have been nice."

Jake didn't want to tell her, but he had deliberately left tea bags in the kitchen back at the house. To bring tea bags meant they needed something to boil water in. That meant more baggage, more things to carry. It was important that they travel with little more than the clothes on their backs.

Following her wishes, he dropped her hair a half a foot from the embers that were still glowing. He was careful to not drop the bundle in the flames, for he didn't want the smell of burning hair to distract them. He then took the rocks that he had arranged for their clothes to dry and scattered them around the land. It was important to leave no clues that would show anyone who was trailing them that they had stopped there.

Turning to his side, he saw her standing next to him. Without her hair, she looked even thinner, even smaller. He was overwhelmed with the feeling that he wanted nothing more than to protect her and to lead her to someplace safe—a place where he could watch over her as her children grew up with him as their uncle. Impulsively, he hugged her, and she took him into her arms willingly.

When they pulled apart, he saw that she was holding the doll that their mother had made her all those years ago. Without a word, she dropped it next to where the fire had been. Then she walked back to where she had slept and sat down to pack what was left of her belongings.

Looking down at the faded embers, he saw the thread-worn cloth that served as a dress and stockings for the doll. Once a deep, deep black, the color was now faded, nearly gray. In some places the cloth was ripped and torn. It looked to him as if they were burying a ghost.

Kneeling down, he moved handfuls of dirt over the doll, the remnants of her hair, and the fire, until it was impossible for anyone to tell that anything had ever been there. Standing, he kicked more dirt around the edges and smoothed over the patch with the bottom of his boot.

He asked his sister, "Where is the blanket?"

"Over by the horse, hanging right next to him," came the reply.

With his pouch slung over his shoulder, he walked over to the horse, patted him along his back, and asked, "Are you ready for another hard day, boy? Are you?"

He took a carrot from the pouch and held it out for him to take. There seemed to be a moment of hesitation as the horse looked straight at him.

"Come on, we don't have much choice now, do we?" said Jake.

With that, the horse took the carrot, his head bobbing up and down as he chewed. Taking the blanket off of the branch, he threw it over the back of the animal. Next he saddled him properly and, taking the reins, led him back to the path they had left the night before.

Over his shoulder, he said, "Come on, Leah, time to get going."

Looking behind him, he saw her kicking dirt and smoothing over where the fire had been. He said nothing.

As she walked toward him, he saw her face suddenly glowing as she walked. A smile now went from ear to ear. Smoothing the front of her shirt, she threw her coat over her shoulders and then placed her hat on top of her head. Without her hair, it flopped around, looking as if it would fly off with the slightest breeze.

She reached into her bag and pulled out several small pins. Placing them along brim of her cap, she did her best to secure the cap to what remained of her hair.

"I don't care right now, but I am sure it looks awful. When we stop tonight, you have to clean this for me. It feels weird, really light. The air going across my head seems funny..." She ran her hand across the back of her head and went on, "Oh, and I assume that you have some plans for boy's clothes. I am still wearing a skirt and leggings, stockings, so the haircut was only part of the procedure..."

"Of course. We will stop by a farmhouse and trade some labor or maybe buy some pants in a small town." With that, he hoisted himself to the top of the horse and then held his hand out to her. "Let's go. We can talk while we ride."

Making a clicking noise with his tongue and snapping the reins as he did, the horse started to move down the path.

Jake knew the Marshes as well as any man. Even with all the studies and travels that he had made, he still felt uneasy while riding through them. There was simply too much hiding inside the wetlands. One moment it was a dense forest—the next, a wide open sandy regions with reeds blowing in the breeze.

He knew that no one had ever accurately defined where the Marsh started and stopped. Many had tried, but the rising and receding of the overflow waters and ponds made the task difficult for even the best of men. With all this in mind and using the sun as a guide, he started for northwest as best he could.

For the first hour or so, he and Leah spoke about the last few years. As time wore on and the land became more challenging, the conversation dwindled, and they settled into a pattern. She did her best to hang on, and he did his best to move in the right direction. There were two instances where trouble occurred. Twice they had started to sink into the wetland when Jake misjudged the depth of the road in front of him.

Both times they had to dismount and drag the horse out of the mire. The second time, the horse rebelled when they wanted him to go further. It took an hour of valuable daylight time for Jake to get him to calm down.

After that, he used extreme caution, and no more problems occurred. For three days and into the morning of the fourth, the land rolled around them. Boredom had become a serious problem, as he was growing tired of navigating around distractions and obstacles.

Jake whispered to Leah, "It's tough going for just a while longer, but we're free, at last!"

"Don't worry about me. We have a good life ahead of us. I will be fine," she said in response.

Without anything to cook, they used that night's fire for warmth and to dry their clothes. Their patience worn thin, they tried to muster some courage, but they found themselves thinking of food…

Suddenly, Jake sat up. He ran over to the branch where his saddle and bag hung. Removing a long piece of rope and tying it around his wrist, he looked at her and said, "There is maybe a half hour of daylight left."

"So?" said his sister.

"About a half a mile away, there were ducks. I wasn't thinking! I should have thought to stop and get them while we could!" said Jake, who continued, "I have been looking for birds that we could eat, but nothing has come our way over the last few days. Everything has been flying over our heads, all of them heading out for winter. I am so used to blowing them off I went right by them and wasn't paying attention...And we couldn't eat a fox or catch a wild boar...I mean there are things to hunt, but that takes time and skill I never developed..."

She put her hand out for him to help her stand. As she rose, he continued, "Hell, we could eat frogs if we had to, but...Maybe the hunger is starting to affect my reasoning because this isn't something I would have normally missed. Dammit! We could have been eating duck for every meal! But I can't leave you alone here..."

It took a minute for Leah to convince Jake that if he were to take off in search of food, she would be fine.

"I'll watch the fire and keep it going so that you can use it as a beacon."

It took him less than half an hour to return with three ducks Jake had shot.

"Build the fire a little higher, and I'll do the rest," she directed.

Having spent a decade in the house of a butcher, Leah knew how to remove feathers from a chicken and cut it as necessary. To her, a duck wasn't that much different.

Wiping her hands on her skirt, Leah said, "Tomorrow is day five. It was good to finally eat something again. Now that we have regained our strength, we can leave the Pripet Marsh and all this mess behind."

Jake assured her, "As we ride, we should see less and less of the wetlands and more and more of the farmlands that lead to Slutsk. From there, Minsk is only a half a day ride away. We can buy some food from the farmers we pass."

For the first time in three days, they fell asleep feeling positive. The morning of the fifth day found them anxious to reach the outlying boundaries of Slutsk as quickly as possible. They rose early and were on the road before the sun had fully risen. Hour after hour, they rode quietly and quickly along a path that grew more open the longer they stayed on it.

Over their heads, the sun had risen and then begun to fall before they realized that the wetlands were receding behind them. Before them, solid land began to stretch out in waves, rising and falling as it rolled onto a new horizon. With less than an hour of daylight left, Leah asked Jake to stop for just a minute.

"I need to walk for a bit. My legs are numb," she said. He had barely slowed down when she jumped off as soon as she felt comfortable. Holding on to a strap near the back of the saddle, she tried not to think of food. Or her bed. Or her doll. Or her Momma…

It was only when she realized that Jake was talking to her that she was roused from her thoughts.

"Leah, we have to find some food while it is daylight. There is no place for us to stop. We haven't got the shelter of the Marsh…"

As if by providence, she turned to her left and in the far distance saw a small dot. Pointing to it, she said, "Look, a house, it's got to be a farm. Maybe we can find some help there."

Looking over to his left, Jake agreed. Seeing a farm told him that they were on the right path. As he reasoned, a farm needs to have somewhere to sell their goods, and that meant a town was within five miles or so.

"Get back on the saddle, there is real possibility for us ahead."

Compared to the Marsh, they were now on a relative flat land. Though he knew the animal was tired, he began to drive it harder. As they rode, he explained to her that it would be safer to reach a more populated area, one where the farms were closer together.

"Who knows how many people that farm has working on it? It is pretty far off the regular path and could be more dangerous than we realize," he said. "Let's stay the course, and I am sure that we will find something more accommodating in the next few miles."

She wrapped her arms around his waist and said quietly, "I am so tired, Jake. Surely, they would not be so unfriendly as to do harm to a fellow Jew?"

He was surprised at what she said. It had never occurred to him that she didn't know what was happening in Poland at the very moment they were riding. Living with the Malkins had kept her isolated from the world at large. Of course, she wouldn't know of the greater dangers! She may not even know about the Communists or the Nazis. To her, everyone was Jewish. To her, everyone was either cruel like the Malkins, or nice like Jake and the rabbi! She had no experience. The world Leah lived in was black and white.

Even he, with all the miles he had traveled and his knowledge of the Marshes and the roads to Minsk, Jake understood that he too was uninformed. There was so much of the world that he didn't know. Yes, the rabbi had taught him to read. Yes, as a man, he had privileges that weren't extended to many women. But in the end, he knew that he was still a boy with many, many days in front of him.

In the world that lay outside the boundaries of Pinsk, he had heard the rumors of camps where Jews were killed in Germany. Even in Pinsk, he had seen anti-Semitism firsthand, when a gentile merchant had denied service because he was Jewish. It hurt him deeply that he was going to have to explain to Leah an ugly truth of life. How do you explain to someone the idea of pure, unreasonable hate?

# FARMERS AND SOUP

With nightfall so close, he rode as hard as he could along the worn dirt path. There had to be another farm or a small group of houses just down the road—anything that could offer them comfort and a roof for just one night.

Leah interrupted his concentration, "When do we stop, Jake? I can go on for a few more miles, but my stomach is torn. I feel it burning with hunger."

As she had the first night, she dug her head into his back and started to slouch behind him. He knew that she was driven down, tired, and torn. He had to make a quick discovery of a dwelling, with kind, sympathetic people. Jake decided that a small farm he had seen about a quarter mile back would be the best place to stop. It looked to be far enough off the beaten path to pose the minimum problem if they called authorities.

Jake was also worried about the horse they had ridden so hard. The poor animal had now spent five days riding at a relatively brisk pace. Grass and water had always been easily available in the Marsh, but the past five hours had been spent on a dirt road. The water and grass of the Marsh was now behind them. Jake had taken care to give him periods of rest. But the journey was, indeed, long.

Comforting her, he said, "A few more minutes, Leah. Just stay with me. It is important that when we talk to the farmer that you look bright and alert."

The voice that answered was sleepy, "I will, Jake, you can count on me." She barely had the energy to dig her head into his back as she usually did.

A few minutes later, he was tying the reins off on the branch of a tree. They stood quietly about a quarter of a mile from the door to the farm. Dismounting, he told her to move into the saddle.

"It will be easier to stay up if you do, Leah."

She did as he asked, and he began walking to the door. About a hundred yards from the door, he heard a voice bark out in the darkness.

"Stop where you are, or I will blow your head off!"

Throwing his hands into the air, Jake said calmly, "No need to shoot, mister. Just looking to trade a horse for some food and some clothes if you have 'em."

The voice yelled out, "Where's the horse?"

"Down the path. My sister is watching it."

As soon as the word *sister* crossed his lips, he hit himself. There had been no point to present Leah as a boy if he was going to call her one when he met a stranger! Then he realized that since she was still wearing her skirt, the mistake would work to his benefit.

"Go get the horse and your sister, and come back this spot as fast as you can."

Running back up the road, Jake debated whether to get back on the horse and simply keep going. The gun made him nervous, and it was clear that the old man wasn't Jewish, for he spoke clear Polish.

The presence of a rifle in any situation was always bad news. But in truth, he had no real choice. Clouds had begun to roll in, and they started to cover what light the moon had provided. That would make any further travel difficult. More importantly, Leah was tired, and neither of them had eaten anything since the leftover duck they had eaten early in the day.

Lastly, the horse was tired and on its last legs. They were lucky to have made it this far. As soon as he reached Leah, the doubt he had felt was over. Before him he saw his sister atop the horse, slumped over and barely holding on to the leather strap at the front of the saddle, her head bouncing as she struggled to stay awake.

"Leah…sister…" he said softly. He saw her look up and then over to where he was.

Her head moved up, and her back snapped into perfect posture.

"Jake, I am really tired. But I can move on if you need us to."

This was one of many times that he would be proud of her while they were on the road.

"Throw me the reins, Leah. They aren't Jewish, but we should be all right."

Leading the horse and the rider down the path toward the lamp, he sent a silent prayer. It was about ten feet away from the lantern when he heard the old man's voice cut through the night.

"Stand where you are, boys."

In the flickering light of the lantern, Jake could see that the lantern was held by a woman, and the old man was now pointing the rifle at his head.

"Damn it, Gunther, if you shoot him, the police or even worse will come! Put the gun down, old man. And I am not going to say it again."

Jake flinched as the woman slapped what he assumed was her husband on the back of his head.

The old man lowered the gun, while she advanced toward Jake and Leah, holding the lantern.

"I will lead you to the barn, and then you can come inside for a minute so we can talk. But you ain't sleeping in my house or barn. We are just going to talk."

Jake understood her offer and followed her as she walked away from the house. Once they were at the barn, Leah dismounted and the horse was tied to the top rail of the fence.

The woman spoke first, "Gunther, look over the pony."

Her husband started to look at the animal closely.

"That isn't a pony, ma'am, it's a full-sized horse," said Jake.

"I know that!" she snapped. "You want to trade it or not?"

"Trade it, ma'am…" was Jake's reply.

"Good, now what you want?" she said.

"We can walk to Minsk, but we can't make it in rotted clothes. So we figured to trade the horse for something decent."

"You'll take what I got, and you'll be happy. Ain't hardly any stores left open in Slutsk. Not after your type was run out."

"Our type?" said Leah.

"Yeah, Jews, darling. The Russians are in town, and the Jews that could afford to do so ran out as fast as they could. Those left behind are doing labor."

Leah looked at Jake but said nothing.

The woman went on, "The goddamn Russians got both my boys for their army. Me and the old man ain't got nothing but the farm now, and I expect them Communist pricks to take that from us soon. So we need all the animals we can get to sweeten the pot."

Gunther told her the horse looked okay but that it was too thin for his taste.

"We can make a horse fat in a couple of weeks," she said in response. Looking at the horse again, she added, "Saddle and the works is part of the deal, right, boy?"

"If the clothes are good enough, sure. I can't carry it." He smiled at her, but she showed no response to his attempt to charm.

Looking to Leah and Jake, she went on, "You say good-bye to your horse, and you…" she pointed at Leah as she went on, "the girl, you come with me." Taking Leah by the arm, the woman started toward the house.

Jake stayed behind and went up to the animal. Patting it on the back, he whispered in its ear, "Thank you." The horse pulled its head back and nodded in his direction.

The old man said, "You got a touch. I can see that. Most animals don't acknowledge me. They work for me just fine, but they don't talk to me. I never had it, the touch with horses. You got it." Putting his hand on Jake's shoulder, he said, "Don't let her scare you, she's a softy. You and me can take him in the barn and pull the saddle off. Then we will get you something to eat."

Taking the reins, he pointed to the side of the horse. "Don't forget your bags here."

Jake untied their bags from the sides they had been hanging on. Then he and the old man pulled the horse inside the barn. It took a minute or two for them to remove the saddle and place it on a bench. The old man held the lantern up and gave it the once-over.

"Don't see no marking, but I assume that it's stolen."

"Stolen from an asshole that tried to rape my sister," said Jake in as threatening a voice as he had.

The old man laughed and said, "Just a yes would have been enough of an answer."

Reaching into his pocket, he pulled out a pile of kopecks and counted out five of them.

Handing them to the boy, he said, "It's a damn good saddle. Take these and whatever clothes the old lady gives you, and make goddamn sure that you never tell people where you sold the horse."

Taking the coins, Jake said, "Yes, sir."

"And here is some advice, boy, don't waste time threatening anyone. Just tell them what you need to, and if they give you shit, cut their throats with that folded jackknife you have in your pocket."

Jake could only nod. The old man put his arm around the boy and turned him to the door.

"Told my boy the same thing once. But the fucking Russians killed him right here in the front yard." Sighing, he finished talking as they walked to the house. "There is always someone bigger, boy. Always someone bigger, so the best thing is to stay out of the way."

Walking through the front door of the small farmhouse, Jake saw Leah sitting in a chair with a sheet around the front of her. The old woman was standing behind her with a pair of scissors, snipping away at his sister's hair.

"She's cleaning up your haircut, Jake!" said Leah.

The old woman told her to sit still and, without looking, said to Jake, "There's a bowl of soup on the table for you. Sit down, and eat it quick."

"It's chicken, Jake!" said Leah.

As Jake sat down, he put their bags next to his ankle while the old man went into a back room. Using a spoon, Jake found a couple of good pieces of meat in the broth and ate those first. After days inside the Marsh and with only last night's duck as a meal, the chicken tasted as good as gold. He was lifting the edge of the bowl to his lips in order to get the last of the soup when the old man came out with a couple of coats, some shirts, and several pair of pants.

Dropping the clothes in the center of the floor, he said, "Finish the soup, and see what fits you."

The woman pulled the sheet from Leah and said, "There, I'm as done as I am ever gonna be. Go over there, and find what you can."

Leah shook the loose hair from her head, jumped up from her seat, and ran to the pile. She pulled a dark shirt and a coat. Holding them up to her chest, she tried to see if they would fit her.

"Those look fine, honey," said the woman, "but if you're gonna pass yourself off as a boy, you need pants too."

Leah knelt down and rummaged through the pile, pulling out two pairs. "Can I go somewhere and try them on?"

The woman walked to the back of the house and said, "Come with me." Looking to her husband, she said, "You get the boy taken care of out here. Hurry up. I want them gone in five minutes."

The old man reached into the pile and pulled out a white shirt. "This'll fit," he said as he threw it to Jake.

Pulling his shirt off, Jake put it on and saw that it was perfect. A pair of pants came his way, and after emptying his pockets on the table, he removed his pants and put them on. As tall as he was, they were still a bit long.

"The boy took after his mother's brother and was a big one. Roll them up at the bottom so you don't trip over them." Reaching into the pile, he threw a coat to Jake. "This'll fit, now clean your stuff off the table, and get ready to go."

Acting fast, Jake did as he was told. Picking up the knife, he noticed the old man was looking at him strangely.

Looking to avoid an incident so late in the deal, Jake said, "Need to cut something out of my pants."

Picking up the pair he had just removed, he cut along the inseam and removed a small packet. Closing the blade, he put the packet in his pocket and looked back to the old man.

"Learn to think ahead, boy. Next time, tell someone you have to piss and cut whatever you are hiding when they aren't looking. A different man than me might take that little bit of gold you're carrying and leave the two of you a mile down the road with your throats cut in a ditch."

Jake started to ask him how he knew what he did but instead just said, "Advice taken, old man. Thanks."

The old man said nothing.

Leah walked back into the room wearing a dark shirt, a black wool coat, and pants that were just about the right size. At the bottom of her pants was a pair of barely warm boots. On top of her head sat a black small brimmed hat.

The old lady saw Jake looking at her boots and said, "Gunther, go get him a pair of Alex's old boots, and see if those fit him. This poor boy's shoes look like they are almost gone."

A minute later, Jake and Leah were walking out the front door.

Before they left the porch, the old man grabbed Jake by the elbow and whispered, "Remember what I told you. Remember everything, boy."

Leah took Jake's arm from the old man, and she and her brother walked into the darkness of the night.

After about two miles of walking in silence, Leah said, "Where are we going to sleep tonight, Jake?"

"We are going to the east where there are some hills to find a dark tree, Leah. Can you go another hour?"

That hour turned into nearly two as Jake pushed her as hard as he had pushed his horse. It was only when he saw her start to drag, occasionally falling behind him, that he pulled off the path and walked up into the hills. There he found a dry spot, and putting her bag down for her to use as a pillow, they sat together.

"I'm okay, but you go to sleep for a little bit, Leah," he said.

"When do we get to Slutsk, Jake?"

"We walked about a mile past it. I didn't want to attract attention by walking through the city. Now, go to sleep, Leah. We have a long walk tomorrow."

It took Leah less than two minutes to fall asleep. After she did, Jake took out his prayer book, moved over into the thin light of the moon, and wrote down the location of the house that had given them so much. After they had reached safety, he hoped to be able to come back someday and thank the old man.

# TOMATOES

In two more days, they made their way through the hills and flatlands that are east of Minsk. As they moved, Jake would occasionally leave his sister in the hills while he ran down to a farm and, taking only what he felt they needed for a meal and nothing more, ran back to his sister with a bit of foodstuff.

On the third night, still a few miles outside of Minsk, his luck ran out. That night, he knew that he shouldn't leave Leah alone with so much light left in the day. But it was clear that the girl was exhausted, and he was starting to feel the dizzying effects of hunger as well.

About a mile before they stopped for the night, he had seen a farm that had a large crop of tomato posts lined up in deep rows. Jake knew that this was unusual for so late in the year. The farmer must be highly skilled, for normally, a good tomato hits its peak in this part of the country in late July or maybe a bit later. To see rows of them so late in the year was unusual. From a distance, they looked to be almost orange. He attributed this to the effects of the setting sun.

Overcome with the desire for a bite of the sweet pulp and looking to avoid building a fire for cooking, he decided to double back and grab what he could. Something told him to just look elsewhere, but it had been weeks since he had enjoyed a tomato.

Ignoring his instincts and rationalizing his decision, Jake told himself, "Leah and I deserve a treat for we have been on the road for so long."

This would be the last time in his life that he would allow himself to make such a careless mistake.

With Leah deep in the wooded area that ran along the path they were on, Jake crept down the hill and toward the back of the farmer's yard. It was clear that he was too close to the main house, so he sat near the edge of the tomato patch until it was as close to dark as it could be.

He waited patiently until he was sure that there was no watchdog or a late working farmhand on the lot. It had been nine days since they had left Pinsk. The moon, a quarter-size when they had left, was now on the diminishing side of being full. That was more than enough light for him to grab a few and then find his way back to Leah.

Once he felt comfortable with what he saw, Jake made his way among the stacks of tomato cages. Slipping through row after row, he paused for just a second.

He thought to himself, *Oh, Leah will absolutely love these!*

For a brief moment, he forgot how tired he was and let the sweet smell waft across his nostrils.

Just as he was reaching for one of the thickest and plumpest tomatoes, something crashed across his left shoulder! The only thing that kept the blow from penetrating his skin was that it had hit along the strap to his pouch.

The blow had come down on him so quickly that Jake didn't fully realize what had happened. Before a second blow landed, he crashed through the tomato cages, blocking his assailant's path. He realized that he had only one option: drop the tomatoes and run!

As he fled, he could hear the farmer cry, "Fucking Russian thief!"

Thinking of Leah, all alone and under the tree, he forgot his injury in his haste to find Leah.

When he got there, he saw nothing—no one. For a second, he panicked, thinking that she had been discovered and was now in the hands of a Russian or been betrayed by a collaborator.

With a sigh of relief, he found the tree he had marked as a guide in the wooded area. There, lying sprawled on the ground, with her head on her bag, was Leah. She was sleeping soundly.

He hadn't been able to see her because he was looking for a figure that was seated! She was so low to the ground that anyone could have missed her. Walking into the forest, he dropped next to her and placed his pouch at her side when she rose the next morning.

He wanted to wake her now, but he knew that she would see his injury and panic. She would demand that he seek help immediately and do something stupid, like leave him behind while she ran to the town.

With his back against a tree so that he could look for anyone approaching, he told himself, "I am not hurt that bad, I will wait until daylight and clean myself before she wakes." In another moment, the pain and exhaustion won its battle for his consciousness.

Jake the Horse Thief slid to the ground and fell to his side into a deep sleep.

# THE SPRING AND LEAH'S CARE

"Jake...Jake!" said a voice in the darkness. He heard the voice but was unable to answer it. Then he felt someone shaking his shoulder.

The cry came out a second time. "Jake...oh, Jake!" Through fog, he heard his name being called once again. Pain ripped through the left side of his body as he tried to sit up, but he had to calm her panic.

"Take off your shirt, Jake! You're hurt!" exclaimed Leah!

"It's not as bad as it looks. "Jake muttered

"Jake...Jake, you are cut! Blood is everywhere! How did this happen?"

It was Jake who had planned the escape from the Malkins. He had led the enemy horsemen into the trap that was the Pripet Marshes, and after temporarily escaping the Malkins, he risked physical harm to prevent hunger. Leah had watched while her beloved brother become gaunt, and now his wound needed immediate attention.

Rushing to his side, she cried, "I'll handle this! Don't you move."

Jake said, "I will wait, you can take care of the wound, there is good clear water in that nearby stream."

Sitting down next to him, she looked over the problem as carefully as she could. The shirt, while torn, was clearly salvageable.

"Let's not waste a good shirt," she said as she began to unbutton it. "Move forward while I take this off," came her swift instruction.

At the Malkins', she had bound up more than one cut that befell the butcher's boys. Leah knew that the thing most injured men wanted was to feel that someone was in charge. For the next few minutes, she put all thoughts of guilt and fear on "her back stove" while she went about cleaning Jake's wound.

In a soft, low voice, she reassured him that all would be well.

"You are a tough young man," she told him, "but you have to let me do this. Now, sit still!"

She washed the wound on his arm as carefully as possible and then bound his shoulder as tightly as possible with scraps of his sleeve. Her training in aiding the Malkin boys around the shop when they knew minor injuries proved very valuable.

"You have to heal, and we have to eat, my stomach is growling! I'm tired, a little nap would help," Leah said.

Jake listened patiently to her reasons of what their bodies needed. Of course, he knew that he needed to heal. But he also knew that they were in terrible danger. Russians were moving through the woods. They were on the roads, and he knew that behind them, somewhere in a tomato patch, was one bruised, and possibly even dead, tomato farmer. They couldn't risk being discovered by anyone.

"We will see what I can do today," was his response to her arguments. "I have the kopecks when we reach the city. Trust me, I won't push myself harder than I can actually go."

As she did what he asked, Leah knew that he was being brave for her.

She also understood that he had years of experience that she hadn't, that he knew the world around them, and that without him, she wouldn't last a day. Her head began to fill itself with all the possible troubles that they may encounter—the loss of freedom, the loss of life, the loss of everything. In her heart, she was sinking.

Once he was sure that they could move, he double checked the area to make sure that no sign of them was left behind.

"We lost a full day on this, and we have to move forward." Though he tried to sound brave, she heard the pain and the sadness in his voice.

For the next two days, they moved through the forest slowly. Jake believed that if they traveled the normal road, someone would see his sling and, putting two and two together, somehow accuse him of attacking the farmer.

"Let's rise early and see what we can find in the city. For now, let's just sleep as much and as well as we can."

She wanted to argue with him, but she knew that if he didn't want to stay, they weren't going to. Moving her bag to her side, she watched his face in the shadows. He looked so much more than his sixteen years. For a brief instant, she saw him as an old man, his hair gone gray and his eyes bearing the lines of age. Scared of what she saw in the fading light, she went to sleep in order to avoid the realities of their life together.

# THE STREETS OF MINSK

The morning came quickly. When she woke, Leah found that Jake was up and anxious to get on the road.

After so many days on the road, she and Jake were wracked by starvation. Her brother's desire to stay isolated meant that they could not venture out for food. Her hunger had been manageable until they drew close to Minsk. As they got closer, the smells of the city began to drift across her nose. There were bakeries, butcher shops, restaurants, and homes all filled with foods and people cooking—all of them preparing food. It all filled her with desire.

*To just have one good biscuit with some watery soup would be a full meal*, she thought.

It dawned on her that the few kopecks that Jake had wouldn't purchase much. The only option she could think of was to reduce herself to begging. The money that her brother had would have to be spent on a doctor. Despite the terrible pangs of hunger ripping through her body, she felt the sacrifice of their simple savings would be well worth it. Fixing Jake's arm was the only thing that really mattered.

Disguised as a boy, Leah could see scant hope for finding the aid her brother so sorely needed. There was no way she could do the labor expected of a young man, especially in her weakened state. To find a day labor job was out of the question.

While Jacob tried to show a brave front, she knew that there was no other course that she could take.

Of necessity, she would be reduced to begging. In order to do this, she would have to reveal herself as a girl, for surely, no one would give a single coin to a strong boy who could earn his own way.

In this desperate strait, Leah plunged into the mass of people making an exodus from Minsk. She had to resist the tide and plunge onward!

As the town limits drew closer, she saw that people of means, peasants, farmers, and storekeepers—all were fleeing the dangers of invasion.

During the time that they had waited in the woods for Jake to heal, he had explained the threat of Germany and the problems with Russia in the east. At first, nothing he said had made much sense. Seeing the people leaving Minsk made her realize how very real the situation was. Thinking of her own life, she thought that, as cruel as the Malkins were, she had been sheltered.

Her life had been spent in servitude. There was little that she knew of the world outside of the butcher shop and the house. She had overheard conversations and read some newspapers, but she had never made an effort to see what the world was really like. As the days passed while he healed, Jake told her more and more about what was happening in Germany under the "Little Corporal," as Jake called him.

Leah was stunned at what she heard. To kill people randomly made no sense to her.

As the number of people on the side of the road increased with every step they took, she finally understood how great the threat was to her and those she loved. Right before her eyes, an entire city seemed to be emptying.

She started to think of all her adventures over the last ten days.

"I cleaned up Jake and held my own in the forest when he was hurt," she told herself. Her confidence began to grow. "I need to help him now."

Her stomach growled so loud that she was worried someone would hear her.

"Oh, if anyone could just give me a few kopecks, I could surprise Jake."

The idea of begging was something new and demeaning. Her mind revolted at the thought of approaching a stranger and humbling herself, but what could she do? Jacob had risked his life to appease their hunger.

The idea of stopping a stranger—someone she didn't know, someone whose eyes she wouldn't want to see—and asking piteously for help in attaining the most basic of human needs made her brain cry inwardly.

"It is the only real option. It won't be a habit. It won't be part of who I am," she wanted to believe.

Taking the initiative, she walked back to the main road. There she watched as people continued to join the ever growing line of those fleeing the city. Hanging along the edges, she took her cap in hand, swallowed her pride, and approached a family near the edge of the procession.

With her hand out, the only word she could muster was, "Please?"

On the first try, she barely mumbled a plea. They walked by without looking at her. Retreating in shame, she believed the idea was hopeless. A minute later, hunger got the best of her, and she approached a young couple with a baby in the arms of its mother.

With her hand out again, she said loudly, "Please?"

The mother looked at her and gestured toward her husband. From the two-wheeled cart he was pulling behind him, he handed her a half a loaf of bread and waved her away.

Shame filled Leah's heart as she put it into her pocket without a question. They were gone before it dawned on her to say "thank you." Now, with such a grand gift, her spirts started to rise. She was determined to not eat a crumb until Jake emerged from the doctor's office.

Another minute passed, and she watched as the young couple disappeared down the road.

Walking against the crowd, she saw an old man with a cane. Hand out, she said again, "Please?" He stopped, went to his pocket, and handed her a single kopeck.

Pocketing the coin, she turned to run back to the roadside, where she saw a very well-dressed gentleman who was walking quickly past the other slower members of the exodus from Minsk. He carried himself as if he was, perhaps, a shopkeeper. To Leah, there was something important in his manner, in the way he moved past the others, that seemed to say he was someone clearly used to dealing with people. From his clothes, he appeared to be more prosperous than many in the rapidly moving throng.

Something told her that she had to act and act swiftly!

"He would surely have something for a poor girl," she tried to believe.

Her nerves steadied by her initial success, Leah accosted the departing storekeeper, and she piteously pleaded with him for immediate financial aid.

"Please, sir, can you help us, we're starving, and my brother is gravely injured, please help us!"

Unaffected by her plea, the man stopped and looked her over. With her hat in hand, Leah clearly looked like a young woman. Her eyes were bright with panic, and her cheeks were rosy from the combination of a brisk walk, and her body was that of a desirable woman.

He was intrigued. In a hurried and condescending tone, he said, "Why should I help you? You're younger than most everyone I can see, and you're a healthy, good-looking girl. Look, if you need help so badly, I want you to walk with me for a minute. I might have a quick job for you." Grinning, he finished by saying, "I have something that you can do for me."

To Leah, he seemed to be a good man. His clothes were clean. His shoes showed little wear, and his hat looked almost new. Thinking of all that Jake had been through for her, she believed that she could do some quick work for the man if it meant a few kopecks or some food.

"Where are we going?" asked Leah.

The man smiled at her and carefully led her down an alley while walking behind her.

Looking up, she noticed that the alley ended in a brick wall. Noticing that a few doors were on each side, Leah refused to let panic set in. On the ground around her, all that she saw was garbage, some discarded tools, and a few loose broken bricks.

*Maybe he will knock on one of the doors. There will be some cleaning to do in one of the buildings...*she hoped.

As they walked past the second door, she began to grow worried. They had gone past almost every door, and he hadn't asked her to stop at any of them. It was then that the reality dawned on her that there was no way out of where they were headed! Fear began to set in. Turning around, she stopped where she was. Neither she nor the businessman said a word for a pregnant minute...

The businessman spoke, "Well, missy, little girl...you want to earn some kopecks?"

His tone changed, and he no longer sounded friendly. To her ears, he suddenly sounded evil, as if something had come over him.

Leah found herself unable to answer his question, for confusion had rendered her tongue-tied. She understood that he had promised her some work, but now she was in an alley and felt trapped. It occurred to her that she could cry out but didn't want to attract attention to herself. It could mean disaster for her and Jake.

The man reached into his pocket and pulled out a handful of coins. He threw them on the ground and told her, "You can pick them all up when you are done."

He then reached out with a massive, sweaty hand and grabbed her at the top of her head, pushing Leah to her knees.

When she fought back at what he was doing, he started to get angry. "Don't tell me that you didn't know this was coming, little girl." He tightened his grip on her hair and continued, "I like the short hair. It's the best of both worlds for me! Part boy, part girl!"

She heard him laughing as she fell to her knees. Too weak to resist his unexpected attack, Leah found herself unable to think. With his one hand still pulling at her hair, he reached for his belt with the other hand and undid his buckle. Next he opened his fly and exposed himself to her with no hesitation.

He kept talking, growing more and more excited with every word he spoke, "You're gonna give me something to remember this stinking rathole of a town by. That's for sure!"

Terror filled her heart as she looked straight at his nakedness inches away from her face. Unsure as to what he expected her to do, she opened her mouth in shock.

"That's right, honey, open wide! Take everything I am giving you, and if you are good, there might be an extra tip in it for you!" Pulling her head close, he bent down and said menacingly, "Now, let's see you how bad you want that tip."

Leah shook her head left and right in order to avoid him. At first she couldn't figure out what he was trying to do. But she wasn't that naive. She had heard the boys talking back at the butcher shop. The idea of what he was trying to force her to do with her mouth made her want to throw up. She could smell his sweat, and being so close, she could see it roll down his body.

He tightened his grip on her head until she felt her hair being pulled down to its roots. Speaking in a low, guttural voice, he bent even closer. Grabbing her in one hand, he pressed against her cheeks, forcing her to turn her face up so that she could see him.

He was spitting as he spoke, "That's it, make me work for it. I like to see a girl struggle!"

She felt him tighten his grip and then force her face closer to his open fly. Tears formed in the corners of her eyes, just as they had when the Butcher Malkin raped her on the night of Jake's bar mitzvah!

Closing her eyes, she thought to herself, *I am doomed to a life of hell at the hands of all men!*

The pain caused by his tight grip made her open her eyes again. She looked up and saw that he was smiling.

"That's it," he said. Spit fell over his lips and hit her in the forehead as he looked down at her. He instructed her, "Look up at me when you open your mouth."

Numbed by his outrageous request and having lost all composure, Leah had never felt more physically and spiritually alone. There was no other avenue of hope that she could explore. She would have to go through with what he wanted, or it seemed as if she would die.

At the very moment that she had lost all hope, something red caught the corner of her eye. Through the tears that were starting to roll down her cheeks, she noticed a hazy, unidentifiable square lying on the ground to her right. Leah summoned all the strength she had and took a chance. She was already afraid that he was going to force her to do something that made her sick. It was obvious that he was so strong that he could beat her senseless if she refused! She had one last desperate chances to save herself from it all.

Forcing herself to smile up at him, she said, "I can't move with you squeezing my hair like this. I can't concentrate and might even bite you. Besides, you are too big of a man for me to do it like this."

He laughed and relaxed his grip. "I knew it! I knew it! You are a real pro. Now, get to work! I want to get outa this shithole!"

He let go of her head and, still looking at her straight in the eye, put his hand on his hips, proudly displaying himself right in front of her.

Doing everything she could to hold his admiring gaze, keeping him preoccupied in the process, she reached up and placed her left hand on his pant leg. He laughed with glee at what he was sure would follow.

At the very same moment that she touched him, Leah was reaching out along the ground with her fingertips of her right hand, feeling along the dirt for the red square that had caught her eye. Once she touched its edge, she knew that it was exactly what she hoped it would be—a brick!

With his eyes glued to hers, she moved her head to his fly. The look of pleasure on his face was almost as sickening to her as what was now an inch away from her face.

In a flash, she picked up the broken half of a brick and, with all her might, slammed it straight up into the center of his crotch.

His hands fell to his side and strained to cover his penis.

Before he could protect himself, she brought the brick up again and then a third time. He started to buckle over, falling on top of her.

She shoved him off of her shoulders and brought the brick down on the side of his skull as he fell. Again and again, she clubbed the man, her eyes blinded with rage, hunger, and fury. She was not going to allow any man to ever touch her in the way that the butcher had!

As the blow after blow crashed down on his skull, she heard bones crack and break. Leah was oblivious to the sickening sound of what she was doing. For a moment, she thought that she saw the image of Mayer Malkin flash before her eyes.

In a violent fever, she brought herself up on both knees, raising the brick straight over her head as she did. Grabbing it on both sides, she brought the rough-edged stone straight down on her assailant's head in one final, bone-crushing blow.

## JAKE THE HORSE THIEF

Her rage left her breathing uncontrollably. She now knelt at the side of the once-living, prosperous shopkeeper. Where his head had once been was now a space filled with only shards of bone and rivers of blood that flowed across the dirt of the alley toward a yellow wall.

All the noise of the world fell away from her ears. There was only silence. Her body was numb. All feeling had left her. Her arms came to rest on each side of her body. Slowly, the weapon of defense fell from her right hand and rolled off of her fingers into the dirt of the alley. It came to rest less than an inch away from his penis.

In the deepest regions of her soul, in the place where she only let God, she felt nothing. No remorse. Not regret. Not guilt. Absolutely nothing.

Down an alley, just a few doors away from where Jake now stood and away from the crowded streets, Leah knelt in silence over the body of a man she had just killed. She couldn't grasp what had happened. Not ten minutes earlier, she had been working toward helping Jake. She had received a charitable kopeck as well as a half a loaf of bread through the kindness of strangers.

Yes, it made her feel dirty. But she did what she had to do, for they were starving and Jake was seriously injured. It was her desire to do what she could to help their very existence!

Now she was a killer in a strange city, and Jake, her brother and protector, was nowhere to be found. Leah experienced the same panic as she felt in the forest when she tried to find her injured brother.

She knew that her existence depended on regaining her composure.

The silence she had enjoyed for the last minute fell away, and the sounds of the city became unbearable. Looking before her, she saw the businessman's crushed skull and understood what she had done. She had killed a man. It didn't matter why; no one would believe her. All they would know was that she had savagely crushed a man's head!

Realizing that her only hope came in finding Jake, she brought herself to her feet. Looking down the alleyway, she thought that she saw Jake's coat walking by. Hoping it wasn't a hallucination, Leah ran to the top of the alley and looked up and down for him. Not five feet away from her, she saw him walking past where she now stood quaking.

A garbled, breathless version of his name crossed her lips, "Jake…oh, Jake…"

Recognizing her voice, he was happy that he had found her so fast. She was a strong, smart girl who had clearly followed his instructions to a tee. With a broad smile on his face, he turned, fully expecting to see her prepared to move on quickly.

Instead, he found a thin, shaking, blood-covered mess clinging to the sharp brick corner of a building that cornered an alleyway. She motioned for him to come to her. When he did, she took his shoulder for support. Her breathing was so rapid that she could barely finish a sentence. He didn't know what had happened, but every good feeling he had just felt disappeared in the second it took to look down the alley.

Leading him down the alley, she managed to say, "Come… with…" before she started to cry. Falling against his shoulders, she tried hard not to collapse completely as she fell into his arms…

He kept asking, "What's the matter, Leah…What happened?" but all she could do was point to the ground in front of them. Looking down, he saw a hat—the type that a business man might wear on an appointment. To his eyes, it looked fine—clean with a near-perfect crease along the top.

Then he went speechless at what he saw before him. Surely, his innocent, inexperienced, and frail sister couldn't be responsible for what now lay at his feet.

Stunned at what he saw, he said out loud, "The man has no head!"

## JAKE THE HORSE THIEF

Leah grabbed at his coat for support as she began to weep uncontrollably. Then his survival instinct kicked in, and Jake took command of the situation. How this horrible accident had happened wasn't important; he could find that out later. Right now, he had to hide the body and get his sister out of the alleyway. Jake grabbed Leah by the shoulders and shook her as he talked.

"We have only a few minutes to get out of this alley! Don't fall apart on me."

Still sobbing, Leah cried out, "It's a gruesome scene, blood everywhere, but notice that the body has a thick jacket, bulging near the seams!"

Reaching into his pocket, Jake pulled out his knife and opened it. Figuring the shirt to be too bloody to take, he looked at what was left. The jacket was of excellent leather and could be cleaned. Rolling the man to his side, he started to remove it. As he did, he noticed something bulging along the side, right under the arm. Cutting along the seam, Jake and Leah watched as a leather pouch tumbled out from the coat.

They looked at each other and then looked back down to the bag before them. The pouch gave evidence that the storekeeper was fleeing with very valuable possessions. Jake picked up the bag and started to open it. Untying the drawstring, he poured the contents out and into his open palm.

There, glistening brightly in the sunlight, they saw not one, not two, but five diamond rings. The brilliance of which diminished the effect of seeing them surrounded by a number of uncut diamond stones.

Without a word, Jake returned the diamonds to the pouch and handed the find to Leah. Spurred on by the stunning discovery, Jake felt around the man's waistband and then slipped down along each of the pant legs. Down below the right pocket, he felt what he thought could be another hidden pouch. Cutting at the seam, he found another, smaller, leather bag. Looking inside, he saw several pieces of fine, sparkling jewelry.

The man that Leah killed had either been a prosperous jeweler or a thief!

Seeing the second pouch, Leah's eyes were as wide as the moon. She sat perfectly still; the shaking had stopped.

Despite the remarkable and completely unexpected discovery of the jewelry, it was not the most surprising thing that they found. After Jake had thoroughly examined the man's pants, he moved back to the jacket to make sure that he hadn't missed something.

In a pocket inside the regular lining of the coat, he found a long billfold. Opening it, he saw hundreds of kopecks as well as the man's passport and multiple business cards. One of which fell to the ground. Leah picked up and read the name, while Jake folded all the bills and put them in his back pocket.

Leah gasped loudly and grabbed at Jake's coat sleeve as she shoved the card under his nose for him to see. He looked over to see what she had found. He read it carefully and saw the name of the man she had killed.

Printed in neat, perfect letters across the top of the card was, "Julius Malkin."

He looked at his sister in disbelief and held the rest of the billfold upside down, shaking it as he did. A picture fell to the ground. The two of them looked down at the same time and saw that it was a wedding picture. Leah recognized it immediately, for a much larger version of that very picture sat on the mantle of the central fireplace located in the home of Mayer Malkin.

Leah Horvicz, one-time servant girl to the family of Mayer Malkin, had just killed his brother!

Jake gave a sharp command, "There is what was a long-ago unused garbage pit at the foot of the left wall covered by wood. It is heavy, but I'll try to lift it—no! I must move it! I will move it! Drag his body to the pit!"

This created a disgusting mess, but the two orphans quickly covered the body with all the trash of the alley. Realizing what this would mean to his sister, Jake grabbed her arm, and together they stood as one.

His instructions were short, sharp, and to the point: "Think of nothing. Walk to the top of the alley. Watch for anyone who walks by. If they do, just pretend you are peeing, and they will cross the street."

She stood motionless next to him, unable to grasp the danger. He grew agitated with her and shouted at her, "Get to the top of the alley so I can bury this bastard! MOVE!"

Reality no longer had any definition in her life. Her inner self cried, "I'm a killer, and I must escape from the picture of the crushed brain!"

Nothing made sense to her. The only thing she understood was that Jake would take care of her and fix anything that had happened. Finally, she realized that she had only one choice.

As she had done so many times over the last two weeks, she did exactly as she was told. Behind her, Jake shoveled dirt on top of Julius Mayer, covering the dead man as fast and as well as he could. Without so much as a simple good-bye, he left Julius Mayer—jeweler, brother, and rapist—in his garbage grave and raced to the top of the alley.

Jake joined Leah as she crumpled near the top of the structure.

Taking Leah by the arm, he led her out of the alley and back to the main road. Once there, they joined the procession leaving the proud city and walked right out of Minsk.

Leah reached into her pocket and pulled out the half of a loaf of bread that the young married couple had given her. She broke it in half and handed a piece to Jake.

Walking among the growing crowd of strangers, they ate their first meal of the day without a word passing between them.

# MINSK TO LITHUANIA

Hundreds walked with Jake and Leah as they left Minsk that day—some, in clean, perfect dresses and suits; others, in torn skirts and pants that were worn from long days in the fields and factories. Some were barefoot, and others wore boots or shoes they had purchased the day before.

Each one was heading west, hoping to avoid whatever was coming. No one was really sure. One day rumors spread that the Russians were leaving the area. The next voice shouted that the Nazis were about to cross the border!

It was a time of incredible uncertainty. All anyone really knew was that war was coming. The details were immaterial to anyone leaving Minsk. Their only goal was to stay alive.

On his frequent secret excursions Jake made to the countryside beyond Pinsk, Jake managed to acquire maps by any means available. Whenever Jake slipped briefly and quietly away from Rabbi Vilnish's humble house, he never left without the latest maps he could find.

Unlike the hundreds that walked with him as he and his sister left Minsk behind, Jake knew where he was going. As they walked that day, he would consult his prayer book. In the margins, on half pages, and across empty spaces throughout the book, he had made small charts and maps to help him. There were notes about how to read trees and how to count the days of the moon for maximum brightness.

Much of what was written was in small letters. Jake's handwriting would not be obvious to anyone trying to interpret it. And of course, he also read the prayers and passages from the Torah. As he and his sister walked from Minsk that day, he found himself taking comfort in his favorite passages from Exodus—most of which he had underlined at the rabbi's insistence. Where the words had once inspired him to travel and help him understand the world around him, they now served as a familiar and reassuring comfort that, despite what had happened, he had made the right decision to leave Pinsk.

Though he had an ultimate goal of isolation in a new land, the only goal he had right now was to hide in plain sight inside the crowd. At some point, he would find a way to slip away with Leah and head for the mountains of the northwest. They needed to get somewhere, somewhere safe, in the next few days because winter could come quick in their destination!

In planning their route, there was the temptation to take the simple way. He thought about following the railroad tracks from Minsk to Vilna. The train tracks were generally flat, which would be easier than the mountains they faced in fleeing north and westward from Minsk. Jake felt that, as easy as following the track would be, doing so would expose them to whatever troops or authorities were guarding the borders.

Traveling through the mountains had one additional advantage. Doing so would offer a greater chance of evading their pursuers. In the back of his mind, Jake feared a vengeful Butcher Malkin ambushing them along any trail.

"Yes," he said to himself, "to stay off the beaten path will be harder and take longer, but it will be worth it."

For days, he and Leah struggled through many grueling woodland miles. Despite the money that he was carrying, hunger once again became a major distraction. Even if there were places to eat, they would have to avoid them for fear of discovery. In one two-day stretch, they were only able to find berries, which they consumed as if it were a feast.

The hunger made him start to doubt himself. Though he believed that he knew the land and the hills, he had to bite his lip in frustration several times. For more than once, he thought that he recognized a same tree or hill that they had passed earlier. And at least twice, he was sure that they had passed the same farm.

Leah, her cap pulled down tight over her head, never took notice or complained. On the morning of the fourth day, Jake took note of how silent she had been.

*This isn't the time for me to bother her*, he thought. *I am sure the burden she carries if far greater than I could know.*

Jake was right. Leah, shattered by what had happened to her in Minsk, found herself walking mindlessly. It wasn't that she had killed a man. She felt that he had deserved it. It was something else that drove her on. Try as she might, her brain told her, "I am unclean, and no man will ever desire me."

As hunger and exhaustion grew, so did her confusion as to what life meant and if it was, in fact, all worth it. It was impossible for her to tell Jake what was in her heart.

"I have to make Jake believe that I am strong and he will not have to worry about me!"

When Jake called out, "Are you okay, sis?"

Leah bit her lip, smiled, grunted, and forced out, "I'm just fine, no need to stop."

There would be a time for her to figure out what her life could be, what it could mean. Until then, she distracted herself by thinking of a day when her legs and feet didn't hurt, when walking would be a restful thing—a day in time when her stomach didn't tear and scream at her from inside.

When they walked, they constantly looked for food. With his body still hurting from his last encounter with a farmer, Jake couldn't afford to find himself in a fight with anyone. He had lost mobility in his shoulder, and his hands still hurt.

As much money as they had, he knew that in times such as this, a thousand dollars couldn't buy a man's last radish. Still, it had to serve some purpose for them. He would be more than willing to give it all away to anyone who could help them at this point.

Leah and Jake struggled through many grueling woodland miles until they came to a village near the small town of Novogoridski. With nightfall coming, they sat on top of a hill underneath a canopy of trees. The chill in the air was enough that they had to button the top button on their coats and huddle together for warmth. Jake saw that the rising moon was only a thin, thin sliver. Tomorrow night it would be gone, and the land would be dark, leaving them physically trapped.

Looking down across the valley and up the next hill, Jake nudged his sister and said, "Leah, there is a shack near the top of this hillside, and I don't see any smoke rising from the chimney. The crops look as if they have been long harvested. To me, it looks as if it is uninhabited. I'm going to see who owns it. Wait here for a moment while I do what I can to find the owner."

Leaving her, he moved swiftly across the upper ridge of the valley until he was a few hundred yards from the shack. Anchoring himself behind a tree, he watched for signs of life. After a few minutes, he noticed a small forlorn individual emerging from the shack and coming toward him.

Understanding that he had been seen, Jake took a step out from his hiding place and stood with his arms by his side.

The forlorn old man who appeared greeted his young visitor with a muffled, "Halloo."

Nodding, "Hello," in response, Jake found himself at a loss for words.

The old man spoke again, "I thought you were soldiers. Be a first time for an army to get this far up in the hills. My family rode out the last one up here and never had a problem."

They stood silent for another minute.

Finally, Jake blurted out, "My sister and I are lost."

He looked at the old man's eyes and saw nothing other than exhaustion. He appeared to be destitute.

Pointing to the man's one-room house, Jake said, "That old shack is falling down, let us have it for the winter, and give me some tools, and I'll fix it up like new."

The farmer brightened up and asked Jake if he was nuts.

The response was a simple, "No, just hungry and tired and in need of a few days of rest."

"With winter coming, I was thinking of leaving, maybe for good." The old man dug his toe in the ground and went on, "If you got any money, it might convince me to let you have it. I got some canned goods in there, and outside, I already chopped up some wood for the cold."

Reaching into his pocket, Jake took out the pile of bills that had come from the jeweler Malkin. The old man's eyes grew to twice their size.

"You a lousy spy?" said the old man.

Once again, Jake should his head no to the old man's question. He counted off three of the five bills he had. The old man took them slowly and held them up to the dying sun.

The old man grew stubborn. Smelling an opportunity, he asked, "You want the tools and it all? I got food in there and a blanket and two towels. You spend the next few weeks gathering some fox or duck, and you could ride out the winter. Hell, neither Germans nor Russians ain't coming through this shithole."

Jake handed him another bill. While he was putting the last one back in his pocket, he told the old man, "I need the last one for when we leave."

Looking him over, the owner of the shack told him, "Paper money ain't worth a shit. I need some coins. Kopecks are always better to travel with."

Without a word, Jake handed him ten kopecks and said, "How fast can you be gone?"

"You go get your sister, and meet me inside as soon as you can. It'll be the moon's last night, and if I am going somewhere, I want to leave while I got some traveling time."

Just as he was ready to turn and head out for Leah, Jake spoke directly to the old man, "Blankets and all. You leave with a coat and an apple. If you don't have an apple, you take nothing. And you stay right here where I can see you. I bought that shack, and…"

The old man cut him off, "You'll be fine, Red. I ain't looking for a fight. You paid me fair. Just go get the girl, and I will be right here."

With nothing else to say, Jake ran to get Leah. He found her asleep. Ten minutes later, they were inside the shack. They watched as the old man stood before them, buttoning up a torn, filthy rag of a coat.

"Fresh water's in the spring 'bout a quarter mile east, maybe less. Been supplying my family for almost sixty years." Opening a cupboard door, he said, "Got some soup, some flour. Few other things. Once a month, I head out for Novogoridski and get what I need. Go southwest, can't miss it." Walking to the door, he took the handle, turned, and said, "I am going to tell Rosenberg that you are watching the place. You'll get along with him. He's a Jew too." With that, he shrugged his shoulders, took a final look around, and said, "Thanks, kids. Been a good home. I may or may not be back."

In a few minutes, it was quiet. All they could hear were owls and a few wolves in the distance. The sun lasted only about ten more minutes. As Jake looked out the window, he saw the man disappear over the hill. Looking back to the cot in the corner, he saw Leah fast asleep under a dark-blue blanket.

On the table in the center of the room was a candle. Jake lit it and sat there for almost an hour. He was too tired to sleep and too tired to open a can of soup. Removing his shoes, he spread out on the floor and pulled his coat over him.

The crushed skull he had seen in the dirty alleyway in Minsk was a vision that made sleep an impossibility. That his sister, his sole loving companion, had killed another human being was beyond comprehension. But it was real, and he would have to live with the awful sight alone, and forever. Also, Jake knew he had an even greater reason to protect Leah for the remainder of their lives. There was the very real need to forget the tragedy and move on.

For Jake, the night was an opportunity to think of where he had been, as well as a chance to plan a destination. The shack was not much of a base to build upon. But it was enough for the time. He could care less about the money. It had come to them through a bout of terrible luck. So he was happy to send whatever he could out into the world and far away from them.

It was at that moment that he decided that money was, in reality, a tool. It can help people, and if the lesson of the jeweler had taught him anything, greed and desire for it can also kill you. He promised that if he could make it somewhere safe with the jewels, he would use the money to help others. That money wasn't his to own. It was his to use to help others.

At first, lying on the floor in a small house, he thought of the years with the rabbi. They had, indeed, gone by fast. He hoped the old man was doing well. Knowing him, he had probably spent the gold piece that Jake had left behind at the synagogue. And Jake was more than fine with that. He thought, *Leaving the money was the first time I was able to help someone with it.*

From nowhere, the brief moment of quiet brought him to the memory of his mother, Miriam. *She had died when I was three years old. I never knew who she was,* he thought.

Looking back to the years after her death, he began to see that his sister, Leah, was more of a mother figure than Miriam. She had taken care of him, cleaned his scrapes, cooked his meals, and told him stories during the years that led up to his father's, Avram's, tragic death—a night filled with lightning and sharp cracks of thunder that spelled doom for his father.

The hut that he and Leah were now occupying reminded him of the small wooden house they knew as home in the outer lands of Pinsk. Both were of wood and mud, calked with some material that barely suppressed the winter's bitter cold. Instead of sleep, he found himself falling into a deep meditative trance that seemed to be real, even though he knew that it wasn't.

There was the lengthy interlude with Rabbi Menachem Vilnish, a time that affected his mental attitude in life. He contemplated his future when this chase, this running, would be over.

He had heard Reb Vilnish speak of the past glories of Vilnius and Kovno Caberna (Kaunas Area). The Jews had been part of the area for hundreds of years. But what would that mean to him? Was he to be a scholar?

While he had been raised by a rabbi, Jake could not conceive of a lifelong career as a student of the holy books, of the Torah and the Talmud. Then he thought of the comments made by the old man who had just sold them the cabin. It was what he said about the shopkeeper Rosenberg being someone, a Jew, that he and Leah could get along with. He harkened back to the doctor in Minsk complaining that he wasn't going to help a Jew. As he had traveled in the past year, he has observed that being Jewish can determine where he would, and would not be, accepted. He thought back to the rabbi's stories of his own encounters with anti-Semitism. He suddenly realized how the non-Jews in Pinsk treated Jews. Many may have gone to Butcher Malkin's shop for the good cuts of meat, but they seldom said hello to him or his wife when they ran into them on the street.

The idea of unsurmountable odds started to creep at the edges of his trance. At this moment in time, Jake did not know his limit physically or intellectually.

*I may think I am wise, but in truth, I am so very young with so much to learn*, he thought.

He had suffered a deflation of his ego when he pushed his luck too far in brazenly stealing the tomatoes from that farmer. Chastising himself, he thought, *The incident had almost cost me my life! Who would be left to care for Leah?*

After that mishap, his sister had reduced herself to begging in order to help him! In the hour that he had to leave her alone, she had been brutally assaulted and killed a man in defense.

The future tore at his soul as he tried to fall asleep. What could he do for her? What skills has he managed to acquire?

Then in a flash of lightning, his inner resolve returned. Jake could not allow himself to think of failing to protect Leah.

"It is part of who I am."

Instead of dwelling on the possibility of losing everything, he reminded himself of his triumphs, how far they had come, how they were now in a shack that provided a roof and a couple of cans of food in the cupboard!

"For the first time in over two weeks, we have a roof!" he muttered excitedly.

Swallowing the last of the "miracle pills," he thought of the jewelry. There were times when they were walking that he wanted to stop and examine the pouch of jewels. Something had told him, there would be no point in doing that; for if he knew the details, it still wouldn't change anything. It was good for the both of them, that they took the found goods in stride. It did not give the rings and their uncut friends any control over Jake and Leah.

# THE CABIN, THE SPRING, AND THE WINTER

The next day held sun and clear blue skies. They ate two cans of soup that they had heated over the stove in the shack. After so many nights under the stars, both found themselves laughing at the suddenly absurd sight of them eating while sitting in a chair at a table.

Unsure as to how long the weather would last, Jake decided that they should find the spring and fill the bucket before they face the day. Together the two headed out, their bellies full for the first time in nearly a week. The spring was closer than the old man had said. Taking off their shoes, the two sat on the edge of the water and cleaned themselves up as best as they could.

After a few minutes, Jake said, "I need to get to town while we have decent weather. So let's cut this short and head back to the cabin."

Once back, he readied himself for the rest of the day. They had enough in the cupboard to last just about three days. With about twenty kopecks left, plus the jeweler's paper money, Jake knew that they should be able to get enough supplies to last for a good while—certainly not enough to last a winter, but more than enough to give them time to rest, regroup, and learn their surroundings.

As he left, he told Leah, "Stay here in the shack, and here is a knife in case someone or something that wasn't welcome comes around. Above all, keep the door shut."

Before he left, Jake kissed his sister and said, "The stove will keep you warm for a long time. I will be back in, maybe, five hours."

From the window, Leah watched him disappear over the hill, just as Jake had watched the old man the night before. For the first time in as long as she could remember, she was alone with her thoughts. First she lay down and fell fast asleep. When she awoke, she was tempted to go to the spring and wash her clothes, but heeding Jake's words, she stayed in the shack.

As afternoon became evening, a wind had blown around the top of the hill they were on. It rattled the loose boards of the hut and seemed to be adding to Leah's growing depressive state. The future was hard to see when her brain was tormented by images of the past.

The only true warm feeling that she could remember was when she had cuddled Jacob so long ago when he was three years old and she was six. Nothing that had happened since then—not a minute of the decade spent with the Malkins and certainly, not anything that had happened over the last few weeks—could come close to the beauty of that singular memory.

As she tried to dream of a beautiful and warm future, she could only look to the immediate past. As much as she wanted to take care of herself and to help Jake, her last attempt to aid her brother had resulted in disastrous consequences.

She asked herself, "My brother, Jacob, has grown into a man. Will he forever be my protector?"

The flimsy hut was bending in the growing winds. Hearing the howling of the wind outdoors, feeling it sneak through cracks in the wall and mud, brought back memories of her childhood with her parents, Avram and Miriam, and their small home. Those beautiful memories came crashing down with the nightmare of what happened near Minsk. Panic enveloped her heart and soul.

"How will I ever be able to escape the image of the stranger yanking my head down to his crotch? I can't believe that I ever did such a disgusting act!" She hoped her thoughts would never be transmitted to Jacob.

She went on, unable to cleanse the sights and sounds of that day from her mind's eye.

"Will I ever be willing to discuss this with a prospective mate?"

Again, she returned to the idea that she was now "unclean."

She asked herself, "Can I ever be near a man without seeing the image of Mayer Malkin? Will I ever know the soft touch of a man's hand, his embrace, his…"

She found herself slipping deeper and deeper into despair. As the thoughts grew more confusing, she looked everywhere for an answer but felt that she found none.

"Why did the rabbi, 'the man of God,' fail me when I went to him after the assault by the Butcher Malkin? Is there such a thing as God? Has he ever visited me? If he exists, can I blame God for my woes?"

The questions flooded in, and her confusion grew.

"No! I can blame no one but myself! I have been a failure for Jacob, he deserves more than I can give him! Of what use am I?"

The darkest of all thoughts tore at her. Ashamed at what she let herself think, Leah willed herself not to shed tears and bring worry to her brother. She must quiet herself for his sake. Wasn't that enough reason for her to erase the sudden thoughts of suicide? Leah was a young woman, but she had experienced immense traumas to her body and psyche, and there was no one—no one—to talk to. In the growing dark of the cabin, she couldn't even find God.

Without Jake near and doubting her own goodness, she felt abandoned. Moving to the back of the small cot, she brought her knees up to her chin and wrapped her arms around them tightly. There she sat until Jake returned. It was dark by the time she heard a door open. Her disgust was so large that she didn't even bother to go for the knife as the figure burst through the door. If it was a wild boar that had thrown the door open, she felt that it was her fate to die between his teeth.

The familiar voice of Jake boomed out in the darkness, "You did well, Leah! I am so proud of you!"

He could not see her cowering in the corner of the cot. She heard a large box hit the ground, and then what sounded like a bag dropped there as well.

Excited to be back, Jake went on loudly, "I knew you were strong. You had the brains to not light a candle, or the stove!"

She heard him fumbling and then the sound of a match being struck. Candlelight filled the room, and as it did, she found the strength to smile at his kind words.

He saw her in the corner wiping her eyes and came to sit next to her.

"I know it was hard to be alone in the dark with all the wind and noise. But you did exactly what needed to be done."

He leaned in to hug her, and she welcomed his embrace with all the strength in her body. For a full minute, the brother and sister held one another.

When they parted, Jake held her by the shoulders and said, "We won't need to be separated for at least a month. I was able to get enough for a long stay."

So began the winter in the hills for the Horvicz siblings.

While the orphans hid from the greater world, that world changed in ways that they could never imagine. The peoples of Central Europe had seen a monumental disruption in their lives. The Soviet Union swallowed up much of these lands of Central Europe in 1940. With hardly a break, the armies of the Third Reich came marching back and invaded much of the land that the Russians had taken. They showed little resistance to the Nazi juggernaut.

# JAKE THE HORSE THIEF

Secure in the hills—out of the normal path of commerce and life—for a while, Leah and Jake enjoyed an idyllic existence. The snow prevented the Russians from coming into their hills, and the Nazis had yet to begin their march eastward into Lithuania and Poland. In a few more months, the problems of the world would come face-to-face with the siblings. Until then, the two lived in peace until everything around them would burst into flames.

Max Rosenberg told Jake, "I'm forced to close my store now. I've heard the Nazis are near, and they're targeting the Jews. About the only thing I have left is a few baked goods. Take them for a few kopecks, and be prepared to move quickly yourself!"

Jake gathered what he could carry and wished Max Rosenberg, "Good health to you and your family," and after a parting hug, Jake made a hasty return to his shack and Leah.

That night, the small, broken shack that had served as a home for them for the last three months felt like a palace. The feast included several slices of bread that Jake had brought back, plus scrambled eggs, an orange for them to split, and much later that night, when the cold had descended on the top of their hill, Leah cut a small pan of gingerbread into six slices.

"It matches the number of tomatoes that you gave up so much for," said Leah as she passed one of the slices to Jake. Raising the fragrant treats as if they were the finest glass of the finest wine in all Central Europe, she said, "No sister ever had a better brother."

"No brother ever had a better sister," said Jake in response.

The next month saw the snows break early. Jake knew it would be time to leave. He hadn't said much to Leah, but on each visit to town and the store of Mr. Rosenberg, he had heard more and more about Germany. It was clear that for a while, parts of Poland now belonged to Germany and parts of Poland had been taken over by Russia. He had understood this when they had been in Minsk. His injuries and Leah's encounter with the Jeweler Malkin had prevented him from learning more.

The one thing that Jake did understand was that they had to leave as soon as they could. Danger was rolling across Lithuania and Poland. Borders were rumored to be changing every day. The maps that he had taken such pains to draw in his prayer books may not be valid anymore.

When he lived with the Rabbi Vilnish, the old man had shared some tales of his own youth. The rabbi had told him of his own younger brother, Mendel. Before the First World War, his brother—with the good wishes of all who knew him—had left Kovna Caberna and went to live in America. When he told stories of his brother, Rabbi Vilnish explained to Jake that Mendel epitomized the experiences of the *Jews Who Were Left Behind*.

Until the Communist takeover ruined the postal system, Mendel had sent small sums to Rabbi Vilnish from his new home in America. The money was meant to aid the impoverished synagogue of the Jews of Pinsk.

In the months before Jake had left, the rabbi had started to speak often of what had happened to Kovna Caberna (present-day Kaunas). Apparently, Kovno had once had a very vibrant Jewish community, but sadly, most of its Jews were slaughtered by the Nazis or had gone to the United States as members of the great migration of European Jews of 1890–1920.

The area had a deep connection with the man who had raised Jake. For many years, Vilna was known as the Jerusalem of Lithuania with Jewish seminaries and a well-stocked library.

Menachem Vilnish had graduated from the renowned seminary in Vilna. He was proud of his education and had told Jake many times that his time there was among the most fruitful and rewarding of his long life.

## JAKE THE HORSE THIEF

The young Rabbi Vilnish would have stayed in his beloved city, but after graduating, he soon found that a rabbinate post did not exist there. In time he learned of the town of Pinsk and considered going there. When the German Army overran Vilnius in 1916 on Yom Kippur, he fled and had never been there again.

Jake envisioned Vilnius, as he had once seen Minsk, as a possible refuge for him and Leah.

It was his hope that, as he had once planned to do in Minsk, they could get lost in the Lithuanian capital of Vilna. Sadly, Jake's knowledge of the city had little to do with the reality. He was a young man who had yet to hear the sound of the world around him. His youth meant that his naïveté might protect him for a while. But at some point, he would have to pay the same toll as so many others had when the events of the world overwhelmed their lives.

With such warlike conditions around them, the two orphans had to virtually disappear while somehow managing to stay in sight. Failure at keeping hidden could mean slavery or worse. Leah knew her femininity would be of critical importance, and Jake understood that he would have to appear as a somewhat older male. To change their appearances, Jake once again cut Leah's hair short. She began to practice binding her clothing tightly as she had previously to suppress her figure. Over the winter months, Jake had grown a full, bushy beard and let his red hair go until it was long and unruly.

He had never said anything to her about it, but he blamed himself for what had happened in that alleyway in Minsk. He should have never left her alone. If he had taken the time to educate her, to let her know of the very real dangers in begging and talking to strangers, she might not have not had to kill the jeweler.

As best as he could tell, they left the cabin on the very last day of February. Their bags were packed; their clothes were clean; and they had enough food for as far as they could make it. Jake knew that the coming journey would be as difficult as the one through the Marshes.

However, this time he had experience as well as a better understanding of the roads and the people that lived along them. It was a good distance to the City of Vilna in Lithuania. He looked for the journey to be long but safe.

He was wrong.

## THE WINTER IN THE HILLS

On the second day of traveling, a wild storm erupted. The wind whipped their exposed faces with ice pellets, and they had to take refuge wherever they could in the woods. In the falling snow, they felt comfortable; but as night came, they froze as the temperatures dropped drastically. Huddling together with only a blanket spread between two tree trunks for a shelter, they still managed to stay warm.

When morning came, the snow was still falling. This caused them to only be able to take three steps for every one that they managed. The extra effort left them more tired than they had ever known. After four days, their food was almost gone. Once again the familiar pangs of hunger returned. The snow finally broke on the fifth day, but it was of little help, for their journey was still made difficult by large drifts in the mountains.

Once they were out of the mountains, their luck changed. Now traveling at a lower altitude, the snow melted quicker. They found themselves walking along drier roads and paths.

Later, they were met by farmers who showed sympathy for the bedraggled orphans by giving them a ride on the back of their truck. That night, Leah and Jake spoke of how many of these people who were helping them were so worn down by their own efforts to scratch a living.

"Yet they still have time to show us kindness," said Jake.

To Jake and Leah, there was little time to dwell on this sad note of poverty. Their immediate quest was to move forward to Vilna as well as to find food and water wherever they could...The area between Belarus and Lithuania is very fertile, and though there was a wartime atmosphere, farms continued sending crops to the market in some quantity.

Jake's experience with farm life proved to be valuable. On the eighth day of their travels, he helped a farmer round up a few pigs that were in distress. They lost half of a day of travel, but it was ultimately worth it. While it was clear that the farmer couldn't spare much, Jake was rewarded with a small sack of foodstuffs.

Now on the road for over a week, the warming days of March began to take hold. One night, when the weather was especially welcoming, they encountered a small lake whose shoreline was temporarily uninhabited. This respite gave them the rare chance to bathe, while each guarded their small, but very valuable, possessions.

Despite the serene beauty of the blue water and forest that surrounded her, Leah found the ugliness of old thoughts reemerging— tormented by what had happened to her at the hands of the Malkin brothers, as well as by thoughts that she wasn't carrying her weight as they moved toward Vilna.

She thought back to the incredible sadness and loneliness she felt in her life, especially that first dark afternoon and night in the shack they had just left behind.

Plunging into the frigid waters of the pond, Leah worked hard to quash the thought of simply dropping to the bottom, grabbing hold of what she could, and thus ending her life. As she entertained the sad thought, it dawned on her that this would endanger Jake's life, for he would most certainly try and save her.

Floating to the top, she began to cry, praying that Jake wouldn't notice.

She thought, *If I die, Jacob will be so alone. That must be my sole reason for living.*

Leah fought her dark thoughts and rose out of the lake, shivering from the gentle air flowing across her wet body. When Jake noticed her fumbling to find clothing, he rushed to find something to control her trembling body. Grabbing the blanket they had taken from the shack, he ran straight to her. Before they realized what had happened, they were clutching each other in a momentary embrace. They quickly separated, and they parted with differing emotions.

To Jake, the physical feeling of a bodily embrace with a woman would never be forgotten. He had never felt the stirring embrace of a female body pressed against him. Though the moment had been a freak accident, completely beyond the control of either of them, guilt at the encounter filled them both.

As Jake dressed, he thought of the jewels for the first time since they had packed them back at the shack. The jewelry they were hiding on their bodies was to profoundly affect their lives and the lives of those they would meet. Knowing of their great value, and how much good he could do with the profits from their sale, Jake vowed silently to protect the pouch that enclosed the large and very antique rings.

When he had bathed, they had stayed with Leah at the side of the pond. He vowed that, out of pure necessity, the pouch would become a part of him. For the rest of their journey, it never left him.

On the ninth day, traveling in a north westward direction, and without realizing they had done so, the siblings crossed an unmarked border into Lithuania. Leah and Jacob were traveling lands that were similar in nature to those being traversed by an invading armed force at that moment in history. The German Army was streaming across Byelorussia and, with it, bringing the promise of hate and anti-Semitism for every Jew in its path.

The two young people walked for another day until finally, after all the miles that they had walked, they now stood at the edge of the

City of Vilnius. Unfamiliar with the language, they spoke to no one. Asking someone for direction was out of the question.

Hiding in the woods, they were amazed to see tanks and military vehicles driving in and out of the city. Each one of them was adorned with red flags that held what looked to Leah to be a black, broken cross.

"What is going on?" Leah asked her brother. "I thought that Vilnius would be welcoming, clean, and…" she trailed off as a long line of tanks moving across the road a mile away caught her eye. "What are those flags? What do they mean?"

It was then that Jake understood that Leah, in all her innocence and beauty and glory, had no real grasp of what was happening in the world. Until he had whisked her away from the house of the Butcher Malkin that rainy night last fall, she had spent her entire life in about a three-mile square radius. While she had been taught to read, she had seldom picked up a newspaper.

"Leah, the German Nazi Army has supplanted the Communist Russians in this area. The Nazis bring with their presence death to all Jews in their path. Until we can find a safe haven, we must become invisible. There is one additional deadly danger," Jake whispered into his sister's ear.

A terrified Leah said, "What else, Jacob?"

"We can't trust anyone, it's obvious that some of the Lithuanians are collaborating with the Nazis to save their own skins."

Now, with the wreckage of the City of Vilna right in front of her, she saw proof of the dangers they were to encounter.

Taking a deep breath, Jake began to tell Leah of what was happening in Vilna and how it related to the much larger world around them. He explained what a swastika flag represented, and he explained why the Jews were being confined.

She reacted in horror to the stories that he told her of camps inside the borders of Germany devoted to the slave labor of Jews.

When he had traveled into town, while they were living in the cabin, he had heard much more of the tragic fate of so many Jews. All of which told him that every mile they traveled was a dangerous one.

He himself could barely understand what was going on. His experience with Mr. L. had given him some inkling of world events. But that was nothing compared to what was before them today. To lie quiet in the woods next to Leah, while dozens of tanks bearing the flag of Nazi Germany rolled by on the road below, was truly frightening. He knew that he couldn't let her see his fear.

When they had finished talking, Leah took her own deep breath.

Looking straight at her brother, she said, "We have to find your friend in Vilna. We can make it there. I know that we can." A look of determination that he had never seen in her before grew over her sunburned face. "I understand why it is so important for us to move forward. I know that we can do this. Look at how far we have come already."

With that, Jake knew it was time to, indeed, move forward. He told her of his plan to slip into the city and find a section that resembled the Jewish sector of Pinsk. A synagogue would have a distinctive architecture, and together they knelt in the woods, scouring the skyline, looking for just such a building.

Heads held high, as if they knew exactly where they were going, the two walked right down the hill and onto a small side road that Jake had noticed. In minutes they found themselves walking among rubble and destruction.

Expecting to find the glory of a century-old city, they were stunned to see only desecration, devastation, and the ravages of war in Vilna. Buildings had been destroyed by bombs and careless tank drivers. Jeeps driven at dangerous speeds had torn up the once-perfect cobblestone roads. Windows were shattered, and roofs lay in pieces in the street. While the physical world was nearly destroyed, on a social level, Vilna would reveal itself as a personal disaster for its Jews. The two orphans were only barely aware of the tragedy that was unfolding before them. Even with the knowledge of the rampant anti-Semitism around them, they were naive about how cruel and immediate enforcement of that policy of hate really was.

In the mountains, every day had a battle for survival to find food, to find shelter, to find peace. They didn't have time to think of anything outside their own small sphere of reference. The problems of the world had been ignored by the siblings for far too long. They needed to come to terms with the unimaginable.

In 1940, the Russians had established Lithuania as a state. One year later, the Germans had invaded. The Lithuanian people suffered greatly under the Nazis. Some were sent to Germany to live and work in slave labor camps. Unfortunately, many Lithuanians were more sympathetic to Nazi Germany than to the autocratic rule of the leader of the Soviet Union, creating an anti-Semitic turncoat class for the Nazis.

Lithuania had been home to several hundred thousand Jews for many generations. But when Leah and Jake crossed into Lithuania, they had soon heard stories of Jews being herded into cattle cars bound for the death camps in Poland.

On the day that they stepped foot inside Vilna (Vilnius), those problems—and many, many others—stared Leah and Jake in the face.

# THE WRECKAGE OF VILNA

From the moment Jake and Leah entered Vilnius (Vilna), their identity as Jews placed them in great peril. It took them only minutes to hear the wheels of German vehicles bearing flags decorated with swastikas rolling down a street. Hiding in shadows, Leah and Jake leaped between doorway to doorway in an effort to avoid detection. On every street they walked, Jake and Leah found nothing familiar to the small town Pinsk that they knew. The austere stone buildings of Vilna that had withstood the bombing and invasion loomed formidably over them—not one of them holding the promise of a welcoming spirit.

The brother and sister looked on in shock at the presence of swastikas on street posts and on banners hanging from the walls of commercial establishments. Each one of the gruesome flags was startling to the two young people and seemed to be a direct attack on their Jewish heritage.

Heightening their fears were the repeated instances of people being stopped randomly. They observed several of these stops from the shadows that they hid in. Leah and Jake watched in silence as sometimes those stopped were questioned, sometimes searched, and almost always herded and taken into custody. Right before their eyes, groups of people were disappearing!

Leah watched in shock as the soldiers were going about this horrendous procedure with little regard for the cries of the protesters. From where she stood, most of the people who were harassed appeared to be Jewish.

The third time that she witnessed such an action, her heart nearly stopped. She saw before her—not a hundred feet away—a small child, barely five, ripped from the arms of his mother. The mother reaching back toward the child, only to be forcibly restrained by a laughing soldier, found Leah choking down muffled sobs…Jake held Leah tightly around her waist to stop her from running into the street to stop the horrendous scene. The cries of both mother and child split the air around them for blocks. It was only when she realized the danger to herself and her brother that Jake could stop her.

"They will take us as well," said Jake forcefully. "This will do no good to run over there and try and stop it."

After a minute, Leah calmed down and fell, crying into her brother's arms. They stood in the shadow of a wall that stood in an alleyway, for five minutes, until she was ready to move.

Clinging to the edge of buildings and doorways, she held tightly to her brother's arm. Slipping between the shadows of buildings and alleys, she and Jake then began to move forward past what they saw.

Looking for a map, or a way to get his bearings, Jake followed the noise of train whistles and the sight of bellowing smoke until they came to the train station. He figured that a map of the region on a large placard would be at the station, just as he had seen one that had been in every city he had ever visited.

This time it was Leah who saved him, as she grabbed his arm and stopped him in his tracks. Pointing to their far right, near a stretch of tracks away from the train station proper, they witnessed men being led into cattle cars and separated from the women. As quietly and unobtrusively as they possibly could be, the brother and sister crept away from the station and made their way as far away from there as they possibly could.

## JAKE THE HORSE THIEF

In terror and panic-stricken and desperate for a solution, Jake walked quickly and with purpose. Block after block, they traveled, until Jake finally saw what he hoped would be their refuge from the stalking force of evil they had found in Vilna. He nudged his sister and pointed to a group of buildings coming up on their right.

As quietly as he could, he said, "There, across the road, I'm sure it's a yeshiva [seminary]! Let's hurry. Maybe the Nazis won't find us there!"

Just as he finished talking, a German soldier appeared from nowhere. Stopping the siblings, he stood before them in a long, flowing leather coat that came down to the middle of his highly polished boots. On top of his head, he wore a broad-brimmed military cap adorned with a gold eagle at the center.

The man spoke as if he was used to speaking with authority. An arrogance, born of power conferred, was in his tone.

Unable to understand what the soldier was saying, Jake blurted out, "My little brother has to pee!" and began to mime urinating on his "brother's" leg.

In response, Leah began to push her knees together like she had seen little boys do when they had waited too long in the butcher's shop.

Unprepared for the absurdity of the scene, the soldier laughed out loud and pointed to a destroyed building two doors down.

"There, pig, among the broken bricks." He walked away and left Jake and Leah alone.

In order to look good if the soldier turned around, they headed directly for the vacant lot he had pointed to and kept walking until they had reached the back. There, Jake did as he needed, while Leah looked out across the ravages caused by invasion. Once finished, they moved back toward a group of buildings that had caught Jake's eye a minute before the Nazi soldier stopped them.

Once there, they discovered that a cluster of important Jewish buildings had clearly been under siege. Recognizing the language written on a sign that had survived the bombing, Jake saw that they had finally stumbled upon a center comprised of a seat of learning—that is, the yeshiva, a library and a glorious synagogue.

Doing their best to act calm, they moved as one toward the structure. Among the ruins, they found that the entire complex appeared to be deserted. In addition to being vacant, the buildings had suffered considerable damages. Due to the massive amount of destruction, it took a minute for Jake to determine which one was the synagogue.

Moving across the rubble and debris, they found a small section still intact. Cautiously entering the structure, they were shocked to find three men huddled in the space beyond the ark on the altar of the synagogue.

The men were hiding in a tiny alcove located beyond the ornate wooden-covered repository where the holy Torah was kept. The altar was placed on a slight elevation facing the congregation. There were the remnants of a gallery set high above the congregational seating. Jacob recognized the gallery as the seating reserved for the females of the congregation.

The men were astonished to see the two orphaned Horvicz children. The shock wasn't just the fact that they had been found; the real shock was when they learned that Leah and Jacob were Jewish.

The eldest of the three identified himself as the rabbi and exclaimed, "When we heard your voices, at first we thought you were the young thugs of the community. These horrible locals have been a greater threat to our lives than the German military. We thought we were hidden. How were you able to so quickly discover our hiding place?"

Jake explained to the rabbi, "When our father died in an accident, Rabbi Vilnish of Pinsk became my foster father. I lived with

Rabbi Vilnish until a few months ago. Though our shul was tiny compared to this great shul, I am familiar with what I see here in Vilna."

The men continued to look on in awe as he went on, "At first, my sister, Leah, and I didn't expect to find anyone here. These buildings looked deserted and are clearly unfit as a place to live. However, something told me that if there was anywhere that people would be hiding, it would behind the ark. What German would have bothered to learn so much about Jewish tradition that he would know to look there?"

Smiling at Jake's ingenuity, the man who had spoken to them shook his head and introduced himself, "I am Rabbi Youssef Kahn, and this is what is left of what was once—and what I pray will once again be—the great Tiffereth Israel Congregation of Vilna, Lithuania." Motioning toward the other two men, he said, "And this is Rabbi Krakowski, who was visiting, and this is my friend, Ben."

Jake and Leah nodded at each member. As he continued, each of them looked at the structure, marveling at what they could see. Leah was in awe at the wonder to be seen in just the remains. For if a building could look so beautiful in such a calamitous state, it must have been a vision of heaven when it was complete!

The rabbi told them, "As you can see, we have had our worlds devastated, just as much by the Lithuanian auxiliaries that were formed to aid the Nazis as by the incredible number of German troops who came marching through here. If you could find us, then the turncoats will also eventually find us here. We must hide in another place I know of. Get your sister, and follow me!"

One of the other of the rabbi's companions protested the decision to flee the approach of Lithuanian turncoats.

"I am afraid to join you, I must stay within the walls of my synagogue, and here the Lord will protect me!" said the man identified as Rabbi Krakowski.

Rabbi Kahn looked at his friend and didn't flinch as he spoke, "As you wish, my companion, for it is your right to do as you chose in this time. For me, I am looking for safety away from the men that chase us, and I believe that God will protect me as I retreat from their guns and bombs."

With that, Rabbi Kahn, his other companion (who was also the congregation's beadle), and the orphans scurried across the compound to the building that, in better times, had served as the library.

The place was once the depository of great books of both Jewish and worldly learning. Yet today, it stood torn apart by ignorance, hate, and stupidity. What the thugs ripped from the shelves, they had thrown into a heap in the courtyard and set afire. Twelve-foot tall bookcases were overturned in every room. Chairs that once supported the greatest of scholars, as well as the youngest at the start of their studies, lay shattered in corners. Windows were shattered by bombs, and glass was everywhere.

Even with all this, the orphans, the beadle, and Rabbi Kahn did not hesitate to enter the building. The rabbi led the way down the hall and a flight of steps to one room in particular. Somehow, the room had managed to stay intact during all the destruction.

Grabbing a tall cabinet, Rabbi Kahn yanked on its edges. Jake saw that it was connected to the wall by thin, nearly invisible hinges. There they saw a hidden stairwell and, at the rabbi's invitation, moved down the steps.

As they descended, he held the door for them and said, "Here we have stored matzo, wine, and canned goods for Passover. We may not be able to stay here for very long, but we should escape the brutes for who knows how long?"

Once secure behind the closed door, he went on, "I've received secret communication that there are small groups of young Jews that are dedicated to help Lithuanian Jews escape the tyranny that now envelopes this land. They are located in caves off to the northwest, off the beaten path." Proving his worth as a leader of his people, he spoke with optimism and hope, "Perhaps, if we can escape detection for a few days, or for a week or two, we may be saved and join them in their struggle to help defenseless Jews."

As they all huddled in secret, Jake and Leah learned how all they saw had come to pass. Horror after horror completed the rabbi's narrative. What he told them forced them to grow up faster than the last six months had. Both Jake and Leah had seen the assaults, the forced arrests, and the terror of losing a child, but what he now relayed to them grabbed them by their spines and shook them senseless.

It became clear to them that while they had been living in the calm and quiet of the shack last winter, the world outside had erupted into insanity.

The rabbi was specific, for he felt that the only way to get ahold of a problem was to know everything about it. He spoke of Jews of Vilna being shot in the street while loved ones looked on. Those that weren't killed outright were now being seized by the turncoat Lithuanian auxiliaries and herded on to trains. The trains had a very specific destination: the death camps in Poland.

"This makes no sense!" cried Leah. "Who allows this? Why is this being done?"

Rabbi Kahn told her in no uncertain terms that it was partially for survival and partly due to greed.

"The turncoats' main reward is not being hauled away themselves, in order to fill the hungry maw of the slave labor camps. If they can collect Jews to do the work, they are left alone for a while. What the poor fools don't realize is that once all the Jews are taken, they will be the next to go."

Seeing the effect that the story was having on Leah, he softened his approach and tried to not speak so matter-of-factly.

"As terrible as it sounds, they are occasionally being allowed to keep the possessions of the Jews who are leaving on one-way tickets to the death camps." He watched as Leah began to cry.

Jake placed his arm around her shoulder and said to the rabbi, "She has had an isolated life. Only in the past month has she been exposed to the world that you see every day of your life."

Handing Jake a cracker for his sister to eat, the rabbi said, "I am sorry for my blunt nature, young man, but none of us can afford to be ignorant of what is at stake."

"You are right, Rabbi. It should have been my job to better prepare her for what I have found."

"Did you know what you would find when you arrived, my redheaded friend?"

"No, Rabbi, I had hoped to find a seat of learning and a comfortable bed for two orphans."

"Then it is not your burden to feel guilt at what she has learned today, for you yourself were unaware of the circumstances. Let's not waste time with guilt when it is beyond all our control."

Jake found himself wondering what his life would have been like if he had been raised by such a man as Rabbi Khan. In his own way, Jake had grown to love Rabbi Vilnish, but their age difference had left a wide gulf between what they could discuss. To Jake, a younger man, such as Rabbi Kahn, would have been more of a mentor.

Leah looked on in shock at what they had seen over the last few hours. It was only as she listened as Jake and the rabbi began to talk of guilt and what it meant to themselves that she could, even for a second, forget the horror from which they were hiding.

She thought, *How often is a woman privileged to hear such conversations? No matter what happens, the learning of my people continues even in the darkest of circumstances.*

Recognizing that this was not the time to panic, she pushed every ounce of shock and depression deep down inside her. The men went on with their talks, while some small amounts of food were brought out, and everyone ate. Distracted by their own minds, they had little idea of what was happening outside of their hidden lair.

Always on the alert for the rewards to be had for turning in Jews, five minutes earlier, two burly turncoats were given a tip that two young people had just been seen running toward the "big Jew buildings" down the broad street.

To the turncoats, this was a clear reference to Tiffereth Israel Synagogue. Seasoned at what they jokingly called "the art of hunting Jews," they found the tip surprising. Many who did what they were commanded believed that all the Jews in Vilna had been surrounded and sent to the death camps. Alerted, the turncoats rushed to the synagogue. It didn't take long for them to find the one poor soul who had stayed behind, with the belief that "The lord will protect me!" It didn't take long for Ben Asher to be discovered and left to his sad fate.

To the turncoats, if there was one Jew in the partially destroyed building, there were three more hiding somewhere.

"They are like roaches," said the shorter one to his heavy friend.

Turning to their prisoner, the bigger of the two yelled, "Jew bastard, tell me where the rabbi and the other two people are hiding!"

The prisoner was so filled with fear that it looked as if he would die on the spot.

The shorter one moved in close and now, mere inches from the shaking man's nose, screamed, "Hurry, and don't lie to me!"

The intimidating assault gained nothing for either of the turncoats except shrieks of terror from the shrinking man.

It was only when one of the turncoats held the poor man's hands down while the other pulled a pair of pliers from his pocket that they learned what they wanted.

"Stop, in the name of God, I can't stand this! I'll talk! You'll find them in the library building," said their victim.

One turncoat turned to the other and said, "Too bad, he didn't tell us in time."

"So true," said his partner in human trafficking. "What is your name, Jew?"

"It is Issyk, sir. My name is Issyk," was the crying man's response.

With that, the collaborator opened the pliers and began to pull the fingernails from poor Issyk's left hand.

Screaming in pain, he cried loudly, "I told you what you want to know. W*HY*? W*HY* do you do this now?"

As the last fingernail on his blood-covered left hand was extracted and dropped to the ground, the turncoat laughed and said, "Since we promised to do it, we had to be men of our word."

The other man laughed as he said, "Men of our word!"

With that, he let go of Issyk's left hand. Blood fell freely from the tips of the man's fingers. He fell to his knees before his assailants, clutching his one hand with the other. Tears fell across his cheeks and then down the front of his shirt.

Pulling him up by the shoulders of his coat, the taller of the two said, "Take us to your friends. For you know that you still have another hand."

"Another hand," laughed the other one.

With that, poor Issyk led the turncoats across the courtyard and straight to the library's place of concealment. Ripping the tall cabinet that concealed the hidden entrance straight from the wall, the two turncoats raced down the steps with a fury.

There, the only people the turncoats found were Rabbi Kahn and the beadle. The noise of Issyk screaming had reached their ears a long minute earlier. The older men knew they were trapped and did nothing to escape. They felt their days were numbered, that no matter what happened, that day or the next, they were both bound to be caught.

Their young guests were caught in the same trap. Jake and Leah had heard the sound of the man crying followed quickly by the crashing of the bookcase. For a second, they looked at each other in panic. To be arrested meant separation, if not death on the spot!

As the collaborators were crashing down on them, the rabbi grabbed Jake by his coat and pointed toward a bathroom at the end of the hall.

"It's locked, but you can break through and climb out the window!" he shouted.

Without a moment's hesitation, Leah followed Jake as he crashed through the bathroom door!

"Don't hesitate, be with me after I burst through that glass window on the other side!" Jake shouted.

After crashing out of the bathroom, there was a meter drop when landing on the ground, outside of the library. Without a thought, Leah followed and let herself fall into her brother's arms. In desperation, the two ran for the nearest secluded area they could see. They stumbled to a brick structure they could cling to. There, they pressed flat against the wall of a small store that was still standing. They hid in the shadows as they watched several German motorcycles with sidecars race past. These were only two wheeled vehicles, but the roar of their engines caused them to shiver in fear where they stood.

Used to working together after a long months on the road and in hiding, they moved with the speed of lightning to what they prayed was freedom. For several minutes, they stayed by the side of the building, trying to gauge what was happening around them. Jake kept an eye on the window they had just climbed through, but he saw nothing. All around them, unfamiliar noises filled the air. Engines, whistles, men screaming—none of it made sense to their ears.

When the moment seemed right, Jake led the two of them to another doorway. From there, they raced to another, until they had raced over three streets in as many minutes. For the briefest of moments, it appeared they would be able to reach the city limits. From there, they could, perhaps, get lost in the forest. From there, they could then move northwest to join other people who were attempting to save other Jews in this darkest of times.

Lithuania was proving to be a disastrous choice for the brother and sister. They couldn't have known that Nazi collaborationists had been hired to set up checkpoints designed to capture young people. The idea was to send the youngest Jews possible to Germany to work in the slave labor camps—the younger and frailer, the better.

For once in the camps, their small, thin fingers were ideal when applying grease to the smaller shell casings on a munition's assembly line. If a child lost a finger or an entire hand, who cared? Certainly not the Germans. After all, the people performing the labor were only Jews!

On the run and in more danger than they had ever known, the siblings attempted to reach the edge of the city by moving from the edges of buildings, straight into the moving mass of the general population.

Jake's racing heart started to slow down as this new strategy seemed to work. Leah and Jake blended in well with the other nationals, who all wore similar dark clothes that seemed to speak of a farming lifestyle. They took a place in the middle of a large group of people, most of whom were carrying farming tools and marching. No one in the group paid a bit of attention to them.

It worked for a few minutes, but a vigilante Nazi sympathizer, looking for reward money and bounty, noticed them as they crossed the street four blocks from the synagogue.

The bullying Lithuanian collaborationists pushed their way through the crowd of farmers. In a second, they were standing in front of Jake and Leah. Not a single member of the group that they had been walking with stopped to see what was happening.

One of the thugs made a remark in scrambled Yiddish, but it was enough to get Leah's attention.

When the thug and Leah made eye contact, he grabbed her collar and pulled her to the curb.

Leah screamed, "Jake, Jake, my love, don't let them part us!" It was to no avail.

Jake had been collared by another Lithuanian collaborationist! They were both in the hands of local informers. There was nowhere to run. Both of them were being held from behind by their collars. The siblings looked at one another with a mixture of separation and tremulous fear in their eyes.

Looking for a possible reward from their German masters, the men who had pushed through the crowd to grab them marched them down to the end of the street to a Nazi checkpoint. The soldier standing guard took one look at them and said, "Good job," to the two collaborationists. He motioned for them to move their captures into the building behind him.

Pushing Jake and Leah through the front doors, the two men told the soldier at the front desk who they were. He motioned toward a German soldier, who had been standing in the corner. He came over and took both Leah and Jake by their collars. From there, they were led into a small, cold room lit by a single lightbulb. It held no chair, no table.

Turning to his sister, Jake said, "I am so sorry that I…"

Leah rushed to his side and grabbed him as hard as she could and said, "Shut up, Jacob. This has been the greatest six months of my life!" She looked up at him with eyes filled with tears. "You did the right thing. I loved you since you were born, and I love you even more today, my dear brother."

The door swung open as she finished her last thought. A man in a white coat accompanied by two armed soldiers and an officer entered the room.

Leah yelled, "Jake!" as one of the German soldiers grabbed her.

She started to yell his name a second time, but the soldier slapped her across the face. Shocked at what happened, she stood silently in place.

Jake started to move toward the soldier when he felt the hand of the other soldier yank him by the collar of his coat. He was then pushed to the man in the white coat.

Without a word, the man looked at Jake once and said, "The boy is in perfect health."

The appointed officer of the Third Reich said, "Good, he will make an excellent laborer." Turning toward Leah, he told the soldier, "Put that other boy down. He is a runt and has no place to go."

The soldier did as he was instructed while the officer spoke again, "Now, let's look at his slim friend to see if his fate lies on a train to the east to serve the furtherer or a camp in Germany."

The man in the white coat approached Leah. Once he was close enough to look her in the eyes, he tilted his head sideways, as if he suddenly had a question. He grabbed at her chest and smiled as she tried to pull away from his touch. Shock rang out in the examination room when it was discovered that "the other, slim boy" was, in fact, a girl!

"Well, who knows what you will see in a day's work!" exclaimed the doctor.

Summoning the turncoat into the room, he asked the soldier if he knew that he had brought the Germans a girl that afternoon.

The man shook his head, "No!" He was as much amazed at the revelation as the officer.

"Well, I certainly can't pay you for something we now have to send back to Poland," said the officer. "Where is the value in that?"

The Lithuanian replied sheepishly, "Sorry, Mein Kapitain. I will exercise much more care in my next capture."

Throwing a single deutschmark at the man, he said, "Make sure you don't waste my time like this ever again. If this happens again, it will be you who is taking a train out of this ugly, gray city. Now, wait with me for a second."

Bowing toward the officer, the collaborationist said, "Thank you, thank you."

With the soldier still holding Jake, the officer turned to the Lithuanian and said, "Search her. I have a feeling about this one…"

While one soldier held Jake and the other stood at attention, the collaborationist was glad to take Leah by the arm and pin her against the wall. Placing one hand over her mouth, he moved his other hand between her legs, feeling up one side and then down the other. In the area closest to her most private parts, he ran across a bump in the fabric.

Turning to the officer, he asked, "How did you know this?

The officer pulled a knife from his pocket and opened it. Handing it to the Lithuanian, he spoke, "The doctor and I have an understanding."

He smiled and watched as the man took the knife to Leah's pant leg. Starting at the knee, he cut into her pant leg and kept moving up the girl's thigh until he was at her undergarments. Once at the edge, he cut into them, exposing her to everyone in the room.

The jewels that were sewn in Leah's undergarments tumbled out, much to the amazement of the officer!

Leah was in no mood to declare where the jewels came from; she was much more interested in covering her nakedness while the men glared with glee.

Knowing full well that there were summary executions if any Lithuanian dared to withhold contraband from the German authorities, her willing assailant quietly reached down and picked up the fallen jewels. The collaborationist, still pressing his hand over Leah's mouth, held the find out for the Nazi SS officer in charge.

Stunned when confronted with the unexpected find, the German quickly concealed the jewels. *In* the back of his mind, he immediately made plans to wait until the war was over and then sell them quietly.

While this was transpiring, the other soldier was still holding Jake. Her brother, Jacob Horvicz, was shackled and unable to help his sister in any manner. Right before his eyes, she had been stripped and searched, as if she were an animal. To the Nazi officer in charge, her nakedness was worth a second glance, but for the officer, it was his sixth capture of the day. And it wasn't even lunch.

It was in that room, under that single lightbulb, that Jake saw Leah for the last time. He would have a hard time remembering that day, for as she was being taken away screaming, tears clouded his own eyes, making him unable to remember the details of her beautiful face.

He did remember her last words. "My brother! My brother! Let me die with my brother! My life has no meaning without him." Her cries of love trailed down the hall until he could hear them no more.

The turncoat did, indeed, take Leah to the train bound for Poland. In an hour, she and several hundred other women were pushed into several open train cars that had once been used for cattle. Unfamiliar with the languages being spoken around her, Leah could not initially understand where she was heading. It was only when the train started to move that an elderly woman recognized what Leah was yelling in the same language that was spoken in Pinsk and told her of their ultimate fate.

Dazed at the drastic change in circumstances, Leah rode the train for as long as she could stand it. Finding no reason to live and determined to take control of her own fate, at two separate points along the way, she attempted to jump out of the moving car. After the second attempt proved to be unsuccessful, the officer in charge all locked the door to each car for the duration of the trip into Germany.

He had left them open in the hope that anyone who was so inclined would jump and save the German people the price of an execution. When they hauled Leah back into the car the second time, he told her she was "too stupid to even kill herself properly."

Leah's fate had been sealed when the jewelry was found. It was obvious that she was in good health. Her hands were thin and strong, and she would have been able to work on the lines that greeted shells. The officer could have chosen to send her into a labor camp.

Greedy and fearful that she would tell someone that she had been robbed while arrested in Vilna, he had chosen to send her to a place called Auschwitz.

The camps were all new, and their cleanliness was deceiving. The purpose of the camps was to handle the growing number of people whom the German government had determined were "problems." Once she arrived inside the camps, Leah and the others who had ridden across the land with her were herded into a large outdoor pen.

From there, they were taken one by one to a barber where their heads were shaved clean. Stripped of their clothes, they had a foul-smelling powder thrown at them in order to help control vermin. Once the process had been completed, the women were gathered together in a waiting room.

In broken Polish, a German officer told them that "they had nothing to worry for, because they were to only receive a communal shower."

It had been almost two days since she had been taken from Jake. Now she stood naked among a hundred other naked women in a small, compact room. Leah made no effort to cover her body, for she was in utter shock and could not fully comprehend what was going on.

As the guards moved the crowd into a small tiled area with a line of nozzles along the ceiling, she continued to stand still. All she knew was that she saw the others moving and understood that she was to do so as well.

Some women were trying to joke about the experience, saying that it was going to be the "cleanest they had been in a long time!"

Just as the door fell shut behind them, the officer in charge said something, but Leah couldn't hear it. She knew that something important had been said, but the sounds that came through her ear were muted, unintelligible. She began to feel as if was if her body was shutting down.

Then, from nowhere, she began to hear only screams. Suddenly, she felt fingernails being dragged across her back. There was no pain to be felt, only confusion.

Turning to the woman next to her, she saw that the woman had been trying to grab Leah as she started to fall. On the floor, before the orphaned Horvicz girl, was a woman writhing in pain, grabbing at her throat as if she was choking.

Looking up, Leah saw that many of the other women were doing the same. Some were clawing at the ones next to them in an attempt to crawl over the growing mound of bodies. Looking up to the nozzles, she saw that it wasn't water coming out, but she couldn't figure out what it really was.

Since she was near the edge of the room, Leah was one of the last to start to smell what was happening.

*It is gas!* she thought.

A strange odor passed over Leah's nose. She couldn't place it, but it began to burn as she took a breath. Then she started to cough. Only she wasn't doing it as violently as so many of the others were. A calm began to spread over every inch of her body.

Leah felt at this time that death would be a release from the misery she had known in this lifetime.

As she began to slide to the floor, she involuntarily grabbed at the easily cleaned tiles that covered the wall. In her mind, as tears filled her eyes and her lungs gasped for air only to find nothing but a burning sensation, she smiled and thought of her mother's face, her father's laugh, what Jake had done for her. It occurred to her that at the very end of her life, she had been allowed to spend time in the company of her loving brother. She saw this as a blessing.

Their time together had been rough and filled with trials and tribulations. But at the very least, they had been together.

As her face started to lay across the cement floor of the "shower," her fingers hit the place where the wall and floor meet. It was at that moment, a second before she took her last breath, that she could only think of one thing: her brother, Jacob!

# AN INTERLUDE ABOUT THE JEWELS

The jewels that had been sewn into Leah's undergarment went on to a life of their own. The German officer who had received them from the collaborator, who had in turn taken them from Leah, was named Hans Fromm. As his career advanced, he would rise to become a midlevel bureaucrat inside the corps of German officers who were responsible for prisoners executed during the war.

These were not the only jewels, art, or money confiscated by Fromm. But they were by far the most important. A realistic and a pragmatic man, in the last year of the war's existence, he could feel that the winds of victory were starting to blow the other way for his beloved Third Reich. His son and two of his nephews began to hide the goods that Fromm's position had helped him acquire. Together the four men stashed paintings, gold, clothes, books, and anything they believed were in farms and houses they owned.

In 1948, a dignified middle-aged man with a German accent sold a beautiful and very unique diamond ring to a jeweler in Amsterdam. Telling various jewelers that he had been a lowly officer solely in charge of maintenance during the war, this gentleman was looking to sell "just a few odd gems that he had stumbled across while building latrines for his superiors, who were, of course, the ones committing such horrible, horrible atrocities…"

Traveling from jeweler to jeweler, and from pawnshop to pawnshop, in the years after the war, Hans Fromm quietly and slowly began selling the enormous amount of contraband that he had accumulated during the decade that he had served the Third Reich.

Almost all the jewelers and auction houses that he contacted, no matter what city or country they lived in, had refused to consider purchasing the gems because of a lack of provenance. That, and the fact that almost all the men contacted felt a moral obligation to not profit from the sad misfortune of millions who had died.

Mandelbaum, a jeweler in Amsterdam, had little or none of the obligations of the other jewelers.

Seeing the unusual ring that Fromm brought into his welcoming shop, that fine day in April, Sam Mandelbaum could do little to contain his excitement.

The ring that this self-proclaimed "low-level officer, who merely did as he was told" laid out before him was the finest-looking piece of contraband that the jeweler had seen since the earliest days of the war. He decided to "cool" the acquisition of this purchase for a month and wait to see if he had anything to concern himself about the purchase.

The jeweler found it hard to believe that such a beautiful ring had fallen into his possession. Since before the war, he had moved illegal contraband among various back-alley acquaintances, hoping to find that one, single item that would give him what he called "the big score." From the minute that he had seen the ring, he knew that it was the one.

It was a month before he was positive that no one had followed the German, who sold him the ring, into his store. It was only then that he went back and pulled the ring from hiding. He brought it back to his store in order to examine it closely.

Within seconds of picking up his loupe and pulling the ring close to his right eye, Mandelbaum found a small jeweler's code inscribed in the band of the ring. Copying it down, he then wrote a detailed description of the stone's highly individualized setting in the ring. Despite his lack of moral compass, Mandelbaum was, indeed, a skilled jeweler. After he found the detailed clarity of its stone, he dug deep, looking for defects, and he noted the strength of its setting.

Over the next few months, he would innocently ask his friends and the few experts that he knew a question here and a question there, until he was able to gather all the answers into one much larger final answer—one that revealed the spectacular provenance of the ring.

He had asked three different experts about the jeweler's code on the ring. The third answer confirmed what he had suspected that first day he had seen the ring. The code was that of a noted designer of jewels who had been based in Paris and Minsk before the war. He had, as so many others, disappeared during the earliest days of the war.

Just before the global conflict had erupted, Julius Malkin had earned a sudden reputation as one of the most brilliant and capable designers of jewelry in the world. Heads of states sought his work, and rich men and women coveted what he created. But there was little of his work actually available. As a result, to see the name "Malkin" on a piece of jewelry was a rare occurrence.

Mandelbaum had a piece of jewelry that was going to change his life. It would also deeply affect the life of Jake the Horse Thief.

# SHLOMO

The Lithuanian checkpoint where Jake and Leah had been detained was in a period of transition. On the day that Leah was taken to a train and Jake was thrown in a damp, dark cell, the compound was being run by a combination of soldiers and locals. The soldiers were happy to not be in a combat position, and the locals were happy not to be packed off onto trains that were headed for slave camps and goodness knows what else.

Inside a cell, unsure as to where Leah had been taken and fearful that his own fate was now beyond his control, Jake now sat on a hard wooden bench with his hands cuffed behind him. The only light in the cell was provided by a single bulb that illuminated the hallway on the other side of the jail's door. The place smelled of defecation and sweat and urine. It hadn't been cleaned in years, and even when it had been cleaned, it still smelled of defecation and sweat and urine.

In the corner of the cell was a lump of clothes that had feet poking out from a pair of torn trousers. A large dark coat, obviously too large for the person underneath it, covered the upper part of the body that undoubtedly lay under the pile of clothes.

Jake said nothing to the pile, and the pile of clothes said nothing to Jake. Every fifteen minutes or so, a guard in a made-up uniform walked by, poked his head through the bars, and walked on. Other than the footsteps of the guard, there was no other noise—

other than the unexpected sound of snoring that erupted from the pile of clothes.

Jake recognized the pile of clothes as a fellow prisoner and whispered.

"Hey there," said Jake in the general direction of the pile of clothes. "Can you be quiet and watch me, we're in a life-and-death situation!"

The small figure entangled himself from the pile and nodded in assent.

"Be ready to watch me, I have a physical plan," Jake muttered.

After about an hour, Jake heard a dinner bell ring down the corridor. The sound of footsteps filled the hall, and the voice of the guard followed out, "About damn time. Hey, Jew! Bet you would love a good glass of beer!"

"As much as I would want one, for I can see from your smile that it must be some of Lithuania's finest brew, I would actually love to have a chance to pee, but I'm afraid to, the urinal in the floor seems to be stopped up. If it overflows, it will stink up this whole damn jail!"

The slightly tipsy Litho jailer sounded, "You're a pain in the ass!"

Jake countered, "Sorry, I can't hold it in, and I'm ready to piss all over the cell floor!"

"Okay, hold it, goddamn it, I'll see what I can do," the sodden jailer answered.

When the jailer stumbled over to the urinal, Jake brought his manacled hands high above and crashed them down on the back of the jailer's neck! There was a loud crack heard as the jailer's body plunged headfirst into the putrid mess.

Jake yelled to the other captive, "Move fast! Get the keys from the slob I've just knocked out. First unlock me, and then I'll do the same for you. But don't hesitate, it won't be more than a few minutes before someone realizes the slob hasn't reported!"

The wiry human in the pile of rags followed Jake's instructions, crying, "Okay, pal, I'm with you!"

The pile of clothes in the corner sprang to life. In a second, what had been hiding underneath the pile of rag slid across five feet of floor to check the guard's consciousness.

"He's out cold! Maybe you killed him?" Grabbing the guard's key ring, the five-foot-five former pile of clothes said, "I am Shlomo."

Taking the guard's keys, the new friend moved swiftly and silently to where Jake was slumped and said, "Turn around so that I can unlock your handcuffs!"

Jake sat rubbing his wrists and said, "If you can get us out of here, I am sure that I can…"

He stopped speaking as he watched Shlomo remove the man's shirt and then throw it to over to Jake. He then dragged the guard's body over to the corner where, not a minute earlier, the pile of rags had been.

Piling the rags that had once hid his own body on top of the dead guard, Shlomo stood and looked straight at Jake as he spoke, "Follow me and you live. Otherwise, I lock you back in here. Either way, they will probably kill you. It just becomes a matter of when."

With that, he turned and walked out of the cell.

"All things in time, my handsome friend. Right now, we have to get out. It can't be found by two men who are in jail or dead."

Shoving the body off to the side, Shlomo put his finger to his lips and stood. He made a motion for Jake to turn around. Then he grabbed his wrists.

"I am putting these on very loosely, so be careful that they don't fall off as we walk." Once again, Jake felt handcuffs bind his wrists.

Opening the door slowly, Shlomo looked out and then pulled Jake into the light of the main hallway. Pushing Jake to the front, he walked behind the six-foot redhead, holding him by the handcuffs as he did. With the other hand, he shoved a pistol in Jake's side.

Through one corridor and then another, they said nothing as they marched. Anyone who saw them would think that they were just two prisoners on a mission to find the latrine.

"Remember, I speak their language, you don't. So don't say a word," said Shlomo in a low voice. "And have your knife at the ready," followed as an unnecessary instruction.

At the end of the hall, there was a stairway that reached past the ceiling. Without blinking, Shlomo, still clad in the guard's uniform and now wearing the second guard's hat, pushed his prisoner forcefully up the steps. The two men went straight up into the first floor. There, the light that fell through the windows to the outside world told them that there was less than an hour of daylight.

With a gun still at his side, Jake saw two armed guards at an iron gate ahead. In what Jake assumed was Lithuanian, Shlomo spoke to the two men. One rose immediately and started to unlock the gate. The other went back to the puzzle that he had been doing the minute before.

Without warning, Shlomo dropped the gun, pulled out his knife with his free hand, and moved toward the guard at the gate. He slit the man's throat so quickly that Jake had no idea it was about to happen! The former collaborator with the German Army fell before he knew he was dead.

The guard who was still at the desk looked up and, seeing what had just happened, went for his gun. Jake broke open the handcuffs and, in a swift motion, pulled his knife from his pocket, flicked it open, and followed Shlomo's example.

When the guard fell dead at the gate, Jake opened the gate, and together the two former prisoners walked out and onto the streets of Vilna. Moving out onto the street, they hurried along one road and then another. After four turns, Shlomo stopped next to a sewer grate.

He told Jake to remove the handcuffs and pulled the gun from his charge's shoulder, saying, "Hurry up. We have maybe a minute."

It was at that exact moment that the scream of a siren broke the dead air over the town.

"That minute is now gone. Get this grate off NOW!" screamed Shlomo.

Working as one, the two men pulled the grate to the side.

Shlomo slipped through first, saying to Jake, "Move it back as fast as you can."

With Shlomo already out of sight, Jake took a few steps into the sewer and pulled the metal lid that covered the entry to the sewer over his head, before descending completely into the tunnel. There, he saw a row of single lightbulbs hanging from long, long wire. It seemed to go on forever. In the distance, he saw a small hulking figure running away from him. It took Jake a second to realize that this was Shlomo.

A voice rang back down the tunnel, "Hurry up, asshole!"

Jake's partner in the escape clearly knew the sewers. It was that hard-won knowledge that kept them alive. They crawled through the putrid slop for several hundred yards until they came to a four-way break in the underground pathway. Shlomo stopped for a second, giving Jake time to catch up.

Once the two men were standing side by side, Shlomo told Jake, "Get used to the smell. This is the only road open to us in Vilna."

For just one second, the men caught their breath. Shlomo then hit Jake on the shoulder and began running down the long tube to the left.

They ran for hundreds of yards, and then they turned again. This pattern went on for almost an hour. Jake struggled to memorize the twist and turns, but the varying depths of water and the odor kept him distracted.

After what seemed to be an eternity, they came to a stop under a fenced-in grate. Shlomo climbed the ladder that hung from the curved wall of the tunnel and, when he reached the top, whispered something that Jake couldn't hear.

The grate was made of cast iron and had been constructed in the same manner as a jail door. Jake watched as his new friend slid it sideways. Shlomo moved quickly through the opening and then, lying on the ground, put his hand out for Jake to grab.

United above ground, the two men sat gasping for breath. Jake looked around as his eyes adjusted from the darkness of the sewer to the brightness of a single candle that flickered in a corner of the room. He heard nothing but Shlomo trying to breathe. As his eyes gained focus, he became aware that there were other sets of eyes all around the walls of the large room.

In a minute, he saw that those eyes belonged to a huddled group of men and women. From what Jake could tell, they were hidden in what appeared to be a partially destroyed large warehouse. One by one, members of the group started to move toward them. His shoulder still heaving up and down from the long run and excitement, Jake began to feel people patting him on the back and saying, "Good job!" or, "You made it!"

He looked over to Shlomo, who was now on his knees hugging a brunette as several small children grabbed him.

Shlomo spoke to all of them, and to no one in particular, "I was turned over to the collaborationists by an ancient sick man I was administering to, when he discovered that I was Jewish. After the arrest, I was rushed to a guard post just before the curfew." Pointing to Jake, he added, "Our new friend made it possible for me to escape."

A hand went out to Jake and pulled him up to his feet.

"Let's get that stink off you," said an unidentified voice.

"My god, he's a tall one!" said a surprised woman.

Jake looked over and saw a blond woman with brown eyes wearing a long black skirt and a babushka down around her shoulders. She was the only one who had spoken. Off to his right, he heard some children laughing. He titled his head toward the woman as if he was trying to ask, "Why?"

"They have never seen a redhead before," came her answer.

As a man grabbed at the buttons on his shirt, Jake stepped back, worried that the jewels he had hidden would be discovered.

The man grabbed him and said, "Take it easy, boy." He then pulled off Jake's shirt and said, "We have to go in the back. You smell as if you walked through hell."

As he walked toward the back with the man, he heard Shlomo say, "He did."

# THE BEGINNINGS OF THE JEWISH PARTISAN GROUP

With that, Jake was led into a small back room with a shower and a few chairs.

The man who had been helping him undress turned on the water and said, "Undress quickly. I will be right back with some fresh clothes…if I can find anything to fit a giant." Laughing a little at what he had said, he added, "There is no warm water, and we have very little water to start with. So you have less than a minute to scrub."

Taking effort to carefully remove the jewels hidden in his worn and ruined garments, he placed them on the windowsill that was built into the wall next to the shower. Next he put his prayer book and knife beside the spoils that had so far cost at least two people their lives.

Less than three minutes later, Jake was wearing a shirt that was a bit too tight and pants that were a bit too loose. While he had showered, his own shoes had been cleaned and set beside the clothes that were waiting for him on a chair. Gathering his belongings from the windowsill, he placed them in his pockets.

From the shower room, he was led into another room where several other men were sitting. One of them motioned for Jake to sit at a small table that was pressed against a wall. The others in the room waved him on as he sat at one of the two chairs.

On the table before him was a bowl of warm chicken soup. It was the first food he had eaten since the crackers that he had been given in the synagogue earlier that morning. A glass of water stood next to the bowl. Jake devoured both without being told to do so.

After a minute, Shlomo and a second group of men entered the room.

Looking up from his soup, Jake said nothing. Returning to his meal, he saw Shlomo pull a chair from the other side of the table.

The man who had helped Jake escape from confinement turned to one of the other men who were standing in the now-crowded room. Without a word, the man stood up and ejected the others from the room. In a minute, Jake and Shlomo were alone. Pushing the bowl away from him, Jake looked over to his benefactor. Shlomo sat as tall as he could. He wore a wicked grin that seemed to be born from an understanding that they had escaped death together.

Together the two men looked to be a study in contrasts. Jake was tall, lean, pale, and freckled and, topped with that, notorious head of rich red hair. Across from him, Shlomo sat so straight as if he had discovered a new part of his spine. Dark, dark hair ran wild across his head in a disorganized mess. It matched perfectly the thick hair that covered his arms and continued down to his hands. His gaze was filled with the thought that the next few minutes would hold the most fun imaginable. Those arms were thick and nearly as wide as his neck. Shlomo was compact, where Jake was expansive.

It was if someone had deliberately placed a barrel at one end of the table and a long rope at the other.

For the next two hours, the men traded stories. From nowhere, a bottle of wine appeared. Jake told him of Pinsk, and Shlomo told him of how beautiful Vilna had been when he was a child. He told Jake of the city's history—how, over one hundred years ago, the gates of the city had helped the Russians to defeat Napoleon. Now, Shlomo believed that the city would rise, as it had back then, and into today's world lead in the defeat of Hitler and the Germans.

As the two men spoke, Shlomo took care to emphasize the urgency of the situation. He told him of how the Germans operated, what their goals were, and how they were going about as they achieved their goals. Jake grew to understand the real danger around him—how the entire world was on edge due to the arrogance and conceit of a single country.

In time they came to the topic of Leah. Though he had finally learned about the evil of the Nazis and seen close-up how they operate, he still planned to leave that night in order to find Leah. Over all of Shlomo's objections, Jake was adamant that she be found. Jake spoke of his love for his sister, how much they had been through, and what their plans for the future were. Shlomo pulled his chair close to the young man from Pinsk.

In the light of a lone candle—with the sound of the wind that passed through the empty streets of Vilna moving across the roof and through small cracks in the wall—Jake tried to understand that, for now, Leah was gone.

"We have all lost people we love. They leave on the departing trains every day," said Shlomo as he placed a hand on Jake's shoulder. "They leave for labor camps or goodness knows where. I mean, we hear the rumors."

Jake stood up and angrily denounced the world.

"How can this happen? We crawled through a sewer for an hour! We can't walk in the open streets? Now we are eating a bowl of soup in an abandoned factory, a warehouse…I don't even know where I am. I was better off in the forest!"

Shlomo stood to meet his new friend eye to eye. Try as he might, he was just too short. But that didn't stop him from speaking to Jake as forcefully as he could. He spoke in whispers, but the burning desire for freedom came through in every word.

"We cannot save those who are taken from us. But we can rise to help and save those who remain."

Grabbing Jake by his arms, he pulled him down so they could look each other eye to eye.

"It is only by being tighter, working as a smart, strong group that we can tear these Nazi pigs down from their self-created tower. Running off in the darkness to chase Leah will only bring you death. They will shoot you in the street. I guarantee you that every soldier in a hundred-mile radius who is wearing a uniform is out looking for a giant redheaded Jew walking through the shadows of Vilna."

It was hard for Jake to understand. To even think that one group of people could do this to another group of their own kind was beyond his comprehension. As much as he wanted to ignore what he saw, the reality of it all had unfolded right before his eyes.

Once Jake had calmed down, Shlomo told Jake that the chances were that Leah was already on a train to Germany or somewhere else. He watched as an understanding of what was real came over Jake's face.

"What can we do, Shlomo? What can we do to prevent someone else's sister from being taken away as Leah was today?"

Shlomo took him by the arm and walked him back into the main room, where so many others were congregated. He took Jake to the center of the room and left him there. A man came forward and put his hand out for Jake to shake.

As he did, the man began to speak, "My name is Simon, and we are a group of Jews dedicated to saving the Jews who are left behind in Lithuania. We move from place to place in the darkness, to hide from the Germans and the collaborationist Lithuanians. For only by staying alive can we honor those who have left and those who will follow us."

One by one, men and women approached Jake and shook his hand. In some cases, they spoke of the ones that they had lost as they shook his hand. Others simply thanked him for helping Shlomo to return to them. As each one finished, they moved to the side and let another approach Jake with what they needed to say.

When they were finished, they gathered around the young man and sat down.

Still standing, the man who had spoken first—Simon—asked, "We are very anxious to hear your story, please tell us!"

Overcome by the welcome he had received and the honesty of those around him, Jake collected his thoughts and started to speak. He spoke briefly of Pinsk and Rabbi Vilnish. Without going into too much detail, he told how he and Leah had been on the road for the last year. In three or four sentences, he came to what was important to him.

"My sister, Leah, was separated from me by the damned Lithos and turned over to the Nazis," lamented Jake. "I despair at the thought that I may never find her. Your group may be my last chance." When he finished, he did his best to stifle his tears at the memory of Leah's smile.

The members of the Jewish Partisan Group moved to embrace their newest member.

# JAKE AND THE BOY FROM KOVNO

This small group of men and women were dedicated to protecting the few, mostly very old, Jews from anti-Semitic Lithuanians and the Nazis. They also did everything they could to help spirit babies and the youngest of their children to safety.

The daring shown by Jake and Shlomo in their escape from the cell soon became legendary among the members of the group. The two men seemed to balance each other perfectly. Shlomo was quick to action, ready to engage in combat at the drop of a hat. Jake looked to use his mind. He wanted to solve a situation with as little blood as possible. But if called upon, the group had no better soldier at their side.

At its peak of activity, the Jewish Partisan Group that had welcomed Jake numbered no more than ten, maybe fifteen. The children that Jake had met that first night were soon sent out of the country through a network of trains and carts and friends that helped the group in their activities.

The group was very young, and each member held a great conviction for the cause in their heart. The redheaded man from Pinsk was a welcome addition. He brought a different set of skills to the team. Most of his adult life had been spent on the run. Swamps, forests, and mountains were familiar to him in his battle for survival. It only seemed natural that he would prove to be good at fighting and hiding. He became a true warrior and a dependable soldier when the group had to fight to survive. If he had to kill, Jake Horvicz would kill.

As the weeks passed and they encountered more and more Nazis looking to capture the resistance fighters, Jake never held back when it came to what needed to be done. In time even Shlomo came to realize that Jake may be the most gifted among them all.

He was the one who set up a dedicated and brilliantly conceived underground network of tunnels, safe houses, and seldom-used roads to conduct many to safety. Thanks to his work with maps, they were able to lead dozens of the elderly, as well those unable to care for themselves, to a better life.

Most of their action took place at night. Jake's years of slinking around Pinsk and exploring the region around his hometown had taught him valuable lessons about how to move in the darkness. After one particularly harrowing mission had ended with no casualties among them, a man named Abe joked that they had found their own legendary Golem.

Through it all, Jake continued to write what he saw and experienced in the margins of his prayer book. The words he wrote speak to the experiences that happened to many others who lived during that tormented period of their life on earth.

Jake learned quickly that Leah's capture by a Lithuanian auxiliary unit and her disappearance into the Holocaust was by no means an unusual occurrence. The idea that something like this could happen to one so beautiful and innocent as Leah drove him to work harder and harder in the fight against this barbarous cruelty.

The years passed, and the group rose and fell in numbers. Some who helped were killed and captured. Others grew weary of the constant pressure and living with the never-ending specter of death. Some left quietly, in order to make a run to freedom on their own. As members came and went, the group was constantly on the move.

In no time, they expanded from initially providing aid to others into more militant areas of the fight against the Germans. Under Jake's guidance, they became proficient at disrupting train traffic that carried arms and materials to the war front. Bridges were destroyed and roads ruined by the Jewish Partisans. Though they had taken up arms against their oppressors, their main cause remained: the protecting the lives of fellow Lithuanian Jews.

As they sought out others to aid in their struggle, they came to find a few Christian clergy who united ideologically with the Jews of the region. One of those special examples of Christian kindness was the attempt to help hide Jewish children from the Nazis.

News of the group spread across the region and inspired many. A monk who lived and served God near the village of Romygala one day found himself quietly reaching out to a man named Yitzhak.

Father Alexei recognized that Yitzhak dressed differently than the Nazi soldiers he saw every day. Hoping that he wasn't wrong, he hoped that Yitzhak just might be a member of a group that he had heard about in whispered tones throughout the town, the Jewish Partisan Group.

Father Alexi understood that the church he served was, at best, holding a tenuous peace with the Nazis that occupied the world around him. As much as he wanted to help the JPG, he was anxious to avoid attracting attention from the Lithuanian collaborationists who roamed the village's narrow streets.

Burning with a desire to help those he could, the monk took the risk of signaling Yitzhak to follow him into his small stone retreat. As they walked down the path, the monk said nothing, keeping his eyes on the roofs that sheltered them overhead in an attempt to determine if they were being watched.

Once they reached the end of the alley, he simply pointed at a pile of cans and wooden crates. The Jewish Partisan fighter was shocked when he looked closely to find a young boy huddled against a wall. The boy was covered by a monk's cloak, shaking from a combination of cold and hunger. As Yitzhak leaned down to inspect the frail, shivering child, he felt that the boy appeared to be approximately thirteen years old. He pulled a piece of bread from his pocket and handed to the boy.

Instead of welcoming the gift, the boy looked to Father Alexi for permission to take the bread.

Nodding yes, the monk knelt down next to Yitzhak as the boy grabbed the half of a loaf and began to chew rapidly. Yitzhak looked to the monk for an answer.

"I am truly amazed at what I'm seeing!"

Without prompting, Father Alexei told him the following harrowing tale.

"When it became evident that the Nazi Army would soon sweep over Central Europe, many Lithuanian civilians became turncoats. They joined collaborationist mobs and often reaped rewards by seizing Jews for the Nazis. One day, a young Jewish couple watched as a small mob encircled their family with the intention of herding them toward waiting trucks in the Romygala square. I watched as the husband bravely created a distraction while his wife raced down the street and into an alley."

The monk stopped for a minute as he played out the scene in his mind one more time.

Clutching at the rosary that hung from the side of his cassock, he went on, "Knowing where the alley led and seeing the bloodlust in the eye of the mob, I impulsively took an alternate route to the direction she was running. I met her at the end of the alley before the mob could learn where she had run. There, seeing my cloak and knowing of me as man of God, she handed the child to me. Without thinking, I took the boy and moved him under the length of my robes. Standing there, I watched as the mob pulled her away from my open arms while she was screaming for mercy. As they took her,

I could feel the boy clutching at my ankles, shaking with fear, but covered by the length of this very robe."

With that, the monk stood and finished his story. "For the past few months, I have been sneaking what I could out of this very alley. The boy lives in the shadows and in his own filth. But I cannot risk helping him any more than I already do."

Though initially indifferent, as the war continued, the Catholic Church had changed its policy in the region and was now doing what it could to save Jewish children. Yitzhak was kneeling before an example of the church's new policy. Father Alexei urged him to be very quiet and related his own reasons.

"I must be very prudent in what I do. I am a member of the Saint Aloysius Monastery up the mountain."

"Why are you down below, near the village?" Yitzhak queried.

"We're attempting to grow blueberries. I must spend time planting seedlings in the vacant lot that is adjacent to this area. When the boy was given to my charge, I couldn't take him up to the monastery, so he hides here and waits for my return every day. I have been afraid that one day, when I come, he won't be here. But enough of that, this is the only time of the day when the German troops are not on constant patrol. They trust me to plant and cultivate on my own." His voice grew urgent, "Please hurry and do something for this child!"

Unable to take the child out into the open, Yitzhak spoke honestly to the monk, "Father Alexei, I thank you for all you have done to save the child. I will try to accomplish this as quickly as I can. But I am not prepared to walk away with the boy right now. It would only get all three of us killed on the spot."

The monk replied with a note of urgency in his voice, "In good conscience, I cannot keep him much longer. There are collaborationists who would turn the child over to the Nazis, and that would damage my relations with the church. I can accept personal punishment, but I must consider other consequences."

Yitzhak put his hand on the monk's shoulder, only to find that the man was shaking under his thick brown robe.

"I can't take the boy with me in broad daylight…I know that this must be done quietly, for the safety of both you and the boy."

The monk looked at him with eyes that were growing red from holding back tears.

Placing his arm around the man's shoulders, Yitzhak spoke with comforting authority, "For the present, having him stay here is the best and maybe the only plan. A vehicle would be too easy to spot. I can see only one way out. We have to come at night and move through the darkness of the forest."

Hearing this plan that Yitzhak had laid out before him, the monk stopped shaking and summoned his courage to make sure that Yitzhak knew all the details.

"I am not even sure that he can walk as far as he needs in order to escape. He hasn't eaten anything but the scraps I have been able to bring him. Can someone carry the boy and still make this dangerous escape?"

A noise behind them startled both of them. They looked to the far corner in time to see a cat killing a rat that had made the mistake of running out into daylight. Yitzhak and the monk exchanged worried glances.

Thinking for a long moment, Yitzhak declared, "We have someone who could approach on horseback through the forest at night to reach this place. He would then carry the boy to our Partisan location. It would be dangerous, but it seems to be the only solution. Make sure that the boy understands what will happen one of these nights. I don't know how long it will take to put in action, but I promise it will happen. He must understand that and not panic when it does happen."

Father Alexei fervently said, "I will pray for this solution, my son."

Looking up and down the alley for any sign of a soldier or collaborationist, Yitzhak ran back to the main street without saying a word to either the boy or the monk. The boy grabbed at the monk, who spoke to him in clear and concise terms. The plan was in motion. With that, Father Alexi returned to his blueberry patch, and the boy returned to hiding behind the crates and under a coat.

It took one rapid overnight excursion for Yitzhak to reach the mountain refuge of the Jewish Partisan Group. He immediately told Jake and Shlomo the unusual story of the monk and the Jewish boy.

"Father Alexei urges us to take immediate action. Collaborationist Lithuanians roam the countryside and do not respect church property. I know it sounds like we would be in danger, but you should have seen the poor kid! We must make an immediate decision!"

After a very short discussion, the group reached the conclusion that the boy's life far outweighed any risk. They looked to Jake for his opinion, for they all knew his story. Jake's experience with horses made him the most logical member of the Partisan Group to rescue the child.

The minute he heard the story, Jake immediately began making plans to rescue the boy. He reviewed the horses available to them, which were hidden in the farmlands of the surrounding countryside.

Among the horses available, Jake had been impressed by a dark bay gelding.

"He probably is not the most fleet, but Yanni is an easy-to-control gelding. It is no doubt that he is strong enough to carry a boy over the distance we will have to travel. And strength and endurance are much more important than speed for this job," said Jake to the Partisans.

The group assembled the provisions they believed necessary for the rescue. They knew that Jake did not regard horses as beasts of burden. To him, they were partners accommodating each other and deserving of respect. Both he and the horse Yanni were fed well before leaving. The horse was brought over, and Jake made sure that he spent time before nightfall alone with the horse, rubbing him down with a brush and speaking to him in low tones about the mission at hand.

Yitzhak briefed Jake on the landscape and the trail that he had thrashed through the forest on his return from the monk's retreat. Mindful that winter was stubbornly giving way to spring and some patches of snow were clinging to the forest floor, Jake took off an hour before the sun was due to set.

Since cold winds blew over the land, Jake wisely covered Yanni with a blanket that would ultimately have multiple uses. They rode across the frozen grounds for hours. The horse seemed to know what was at stake and performed perfectly under Jake's control. It was deep into the night when the rescuers finally neared their mission. The horse and the Partisan warrior carefully walked their chosen path as they neared Father Alexei's retreat.

As they came upon the monk's blueberry patch, Jake dismounted and nuzzled Yanni, tethering him to a stake among the seedlings. Their journey had been timed to make sure that they arrive at Father Alexei's retreat during the middle of the night. He carried the horse's blanket with him to warm the boy and to help the horse establish familiarity with the boy, lest the child panic.

With good reason, Jake had never warmed to the idea of walking down an alley. In his life, nothing good had ever come from any time he had spent in one. Proceeding with stealth and caution, he moved slowly toward the end. There he found the group of boxes and a group of bottles and cans, just as Yitzhak had told him four hours earlier.

He looked down at the mess before him and whistled a low, nearly silent note. He then crouched down and poked at the pile with his finger. He watched as the top of the coat began to slowly slide down, revealing a head covered in brown hair that soon revealed tired, dark eyes and a small running nose.

Jake put his hand out, and an arm reached out from the coat to take it.

"Let's go, son," said Jake.

Taking the boy's hand, Jake pulled him to his feet. As part of his preparation Jake had brought a few small strips of chicken. He unwrapped the paper that held them and, one at a time, handed them to the boy. He watched as the boy nibbled at the first one and then looked up to meet Jake's eye, hoping for a second as he looked up to meet Jake's gaze.

Then the boy smiled and held the last one out for Jake to take. Shaking his head no, he watched as the boy took the paper from Jake's hand and wrapped the last one up. Jake then wrapped the blanket around the boy's shoulders and led him out of the alley.

Yanni was waiting exactly where Jake had left him. Jake lifted the boy to the horse's back. Taking the reins in his hand, he walked the horse and its new rider away while he carefully measured his steps away from the blueberry patch. The land was cold and hard. To ride at full gallop would scare the boy, and the sound of the horse in full flight might bring someone out to see what the commotion was.

Jake knew that their greatest danger was Lithuanian collaborationists who patrolled the streets and countryside at night looking for easy prey and big rewards. Jake moved quietly, first calming Yanni, then he wrapped the boy in the blanket that the horse recognized, and lifted him onto the horse's back.

Walking under the barest of moonlight, he led the boy and the horse over two long miles through the cold until they were close to the edge of the deep forest. It was only then that Jake felt he could mount the horse himself.

When he returned to the group that morning with the boy, the group celebrated their arrival. Jake the Horse Thief had accomplished a monumental task. Single-handedly, he had rescued the boy, avoided detection by the collaborationists, shielded the monk from discovery, and led the horse and boy by foot over many miles to the lair of the Jewish Partisan Group of Lithuania.

It was rare for Jake to sleep, but this time, he took a swig of Shlomo's bottle and walked over to a dark corner with the horse blanket around his shoulders. There he slept until the darkness had fallen.

# THE RABBI AND THE BOY

The Partisan group ranged over a far-and-wide territory in Lithuania. From the sandy shores of the Baltic to the mountainous region of Western Belarus, they did what they could to help Jews everywhere. They began to set up small, hidden stations in the caves and forest areas found around the Aukstazya Hills—which is located in the easternmost region of Lithuania. The region was the perfect place to hide fellow Jews from the pogroms of the Lithuanian turncoats and for the group to rest and make plans for the future during the bitter months that made up the cold, cold winters.

Never one to talk much, Jake had seen something inside the boy that touched a nerve. The successful rescue had given Jake a renewed sense of hope that all their work might someday pay off.

In the weeks that followed his rescue, the boy had regained his strength with alarming speed. Once he was comfortable speaking to them, he told them that his name was Victor. Soon, it was as if he had never been lost and abandoned in an alley. The boy had grown healthy so fast that he had soon reached a point where Jake was comfortable taking the boy out on horseback.

As the boy Victor grew back to full strength, the Partisan Group committed themselves to the rescue of a group of elderly Jews who were escaping from deadly turncoats in the City of Kovno.

Riding a wave of good luck that began with the rescue of the boy, the rescue went like clockwork.

Unsuspecting local collaborators were caught off their posts, while Shlomo, Yitzhak, and two others had slipped into the containment area of elderly Jews. They spirited away almost a dozen of the men and women held there, when Partisan member Nahum created a major diversion among the collaborationists by throwing a stink bomb in their kitchen and food supply compound.

Among the elderly men rescued, when the group returned to their safe area, was a rabbi. An introduction was made between him and the young boy named Victor. They connected immediately. It was as if the two were fated to meet each other in order to complement the other. The parental relationship fell together, as if by preordained providence.

Rabbi ben Israel bowed to the boy and said, "You are the kind of boy I'd wish my grandson to be."

The boy threw himself into the old man's arms and sobbed, "*Zayde, Zayde!*" (Grandpa, Grandpa!).

Within hours, the boy had become a doting grandson to the old man.

The rabbi would see to it that the boy completed the education needed in the matter of Jewish tradition and that he would lead Victor to become bar mitzvah. Jake had told Shlomo that the boy was very well educated and only needed to be pushed into that direction to possibly become a scholar or historian for his people.

The next day, Jake called the boy out to the yard and, using the very horse that had rescued him not a month earlier, patiently he went over the rules that he had taught him on how to treat a horse on the road. They reviewed the parts of a saddle and when to stop a horse before exhaustion could set in.

Jake removed a carrot from his pocket and handed it Victor. "Make friends with Yanni," he told the boy. He stood back and watched as the boy balanced the carrot flat on his hand and held it under the animal's nose.

Behind them, a wagon filled with the men and women who had been rescued by the Jewish Partisan Group not ten days earlier was pulling into the flatland in front of the small farmhouse. One of the Partisans who had rescued them from Kovno, a bright and affable man named Wallach, was sitting atop a small gelding dressed as a native Lithuanian. He nodded at Jake.

Looking over to Victor, who was still standing in front of Yanni, running his hand across the horse's neck, Jake said, "Go get your things. You are riding out with the rabbi and Wallach to take the others up across the border."

With that, Jake turned and walked back to the barn.

Victor had grown to understand the men who had rescued him from that dark and dangerous alley. Without a word, he ran inside to where he had been sleeping. There, across the small straw cot, he found a shirt and a pair of pants that would make him look as if he had been born and raised in Lithuania. Changing quickly, he ran out to join the wagon.

Approaching Wallach, he asked if he should sit with those in the wagon or with him on the back of the horse.

Pointing to where Yanni had been standing, Wallach told him, "Go grab Yanni. You are riding next to me. And hurry up, we are already running late."

Stunned at what he had just heard, Victor looked around the yard but saw no one. Moving to the horse, he wanted to yell out to all that he loved them. But he knew that everyone who lived in the compound was forbidden to raise their voice, lest it carry out over the countryside and catch the ear of a passing stranger.

Looking around quickly, just in case he saw anyone looking out, he got on top of the horse and rode to Wallach's side. "When you come back, tell Jake, 'Thank you!'"

"Neither one of us is coming back, boy. We are taking this load as far as we possibly can. If we are lucky and everything goes well, we will be standing on the edge of the Baltic Sea, waiting for a boat sometime in the next week."

From the corner of the barn, Shlomo and Jake stood next to each other. Shlomo slapped his friend on the back and said, "Sometimes it works, Jake. Sometimes it just works."

Jake said nothing. Inside his heart and mind, he sent a prayer out to the soul of Rabbi Vilnish. More than anything, he hoped that he was still alive to hear his wishes.

With that, Victor was able to join the group of *Jews Who Were Left Behind* on their way to a new life.

# THE UNSPOKEN LEADER

While Jake was ostensibly the hero of the outfit, it was Shlomo Levitz who was the leader of the Partisan Group. For decades, he and his family had lived and prospered as shopkeepers in Lithuania. He was the one who understood the region and could safely navigate around the obstacles that arose when crossing the country.

As they traveled, Shlomo' knowledge of the land was extremely valuable. When the Partisans elected to move the group across Lake Vistytis to safety, it was Shlomo who led the way. His grasp of the myriad ways to navigate the land and waterways aided them immeasurably. He planned their route in anticipation of the problems that their enemy would face when they would reach the lake's rocky shores.

Once there, the Germans who were pursuing them had trouble casting off from the jagged rocks.

As the attackers floundered behind them, Jake and Shlomo smiled, while the *Jews Who Were Left Behind* were led to safety.

Lithuania's shoreline on the Baltic is narrow and very sandy. In the early days of the war, there were a few very daring Jewish fisherman who risked bringing their boats close to shore in order to aid the process of smuggling Jews out of the country.

When the war continued, the cooperation with the Jewish fishermen had become too dangerous for them and their cargo. German Luftwaffe sank shipping that resulted in over a hundred thousand fatalities. As those statistic increased, each mission was weighed against the potential cost and damage. The *Baltic Coast became a death trap for a fishing boat, and another plan had to be devised.*

Constructing these plans required leadership, and the Lithuanian Jewish Partisan Group found its leaders in Jake the Horse Thief and the quiet but forcible Shlomo Levitz.

In the middle of a mission, Shlomo had no equal when it came to determining action that needed to be taken in precarious situations. As stories grew of Jake's reckless and thrilling stunts and exploits, they grew parallel to the wonder that men found in Shlomo's resolve and ingenuity.

Over the many decades that Shlomo's large family group had lived in Lithuania, they had established deep and loyal commercial relations with many of their customers and clients. When the Communist Government took over in 1940, those relationships fell apart. They had only grown worse when the following year the Nazis had easily supplanted the Russians.

In the few years that preceded this maelstrom of change, many senior members of the Levitz clan had recognized the perils they would be facing, as the rumors of invasion and even war came across the continent.

They chose to flee to other European states, and some of them settled in England. Shlomo had a chance to leave. Instead, he elected to stay behind with a small contingent of young Lithuanian Jews that stayed and wanted to protect Jewish institutions. They also wanted to make sure that the very old and the very poor among their compatriots were cared for and rescued.

The driving obsession for this group of Jews who stayed behind was to find liberty after the war ended. They longed to live in a Jewish friendly state. Many among them saw the land of Israel at the end of that dream.

Though raised elsewhere and under different circumstance, Jake also believed in a homeland. But he had a secret ambition that drove him even harder. Despite what he had been told over the years, despite what he had seen over the years, it was his prayer that he would find Leah.

With each mission, with each person he helped find freedom, this dream became less and less real, as the maelstrom of trouble escalated. The realities of a mission that never seemed to have an end in sight hung over his head, preventing him from experiencing much joy during the Lithuanian Jews' relentless campaign for freedom.

# MARISSA

Across the years of the war, membership in the group rose and fell as it attracted and lost those who stood with Jake and Shlomo. From the start of their battle, their existence had been built on the most precarious of standards. Each man and woman involved knew and accepted that at any moment, they could be facing a violent death...

Every one of them lived from day to day, knowing that the person who was standing next to them could die tomorrow. It was only natural that in a group of young men and women living together without pause, there would be frequent physical attractions between the sexes.

Among the fighters who joined them was an unusual young woman named Marissa, who served as valiantly as any man in the group. She had grown muscular from carrying heavy arms and running long miles without a stop. This addition to her previously scrawny physique had only enhanced her naturally striking, dark, and swarthy beauty.

In her first few weeks with the group, little was known about Marissa. She kept to herself. Outside of one or two self-styled Lotharios in the group, each of whom she put in their place with no problem, the others left her alone.

This was the way of the group. They respected each other. With death at every corner, those with experience knew to not grow to close to anyone for too long time. Later, they might have to leave them behind as they lay dead, or captured, in some better-forgotten place.

One thing was never questioned by virtue of Marissa's volunteer status. Everyone understood that she was dedicated to the cause of the group. Even as a new member, Marissa was unusually silent and uncommunicative. This continued until one night when the group found themselves unable to stop a line of train cars that was crowded with humans. Every member who watched the train pull out that night knew that it could be headed for Poland and the crematoria of Auschwitz.

While she watched the train speed along toward its fatal destination, Marissa had begun to sob quietly to herself. As unforgiving as he normally was, Shlomo probed the young woman about her emotional reaction at that moment.

"You must tell me what is bothering you, and you must spit it out now!" Shlomo stared at Marissa with unwavering eyes. When there was no immediate response, he continued, "One weak link endangers all of us!"

"One month before I joined the group, I saw my parents herded into a car headed for Poland, just like the one that just passed us, I couldn't control myself…It won't happen again." Marissa wiped away a tear and bowed her head.

Shlomo embraced the young woman and knew that she would be a valorous member of the group dedicated to aiding the *Jews Who Were Left Behind*.

Jake's reaction to the new member of the group was different. He didn't doubt that she was trustworthy. He knew that anyone who decided to take part in their covert and dangerous activities could only be one of two types.

The first type was devoted to the idea that helping other Jews was not an option but an obligation.

The second type was a person who had ulterior motives, something along the lines of infiltration and betrayal.

To Jake, anyone who had such action in the back of their mind would ultimately betray their motives quickly. For both he and Shlomo kept a close watch on even the most loyal. To fool one of them was possible. To fool them both was nearly impossible.

A naturally guarded man, Jake couldn't deny that he did find the woman attractive. The fact that she was beautiful was a matter of course. What drove Jake toward her was something else. He quickly realized that her commitment to the cause was nearly as great as his. She was a creature he had never envisioned: the perfect combination of beauty, skill, and loyalty. He saw her as a comrade in arms.

Soon they took off on patrols together. Then they started to share meals and finally, a bed. In the highly volatile atmosphere of the Partisan Group, this was not unusual. The understanding that almost any day was a gift and that almost any hour could be someone's last resulted in relations that were all-consuming in their physical intensity.

There were no moments for poetic words or adoring sighs between two lovers, with the ghost of death in the next bunk.

After being in Marissa's arms, Jake asked himself, "How much does this love that we've found so quickly mean to me?" In the quietest of their shared moments, he would think, *What will it mean when the war is over?*

The closeness they developed as a couple was only enhanced by the fact that they shared so many missions together. The two activities, their private shared moments and the thrilling escapades of their group, fed off of each other. The adrenaline found in their missions filled their lovemaking with energy and a sense of abandon. In turn, the closeness of their physical relationship heightened their natural sensibilities when they went out on missions.

Nothing prevented them from participating on missions that were extremely dangerous and fraught with fatalities. One night, Marissa and Jake led a small group in the rescue of three elderly Jews who were in jeopardy in the large City of Kaunas.

The outburst of anti-Semitism that had occurred in the city square of Kaunas that day was just one small occurrence in the Holocaust of Lithuanian Jews. During this time, the genocide rate of Jews in Lithuania was 95 percent to 97 percent. This inconceivably high number was one of the highest in Europe. Much of this was primarily due to the widespread collaboration of non-Jewish Lithuanians with German authorities.

Nazi propaganda of the time had been designed to blame the Jews for the activity of the Soviet regime before 1941. Misinformation, such as this, was only one of the reasons why so many Lithuanians had decided to work with the Germans toward the liquidation of the Jews. With the entire country of Lithuania under the command of the German Officer Adrian von Renteln, the people became ruthless in their pursuit of Jews. In his time, the Vilna ghetto was liquidated, and Kaunas was turned into a concentration camp.

The paramilitary operation that had been planned by Jake, Marissa, and Shlomo in order to rescue the elderly of Kaunas was complicated, even by their standards. The main problem was that the rescue required rapid movement through an area sympathetic to the collaborationists. This time spent in the city was one of the most dangerous missions that the group had ever undertaken. Through meticulous attention to detail and near-flawless teamwork, they located the three elderly Jews and, through subterfuge and distraction, managed to get them to the outskirts of town.

It became necessary for the rescuers to ford a small stream that feeds into the Niemen River. As they aided the three elderly men, shots rang out from a small wooded area about two hundred meters away. When rifle shots shook the air, the group was forced to scatter.

Each member of the Partisan Group took charge of one of the people they had rescued. The others went their separate ways.

When they reached a safe house near Jarbarkas, they discovered that Marissa and her charge were missing. When they reviewed the details of that hard-fought night, one of the group told his partners that he heard a body hit the water during the escape and heard a cry, "That's for Julius!"

The news of Marissa's loss was met with deep sadness by the group. Her killers had struck fast and in their retreat had moved quickly. With each member of the group preoccupied with their own escape from Nazi soldiers, there had been no time to look for clues as to where she may have fallen or who had made the strange cry. Jake, with much bitterness, knew of its origins.

There was just as much a chance that she had been captured. Every single member of the group knew what was at stake for Marissa. When a male member of the group was captured, he was summarily executed on the spot. The fate of a female companion was infinitely worse. Typically, the collaborationist Lithuanians raped females, tortured them, and then turned them over to Nazi SS officers for rewards. During the war, few women were safe from this horror.

With heads that ached with remorse, each of the rescuers slowly became resigned to the idea that Marissa would never be heard from again. While Jake knew the realities of their battles in this war, he found it nearly impossible to accept the loss of Marissa. Over the next few days, he became inconsolable. He stopped speaking to anyone—even Shlomo.

All he could think was, *Once more, I've lost the woman I've loved. First, Leah, and now, I've lost Marissa!*

Struggling to contain his tears and feelings of guilt, he obsessed over what had gone wrong that night. When that subject exhausted itself, he continued to think of what had happened in his life.

Jake understood that so much of what he felt responsible for was beyond his control. But the nagging feelings of loss and failure never stopped.

"Will women I love be doomed? Should I never love a woman?" with his depression deepening, Jake drew within himself.

Those who knew him at this time whispered of their fears. They watched him become even more reckless on missions. It was as if he had developed a death wish. It ultimately took Shlomo, a dark night in the forest, and a bottle of wine for Jake to make even a partial return to his former self.

"You have to snap out of it! Our group needs your leadership!" Shlomo muttered in Jake's ear.

The two old friends then shared a crushing hug

Some felt that he had become meaner, colder, after Marissa's loss. They were wrong, for her presence in his life had made him warmer and more open to life. His ever-present shell became harder to penetrate. Those he chose to let in found a man who loved life and was happy to have found so much love in his short time on earth.

# THE GYPSY AND THE GAON OF VILNA

"Do we really know what is going on in the world? Do we know what in the hell is happening to our world?"

These questions bothered Shlomo as he dined with the Partisan Group one day in their early years.

"What in the hell is bothering you, Shlomo?" asked Simon

"I can best answer you by reading this article in the *Minsk Daily News*," Shlomo answered. "Here it is."

From the very beginning, the National Socialists (Nazi Party) has made the idea of ethnic purity part of their campaign. The theories and practices of eugenics are just part of their drive to "purify the Germanic State."

Using brutal campaigns of intimidation, sterilization, and most certainly, murder, the Nazis have taken it upon themselves to rid their country and the world of those they considered to be lesser people. Among the members of this list are the mentally ill, the disabled, the handicapped, the homosexuals, the physically sick, and essentially, anyone they deemed to be non-Aryan. This last category includes Jews, Blacks, and Roma. Many today know the Roma as Gypsies.

As early as 1933, the German government had begun registering the Roma as being genealogically unfit. One survey that the German government had conducted determined that Roma blood was less than 10 percent German. This has led to a program to have all Romas register with the German State.

The adaptation of eugenic theories was so frightening that many families and individuals who considered themselves to be classed as Roma ran to neighboring countries, such as Byelorussia and Lithuania, in order to find refuge and safety.

Two years after the command for Romas to register had gone forth, a Jewish farmer who lived near the City of Kovno decided to clean out the second floor loft of his barn. There, hidden in the corner, he found a young girl shaking under a large pile of old hay. From her condition, he could see that she hadn't been there long, for she was still wet and cold. Shivering uncontrollably, constantly pulling her thin, threadbare shawl over her shoulders, she was doing her best to stay warm.

The frightened young girl looked up at Herman Mermel. As she did, he saw dark-brown eyes that certainly held fear but above all revealed a deep well of hidden resolve. Caught off guard and nervous at finding such a young girl on his property, Mermel began firing a good number of questions at her in such a fast manner that she had no chance to reply.

As he rattled away, the girl began to push herself as deep as she possibly could into the corner. Pulling her shawl close and covering herself with bits of hay as she did, the girl never let herself lose eye contact with him. If he had taken a second to look at her, instead of screaming questions, he would have seen a face wracked by fear and hunger atop a body worn thin from starvation and longing.

He practically spit out each question as he spoke, "Why are you in my barn? Where did you come from? Have you been sent by them?"

Leaning against the wall next to him, there was a three-pronged pitchfork. Without breaking from the gaze of the terrified girl,

Mermel reached over and grabbed it. As he went on yelling, he pointed it straight at her.

Questions and statements, such as, "Is there anyone else up here with you? If there are, they need to come out now!" came out as a vicious threat. "I will run her through!" he promised as he looked to his left and right, fully expecting to see others in her company.

Seeing that no one had emerged, he went back to the girl, "Where are your parents? How much have you…"

The farmer was unable to finish his last question, for the girl cowering before him had finally summoned the strength to speak.

"Please, sir, help me, I'm cold…" she blurted out before tears overwhelmed her ability to speak. Her chest began to heave as she gasped for air.

Taken aback by her sudden outburst, Herman took a step backward. Dropping the pitchfork to his side, he watched in confusion as she struggled to control her sobbing.

Between breaths, she tried to complete a sentence, "I…haven't…eat…en in…so…" Exhausted by the effort, she covered her face and continued crying into the palms of her hands.

Without as much as another word, Herman leaned the pitchfork back into position against the wall. Removing his coat, he knelt down beside her, gently placing it over her shoulders. Not sure what to do next, he started to brush away the loose hay from her shoulders. Then Mermel began to pick at strands that were loosely sticking out from her hair.

Looking into her eyes and at a loss for what to do next, Herman Mermel began to hug the girl. Not in any deeply personal way, just enough that she would know that he was there.

For a few minutes, she clung to his shoulder, just long enough for the shaking to stop. Then she started to pull away.

Looking up to him, she said nothing.

# JAKE THE HORSE THIEF

In direct contrast to the fierce explosion he had shown her a few minutes earlier, he spoke quietly, "I am going to have you come into the house. Can you walk down the ladder?"

She shook her head yes and started to stand.

Still on his knees, he moved toward the ladder, assuming that he should go first. That way, he could catch her if she fell. As he placed his foot on the first step, he looked over to where she was still sitting. When she stood, he could see that she wasn't more than five feet tall. Bone-thin, her sharply detailed face looked as if it had come out of an old German woodcutting. Her feet were bruised, and the left one was bleeding from a gash along the side.

He made his way down the ladder and waited for her at the bottom. She descended slowly, as if she was worried that he would try something cruel as she approached him. Herman backed up so that she could land on the floor under her own power.

As she stood before him, she seemed at a loss for what to do.

He extended his left arm and told her, "This way."

As quiet as the moment on the second floor of the barn was, Herman Mermel did not consider himself a fool. He knew full well that he needed to be wary of any stranger, no matter how small and cold they were.

In deference to her damaged foot, she walked past him with a limp.

Herman took a step to her side and told her, "I am going to put my hand around your waist. It's obvious you need some medical attention."

She said nothing. As he took her by her side, she placed her head against his arm. Together they walked across the back of his farm to the large, bare, well-kept house he apparently shared with no one.

Sitting her down at the kitchen table, Herman made tea and then put a plate of biscuits in front of her.

"I have some soup I will heat up. I don't recommend that you eat too fast," he told her kindly. "Once someone has been starving, you must respect the stomach. It has its own rules when it has been mistreated. You can't just pile food in."

His unexpected guest sat there, sipping the tea, staring at the biscuits as she did.

With his back to the table, Herman spoke as he opened the iron door on the side of the stove. Lighting a match, he asked, "Now tell me all about how you found yourself in my barn."

The girl hesitated and then began to eat a biscuit. She kept her hands folded around the cup, hoping that the warmth would spread to the rest of her body. While she sat eating, Herman poked around at the wood inside the stove, looking to where she sat. In a minute, the fire caught on, and he moved a cooking pot to the top of the heater. Opening a container, he poured what remained of last night's soup into the pot.

Once she had taken a few mouthfuls of biscuit, washing them down with tea, the tremulous little girl began to recover her bearings.

"Thank you so very much," she said with deep sincerity. "I don't think I could have lived much longer!"

Putting her hand out to Herman for him to shake, she went on, "My name is Georgina Lupescu, and I am a Roma, you probably call us Gypsies in this land."

Taking her hand, Herman then put a bowl and a spoon before her. Sitting down in a chair near her, he told her, "Indeed, we do call your people Gypsies."

Still eating the biscuits, Georgina spoke quickly and with more than a hint of awareness of who she was.

"But have no fear! I know many think of us as thieves, but don't worry, I won't steal from you!"

Mermel nodded, and she went on.

She told him, "My story is a long and desperate one."

He told her, "My day is a long and a boring one. Speak freely, please."

With crumbs falling from the side of her mouth, she stared at her host as if she was trying to figure out a puzzle. Georgina decided it would be best to start speaking from her life's beginning.

"At the end of the last century, 1899, my people were subjected to a central registry practice in Germany, that beautiful land that I just ran from. Later, after the registry took effect, they began a police action against Roma in Munich. The people in charge instituted harsh conditions against our people that clearly predate the policies that the Nazis are now enforcing in strictest detail."

The soup seemed to have a calming effect on her, for she began to slow down as she spoke, "People who practiced our lifestyle were labeled Gypsies, and as the Nazis gained power, the persecution of my people began increasing. The government would quote studies that they alone had made. The Romas were singled out. They said that 90 percent of our people were judged to be of mixed blood, and we, as a whole, were declared to be a danger to the German people."

Georgina put her spoon down and looked Herman Mermel straight in the eye. As she continued her story, she grew excited.

"Those statistics they quoted led to a program that demanded the forced sterilization of Roma women. You can understand why I wanted none of that! I had to escape! And escape I did!"

She hit the table with a small fist, and then, as embarrassment brought a rush of red to her cheeks, she caught herself. Watching for a reaction from Herman, she paused for a second.

Seeing none, she sat back and crossed her arms. It was then that he realized that she was still shaking.

Rising from his chair, he went into the other room and returned with a blanket. Wrapping it around her shoulders, he sat down and nodded for her to continue.

She sat back down and went on with her story. As she spoke, she rubbed her hands together under the blanket. The desperation that he had seen in the girl in the barn was now replaced by determination fed by a charming, natural type of confidence as she resumed her story.

"Practicing a medical experiment on my body would be the worst kind of death that I could imagine. I could not concern myself with any concept of morality! They had already taken me from the streets where I worked and forced me into one of their hospitals. I knew that either sterilization or death lay ahead of me. They called it a hospital, but in fact, it was a compound surrounded by barbed wire. From the brick rooms that dotted the grounds, I could hear the screams of the other girls they had taken before me. It was then that I decided to take desperate measures."

She waited as if she expected to be told to carry on. Herman found no reason to interrupt the girl and said nothing. He did point to the bowl before her and motioned with his hands that she should finish her soup while she continued.

Then, in a strong voice, Georgina Lupescu told Herman Mermel what remained of her story.

"I had only one weapon to use in an attempt to save myself… Ironically, it was the thing they were trying to penalize me for having. That was my female body. I already knew that men and boys looked at me with desire in their minds. With that in mind, I planned on using their lust as an asset. You are kind, but you are a man, and I do know what you are thinking."

Looking right into his eyes, she took a sip of her tea and set the cup back down.

Now, it was his turn to blush, for she had hit a nerve. As he sat there, listening to this girl tell her story, he could see that she was coming back to life in front of him. Just to have the company—

someone smart, someone who could tell a good story, no matter how bad it was—thrilled him.

Herman Mermel was, indeed, feeling pangs of loneliness. His wife and their son had left for Switzerland. From there, it was hoped that some small part of the Mermel fortune could help them gain passage to America. There was a scourge coming in from Germany, and he wanted to keep his family from having to face it. The plan was for him to join them, but obligations to the farm and others in the family had kept him at home.

While the girl was clearly in pain and troubled, he was thankful that she had appeared in his life. For she was the one thing that he craved in his life—company.

There was a measure of intuition in the girl. Sensing Herman's embarrassment about what she had said about men, Georgina did not push the point she had made about men. Still, her anger at what she had faced did not disappear.

Holding that note of outrage in her voice as she spoke, she continued, "If I had to sell my body to avoid what Roma women were experiencing at the hands of the German scum, I would. Gypsy women pride themselves on their virginity. It is meant for only marriage, but I was not going to *die*!"

Her eyes were now filled with excitement, as if the choice that she faced was there in front of her once again—that this outrage needed to be addressed that very minute. A combination of anger, calculation, and fear began to move through her bones with every word she spoke.

"One of the young Germans guarding our compound had lost no opportunity in trying to get my attention. He winked and smirked at me as I walked past him. But he didn't need to be so obvious, for his intentions were clear." She waved her hand as if dismissing a waiter and said, "Phffft…"

"Knowing exactly what he held in his heart, I feigned illness, slumping to the ground right where he was standing. When this young, cocky know-it-all bent to assist me, I whispered to him, 'Meet me tonight beyond the latrine, and then we can have a party.' As I rose, I made sure to brush against his crotch. Smiling at me as he so gallantly helped me from the ground, I heard him whisper, 'Okay, after lights-out.'"

She stopped and watched Herman for a reaction to her bold choice of plan. He conveyed neither judgement nor acceptance. Picking up where she had left off, she had started shaking at the memory of it—which, ironically, was in direct contradiction to what she was saying.

"With that, I made a great effort to calm my nerves. My life was at risk from both sides, for if I couldn't follow through on my plan, I would most definitely have to follow through on his. The hours passed slowly that day as I awaited nightfall. Slipping from my bunk, I ran in my nightclothes to the appointed meeting place. I had put some regular civilian clothes—nothing that could identify me as Roma—in a small bag and, having made sure to arrive before he did, dropped it on the side of the building.

"In no time, Fritz unlocked the door, and together we stepped into the latrine area. I put my finger to my lips and smiled in an effort to quiet him. Up close, I could see that he was just a boy—taller and broader in the shoulders, yes, not still much older than me. Looking straight at him, I wrapped my arms about him and pulled very close. He began to slowly push his arousal against the nightshirt they had given me.

"Whispering in his ear, I said, 'Let's have a real party!' After a kiss on his cheek, I opened the latrine door and pulled the bag into the small building. I opened it in front of him, and he stepped back as if he was going to hit me. I smiled and said, 'Caution, lover, look what I have brought for us.' With that, I took a small bottle of wine from my bag. He was surprised, but the sudden smile on his face betrayed his stupidity."

She stopped to draw a breath. As he had since the beginning of her tale, Herman said nothing. He sat motionless.

Leaning in, she drew the blanket tightly around her as she spoke in a hushed tone, "As I undid the cork, I let his hands wander over my body." She continued to shake as she recalled the moment. "It felt as if a cold ghost was touching me. I then encouraged him to have a drink of Roma Rum.

"'Let us have a sip of my German bear before we move on. I like the mood to be set by a good stiff drink.' He took one of his hands off my behind and grabbed the bottle. I watched him raise the bottle to his lips and throw his head back as he drank. I felt his other arm pull me closer to him while he guzzled what he could from the bottle. Through the thin cloth of my nightshirt, it was obvious that he was ready for me. I felt panic in my heart, for if my plan failed, he was going to take what he wanted from me.

"When he pulled the bottle away, he handed it to me and said, 'One for you now, my Gypsy whore!'

"As I put the bottle to my lips, I whispered, 'Kiss my neck you beautiful, beautiful man.' I did, indeed, raise the bottle, but I pursed my lips tightly, not allowing a drop to pass over them. For the bottle had been effectively laced with something that I knew would knock him out in twenty seconds. You see, my mother, before she had been taken, had taught her daughter the secrets of herbs and potions. A few ground-up mushrooms and a few leaves that I had in my pocket when they had taken me and…"

She snapped her fingers and then smiled as she went on.

"His arousal died first. Then in seconds, his body slipped through my arms. I placed the bottle by his side so when he would be discovered, it would look as though he had been drinking. Changing into the civilian clothes, I opened the door slowly. And yes," she said defensively, "I did check his wallet for money. Anyone would do that! Such an activity is not exclusive to a Gypsy. I was escaping certain death, and money always helps."

He used her defensiveness as a reason to interrupt her. "I said nothing, Georgina. You are putting thoughts in my head," said Herman. Offering her a smile of his own, he added, "I hope you took his gun as well."

"Don't think I didn't consider it! But if his gun was gone, the authorities would know that it was a robbery and look for an escaped prisoner. The compound would go on alert, and cars and trucks would be sent to look for me. If I leave the gun, he is a drunk."

Herman said nothing, but his smile stayed.

She went on, "I prayed that he would not die but would sleep until the dawn. Once changed, I quickly fled into the surrounding land, making it finally to the nearby streets of a poor German neighborhood that was two miles distant!"

Her body was now trembling as hard as it had fifteen minutes ago, when he had found her. To him, it was clear that regardless of her bravado, the Gypsy girl was on the brink of collapse.

Concerned, Herman pointed to another room and said, "I have a cot for guests, please take some time and rest. No one will discover you in my house."

Georgina shook her head no. Reaching for the tea that was still on the table, she picked up the cup and wrapped her hands around it. Taking a sip, he could see that she was making an effort to calm herself. After a pause, the young woman continued her story.

"On the outskirts of that town, I spotted a large farm wagon heading north. The farmer had paused by the side of the road so he could pee. I jumped into the back and pulled as much hay over me as I could, lying there quietly until I felt the wagon move. We drove for what seemed like hours. I had no idea in what direction or even where the sun was in the sky, for I did not want to poke my head above the blanket I had made.

"Finally, I could feel the wagon hesitate near what I assumed was a crossroad. As it turned, I snuck a peak and saw that we were now heading next to a heavily wooded area. Without a noise, much less a 'thank you for the ride,' I jumped off, scurried into the woods, and hid until it was absolute darkness. With the cover of night, I started walking slowly, holding close enough to the road that others couldn't see me but I could see what was coming.

"I was too afraid to even consider stopping for sleep. I wanted to use all the energy I had to get as far away from Germany as possible. After about two hours of walking, I finally saw the familiar markings of a Roma family wagon. From where I was, I kept up with them as best I could, watching every movement they made. Thankfully, they eventually stopped for a bathroom stop. Tired from it all and knowing that I should be safe, I took a chance that they would realize that I was one of them. Speaking to them in the right accent and with the right words, they knew that despite my unfamiliar clothes, I was Roma.

"They offered me a seat. They told me that they were fleeing from what the Germans were doing to our people and had decided to travel through the Pripet Marshes to reach the Ukraine. They continued on a route that they were traveling through darkness."

Georgina paused, set her cup down, and took a breath.

"Another cup, Georgina?" asked Herman.

"No, sir." She gathered herself, and then, her energy almost completely exhausted, finished her unbelievable story.

"Not wanting to burden them, I told them that I felt I should continue on my own. It was light, and they had let me sleep in the back of the wagon for a few hours, so I was ready to continue. The father asked me to stay with them, but I declined. With that, he pulled a piece of paper from his pocket and showed me on a small hand-drawn map that if I went straight through the forest that we were riding parallel to, with his instructions, I could be across the border in a few days. He knew that, burdened with the cart and their children, a good week or maybe more of travel lay in front of them."

"The placement of the moon in the sky and few stars that my father had taught me before they had taken him…" she began to choke up at the mention of her father. Her shoulders shook, and tears filled her eyes. Despite the fact that she had declined his offer to refill her cup just minutes earlier, Herman picked it up and turned his back to face the stove. He fiddled with the teakettle for about a minute so that she could have a minute to collect herself.

She was talking again before he had set the cup on the table and returned to his seat.

"I decided that the nearby forest area would be a place to get away from Gypsy life! For after all I had been through, I didn't want to risk capture by being found in a wagon filled with Roma. Selfish as it sounds, I didn't want to abandon those who had been good to me. I thanked my fellow Romas and gave them a few coins that I had taken from Fritz, the German guard!

"I then traveled onward alone but free. I found strength in the hope that I had distanced myself from the filthy Germans. I soon stopped to rest in a wooded area. After only a few hours, I awoke and went on. As I traveled, I stayed close to the forest. When I needed to, I stole food from the orchards of farmers on a road that traveled eastward. I slept for only two nights out of four, as I walked on endlessly.

"The final result of it is that I now sit before you, broken, bleeding, cold, and tired. All I can offer you in return for your kindness is that I will help you with chores or what I can within reason."

Taking the last bucket from the stove and pouring it, he said, "Your feet may be infected. It is important that you wash them and inspect them before you fall asleep. The cot in the other room will afford you some privacy."

He handed her a towel that he had pulled from a shelf above the sink. "Call me when you are done. I will show you where you can rest."

"No," she said. "Stay and talk to keep me awake as I clean. Tell me your name, and now you must tell me your story because I have told you mine. The world stays balanced when people share."

He sat and began speaking in a strong voice, "My name is Herman Mermel. You are now in Lithuania, and it is 1935. This is a proud Jewish household, and it exists in a proud democratic state! You will be safe in this house."

Sadly, five years later, these proud words would prove to be a false prophecy. In that time, restrictions on travel would keep Herman on his farm for far longer than he had hoped. As the power of his contacts dwindled and the family fortune became tied up in currencies in Switzerland, his own situation became troublesome. It became clear that his wife and child had deserted him.

Myra (his wife) had written to him ten days after she arrived in New York City:

> I have family that is financially very capable here in New York. My parents are worried about conditions in Europe and believed it was best that I and our son had to leave Lithuania. Furthermore, I do not want to face a future as a farmer's wife in Kovno. I have cleaned out our joint bank account. Good luck to you.

It was signed, "Myra."

The day after she had been found quaking in the barn of the Mermel family, Georgina Lupescu awoke from a deep sleep to find clean clothes laid out on a table next to her.

Changing into them, she began to call out, "Herman, Herman...?"

Finding no one answering her call, she looked out a window and saw that Herman was working with a farmhand, rebuilding a fence. She watched as he moved the wood in place and held it firmly as his helper tied off the end and then nailed the long board to the post. For minutes she stood there, looking longingly out the window and wondering if she would ever be able to settle down in one place. So deep were her ties to an itinerant lifestyle that she doubted it would ever happen.

Eventually, she sat down in a chair next to her bed. Looking to her left, she found a book of stories that had once belonged to the child of the house. She had never heard of the Brothers Grimm, but after reading one or two of them, she could see how these tales were as much part of her Gypsy upbringing as they would be a Lithuanian's.

In time Herman came into the house and discovered that she was awake. After asking her if she slept well, he said, "I am going to fix lunch. Maybe now is the time to tell you my story."

As they ate, he told her of how his wife and son had slipped across the border and onto a boat bound for America. His concern for them was apparent, as he grew distressed when he told her that it had been over three months since they had left.

"So great was my worry about what is happening next door in Germany that I felt drastic measures were needed. As demonstrated by your own harrowing tale, the rumors cannot be that far removed from the truth."

The lunch turned to evening as both of them spoke at length. Herman told of his family's history—how his grandfather had taken a single small farm and, with the help of his sons, had made it into the big business the family enjoyed today.

"When I was a young man, I had a facility for shopkeeping. Working at the small shop that my father had started in town, I built it up into a small run of other shops, which are now located in several surrounding cities. That profit, I converted into investments that my father and grandfather had begun in the Netherlands. Today I am afraid that if I stop working, it will all disappear, just as my family has. How can we know what the Germans or Russians will do next?"

She told him of how her father had been taken from her in the town square of Augsburg, a city they were simply passing through on their way to a better land.

Herman, Georgina, and the farmhand finished building the fence.

By the end of the first week together, the two had become lovers. She loved that he told her stories and took care of her. He loved that she had the energy of three women. In the next few years, the farm achieved more success than it had ever seen under his father's ownership. Whatever he showed her, he only had to show her once. The twelve-year age difference meant little to either one of them, for they truly enjoyed each other's company.

Her mind was active, and she quickly learned the ceremonies of the Jewish faith. Herman, in turn, began to appreciate Roma lifestyles. Those who objected to their living together were initially ignored and then squelched when it was seen that the two honestly belonged together.

The question she had once asked herself about being able to stay in one place for more than a short while had been answered. It would be no problem for her, if she was allowed to be with someone as interesting as Herman Mermel.

As he saw the vehicles of German occupation approaching, Herman discovered that their estate had been singled out as desirable by a jealous neighbor. He had been betrayed by a collaborate Lithuanian local, who was doing so in order to save their own farm. Recently, he had heard of people being given rewards for helping

Germans find wealthy Jews. With his faith in the inherit goodness inside all men, he had dismissed them as fiction, but to no avail.

In the desperate final minutes of his forced departure, Herman pulled Georgina close and told her, "Hide in the place I've excavated in the barn, and there you will be safe until I return!"

With a choked voice, Herman told his Gypsy companion, "When a moment of safety comes, look in the corner of the space. I've hidden a very valuable box for you to protect with your life! We cannot let it burn!"

Herman kissed Georgina and gave her one final ray of hope as he pushed her toward the back door. "I will fight with all my life to return to you. Right now, the Nazis are ready to set fire to the house, and you must hide as soon as you can. They won't damage the barn, for they will want the foodstuffs." Slipping a handful of gold coins into the pocket of her apron, he said, "Money is a tool for good."

With that, he pushed her out of the very same backyard that, five years earlier, had provided a doorway to her freedom. Now it served as her exit from one life and into another. As she ran to the barn, she could hear the trucks and cars pulling up. The smell of diesel fuel was now heavy in the air.

With not a second to spare, she made it to the large barn door. Pulling it behind her, she looked back through a crack to the outside world. There she saw a dozen six-wheeled trucks tearing up the path that Herman had so carefully lined with brick two years earlier.

Running to a corner, she dug into a large pile of hay and looked for a small nick in the wood of the floor. It took a second, but she found it. Pulling a screwdriver from her pocket, she dug it into the crack and pulled with all her might.

A large, flat segment of the floor that looked to run perfectly along the cracks in the wood opened to reveal a deep pit. This is where she would lay until she was sure that the Germans had left. Slipping inside, she gathered fallen hay from around the edges and placed it over the edge. Then she let the heavy floorboards fall over her.

While the woman he had grown to love lay in the cold ground, shivering, just as she had when she first met him, Herman Mermel was standing on the porch of his house with his hands up. He was awaiting arrest.

Without moving, he watched as the trucks pulled onto his estate. Leading the way was a group of German soldiers who had pulled up to his porch in a Type 82 Bucket Car.

With the car sputtering loudly, the driver kept his hands on the wheel and looked Herman Mermel straight in the eyes while the other two soldiers who were riding with him raised their rifles.

No shots were fired, but he could feel the desire to pull the trigger in the way that they looked at him.

As he stood there, fully conscious of the display of power before him, he could only worry about what would become of Georgina. A German officer pulled up in a second car and came to a stop directly in front of Herman.

Standing behind the passenger side of the car, he looked at Herman and spit on the ground. Next he told his soldiers to arrest the "Jewish rat" for being an enemy of the German people. His next order caught Herman off guard. It was that they were to set the place afire.

Yelling over all the noise of the trucks, the soldier who was driving the car asked, "What about the barn?"

"Forget the barn. Burn it as well," came the brief reply. The officer then swatted at the side of his car with his leather crop, and he fell back into his seat as the car raced away.

In seconds, two of the soldiers jumped from their car and onto the front porch. Grabbing Herman by his arms, they threw him to the ground. He saw one soldier raise the butt of his rifle, head high, and start to bring it down on his head.

In the last seconds of consciousness, he thought of Georgina shivering in her blanket, the very first day he had met her.

Torches appeared from nowhere, and as the flames rose around the estate that his family had owned for over fifty years, Herman Mermel became another one of the *Jews Who Were Left Behind*.

Just one of the many who would be so difficult to find after World War II.

# THE GYPSY IN THE BARN

Inside the barn, Georgina lay shaking below the wooden floor. The years had made her strong, but the insanity found in the idea that someone could drive up to your house and take it all while killing you made no sense to her.

Sheer terror had driven the ability to cry from her body. For minutes, she lay as quiet as she could. With her right hand, she felt for the edges of the box, about which Herman had told her. She had never heard him speak of this previously. Questions raced through her mind.

Then she smelled smoke. At first, she assumed that it was just the main house that was on fire. As the heat of the floorboards above her rose, she thought, *Herman had been wrong! The Germans are burning the barn!*

Then a second thought came to her, *Or maybe he had just lied to me so the Germans couldn't find me. He didn't want me taken away to the labor camps that had been written about in all the newspapers.*

Concentrating as hard as she could, she listened for the sound of footsteps racing through the barn. All she could hear was the noise of engines and men laughing and screaming. In a minute, it had all disappeared in the distance, but the heat from the fire was now becoming unbearable.

Now she had to decide whether to lie there and die of suffocation as the smoke built up around her or risk it all and make a run for it. Feeling around the edge of the box, she found a rusted handle and grabbed on to it with all her might.

"If Herman told me to save this box, I will die trying," she told herself.

Waiting until she could no longer endure the choking smoke and melting heat, she rolled over and grabbed the handle of the box. Using her legs, she took a deep breath and, with all her might, pushed the heavy door up. She had managed to lift it a bit, but ultimately, it fell back with a resounding thud. She tried again and then again. Every single time it fell back, it effectively locked her in the hole in the ground. With every effort, she could feel the heat racing across the barn floor, scorching the air around her.

On her fourth attempt, fueled by fear and determination, she was finally able to push it aside. The second that she had moved from the cool of the ground, she had felt the flames. Now lying on the floor, she could see that each wall was engulfed in a red-orange curtain of flames. They were racing upward from the base of every wall in the barn. Dragging the box behind her, she moved out in the burning air that filled the barn. The heat forced her to her knees and then to her stomach. As she tried to breathe, she felt hundreds of needles poking at her lungs.

Rolling over on her back, she could saw that flames were tearing across the roof as well.

"Someone must have thrown a torch up there!" she thought.

Flipping back onto her stomach, she began using her arms to pull herself across the floor to the back of the barn. It was her plan to get out as fast as she could and race for the line of trees that marked the end of the Mermel property in Kovno.

She had barely moved three feet when she dissolved into a coughing fit. Her mind raced with possibilities.

*If there was even one German left on the property, I will be shot… Why couldn't we have left one day earlier…Oh, poor Herman! He was so gentle, so naive! I had pleaded with him to leave…*

She was now coughing so hard that any thoughts she tried to hold slipped from her mind.

Miraculously, she finally crawled to the back door and kicked it open. A sudden, short burst of air rolled over her body.

As she dug into the floor with her legs, a nearly spent Georgina dragged the box by both hands. Now outside the door, she looked to her left, only to spot two men walking across the tree line about twenty yards away from the back of the barn. She wasn't sure, but she believed that one of them had seen her.

With the box and her legs still inside the barn, two opposing walls of the barn suddenly collapsed in on each other. The result was a cascade of flaming beams and bricks falling to the ground on nearly every side.

Georgina was caught half in and half out, knowing that the next fall would kill her. As she pulled with all her might, she could see that above her, flames were now dancing across the roof and straight to the back wall. It was possible that the frame of the doorway might protect her, but when the two walls had started to fall, the force of it shook the ground, causing her to let go of the box. It was now trapped in the mud and surrounded by flaming timbers, just a foot out of her reach!

Frozen in place by the force of her recurring coughing fit, she pounded at the ground in frustration as the sound of the barn collapsing drowned out everything around her. She felt as if the heat was putting needles into her skull.

Involuntarily, her arms rose over her head in a desperate attempt to deflect the boards and panels as they fell. Before she could jump, her legs were suddenly pinned in place by a beam engulfed in flames.

She felt the fire jump to her skirt and start to burn through to her stockings. A twelve-foot beam, one of the main supports for half of the roof, crashed loudly to her left.

Instinct for survival kicked in, and she cried for help.

From nowhere, she felt two hands grab at her wrists. They struggled to pull her forward, tearing her arms from their sockets. She expected to hear a popping noise in her shoulder. The strangers dropped her arms. The beam that had fallen across her legs was too heavy. They could not move her.

As her arms fell free, he heard one of the men shout, "We are letting go of you!"

Assuming that it meant they were leaving, Georgina began to pray for Herman, that someday he would be reunited with his family and find happiness. As the pain in her legs grew, she twisted and fell face-first to the ground, pounding in regret at her failure to save what Herman felt was so precious.

"I let you down!" she screamed for anyone to hear.

Suddenly, she felt free! There was no weight across her legs!

Without a second's hesitation, she began pulling along the ground with her fingers and then with her hands. In a few seconds, she was finally crawling with her arms along the ground in front of her. The sound of the fire suddenly raged in her ears. She wondered why she hadn't heard such a loud noise just a second before.

Putting one arm in front of the other, she dragged herself into the mud until something began tugging at her wrist. At the same time, her legs were starting to kick out behind her, as if she was trying to stand. A voice rang out above the noise of the falling wood and incessant crackle of the burning flames.

"Don't worry, I'm not a German, I'm here to help you!"

In the confusion, she still knew that the voice was speaking in a familiar Yiddish accent!

It yelled at her again. "Please stop crying!"

Georgina didn't know that she had been crying, for she felt nothing. There was no pain in her legs, no sensation of cold in her exposed arms, and no feeling of weight in her body. It was as if she was moving forward in a strange trance—dancing on the tips of her toes as if suspended without sensation above the ground itself.

Then she felt another hand reach out and grab her by her other arm. In a second, she was being whisked away from the heat of the burning barn. Looking up, she recognized the line of trees that formed the back line of the Mermel property.

Yelling as loudly as she could, she said, "I have lived with the Herman Mermel for many years as if I was his wife!"

A coughing fit suddenly overtook her entire body as her rib cage and lungs shook from the violent force of the action.

Through it all, she began screaming, "The box! We must save the box!"

One of the voices said, "What? What box? Where?"

Rising to her feet, she tore one of her arms from his grip and pointed to where the barn was still falling.

"I left it by…" the coughing fit left her unable to end the sentence. "I left it…" Again she fell to her knees, still ripped apart by the smoke.

One of the men grabbed her by the arm and yelled, "We have to get away from the flames. If a cinder leaps to one of the trees, we will all go up in seconds!"

He pulled her to her feet, and again, she tore herself away from him. The two men watched in amazement as she raced straight toward the very place from which they had just rescued her!

One of them, the shorter one who had done the talking, ran behind her. He was there a second after she had arrived at the spot where not a half minute earlier stood the door to the barn. Around them, fire raged as boards and beams and hay burned wildly. With the eyes of a madwoman, she looked around the ground and began kicking at the debris.

"It is here somewhere! Herman said to guard it with my life!" The woman looked up at her companion as if he was supposed to know what she meant.

Shlomo Levitz figured that the shock of the fire, coupled with the loss of her husband, had caused her mind to snap. He had already been on at least a half a dozen rescues that day as the Germans rolled into Kovno. This had to stand as the most difficult. He couldn't risk their entire rescue operation for just this one woman. He made the snap decision to throw her over his shoulder and cart her out. If she screamed, he would simply knock her out with a punch.

*She's small, it won't take much*, he thought.

It wouldn't be the first time that he had done that in the past week. The rest could sort itself out later.

Just as he was about to tackle her about her waist, he saw it—the box that she had been screaming to save!

There it lay, covered in smaller burning boards, their flames jumping all over the eighteen-by-eighteen-inch iron box. He saw that there was a handle on opposite sides and another larger one on the top. Without thinking, he grabbed one of the handles and lifted the box from the muck and debris. It was hot to the touch, but he held on.

Above him, he heard a beam start to fall, and based on the sound, he jumped as hard as he could to his right. Something had made him hold on to the box. For when he looked up, he saw that the beam had fallen exactly where the box had been not a second earlier!

From behind him, he heard her yell, "You found it!"

The weight of the box grew lighter as Georgina grabbed the other handle of the box and, picking it up off of the ground, started to run with Shlomo toward the tree line. Together the two of them moved as one until they had dragged both the box and themselves a good twenty feet into the forest.

"This way!" she yelled as she pointed to their left with her free hand.

Shlomo's companion, Simon, reached out to her and took the box from the woman. With her leading the way, the two men awkwardly ran in the direction she was now moving. In three minutes, they were at the edge of a small stream. She jumped right in and yelled for them to put the box down and do the same.

Shlomo hadn't even realized that flames were moving across his pants. Looking to Simon, he saw that half of his friend's shirt was gone, as a glowing border of cloth was racing toward the man's beard.

Dropping the box, the two men waded in and started throwing water onto each other.

Georgina, who had waded to the center of this small, flowing body of water many times with Herman, knew it well. She simply lay down and rolled back and forth over the rocks that dotted the bed of the stream.

After a minute, she rose and walked to the side where the box now lay. Collapsing on her back, she spread her arms out and let the smoke that was still trapped in her lungs rise until the coughing stopped completely.

"Who are you?" asked the same voice that she had heard when trapped in the barn.

Without moving, she told him what he wanted to know. "I have lived as the wife of Herman Mermel for the last five years. That was our home that the Germans just burned to the ground. It was in my husband's family for over fifty years."

Silence greeted her reply.

Knowing what they were thinking, she spoke in a hushed tone, "Yes, I am a Roma, but I now consider myself Jewish. My husband and I never officially married, for neither of our worlds would let us.

We respected tradition too much to deny that fact. But we also loved each other too much to live without the other."

With the coughing fit growing less and less frequent as she spoke, she was able to sit up.

Her rescuers looked on in awe as she spoke directly and as honestly as she had to Herman, that day so long ago when he had taken her into his kitchen and fed her a bowl of soup.

"Herman and I were preparing to leave just as the Nazis attacked. We knew they were coming, we just waited too long. In the months before they arrived, he and I had had prepared for the inevitable. My husband had carved out an underground shelter below the floor of the barn. He told me to hide here if the Nazis attacked before we could leave! He also told me to guard this box underneath me, with all my life!"

Shlomo was impressed with the woman's resolve and focus. He told her, "Yes, it is clear to us that you are not Jewish, but please tell me your name. Who are you?"

"My name is Georgina Lupescu. As I have said, I have lived with Herman Mermel, and that was our world falling down in flames. Thank you for being there. But I now must ask, sir, who are you?"

Shlomo looked at his partner, Simon, and saw that his partner's reaction was as suspect as his own. Regardless of how he felt, her straightforward introduction deserved a positive and quick response. He nodded at Simon and let his partner do the talking.

"My name is Simon, and I am a member of a Lithuanian Jewish Partisan Group. We are dedicated to help *Jews Who Were Left Behind*."

"Good!" said Georgina. "Despite my life story, I am what you may call a 'Gypsy.' My heritage is that of an often a despised group." She rubbed her eyes as she asked her next question, "Where do I fit in with your people?"

Simon looked to Shlomo for a response. His leader said nothing but did smile. Taking that as a positive confirmation, Simon told the

Gypsy, "We don't have time to discuss who you are. It's more important to save our lives at this time. You have already proven yourself as brave." Moving over to the box, he went on, "We should see about the valuable box that Herman Mermel wanted you to guard with your life! If it is junk, we will bury it for the Germans to find later."

Pulling the cuff of his sleeve over his wrist, he began to wipe across the top of the box.

"Here, you two, help me scrape away the dirt that is covering this valuable artifact that nearly cost us all our lives."

Once it was cleaned, the top revealed no secrets as to its contents. There was no writing, no etchings, and no decorations—nothing so much as a sticker.

"If I had something to open the lock with, it might help," said Simon.

Pulling the same screwdriver from her pocket that had helped her gain entrance to the hidden room below the barn floor, Georgina pushed the point into the slot at the side. Deftly moving it left and then right, the latch slipped out of its casing.

Shlomo and Simon looked at each other and smiled.

Speaking for the first time, Shlomo said jokingly, "Every good Jewish wife should carry a screwdriver."

"Every good Jewish wife should be lucky to have Herman Mermel for a husband," said Georgina in response.

Reaching into the box, Simon and Georgina pulled out what appeared to be a smaller box wrapped in several layers of cloth. She held it in her lap as Simon closed the lid. She then placed the contents on top of the box.

Shlomo suggested, "We should take this slowly. I feel something odd about this. It clearly isn't anyone's family fortune, and it was too light for it to be gold."

As the final layer of cloth fell to the side, Shlomo and Simon gasped, for each of them recognized what appeared to be, without a doubt, an aged Jewish Holy Book. Covering the easily discernable scroll was beautiful silk cloth with silver thread writing. Without a doubt, it was—at the very least—an object of stunning beauty.

The three of them were rendered speechless at what they saw. None of them could bring themselves to touch it anymore, lest they damage what lay before them.

Shlomo, realizing his own limitations as a scholar, turned to Simon. His bearded friend knew that they had undoubtedly found a treasure of the Jewish people. But he was unsure as to exactly what it was.

"I really haven't got a clue on this…" he said with reverence. "But there is no doubt that something must be done to preserve it!"

After all the discord of what had happened over the last half hour, the sounds of nature provided the perfect backdrop to what they had just found.

"There is no doubt in my mind that your husband cared for the Jews of his community," Shlomo told Georgina. He started to wrap the scroll back up in its cloth coverings. Looking at her, he said, "This is your responsibility as his wife. He has asked you to care for it, and we are bound to honor the wish of a fallen hero." Shlomo told her, "Gather all your belongings into one easy-to-carry coat. As we travel, we must do everything we can to protect this. And stay very close to me. Judging from the way you fought the fire, I am more than sure that you will have enough strength to keep up with me, until we meet our friends."

Georgina did her best to not cry at the memory of her dear Herman. In a minute, she was ready to travel.

With Shlomo's help, Simon tied the box with its valuable treasure onto his back. Soon, they were headed back to where they had just come.

"I don't understand," she asked as they came upon the still-burning buildings that made up the Mermel estate. "Why would we go this way? Won't the Germans still be looking for...?"

Shlomo held his finger up to his lips. Pulling himself close to her ear, he whispered, "The Germans have already been through here once. They have so much confidence in their ability to destroy that they seldom go backward. Georgina, follow me closely. I know that this route must bring back memories, but we must not tarry!"

Steeling herself against the memories found in the Mermel estate that she was now walking past, Georgina looked around at the smoking remains of what she and her husband had worked so hard to make beautiful. Without a tear, she led the two men down the brick path that Herman had built not two years earlier.

In minutes, she and the two resistance fighters were moving into the hills bordering the west side of Kovno. After the escape from the burning barn, it was an arduous journey for all. But the path chosen for their journey to the hidden quarters of the group more than served its purpose. The obscure and hidden side roads that they traveled kept them well hidden from the German patrols.

After hours, with the sun moving toward the edge of the horizon, the three exhausted travelers came across the caves where the Partisan Group was hiding from the onslaught of Nazi tanks and trucks, soldiers and cars. As members of the group watched the three of them walk into the hidden dwelling, they greeted their friends' friend with cheers and hugs.

"Simon, as always, we are happy to see you and Shlomo return safely. But who is this woman that you have brought with you?" Jake asked.

"And what the hell is that box that she is hugging?" Nahum shouted.

Shlomo raised his hands to quiet the members of the cave and told Georgina and Simon, "Rest for a moment. Both of you should have a cup of tea and some food. Then we'll talk." To the group, he said, "You'll hear all about it very soon."

In response, the members of the Partisan Group surrounded the young woman and Simon, each of them offering comfort and refreshment.

While Simon and Georgina took time to wind down from the harrowing adventures of the day, Shlomo kept working. He took charge of the box and showed its contents to a few of the fighters who had more experience in the history of the Jewish people.

After giving Simon enough time to eat and relax, he asked the young fighter to join the small group that he had assembled. Shlomo knew that among them, Simon, even though he was one of their youngest members, should be the best one to evaluate what had been found. Before the invasion, he had spent several years as a student at the Vilna Library.

As Shlomo carefully opened the box and showed them the contents, audible gasps rose from some of the older members. While not as educated as Simon, some of the members were able to read the markings on the book.

In the light of bright candles and two lanterns, the contents of the box became visible. Inside the cloth wrapping, there was a very large scroll that was clearly wrapped with care. Someone had definitely wanted to make sure that the parcel would last for centuries. The wrapping was that of a sheep's skin that had been specially treated.

Looking closely at the scroll, Simon asked permission to handle the book.

"I believe that there is much to discover about the book's origins and content. But I can't be sure without a closer look. The inscriptions are very small and written in Hebrew. But they appear to be from an earlier time than I may not truly understand."

There was some minor discussion before all agreed that Simon had the best ability to read the Hebrew as it appeared on the scroll. Lifting the material carefully from its base, he placed it on a cloth that had been spread out on the table in front of him.

"This book concerns the secular opinions and teachings of mathematics by the Vilna Gaon. It looks to have been was published in 1801, just several years after the Vilna Gaon's death in 1797."

Each man had his own reaction to Simon's translation. One or two members were skeptical at Simon's announcement, for how could such a valuable document fall into the hands of Lithuanian farmer—albeit a rich one, but a farmer nonetheless?

Many nodded their heads in agreement while Simon continued with his review of the document.

"I am somewhat puzzled by another sentence…" Simon hesitated as if he wanted to phrase the question exactly perfect so each of them could understand. "If my translation is correct, the Gaon refers to Euclid and also the Pentateuch.

"We must, without a doubt, find a rabbi with knowledge about the works of the Vilna Gaon. He must examine the book when we remove the sheepskin cover. None of us can risk damaging this book, for it may prove to be a stunningly important artifact of our faith," Simon concluded.

Another member of the group spoke up, "Considering how we have found this book, and what it may contain, we must guard the book as the treasure it appears to be!"

Simon went on, "We must remember that it was being held by Georgina when we found it, and she has an allegiance to Herman Mermel for its safekeeping." Looking to Shlomo, he asked, "Can we have her come in here to answer a few questions?"

Shlomo made a gesture toward one of the younger members of the group, and the boy ran to bring the Gypsy girl to them.

Simon went on, "Regardless of the details concerning its discovery, let's find a rabbi or someone from a university who is able to detect the meaning of what we have found. Shlomo, isn't there a rabbi nearby that you know can help us?"

"Yes, I believe that Rabbi Yaakov Muntz, though elderly and frail, can help us. Having spoken to him many times, I know that he too was educated at Vilna," answered the group's leader.

Looking to one of the older men, he gave a quick and decisive order.

"Yitzhak, please accompany me in a few minutes as we leave to find the rabbi. This isn't something we can waste time debating."

Georgina entered the dwelling just as Shlomo finished talking. The questions began to fly so fast that Shlomo had to take step in and take charge lest the tired girl be overwhelmed by the attention.

"Everyone, stop for a second!" said their leader.

They all fell silent at their leader's request.

Turning to the Gypsy girl, Shlomo asked, "Now, first, it's Georgina, isn't it?"

"Yes," replied the girl.

He was impressed at the way she was handling herself. She showed no panic, and even though she had been through a rough day, she didn't hesitate to help them when asked.

*This is a sturdy girl*, thought Shlomo before he went on.

He asked her to tell everyone the story of how she had come to be with Herman.

Leaving out certain details that might bother some of the more traditional members, she told them of escaping from the German program of forced sterilization. Reducing her story to a few brief sentences, she came to the heart of the matter quickly.

"Herman told me that I wouldn't understand the contents of the box. Even though I wasn't Jewish by birth, I still could feel the special reverence he had for the book. He told me, when we had placed it in its hiding place, 'It holds secrets that are hundreds of years old! We must take care to make sure that it falls into the correct hands.' In all the time we spent together, I had never heard him speak so strongly before!"

One of the men who had been listening asked her, "Do you consider yourself Jewish?"

"Herman and I lived together as man and wife for over five years. My attraction to him was instant. I had never met so kind a man and doubt to ever do so ever again. From the first day, he included me in all household events. I enjoyed Passover, and as our time together passed, I learned to cook for it as well as I could. As the other holy days came upon us, he would explain their meaning to me, and yes, I did fall in love with the beauty of the day—if not the beauty of what those special times meant. I made an effort to learn Yiddish, but the language never felt natural rolling off my tongue."

She smiled to herself for just a second at a secret memory. Realizing that she had stopped talking, she looked up to all those who stood in judgment before her.

"Herman would laugh when I mangled some of the words. But he knew that my heart was in the right place." Sadness then began to cross her face. She closed by asking the group, "Does this make me Jewish?"

She raised her hands with their palms upward and shrugged her shoulders as she finished, "Who's to say?"

The frank and straightforward way in which she had answered their questions caused many of the members of the Partisan Jewish Group to stare at her in wonder. It was an odd experience for some of the more traditional members to hear a woman speak so openly and with such force.

Shlomo stepped forward, and he was smiling as he spoke, "We thank you for all you have done for us. Whether you are Jewish or not is immaterial right now. The Nazis are looking to kill us both for no reason other than being born. That makes us the same." He patted her on her shoulder as he went on, "For our security, as well as yours, it will be crucial that you stay with us for a good while. I am sure that I speak for all of us when I say that we will try to make you as safe as we are safe."

Georgina asked if she may lie down for a few moments. The same young man who had brought her before the group escorted her to another part of the cave that had been outfitted with cots. In minutes, Georgina the Gypsy Girl fell asleep.

As Shlomo and Yitzhak started to ready themselves to look for the rabbi, he pulled Simon aside and gave him very specific instructions.

"You guard this and let no one else open the scroll. When I come back, you can grab a bite. But I want either you or me in front of this box at all times. We have some very nosy friends among us."

Simon nodded and pulled a chair over to where the box was.

With that, Shlomo pulled Yitzhak by his arm and said, "Let's head out."

# THE RABBI AND THE GAON OF VILNA

It had taken nearly a full day, but Shlomo and Yitzhak had finally returned to the group's hidden quarters with their charge in tow. Several times in their travel, they had barely escaped detection and capture by both the Germans and the collaborationists.

The two members of the group went about their mission. After another hour, they found the Rabbi Muntz hidden away in the crawl space of an attic just two houses over.

It was only on their return that the pair of soldiers who served the group could afford to take a deep breath.

Moving toward the camps, they found comfort in the familiar surroundings of the farmland that led to the caves. It had been almost two days since Shlomo or Yitzhak had slept. Still, they took care to show respect and restraint as they led the rabbi from the back of Shlomo's horse to inside the cave where the group was hiding from the Nazis.

"Please use caution as you walk with us, Rabbi," said Shlomo.

Taking the arm of the frail old man, he began to patiently walk with him to where their group was hiding.

Hoping to excite the old man with what lay ahead, Shlomo went on, "For all the discomfort the ride has placed on your bones, I believe that your mind will be rewarded tenfold when you see what we have recovered."

The frail and worn Rabbi Muntz wondered what could possibly be so important as to take him from his afternoon study. Smiling as the young man pulled at his arm, he couldn't help but think, *Ah, to be so young and filled with the idea that time will bend to my will!*

Together the young fighter and the elderly scholar walked as fast as the old man's legs could carry him. Entering the cave, the rabbi covered his eyes as he tried to adjust to the growing darkness. If he had been able to see what was around him, he would have found a guard posted along the wall every hundred feet or so. Some of those who stood there had been members of his synagogue.

In time they reached the far corner of the cave where the book was stored.

By now, the rabbi had adjusted to the darkness. Pushing his glasses down to the tip of his nose, he thought that he recognized one of the young men who now stood before him.

"Simon? Young Simon? Are you the reason that I am here?"

Simon stood to greet the rabbi and put his hand out for him to hold.

"It is I, Rabbi. I am honored that you would remember me after so many years away from the door of your classroom." While he spoke, he led the old man to a seat at the table. Holding a chair out for his former teacher, Simon went on, "I do not have the understanding of our shared history to say for sure what is before us."

"Well," said the rabbi in reply, "let us both see what causes such concern among the brave men and women who brought me here."

Simon pushed the scrolls toward the rabbi and asked him if he would need more light.

"No, Simon…" was all that the rabbi could say.

Tired from the ride and unsure as to why he had actually been summoned, the aged rabbi struggled to stay awake as he began to examine the scroll. With hands that shook from exhaustion and age, he slowly moved his finger across the words that he saw along the outside of the scroll.

It took less than a minute for him to grow excited at what he read. The sense of discovery filled his body with energy. Suddenly, the rabbi felt as if he had become wide awake. Everyone in earshot could hear the elation that filled his voice as he sat back and spoke to Simon.

"I can see that you are wise in your own way, Simon." Holding his finger at the end of a sentence on the scroll before him, he watched as the young man leaned in to hear what he was saying. "What did you think this was when you began to read these ancient words, Simon?"

In the time-honored tradition of teaching through questions, the rabbi looked at his former student.

Simon replied quickly, "My impressions are that of an amateur, Rabbi. But I believe that my suspicions have been confirmed by the way you sat up so quickly. The announcement and confirmation should come from your lips alone, Rabbi, not that of a student."

Smiling at what Simon had said, the rabbi placed a hand over the scroll and held the other up as sign that no one else should speak. Taking a deep breath, he announced to all, "This is surely a lost work of the Vilna Gaon!"

Filled with awe at what the rabbi had revealed, Simon sat tall in his chair and found himself unable to speak.

"Do you know what that means?" asked the rabbi as he looked toward Shlomo and Yitzhak.

The two soldiers shook their heads in equal measures of uncertainty and disbelief.

"This is the work of one of most of the important scholars in the modern history of our people. He is known to many as the Gaon of Vilna."

The men in the room looked on with confused faces.

The rabbi went on, "*Gaon* means 'genius'! His works in defining the Torah and the Talmud have lived since his death in 1797, and his works should live forever! This could very well be a book that, for many years, was considered to be lost. When the Lithuanian hooligans and collaborationists began ransacking the Great Synagogue and Library in Vilna, they destroyed everything they could. There were works in there that hadn't been seen in decades or longer. Their existence was known only to scholars."

Shlomo looked at the book in awe.

"Who is the man who wrote this?" he asked the rabbi.

"So good a question, young man. Let me tell you that the name *Gaon* was once an adjective that meant 'incredible genius' or 'great one.' So defining was this man's work as service to the world of Judaism that in time, the word came to mean him as an individual. He lived in Vilna, which was at one time considered to be the center of learning for European Jews. It was there that he changed the way we study the Torah."

He took a second to catch his breath. Tears began to fill his eyes.

"This is a treasure beyond description. How did you find this book?"

Yitzhak told him the details of how the book had come to be in their possession. When the story was told, the rabbi asked if the young Gypsy girl was still with them.

Shlomo nodded, "Yes."

"Please bring her to me, young man."

The leader of the group ran from the room to do as the rabbi had asked.

Simon asked the rabbi to tell them more of the importance of the Gaon of Vilna. Just as the rabbi began to speak, Shlomo returned with Georgina. The old scholar waved for the girl to approach him.

As soon as she was by his side, he beamed and warmly addressed her, "You are the young woman who brought this treasure to us?"

She shook her head and said, "Yes, Rabbi. It was at the express request of my Herman."

"Mermel?" asked the rabbi.

"Yes, Herman Mermel," was her reply.

"The Mermel family was one of the wealthiest and most active of the Jewish families who lived in the land between Vilna and Kovno. It appears that they have made a supreme effort to save this wonderful book." He smiled at the girl and said, "I have heard of your valiant struggle to save this book from the fire and bring it to us."

Georgina could only return his gaze. She felt unworthy to speak in the presence of the old man. Seeing her modesty, he motioned for her to sit next to him. Holding her hand, he asked her how she had met Herman Mermel. As she had twice earlier, Georgina spoke of her life over the last five years. When she was done, she bowed her head.

The rabbi took her by the hand and led her to a seat next to him. "You will sit with us and learn as we talk."

Seeing the concern on the faces of the men as she took her seat, the rabbi spoke to none of them in particular but to all of them at once, "Our dear friend fights by our side, and so she can learn with us as well." Looking to Simon, he asked, "Do you have a pencil and paper?"

From the front pocket of his trousers, Simon pulled out a folded piece of brown wrapping paper. He had taken it from the counter of a butcher shop two days earlier.

Feeling around in his pockets, he looked to Shlomo as if to say, "Got a pencil?"

In seconds, one was in his hands, and he began to take notes as the rabbi spoke.

"Eliyahu ben Shlomo Zalman, the Gaon, was noted for many accomplishments—including making greater sense of the Talmud and encouraging his disciples to learn about the secular world. Now, please know that the word *gaon* does, as I said earlier, mean 'genius.'

But so great was the breadth of his learning that in time, those who uttered the word were understood to reference only the man. His studies were so wide, ranging that in his work, he dealt in mathematics and the works of Euclid."

Yitzhak interrupted and said, "I remember studying math and the works of Euclid, but do you think the Gaon translated Euclid into Yiddish or Hebrew?"

"Yes, he did!" came the answer. Touching the scroll, the rabbi said, "This book could possibly be a Gaon's treatise on mathematics. If that is true, it will be worth an unimaginable fortune. However, none of us should profit a single coin by it. It belongs in a museum that is dedicated to the works of Eliyahu."

For the next hour, he told his captive audience many stories and facts in the life of the Gaon of Vilna. He spoke of the Gaon's legendary photographic memory—how the man would sometimes work twenty hours a day in service to his studies and writing.

"The texts that we have today were corrected and developed by this man. He kept our traditions alive while also protecting the texts from those who would destroy their deeper meaning in the pursuit of extremism. We know that he brought insight to almost every single word that is written in the Bible."

Simon wrote furiously as the energy of the eighty-year-old rabbi seemed to grow stronger with every word he said about the Gaon. There were comparisons with other scholars, such as the Gaon's contemporary—Moses Mendelssohn. The rabbi caught himself and slowed down when he told them of texts that had been written about the Gaon's work so that Simon could notate the exact title of the books for future reference.

They each listened as he spoke of how the Gaon would fast when he attempted to amend the holy works.

"For only then did he feel that he had the support of heaven as he worked."

Only once was the rabbi interrupted. It was Simon, who asked him to clarify a point about how the Gaon had worked to apply all knowledge he could to the Torah.

"The Gaon felt that one could only understand and interpret the books if one knew of linguistics, how words change and how they grew. He made it a point to speak of how different peoples understood the concept of communication. He was said to bring astronomy, mathematics, and all sciences into his work."

The Rabbi Muntz continued to speak for another half an hour after Simon had flipped the paper over to continue taking notes.

Through it all, Georgina sat in rapture at what she heard. Not once did her eyes leave the face of the rabbi as he spoke at length. She watched his hands flutter delicately through the air when he became excited at a something he had to relate and how, as the time passed, his hands had started to fall into his lap while as his voice began to fade.

After over an hour, the rabbi finished by telling them all, in a weak and strained voice, "It would be extremely dangerous to lodge something so valuable in Vilna when it has become such a closed and secure place now. It is up to you, young people, to save the studies and knowledge that this man gave us, for it spans centuries."

His head began to nod as he fell into a state of exhaustion.

Shlomo, knowing that the rabbi was nearly undone by the effort of teaching them everything he could, asked one last question, "Is there any place else for the book to find a home?"

"Yes, there is such a place, and carefully listen to me. From 1802 to 1810, the disciples of the Vilna Gaon made aliyah in what is now Eretz Yisroel." Rabbi Muntz sighed and continued, "This is an institution dedicated to the works of Eliyahu ben Shlomo Zalman, the Vilna Gaon. If it should fall into the hands of those who kill and persecute those of our faith, it will surely disappear forever. The future of his legacy and of all Talmudic study is in your hands!"

With that, he crossed his arms and fell into a deep sleep.

Shlomo stood and asked quietly if Yitzhak would get a blanket for the rabbi. "I will stay here with him and keep watch."

As Yitzhak turned to leave, Shlomo made one more request, "When Jake returns, tell him to come straight to me. And all of you, pay attention to this as I speak. It is important that we let no one else in the group know what we have here."

Simon folded the paper that he had been taking notes on and handed it to Shlomo. "If we have nothing further to speak of, I am going to get some sleep."

After Yitzhak and Simon had left, Shlomo turned to see Georgina standing beside him.

"May I stay in here to keep watch over the rabbi?" she asked. "While you had gone to retrieve him, I was able to catch a few hours of sleep. I know that you could use some rest as well."

"Why don't you get us two blankets, and I will stand watch by the door while you sit by the rabbi in case he stirs. I figure we will have to move him soon anyway. So it is good that you stay with him as well."

She left to do as he wished. In time the rabbi was covered with a blanket, and Shlomo found himself seated next to the door, wrapped in one of his own. Despite his best efforts to stay awake, he fell asleep in minutes.

# JAKE, THE GROUP, AND THE SCROLL

The next thing Shlomo felt was a gentle touch on his shoulder. With one eye opened, he looked up to see it was Georgina reaching down to rouse him from his sleep.

Pulling his blanket to up around his shoulders, he asked, "Has Jake come back yet?"

"Yes, I am over here," came the reply.

Shlomo stood, looked over to the table, and saw that the rabbi was gone. In his place was Jake, eating a bowl what appeared to be soup. Shlomo joined Jake and asked him if he knew about the discovery.

"Simon told me everything, including the story of the girl who just brought you your soup. Sounds like my mission was as boring as yours was exciting."

"Everything work out?" asked Shlomo.

"Yes, all four of the women were sent out through a small train that should have crossed over the border about five hours ago."

"How long have you been back?"

"Long enough to know that you slept for ten hours."

Putting his spoon down, Shlomo threw off the blanket and told his friend, "Good. That means we can get right to work!"

He called out loudly for Simon and Yitzhak to join them at the table.

"Now, let's start the discussion. I believe that we have to leave the book in this cave for as long as we can. It is burdensome and too dangerous to carry it in our activities. We are together for one purpose and one purpose only, to rescue Lithuanian Jews from collaborators. There are a pitiful few, mostly elderly, who had managed to survive in the cities of Vilna and Kaunas. It is to the living that we must devote our time."

Simon looked to them and said, "Without our heritage and the knowledge of this book, our people are diminished. We cannot leave it behind!"

"At the sacrifice of the living?" was Shlomo's reply.

Jake stood and cried, "Isn't this the kind of thing that the group is meant to do?"

"You are correct," said Simon in agreement. "All that is left to decide is whether we wait until the war is over to decide where it should be permanently placed. Or do we act now?"

Shlomo immediately asserted, "I am glad to hear of your commitment to what has fallen into our laps. For I wondered if the enthusiasm of last night had dissipated in the morning sunlight."

"You slept through the day, Shlomo! The morning sunlight is behind us!" yelled Jake. "Now, stop the dramatics, and let's figure out how to get this treasure into safe hands!"

Shlomo was the first to laugh at what had been said. He had always felt that a leader should be aware of his own faults and smile when they became obvious. Looking out among the people that he led, he began to speak with a smile on his face but grew serious as he went on.

"A rested soldier is a strong soldier, and it appears that I have done my duty well so far. Now, how do we solve the problem? We can't take a chance to keep this book, we are constantly on the move, and it may be difficult to maintain its safety properly!"

The others grew quiet as they each considered a solution.

After a pause, Shlomo continued, "When the rabbi told us of the Gaon last night, he spoke of the great man's disciples. Simon, do you remember what he said?"

"Yes, Shlomo, I do. The Gaon's disciples made aliyah to Eretz Yisroel, that's where it should go!"

Yitzhak jumped up and said forcefully, "I agree! We must immediately discover who remains among the Gaon's disciples in Israel. Once we know that, we can decide the best way to get the book to them."

Shaking his head in agreement at what they both had said, Shlomo then asked for plans on how to accomplish this.

For minutes, the light of a single lantern danced around the walls of the cave. No one spoke as they all considered what might help to advance the cause. Finally, it was Jake who spoke up.

"Shlomo, you've mentioned that members of your family have escaped from Lithuania and made it to London. Using our contacts in Kovno and beyond, we will try to contact them. They will be able to discover where the Vilna Gaon disciples live in Israel. With that knowledge, we can plan how, where, and when we will transport the book to them."

"You make it all sound so easy, Jake!" said Shlomo.

They all laughed, for they knew that the actual task would be far harder than that.

Jake's suggestion was as close to perfect as it could be. He knew that Shlomo, a member of the famed Levitz family, had connections that the others in the group didn't have. For many decades, the Levitz chain of general stores had prospered throughout Lithuania. Farmers, tradesmen, builders, and sellers knew that the Levitz name on a general store meant a fair deal in exchanging crops for necessary supplies and equipment. In turn, those crops were sent to larger areas for processing. The end result was a fair and equitable deal for all.

A decade earlier, when senior members of the Levitz family heard of the rise of Adolph Hitler and what he believed, they had begun to transfer their wealth to Amsterdam and, later, London. In time many of them had followed that money to safety. Now living outside of Central Europe, the relatives of Shlomo Levitz had not forgotten their homeland. Their money and name had become a valuable tool in helping those in need.

Shlomo answered the call to action. "It will take time, but it will get done! Also, since we all know that it is impossible to bring money into our country at this time, we must find a way to pay for this action ourselves. It is one thing to use a small bribe to help a couple of the elderly find a seat on a friendly train going north. It is another to move something so valuable across so many borders and into Israel. This will require lots of dough, we'll have to raise that somehow."

Jake thought for a moment. He was hesitant to reveal the extent of the riches that he had been carrying with him all the while. Shlomo knew of the jewels, but the others in the group had been deliberately kept in the dark about what he carries. He and Shlomo had decided early on in their friendship that what he carried belonged to Jake and were his to do with as he saw fit.

As the group broke up and went about their normal duties, Shlomo signaled for Simon and Nahum to stay behind.

As the others mulled around, Jake approached Shlomo and spoke quietly, "I have a means to acquire some money. How much, I do not know. But it may be enough. It will be risky, but it can be done."

His admission brought the sad recollection of Leah's confrontation with the stranger on the road to Minsk back to Jake's mind. He hoped that using the money and jewels that he carried would go to some lengths in paying back what it had cost so many in his travels.

Simon nodded to Jake that he understood. Standing, he removed a map from his back pocket. Unfurling it before the table, he moved his finger across it as he spoke.

"We have now seen the start of a great war offensive by Germany that is rapidly moving eastward and straight in the direction of Russia. No matter the direction we move in, we will certainly be confronting warlike conditions. And no matter what we do, time will always be against us. That said, I think our best bet is getting to the sea."

Simon went on, "Look, the shortest and most practical route is straight across to the Baltic Sea. We don't have much of a choice, so let's examine the map."

Nahum broke in, "If you mean to Memel, that's possible, but then what?"

Shlomo had kept him back, for he knew that few in the group could match Nahum's knowledge of maps and the terrain.

"There is only one possibility, and I have an idea that could work," said Shlomo. "But it will require contact with the Allied Forces. My family's connections could possibility be helpful."

"Please explain!" cried Jake.

Shlomo continued, "There is only one way to get the Vilna Gaon's book out by sea, and that is by submarine. The Baltic is impossible by ship. Ships are being sunk every few days by the Germans."

"How in the hell can we get the Allied Forces to do this for a few young Jews?" asked Simon.

"I've thought of that," Shlomo answered. "We have diagrams and drawings that our friend Nahum has acquired, which we have used in our goal of helping the *Jews Who Were Left Behind*. This is important information that covers military land, sea, and air operations! Nahum has accumulated this in his own code of Hebrew and Yiddish. This information is valuable to those planning attacks from outside our borders. These works will serve as a great inducement for the Allies to help us with the movement of the book. If we could combine our mission to include both the book and Nahum's valuable records, we could kill two birds with one stone. The success of our plan would be in getting Nahum, his works, and the Vilna Gaon's book out together on a sub."

The mention of meeting a submarine and sending Nahum out in such a ship was greeted with quiet. The danger of crossing north to the sands of the Baltic Sea was unimaginable. As hard as it was to imagine, it was truly the only logical way to approach the concern. Simon started the ball rolling with a question about the first step in the process.

"How fast can you reach your family in London with this plan?" asked Simon.

"This will take time. Weeks, maybe months, for the war changes what we can do every day. It is imperative that we stay focused on what this means to us." He turned to the map keeper, Nahum, and asked, "Will you make sure to keep all current maps and codes and language that you find? For though we may wait for months for an answer, we will have to leave on a minute's notice when called upon. You know that you will be called to go with us on this most dangerous of missions?"

The small man, whom they had all grown to respect, nodded yes to what he had been asked.

"Good to hear, Nahum," said Shlomo. "Starting tonight I will work closely with Hershel to use his radio in order to see which one of our contacts can help us the most. We must be patient, for we may not get direct contact with London. But we can certainly find someone to relay our message. Now, let's review the proposal and cement our general plan. Simon, what's the ride time to the Baltic?"

"It will take several days to get to Memel, two at the minimum, maybe as many as a four, especially while carrying such a large package. Escaping detection will be nearly impossible with such a mark on our backs," said Simon.

Jake picked up the idea. "We will need three men, no more, no less. This way, the riders can trade off with the package every four hours. I believe we will have to arrange to have fresh horses along the route. So someone will have to set that up once we are cleared among the roads. In addition, we should be ready to commandeer a vehicle at any opportunity. The Allies certainly aren't going to wait for us if we are late."

"Who among us should go on such a mission?" asked Shlomo.

Jake was the first to speak, "I traveled extensively over lands such as these, more so than any of you in the group. I will lead the journey."

Shlomo started to speak, "That makes sense, Jake, but you are the most valuable among us. Time after time, you have rescued those who needed our help. To lose you would mean…"

"Oh, can it, Shlomo. We both know that you and I are going, so let's not waste time. Just name Nahum as the third, and let's get to work," said Jake.

Simon agreed with Jake, "The two of you have the money and connections that the rest of us lack. Nahum has the strength, and he also understands both radios and maps."

There was no more discussion. It was to be Jake, Shlomo, and Nahum who would travel to deliver the Gaon of Vilna's scrolls to the Allied meeting in the Baltic.

Many among them were happy to see that Nahum was given such responsibility, for he had proven himself time and time again on countless smaller missions. Normally, his work had been confined to mapping and reconnaissance. In spirit, he was an easygoing man who never uttered a single bad word about any of the others. He was loved for his easy laugh and his consistently pleasant disposition.

Many who felt the stress of missions to be too much for them to handle had sought his evenhanded counsel. It was considered good luck to have him travel with you on a mission. His natural charm and smile were an asset during long nights of discomfort and long days of silent movement.

With the team decided, Georgina finally spoke up. She had been silent for so long that the others had almost forgotten that she was in the room.

"I know the roads in this part of the country as well as any of you, if not better. Many was the time that I accompanied my dear Herman on the way to other stores and to other houses he owned as far north as the Baltic. I watched my Herman die on the porch of his house for this book, and I will watch over it as it leaves for a new home. I want to accompany this mission!"

Simon coughed and then spoke quietly, "When Marissa—of blessed memory—perished, it was one thing. Even then, I was uncomfortable with a Jewish woman in our midst. But she was, indeed, exceptional. This plan will leave our friend, the Roma girl, as the only female with our group, and that presents an ongoing problem. We should find a place for her to live." Looking to Georgina, he added, "I am sorry to insult you. For your bravery is without…"

Jake interrupted his fellow crusader. He sounded as if he was working to control his anger as he spoke, "When Marissa was with us, we got along okay, didn't we?"

"Yes, but…" said Simon.

Shlomo stood and spoke firmly, "Simon, we can't carry memories and pains in our actions. We are committed into our ideal of protecting Jews. Many others from Catholics to good Lithuanians have helped us in our quest. Now we have another commitment to find a home for a great Jewish book. We must cement our trust in each other. If Herman Mermel trusted this woman, then we should as well."

"I respect all Jewish traditions," said Georgina as she looked out across them all. "But we are at war. Both Jews and Romas have lost unimaginable numbers of our peoples. When the guns and bombs that kill our families are quiet is when we can go our separate ways. Until then, we work as one. I will stay behind and help with the group as much as I can. I will stand beside Anna and cook as needed. If called to fight, I will do that as well."

Shlomo looked at the others and said, "Any further questions?" Seeing no one answering, he then went on. "Good. Let's tighten the details of our plan. Simon, go get Hirsh, and bring him to us. We need to solidify our message and come up with a list of most valuable contacts."

Alone with Jake, Nahum, and Georgina, Shlomo spoke quietly, "Simon is a strong traditionalist. I am as well. For tradition is what binds us together. But in times such as this, we must, indeed, work together."

She nodded in agreement as Shlomo went on, "Now, understand that if at any point, I feel you are a burden…we will have to find a safe house so you can be moved elsewhere."

He said nothing for a full minute. No one else spoke.

"Glad we understand each other.

As the months passed, waiting for word from England, the box and the scrolls it contained were stored in secret and tended to on a daily basis by both Simon and Georgina. As the spring came, the radio came back to life. Within days, word was received that it was time. Thanks to Jake's clandestine help, payment was arranged and, in a magnificent act of trust in their contacts, sent ahead to the port.

Shlomo, Jake, Nahum, and Georgina took to a back room and went to work.

Nahum observed, "The damn collaborationists are too much in evidence on the roads that lead to Vilnius and Kovno. But I know of a series of small unpaved roads that lead to Memel."

"They have not been traveled in a while. I was last there in the fall with Herman, and no one was using them as an escape route.

Everyone was thinking that the Germans might come down those paths. Now we know that they didn't," said Georgina.

"Yes, the Germans came from another direction. I know these roads to be as she has described," replied Nahum.

"Good," said Shlomo. "How should we dress while we travel?"

Jake spoke up, "We must dress so that we do not look like the wandering Jews that we are! Traveling at night and staying away from well-traveled roads is preferable, but it will not always be possible. We will have to look like down-and-out farmers, or bums, while at the same time carrying the book."

Nahum and Shlomo nodded as Jake continued, "I have seen soldiers carrying heavy packs over long distances. We can disguise the box with fabrics and printing, until we look similar."

Nahum spoke, "We have all had experience with the land, and it should serve our purpose. As always, we will only have one real worry in that region. The damn turncoat Lithos still patrol, hoping to find a lost Jew to turn over to the Nazis and get rewards." Nahum pointed to the map and said, "Still, I think our best route is to aim for Memel after reaching the Curonian Lagoon."

"We should bypass Tourage. My last contact told me of heavy vehicular traffic that can be found there," noted Shlomo. "If we bypass Tourage, there are several small streams and two little lakes to concern us. We cannot afford to lose our precious cargo in the water."

Jake said, "I've done this before, we can build individual rafts over our heads to carry our valuables and dry clothing. Branches from small trees and reeds can be made to make the rafts."

The night wore on. Shlomo went outside with Hirsh to try and raise a connection to London on the wireless. Georgina took charge of the clothes. In hours, she had created a series of outfits that would make them all look as if they had been ploughing the earth since the first day they worked.

Jake began an inventory of the foodstuffs and packed the barest of minimum that they would need for a three-day mission. Simon gathered the others and let them know that the move to a new safe house would overlap with the new mission.

At one point in the evening, after they had successfully raised London and relayed the message, Shlomo pulled Simon aside and told him that he was going to take Georgina for the first few miles.

"I told her this late today. There is a train that we are passing on the way. Normally, I wouldn't risk it with our regular cargo of escaped Jews, but she can be disguised. Plus her youth will give her an advantage if she is caught. She can run!"

Away from them and in another room, Jake was double checking what he had assembled for the trip. Looking up, he was surprised to see Georgina standing near a doorway.

"I have a favor to ask," she said. "I need your help."

"Of course," came Jake's reply.

He watched as she gathered her long locks into a one ponytail and pulled it tightly away from her head. Jake began to shake. He knew what she was going to ask. A few years ago, he had to do the same thing for his sister, Leah. The memory of that day in the Pripet Marsh paralyzed him where he stood.

So skilled was Jake at masking his emotions that the Gypsy girl had no idea of how quickly he had become upset.

Looking at him, as she pulled at her hair, she said quietly, "I cannot look like a woman on this trip. Undoubtedly, you know that I am being sent out on a train about fifteen miles from here. I am going to travel toward Russia on the rails and then double back north to another port on the Baltic. Part of the plan is that I will bind my own body, but I cannot rid myself of this tangled mass." She paused and continued, "I know that we don't really know each other, but it is obvious that you are the most skilled among us with a knife. If

I am to be accidently cut, I would rather it came from the hand of an expert."

Jake swallowed hard and, without saying a word, walked behind her. Pulling his knife from his belt, he took what she had been holding in his hand. Placing the blade against the back of her neck, he began to saw at her hair near the root.

In an instant, he could remember the texture and feel of his sister's hair. It was as thick as the Gypsy girl's was but considerably longer. Leah's had reached to her waist when Jake had cut it all those years ago.

Georgina said nothing as a draft that always seemed to be flowing through the cave suddenly drifted across her neck. In less than a minute, Jake had finished the job. Without looking at the girl, he handed her what he had cut, wiped the blade of his knife on his pant leg, and walked back to the box of foodstuff.

"Thank you, Jake," said Georgina.

For a second, he thought that he heard sadness in her voice. With his back still to her, he raised his hand and waved to her that he was going back to work.

His attempt at privacy didn't work. She was now in crouching in front of him, holding the large, knotted jumble of hair across her lap.

Gently, she asked him, "If I had known that you had done this before, I would have asked Shlomo." Taking a deep breath, she asked him what he didn't want to be asked. "Who was she?"

Jake drew his sleeve across his face and said, "What are you talking about?"

"You have done this before. I can tell. Your manner was so gentle that I didn't even realize it was over until you handed my hair to me." She paused and asked again, "Who was she?"

"My sister," came his muted reply. He focused on the cans of beans before him and acted as if he was counting them.

"She was lucky to have you as a brother." With that, Georgina stood and walked out of the room, leaving Jake to his memories.

It was close to morning when Hirsch came running to find Shlomo.

"We have London calling," he said breathlessly as he touched Shlomo's shoulder. "It's still dark there, so they are active."

Jumping up, Shlomo ran outside to deal with the communications. Ten minutes later, the word went out for all to gather in the larger meeting room. Standing in front of the small group he had led for the past few years, Shlomo was brief and to the point.

"Undoubtedly, many of you have seen the activity that has sprung up from nowhere this long evening. I ask that you all listen carefully."

With that, he handed out the assignments and offered no explanation to anyone. They knew better than to question his judgment, for he was the one who had kept them all together and alive.

When he was done, they all nodded.

"Good. Now, Simon is in charge. As to Jake, Nahum, Georgina, and I, we will be leaving in ten minutes. It is imperative that we take advantage of the moonlight. By morning, all will have changed."

# CARRYING THE WORD OF THE GAON

Leaving their fellow group members behind, the three Jewish Partisan Soldiers and the Gypsy girl began their journey north to Memel (Klaipeda) located on the sandy Baltic Coast of Lithuania.

They rode through what remained of the night and into the day. Keeping well off of the beaten path, they planned to continue until they could find a place to stop until daybreak. The night was their friend; the daylight brought the eyes of the dreaded collaborationists.

All four looked as if they had spent years in the dirt. Both Jake and Nahum had shaved their beards and trimmed their hair. Georgina had undergone an amazing transformation. Unrecognizable as a woman, she sat straight and tall in the saddle as she rode.

By the end of the day, they had come to the point where the Gypsy girl was to meet her train to the east. By this time, she had spent over six months in their care and company. They all began to understand how fast time could move, for it seemed as if it was only a day ago that she had first come into their midst.

In that time, she had grown to be an invaluable part of their team. She had cooked, sewn, taken care of the horses when other men were tired, and not complained once. Her knowledge of foodstuffs and her ability to find food even in the snowiest and darkest of times was almost magical. Looking at her as she watched for the train, Shlomo began to think that he had made a mistake in deciding to send her off.

At that moment, the sound of the whistle came around the corner. The plan was that the train would be going slow enough when rounding that corner so that she would be able to jump on one of the last two cars. Once onboard, a friend of the underground would contact her and whisk her to safety.

Hidden by shrubs and cut branches, they said little to each other. With the whistle growing louder, suddenly, they each felt as if they had volumes to relate to the Gypsy girl. She quieted them all with a finger to her lips.

Standing, she uttered a single word, "Shalom."

With that, she raced to the train. Jake and the rest watched as she grabbed the handrail of the second to last car, just as she had been instructed. With that, she was swept up in the darkness and speed of the train.

From the safety of the bushes and shrubs that hid them from view, the men watched the light from the windows of the car swiftly pass them by. In seconds she was gone.

They walked their horses for miles until it was past midnight. No one spoke. In time they came across the small shack that they had arranged to meet on their way. It would be their last chance to get fresh horses and sleep under a roof.

That night they ate a biscuit, and each were given a glass of wine. Their host asked them why they were so quiet.

Their glasses half filled, Jake raised his glass and said, "To the Gypsy girl, who walked tall and rode so well."

Shlomo and Nahum raised their glasses in silence. A half hour later, Shlomo and Nahum were asleep as Jake took the first watch. As he always had, he found it easy to get by on three or four hours of sleep.

Standing under the spring sky, with at least three days of travel ahead, he looked up to the stars and thought of the weight of the

Gypsy girl's hair in his hand. As he had wanted to that day, he finally took time to cry for the memory of Leah.

He promised, "In time I will find you, my sister. Your memory will help so many others."

The next night, they started early. Whenever they stopped to rest, one would stand guard over their precious cargo. Riding through the night, they knew that they would have to sleep through much of the day to avoid the Lithos and Nazis. When the sun was at it hottest, they looked to escape it in the shade. Over the next two nights, they moved silently through the forest and alongside the occasional road.

Conversation was kept to a minimum, and any campfire, if they needed one, was extinguished once they had cooked what little food they had.

Shlomo and Jake had never traveled with Nahum over such a distance. He had always been their map person, staying behind when they had ridden on a mission. Over the days, he had proven every inch their equal. Together the men quickly grew to become one mind. They sped up when needed and had enough sense to not drive their horses. They had built an extra two days into their schedule to account for rains and any unexpected problems that they could conceivably encounter.

Only once did they lower their guard. Moving through the forest at night, they were accidently spotted by two drunks who had staggered away from a tavern in the small village of Upyna. They failed to notice that Jake had slipped off his horse and was making his way behind them.

Moving with the quiet of a fox on the move for prey, he picked up a thick, strong branch that had fallen nearby. He hit the first drunk so hard that the branch snapped in two as it connected with the man's skull. A sharp crack filled the air as the blow landed. The drunk went limp and began to spit blood as he fell.

Hearing the noise, the second drunk turned to see what had occurred. Before he knew what had happened, Jake crushed his neck with one swift two-handed blow. Without stopping his rapid assault, Jake dropped the unconscious man and turned back to the drunk he had hit first. Lifting him into the air, he threw him headfirst into the ground.

Jake's entire action took less than sixty seconds.

The riders Shlomo and Nahum, seasoned fighters on their own, were awed by the speed and ferocity of Jake's actions as he dispatched the two drunks. Neither of the drunks had time to sound a warning.

Taking the reins of his horse, the redhead moved to where Nahum and Shlomo were steadying their steeds and cried, "There may be more drunks. We are too close to a tavern. Let's get the hell out of here!"

Jumping back on his horse, he motioned for Nahum to do the same. As they took off, he took over as the lead rider. Looking at each other in disbelief, Shlomo and Nahum moved quickly, to catch Jake's growing lead. They followed Jake, and together the three men took their precious cargo into the deep forest. None thought to stop to see if the two drunks had survived Jake's onslaught.

This was the only real encounter with people that they had on the entire journey. The real battle was with fatigue, and the landscape for the journey to the Baltic Sea was long and arduous. Their trail to the Baltic Highlands had swept through streams, small lakes, bogs, and forests.

Adding to their difficulty was the need to protect the Vilna Gaon's fragile book. They worried that every jarring motion might bring damage to what they bore so carefully. The journey was an example of the dedication of members of the group of young Lithuanian Jews who were protecting not only the *Jews Who Were Left Behind* but the history of them as well.

They traveled on in darkness and ate only occasionally. After experiencing dawn break two consecutive days, Nahum carefully checked their map and discovered that their main objective was close at hand. Finally, after having traveled almost twenty-four hours without sleeping, they skirted the edge of the Curonian Lagoon. Then it took them another two hours to reach a secluded wooded area behind the sand dunes of the Lithuanian beach.

There they camped in a small group of bushes that were as close to the sea as they could risk. Every minute was spent aware of the dangers of the traffic heading in and out of the bustling commercial port of Memel, which lay not two miles away from their scheduled rendezvous point.

This dual-nation giant action—comprising Great Britain (itself engaged in a desperate conflict) and the group of Lithuanian Jews (who were courageously struggling to save the *Jews Who Were Left Behind*)—they could only succeed with minute timing and great care. All this while the Nazi war machine controlled the Baltic Sea Coast of Lithuania!

Every fifteen minutes, Nahum attempted to signal their contact on their portable wireless. After four hours, Shlomo took over the radio duties so Nahum could rest. On his third attempt, he was finally able to get a confirmation from the Allied submarine in the Baltic Sea.

The message that came back to him explained in brief, clipped words that the transfer of a single man and the precious book of the Vilna Gaon could only take place at night. The travelers knew there would be too much commercial and military traffic on the beach during daylight. Even a small rubber raft would be sure to attract attention during the daylight hours.

It was clear in that first transmission that it would be impossible for the submarine to say with certainty exactly what day they could send the miniature transport. The plan was for the small craft to race to shore in between the sweeping motions of the giant lanterns that the Nazis were using to monitor a massive stretch of the beach.

Those lighthouses were limited in their range. The group had been given exact coordinates, which would place them just outside of the range of the lights. To be even five hundred feet off would place them all in jeopardy.

The immediate problem was the sub's inability to tell them exactly what day this would take place. This meant that the group could be hiding for a week, maybe even more. Each of them knew the limitations of the foodstuffs, so they never spoke of it. Why address the possibility of hunger when it was inevitable?

As they waited, the group studied the details over and over. The range of the submarine was limited.

There were factors that control how close the submarine can get to the shoreline tides. These could only be calculated when they received the signal to move. To do so beforehand was a waste of time, for conditions such as the weather, force of the tides, and their own ability to escape detection changed on a minute-by-minute basis.

They had to watch the moon as well, a skill with which Jake was familiar. A dark cloudless night was preferable for both the sub as well as for the rubberized raft. On their first night, Jake had calculated that total darkness was four days away. That meant a long, long wait.

In preparation, each man took his own duties. Nahum and Shlomo studied the tides independently. By comparing notes, they were able to determine exactly when tides rose and fell.

Jake monitored the flow of traffic to and from the port during the day. At night they all took turns watching the roads. Using a stopwatch, Shlomo timed the rotation of the spotlights that swung out in a wide path along the sandy shores.

That first night, he told Nahum, "I am counting once very seven minutes."

Taking the watch, Nahum found that after eleven o'clock, the lights began an alternate rotation, moving every nine to ten minutes across the space they had to reach.

"That must be a shift change with the operators. It would be ideal for us to get the call after eleven, but it is beyond our control. Let's review in our minds what it takes for us to meet the raft in seven minutes or less," said Shlomo.

In turn, they each detailed their own vision for how the landing would go. In time they agreed that Nahum should have the box strapped to his back as he ran to the awaiting craft. He would take his place while Jake steadied the precious cargo! Shlomo would keep watch for any signs of trouble from the Nazi patrols that sped along the roads.

That night came quickly as they each took turns sleeping through the day while the others kept watch. It was Nahum who kept their spirits up. He was a constant source of positive feelings and never did anything without a smile. It was the same when he had been back at the caves. Shlomo couldn't remember a time when Nahum hadn't taken time to be the light of the group. It was obvious why so many in the group valued him.

As the sun set, they began to fear that the call wouldn't come. Then, just as the last sliver of light hung in the sky, Shlomo felt the radio begin to shake with the signal that a call was coming through.

The prayers they had made the night before were answered.

The captain of the submarine signaled to Shlomo that fifteen minutes before ten o'clock, they were scheduled to send a rubberized raft with a small motor to a prearranged spot near the shoreline. The captain could only give them a general place where the raft would stop, as the shifting tides could throw the exact spot of their arrival off by as much as five hundred yards. The utmost care had to be taken when monitoring the swiveling lanterns two miles away at the beach.

To reveal their attempt to board would compromise the submarine as well. It was understood that, at the slightest inkling of trouble, the submarine would leave without as much as a warning. It was possible that after Nahum had boarded the raft, he would not be able to board the submarine.

The raft had been instructed to stay at the sandy beach for no longer than three minutes. At precisely three minutes, the driver would return to the submarine, never to return. If they were to wait any longer, they would undoubtedly be caught in the spotlights.

The signal ended as quickly as it had come. Shlomo looked up at the sky above. The previous evening had seen the moon hidden by clouds for almost the entire night.

Asking for one more answered prayer, Shlomo said, "I hope that tonight will be as dark as last night."

Shlomo began to check the assignments, adjusting them as new ideas occurred to him.

"We won't need the radio on our way back on land. I will bury it in the minutes before we break for the beach. We need someone to take the binoculars and watch for the raft as it approaches. We must also keep an eye on the roads."

The men nodded to each other in agreement.

Shlomo asked Nahum, "Do you have the valuable pack of maps and codes that the Allies expected?"

The little man gave him a smile as big as his head and patted his top-right pocket.

"What an adventure, eh, boys?" he asked Shlomo and Jake as they waited together in the reeds and bushes.

His friends shook their heads back and forth, while admiring their friend's bravery. He was the one going out in the choppy waves to ride in a metal vehicle that crawled near the bottom of the ocean.

When the assignment had first come, Nahum had told them laughingly, "I have never even been in a boat that crossed a wide stream. I believed in walking across a bridge. It is so much safer! How much fun is this going to be?"

In a few moments, the sun was gone. Darkness revealed a clear and cloud-free sky. The moonlight was considerably less than a quarter full. Even in its diminished state, it was certainly enough to aid anyone searching for people on the beach.

Nahum, not ordinarily prone to an outburst of any kind, was heard to mutter, "Shit," as he looked to his friends.

Shlomo and Jake looked at each other and smiled.

For two hours, Shlomo kept an eye on the rolling surf. Beside him, Jake alternated between the dunes and the forest behind them as he looked for signs of activity. Every fifteen minutes or so, Shlomo pulled out his watch and checked the time in the glowing moonlight. Ten o'clock was drawing nearer and nearer. None of them had spotted any movement on the water. Periodically, one of them checked the radio to see if it was still working.

The appointed hour came and went.

Nahum whispered to the group, "This is great, for in another few minutes, the Nazi spotlight shift will come on, and we will have the advantage of a greater window of opportunity on the beach."

It was just then that he elbowed Shlomo.

Handing him the binoculars, he whispered, "About forty yards to the east of twelve o'clock."

"I see them," he said.

Putting the binoculars down, they each sprang into action.

Jake stood and pulled up Nahum. Hampered by the weight of the box, Nahum wobbled a bit as he stood. In seconds both men were moving across the dunes, following a path straight toward the raft as it approached them across the water.

For three days, they had waited in the small, confining area of the brush less than one hundred yards from the beach. They had sacrificed comfort and mobility in order to get as close to the water as they could. Now all they had done was about to pay off.

Shlomo buried the radio in the sand, as well as the binoculars. Then he ran out low, in order to join the others. His need to hide any traces of their stay in the brush had given the others about a thirty-second head start. As he moved across the beach, he watched the path of the spotlights. Allowing for a variance of roughly a minute, he figured that he and Jake should make it to the beach and back to the safety of the brush with time to spare.

Shlomo moved quickly to make up the distance between him and the others. He saw that the raft had hit the beach about fifty yards from where they had calculated its arrival. His companions had adjusted their approach accordingly. A few seconds later, Jake and Nahum had reached the side of the raft and were wading into the water.

Shlomo realized that Nahum was too short to make it all the way through the water. He was going to get the box wet! All this planning, and it was going to go for naught as something they had never thought to consider was going to trip them up!

The sound of a small electric motor caught his ear. He knew that would have to be what was attached to the boat.

Shlomo did what he could to calm his nerves when he saw his friends so open and exposed on the beach. Both Jake and Nahum were now wading as fast as they could to meet the raft. He was still running with twenty yards of beach in front of him.

Shlomo wanted to yell at them to get Nahum out of the water, but he couldn't risk betraying their position.

Suddenly, he couldn't see Nahum!

He immediately had visions of his friend and fellow soldier having slipped under the raft, the poor fellow's leg being torn in the blade of its small electric motor as he drowned in the surf with the book of the Gaon of Vilna.

In the moonlight, he watched as Jake, aware of how deep the water was, had picked up Nahum from under his shoulders and saved the box from the surf! He was trying to put his fellow soldier straight into the raft! The man who was holding the small craft in place was unable to help them, as he had to struggle to hold the motor in place.

Suddenly, a gunshot rang out! A second one quickly followed. Then the sounds of man screaming in German filled the air. Time began to almost stand still as Shlomo watched what unfolded so dramatically before him.

Shlomo saw Jake grab his arm. It was clear that one of the shots had hit him square in the shoulder. In the brilliant light of the sweeping lanterns, Shlomo could see for just a second the pain rip across the face of his tall friend.

Then he saw that blood was drifting over the edge of the raft. He just couldn't figure out where it originated. Jake was holding his shoulder and was now standing a good three feet from the boat.

Suddenly, the entire beach lit up as if the heaven's had been lit by silver fire! The spotlight that had gone over Jake had now discovered them!

Looking to the boat, he saw the figure of Nahum facedown in the boat. His right arm was hanging over the fat lip of the raft. Shlomo realized where the blood he had seen a second earlier was coming from. It was pouring out from Nahum's back and falling over the edge of the boat into the water.

Light stayed on them as the boat attempted to turn around as fast as the man at the handle of the small motor could make the rubber craft turn.

A third shot rang out, but Shlomo couldn't figure out where it came from. Instinctively, he pulled out his own pistol and shot flat at the beach. He looked to his right and saw that Nahum had been shot a second time. The blood, dark and flowing swiftly from the side of the poor man's head, had covered the right side of the boat.

The driver was screaming at Jake as he gunned the small motor, "Get the hell out of here!"

For a brief second, everything was plunged into darkness when the spotlight left them.

In an instant, it was back on, and the entire world shone before Shlomo with crystal clarity. The boat was racing across the water back into the Baltic. Just as it slipped into total darkness, he caught sight of his friend. He was now hanging halfway into the water. As it did, Nahum's head was bouncing off of the waves, as his arm waved wildly in the air. The box was still attached to his back and now served as a weighted anchor, which held him in the boat. It bounced left and right as the boat moved forward. Every time it did, the weight dragged the body of Nahum with it.

Shlomo rushed to the beach and found Jake trying to crawl toward the shore. The gunshot wound to his shoulder was preventing him from making much headway. His efforts to help Nahum had almost dragged him under.

Once he reached Jake's side, Shlomo found himself almost up to his shoulders in water when he reached down and grabbed his friend by what he hoped was the shoulder that hadn't been shot. With the help of Shlomo's powerful arms and back, Jake was able to come to his feet.

Once ashore, Shlomo paused to make sure that Jake was able to run.

As the sound of the small engine on the raft passed into the blackness of the Baltic, Jake yelled in his ear, "We can only save ourselves now, Shlomo! Run for all you are worth!"

Together the men ran as hard as they could back up the beach and past the dunes. They knew that the spotlights could only follow them so far up the beach. Standing in darkness, they struggled to find the raft.

It was Jake who said, "The driver moved past the range of the searchlights. They are going to be fine."

Shlomo knew that Jake had made a mistake when he had said, "They are going to be fine," for there was no *they*. From where he had been standing on the beach, he had seen the last shot hit Nahum in the head. As they ran, he saw no point in telling Jake what he knew as a certainty.

Their beloved friend Nahum was, indeed, dead.

Running past the brush that had been their home for the last three days, the two survivors kept running until they had reached the wooded area. Once undercover, Shlomo ripped off his shirt and fashioned a makeshift sling for Jake. It took them more than five minutes to locate their horses.

With only one arm, Jake had a hard time mounting his horse. Shlomo steadied his friend and then, once Jake was in the saddle, ran to Nahum's horse and made sure that it was still tied off. To have the horse be found wandering around might point the Nazis in their direction. Leaving him tied up was, indeed, a cruel measure. But the horse would be found eventually.

It was only when they were both in their saddles that they could hear the sound of trucks and engines coming down the road, which lay more than a mile to their right.

Leaving Nahum's horse behind them, they rode out of their cover and moved to the open dunes. It would be a tougher ride, but it would ultimately get them out of sight much faster than going along the outside of the forest line.

Once inside the main body of the forest, they could move as swiftly as they needed. Their clothes wet and their hearts beating faster than they had ever done before, the two men rode for miles. When they finally stopped to see what lay behind them, the sun was already starting to rise.

Daylight had come, and neither man had been able to see it.

Shlomo asked Jake if he could ride, and Jake nodded yes.

Clicking his tongue, Shlomo turned his horse back to the road.

Jake followed the man as he had so many other times in the last year. His shoulder throbbed with every bounce and jump that his horse made. But he had been in pain before, and he knew that somewhere down the line, it would stop.

# THE RIDE BACK

On the ride home, neither Jake nor Shlomo could bring themselves to address the loss that they had just experienced. What they had left behind on the beach of the Baltic Coast was not something they could have ever predicted. Both wore the scars of a battle-hardened lifestyle and considered themselves as tough and cold as men could be, who were trapped in war.

Both men had been shot at countless times. They had seen other members of the Jewish Partisan Group succumb, and they had seen countless friends and loved ones disappear into rail cars, never to be heard of again. They had seen the dead bodies and all the detritus of war up close and disintegrating with its stench.

Seeing their friend Nahum lying motionless with his lifeblood flowing out across the side of a raft had broken something in each of them. The hard-won logic of battle told them that being discovered by the spotlights, the bullets flying, and the panic exhibited by the pilot of the raft were nothing they could have ever imagined.

As they rode, each man tried to rationalize, and maybe even hope to explain, what had happened. Both were intelligent men who had dealt with much in their lives, but the words needed to understand what had happened to them were out of reach.

They knew that in war, soldiers—both good and bad—die. It was an unspoken truth that in war, much of what is experienced is truly beyond anyone's control. Experience had taught them that much.

But experience is by no means a guarantee for success. At the base of it was that their hearts and minds were in shock at what they had seen.

Near the end of the second day of traveling in silence, they came upon a small farm that was situated on the edge of a small town. With a few coins and a smile, they were able to purchase half of a cooked chicken, a few slices of bread, and a small amount of cheese.

"Do you want some wine?" asked the farmer. "We have a very small number of bottles that we can part with." When both Shlomo and Jake declined, the farmer told them, "That's good, they will sell anyway, although it has been hard to get anything through in the past few days. About thirty miles away, two drunks got loaded, and one of them was found dead. The other has a memory lapse. It seems that the dolts were wrestling in a field by a small bar. The one guy slammed the other down, broke the poor bastard's neck. Now he claims he doesn't remember. Naturally, the Lithos blame anyone they can except, of course, the drunk who did it. So for the last few days, they have stopped the flow of goods, such as the wine and chicken, to outlying regions. I was lucky to be able to give you the chicken!"

Knowing that the story was a little richer than the farmer understood it to be, Shlomo and Jake gathered their goods, thanked the man, then mounted their horses and rode away.

For another five hours, they put as much distance between that province and themselves as they could. It was twilight when they stopped. It was warm enough that they didn't need a fire for warmth. The chicken was just fine cold. A nearby stream provided them with fresh water. After tending to the horses, each of which was as tired as their riders, the two men sat down.

Handing Jake his half of the chicken, Shlomo asked, "Bread?"

His friend nodded yes, and for the next half hour, the two men ate.

Jake began to review what had happened on the beach that night. He went over every detail. Did he cause them to be discovered? Could he have run faster? Could he have yelled sooner? Could he have drawn his pistol and at least tried to shoot out the massive spotlights that allowed the shooter to take aim at Nahum?

With Shlomo sitting quietly across from him, his mind raged with doubt and sadness. He had always prided himself on his ability to keep calm in even the most out-of-control situations. This time he felt he had panicked. Questions flooded his mind.

Did his panic cause Nahum to die? Were there signs that he missed? What could have caused the spotlights to find them? How come he couldn't figure out where the shots were coming from?

Shlomo saw his friend and broke the silence that had lasted for too long.

"It was beyond our control, and all the backpedaling in the world won't change that."

"I can't accept that," said Jake excitedly. "There was something we missed, Shlomo. There was a mistake we made! Something that could have prevented..." He swallowed the last sentence.

By finally speaking out loud, all his sadness sounded absolutely selfish to him. They had, indeed, done what they could. In his heart, he knew that Shlomo was right about this. Despite this realization, his frustration was growing.

"Was it worth it?" Jake cried bitterly. "Was a damn book worth the life of Nahum?"

"Cry, do what you need to. But make no noise if we want to live," said Shlomo in a low voice. "We have no idea if there are Lithos ten feet away. Remember where we are."

Jake sat back against the log he had been leaning on. He watched the stars above start to become sharper as the night began to fall in earnest.

Shlomo quietly whispered to Jake, "From the beginning, we have always been fighting to save the *Jews Who Were Left Behind*. The book contained the words of the great Vilna Gaon. They will provide knowledge and inspiration for ages to come. That is more than enough of an inducement to have saved it. For a world without culture and art is empty."

Jake told Shlomo, "My foster father is a rabbi, and I carry a siddur with me always, but I don't see where it values a book over the life of someone like brave Nahum," he told Shlomo.

"It isn't the physical properties of the book—the paper, the cover, the lettering. It is the ideas that the book hold that they represent. In the rarest of instances, they can come with a heavy, heavy price," said Shlomo. "And don't forget the maps he was carrying. They will most assuredly help countless others. Now, look, we have another long ride in front of us. You know that my heart is as heavy as yours. And don't think that I don't understand what you mean. There is some truth in it."

"Yes, I know what you mean. I am not debating what we did, I just think we could have done it better."

"Your relentless drive and deep devotion are just two of the reasons that you are one of the few I honestly trust, Jake. But when we return, it will be time for us to be leaders. Any doubts we have must stay behind in these woods, by this stream."

"Yes, those doubts most definitely must stay with us Shlomo," replied Jake. Pointing to the deep, dark, star-filled sky that was now over their heads, he added, "But these stars will always know what they have seen. What they see is not something we can ever leave behind."

Shlomo sat up. "My friend, those same stars see the atrocities and hate that we fight every day and every night. And if they judge by the weight of responsibility, I do think that the scales are in our favor."

"So much death, Shlomo…so much death," muttered Jake. "It will always be there, but I don't think that I will ever get used to it."

"The day that you do is the day that is a cold day. When it comes, you will be as dead as those that drive us to hide in our own country. And I know you too well to think that day will ever come. Now, let's get some sleep and hit the road early. You want the first watch, as always?"

Nodding yes, Jake said nothing else.

"Good. The last two days have finally caught up to me. I don't know if I could stay up another ten minutes."

With that, Shlomo patted the side of the blanket that he had folded into a pillow and lay down on the ground. He propped himself up on an arm and said one more thing to Jake.

"You are the finest soldier of us all, Jake. You did everything possible. It was time for Nahum to leave us. You cannot argue with the stars…they hold more knowledge and have seen so much more than we can ever imagine. Now, wake me in two hours so you can sleep. And above all, stop beating yourself up, man."

Jake assented, but as his friend fell asleep, his mind entered a separate place—a place solely his own which no one could enter. Thinking of Nahum, he moved to the memory of Marissa's soft hair, the warmth of her embrace. How after their time together under stars in moments of peace, she had always draped her arm across his chest before she fell asleep. As he went through the times of his life, everything always came back to one specific memory. It was Leah's smile and the way she would laugh at stupid things. Looking up to the night sky, he could do more than dream of the life that lay ahead.

It was another two and a half days before they were able to return to the Partisan Group's hideaway. As they walked into the cave, those who had been waiting could see the sadness that hung over their tired, slumping bodies.

It was then that the member of their group began to realize that a tragedy had occurred.

Simon asked, "Did Nahum make it?"

The others looked on eagerly as they hoped for a positive response.

For a brief instant, Shlomo—looking out at the hopeful faces of Nahum's friends and fellow soldiers—found himself unable to speak. An uncomfortable silence spread among the group as several of them clung to each other for support.

It was Jake who told the group of the boat that had been sent to take Nahum to the submarine. He told them of the bright spotlights that burst out unexpectedly and how the gunshots had raced through the air.

He spoke honestly and without emotion, "He died while he was climbing in the boat. He did everything he could do to keep the cargo and information dry. Even as the shots rang out, he was struggling to make sure that the transfer was completed."

With the story of Nahum's death told, the room went silent.

Jake continued, "He was a friend to us all. Let us keep his memory with us every time we move to save another Jew."

Shlomo stood up and announced, "We will remember Nahum with prayers and stories. We will not let his life pass without meaning. We will pray and remember, and then we will fight as hard as we can."

Every member of the Jewish Partisan Group nodded their head in agreement. Some began to move about in an effort to make a small table ready for the service. As they all did what they could to manage their grief, Shlomo asked Hirsch to walk outside with him. There he explained that it was imperative for them to raise London as safely and as quickly as they could.

"We must know the resolution of what happened on the submarine. Every fifteen minutes, ring for our contacts. Let them know that we are in the dark. When you can't make the contact, ring me, and I will work while you are asleep."

"And, Hirsh," said Shlomo, "keep this between you and me. No matter the outcome, we need to keep the group focused on the next mission."

Hirsh, not a man who was much for words, nodded that he would keep Shlomo's confidence.

It took almost three weeks before the outcome of Nahum's mission was known. It was learned that the pilot of the boat had been killed as well. The raft had miraculously floated against the side of the submarine for fifteen minutes before it was finally pulled onboard. Once there, the bodies of the two men were examined. The maps carried by Nahum were found by a vigilant sailor who knew the details as well as the importance of the transfer.

The book that they had struggled so hard to save was, indeed, the Vilna Gaon's treatise on Euclid. This invaluable document was to be held in London until the war ended. The plan was to transport it to Israel where it would find its desired place among the group of the disciples of the great Hebrew scholar.

The papers, maps, and notes that Nahum had produced for the Allied cause proved to be of such great value that a letter of commendation was later sent to the Jewish Partisan Group of Lithuania.

When the honor arrived, the group had already lost two more members. Shlomo spoke briefly to the group of the collective sacrifices made by all involved. By this time, death was so familiar that few had the strength to even shed a tear. All who served as members of the Jewish Partisan Group were exhausted and pushed past their own limits. Still, they rose the next day and fought another mission.

The Jewish Partisan Group in Lithuania was not alone during World War II. Other underground groups were fighting Fascism throughout Europe. Many men and women fought and died with little or no desire for recognition. They are a shining beacon that struggled against the worst period of inhumanity in recorded history.

# AS THE WAR ENDS

The long years of battle and conflict drew to an inevitable end. While the battlefields were growing quiet, the fate of Jews in Lithuania was still problematic. However, the cessation of combat had left the Jewish Partisan Group in a position where their clandestine operations were no longer needed.

With Germany defeated, everything they had done was now coming out and into the open. There was no need for anyone to hide in caves, trees, or behind the walls of houses. The roads were clogged with retreating truck, tanks, and armored vehicles. The factories were trying to retool operations as swiftly as they could. The farms were doing what they could to clear their land of debris and unexploded bombs and land mines so they could once again return to the business of growth and life.

People were attempting to return to what was left of their lives. With the Nazis defeated and the news that the concentration camps were emptying, there was hope in the lives of the Lithuanian Jews who were still standing.

With their service as a rescue force no longer needed, the members of the group joined together in prayer one last time. Holding each other's hand, they prayed for every member who had lost their life in the fight to save those they could. Marissa, Nahum, and the almost-forgotten Nathaniel, who had been the first member to perish in combat, were singled out by many as among the bravest ever seen among their ranks.

When the service ended, it was time for each of them to move on with their own lives. They had not known one another before the group was formed, but the years had forged an undeniable bond. Each one of them would always be joined together in the memory of their efforts to save the *Jews Who Were Left Behind*.

An unexpectedly high number of the members of the Partisan Lithuanian Group evinced a desire to be part of a Jewish State of Israel. After each of them had said good-bye to the towns, cities, and villages they had lived in before the war, they met each other once again on the road. Together they traveled the road and water to their new homeland.

In the end, the bond between Shlomo and Jake proved to be strong. Their friendship, cemented in times of dependency on each other for their safety and very lives, continued. Between them they had developed an understanding. For Jake, Shlomo was the only one in their group that appeared to understand his wish to have a private world that at times no one could enter.

The turbulence he felt in his very existence seemed to be never-ending. The confusion posed by the question of the future was something with which he was familiar. When his father had met his untimely death, six-year-old Jake was plunged into a bewildering state. Schooling and living with Rabbi Menachem Vilnish created new ideas and new language to absorb. His earliest experiences seemed to create a template that would contain little permanence in his life.

From the moment Jake and his sister, Leah, hastily left Pinsk, Jake felt he had never once stopped fleeing danger! There hadn't been any permanence in his life since his sixth year, and except for the few, somewhat puzzling, years with Rabbi Vilnish, there hadn't been anyone he could depend on for guidance and counseling.

Other than his sister, Leah, Jake had never depended on anyone else. He had built a wall of privacy around his innermost self. Even with all he could see about his life, he knew that self-pity was not the answer. What good would that accomplish? What had occurred in his life could only be valued as valuable lessons to be filed away as reference material. His relationship with others would always be seen from the wall he built around his inner self.

As far as he could see, he wasn't the only one that lacked permanence. The military seemed to be always on the move. Everywhere he looked, civilians were either fleeing or preparing for evacuation.

With the exception of Shlomo, there was not a note of constancy with any of his companions. A few, including Shlomo, talked constantly about "Eretz Yisroel!" But even that faraway land appeared to have an unremitting foe. From what Jake could understand about the situation in Israel, there would always be the Palestinians and the entire Arab world to contend with in the future.

When he and Shlomo took to the road, Jake found that he could only think of the important questions.

"If I do travel to this new land, would I once again be in mortal combat with a foe that vastly outnumbers my people? Would life there just be a repeat of what it had been in Lithuania?"

The two walked for days, and those days became weeks. Over the course of their time together, Jake found himself wrestling with his place in the world. The peace held in the countryside, the idea that they could essentially walk through their country and lands without fear of attack, brought time for reflection—the first time he had to do such a thing.

While, by his own admission, Jake's understanding of the world was limited, there was only one place that seemed to be a beacon of stability and normalcy, the United States.

As he and Shlomo walked to destinations unknown, he thought, *Is the United States a place I should set my heart upon? There are known and unknown enemies that I may have to always contend with in Europe, but I won't face the same enemies in America, will I? Perhaps I will find a new life in that "promised land."*

Jake was not alone in having conflicting thoughts about the future. Shlomo understood his reluctance to commit to one place all too well. They saw that with World War II ended, military alliances were already crumbling and being replaced with political and social philosophies that were fighting for power. Many of which had lain dormant during the war.

Jake the Horse Thief had more practical observations than most citizens of the world. The simpler people expected the world to return to what it once was. He knew that wasn't going to happen.

To him, it was obvious that the engines of industrial commerce had been severely damaged and would take many years for them to be once more up and running at full, prewar capacity. He and Shlomo had seen the devastation of Europe up close. They had run through torn and destroyed streets and cities. They saw the damaged pipes and crumbled buildings. He knew that there would be a shortage of housing and water and of fuel and food. There would also be a shortage of men to do such labor. But Jake wanted more than to just carry pipes or to dig a new hole in the good earth.

Jake firmly believed that his survival depended on keen observational skills and informed decisions. As he read what was taking place in the aftermath of the war, he became deeply impressed with the advent of the US Marshall Plan to help rebuild a desperate Europe. The early emergence of such a solid program had a profound effect on his wish to immigrate to America.

Even with this understanding and growing awareness of the world, and his wide range of experience, Jake faced a serious problem. He had little, if any, real formal education. As a soldier in the Jewish Partisan group, he had not developed solid occupational skills that could be immediately transferred into civilian life employment.

His sole focus had been on helping and hiding those who needed his skills in combat the most. He didn't see any need in a peacetime world for a man who could sneak a group of small children on a train at three fifteen in the morning…

He knew that his wartime movements had given him a million new skills. He had a working knowledge of different European languages and terrain. There was his ability to handle and care for horses. In some of the missions, he had learned the basics of car mechanics. When it came to foodstuffs, he had become an imaginative cook. There was a lot of positivity in what he had done. These were a wide-ranging set of skills that could never be taught in a classroom.

One factor he quickly became aware of was his own restless nature. This meant that a permanent job wasn't really something he could consider. At the very least, his back was strong. Together he and Shlomo traveled endlessly across different lands and regions, mostly picking up steady work as day laborers.

Over the course of their travels, they became aware of the fact that anti-Semitism was still very much alive. Certain jobs were denied them, even though the advertisements had said, "Anyone Welcome."

In several instances, a yard boss who was desperate for laborers had told them flat-out, "We still can't hire Jews. Sorry, boys, but the owner is a prejudiced asshole."

While the statement was made in the most honest and respectful manner by a man who felt the same way that they did, it was still a hard pill to swallow. The idea that an entire war could be fought with the extermination of Jews as one of its main goals and that once it was over, people would still go out of their way to slight Jews was incomprehensible to them.

The struggle for identity tore at Jake. It was a problem that he found deeply perplexing. He was certainly a citizen of the world. He had fought in the largest and most devastating war ever held—a war that, he would learn, had traveled across nearly every continent. In the end, as much as he was, indeed, part of something so much bigger, that struggle he felt internally was something simple, something basic—a fight that came down to what he felt in his soul. What kind of Jew was he?

As he walked with Shlomo, he tore at the constructs of his identity in an attempt to rebuild a better one. One of his earliest teachers was Rabbi Vilnish, the man who had given him the only home he had ever known. That took sacrifice on the part of the rabbi. No one had asked him to care for the newly orphaned six-year-old Jake. No one had told him to do such a thing either. He did it out of charity and kindness.

"That tie to the rabbi is among the strongest I have ever known. His was a selfless world, and he let me in with no question. I have to learn from that."

Touching a small square shape that had rested in his pocket for so long that the edges of the book were etched in the very fabric of his garment, he went on.

"The little siddur, my prayer book which the rabbi gave me, is always with me. It was, for many years, the only book I read. I have written my diary on its margins. What is found written on its pages have had a profound effect on me. For many years, what I read in that book were the only reminder of my connection to Judaism that I had. It has been my comfort as well as my guide in times of crisis."

The act of joining the Lithuanian Jewish Partisan Group had given him a strong identity of being Jewish.

"The group's clearly stated goal of saving the *Jews Who Were Left Behind* made me proud of the personal label as a Jew."

As they traveled mile after mile, Jake took care to keep his personal debates within himself. He fully understood the Judaic tradition of discussion and questions, but he also felt that for some that tradition must be held to an internal dialogue. His ears would remain open to what others said, but as to what he would share, it was his nature to keep to himself.

"There is nothing wrong with this. It is my nature. Just as some don't like certain herbs, I don't like too much discussion. Talk is, indeed, food, but I prefer to keep it to my own tastes."

There was another factor that he tried to address. He felt it might have been the most important thought of them all. The hardest part for him was his personal relationship with God.

"Does being a Jew mean any type of real relationship with God? When our Lithuanian Jewish Partisan Group lost the brave man that was Nahum, when he lost his life saving the works of a revered rabbi, the Vilna Gaon, was the treasured book worth Nahum's life?"

It was the same problem that he had tried to articulate, that night two days after he and Shlomo had finally stopped on their ride away from the dunes of the Baltic Sea.

It was hard for him to reconcile his relationship with God when he had seen and experienced so much that had brought pain to him and loved ones.

"My sister's, Leah's, death was a direct result of being a Jew. If she had been a Lithuanian Catholic or Protestant, she would probably still be alive. Those in power had taken her for the simple fact that she was a Jewish woman."

From this question, he rationalized, "So I remain a committed Jew, at the risk of my identity and my life. Men and women have retained that commitment over thousands of years. Haven't they wondered why they remained Jewish? It is certain that the Jews' relationship with God over the ages can't be denied. My own identity as Jacob Horvicz, a man who is a Jew, is most definitely a positive factor in my life. What has gone on before has made me what I am today. Regardless of my relationship with God, I will always remain a member of the Jewish people."

There was the bitter knowledge of being born anew at of the loss of Leah, Marissa, Nahum, and others. Running side by side with those memories was the joy in his growing understanding that his life had meaning—that despite his loneliness, he was, in fact, connected to something so much bigger than himself.

It took him a few minutes, but Jake managed to compose himself as they went on.

His companion, Shlomo, knew the weight that Jake carried, for he carried a similar weight. His friendship with Jake was based on respect. He knew that if Jake wanted to talk about what he was thinking, he would.

*A good friend never pushes another friend*, thought Shlomo to himself. *However, there are times when it is okay to nudge someone...*

This wasn't one of the times that Shlomo felt he should nudge Jake.

So they went on. A long trek to Warsaw brought them face-to-face with the horrors that Polish Jews had met in the ghettos of that beleaguered city. The details were even more gruesome than they had ever imagined. In their travels, it was Jake who had insisted that they visit Auschwitz. It was his hope that once there, he could find some evidence of Leah's fate. He had continually tormented himself for allowing Leah to be lost in the millions of Jews who were led to places of extermination. Nothing could assuage his grief in losing her.

Neither Jake nor Shlomo were prepared for what they saw at Auschwitz. It was there that they came face-to-face with the stunning enormity of the Nazi killing machine. To see the buildings so carefully laid out; to see the construction that had been made with the idea of permanence; that someone had felt that such ovens and showers would always be needed; to stand where so many had walked their last steps; to breathe the air that Jake felt still held the stench and despair of death; to see so much and then realize that it was only a small group of human beings that had created all this for the sole purpose of killing other human beings—was beyond their ability to comprehend.

The devastating nature of the experience did not deter Jake from his main reason for coming there. Moving from building to building, he sought every possible record he could find. Time after time, he drew his finger slowly down the list of names that the Nazis had methodically entered on their ledgers.

As he scoured the records for anyone named Leah that he could find, he began to feel that the act of touching every name in these decrepit books was bringing him closer to those who had died. While name after name passed before his eyes, he found himself offering up prayer after prayer in their memory—that they, at the very least, be acknowledged for their sacrifice in the war. To allow so many to go unnoticed or forgotten would be a sin of the highest order.

In the end, as they walked away, hoping to leave the images and ideas behind, both men fell to their knees in silent prayer—each one unashamedly crying at what had gone on while they had lived in caves and ran through bombed-out streets.

Standing again, Shlomo took Jake's arm and said, "If I had any idea that this existed, I would have come here and killed every one of the bastards that I could have…" Tears began to overwhelm him a second time as he tried to speak of his anger.

Holding the hand of his friend, Jake told Shlomo, "We were where we were supposed to be. That is all we could do. What we did saved hundreds, maybe thousands. To die in a hail of endless bullets would have done nothing. Be glad for what we did accomplish in the fight for freedom."

"Again, you surprise me, Jacob, just like you did that night we were returning from the Baltic North. That wall you have around yourself is, indeed, considerable. But when you do open a door, it is something to hear and see."

He put his arm around his friend, and they walked on in their search for work.

They continued on to Cracow, and from there, they found transportation on the Vistula River into what is now called the Czech Republic. In their quest for new lives, the two went on to seek employment in Prague. The need for cheap labor was there for the rebuilding of the war-torn Czech Republic. Even with the labor shortage in Prague, they encountered the same familiar experience. There was little welcome for a Jew, no matter how strong they were.

It was there in Prague that they found a few Jews who had managed to survive in the Czechoslovakian underground. It was only natural that Jake and Shlomo would find refuge in a group that was hiding, for they had spent so much of the war hiding themselves. It had almost become all they knew.

It didn't take long for the group to realize how much of an asset Jake and Shlomo could be. Focused, strong, and ready to do what was needed in order to survive, the men understood better than almost anyone else what it took to survive in such an unfriendly environment.

They made friends quickly and within days were running small excursions in search of food and whatever they could find to stay alive. Hiding in the bombed-out buildings and in small spaces, hoping to avoid detection, the group drew close to each other quickly.

Through it all, Jake kept the idea of America open in the back of his mind. Through what he could only consider to be a miracle, he was still carrying the jewels of the Jeweler Malkin. He was almost certain that he would never see a member of that family again. If he did, he was afraid that he would wreak vengeance on them for what they had done to Leah in her youth.

It was only a matter of time before a window would open, where he could trade what he had for passage to the United States. In the meantime, he would do everything he could to help his new friends in the Czechoslovakian underground.

# JAKE THE HORSE THIEF

It was his nature to keep his distance from people. He spoke little and stayed by himself in the safe houses they occupied. Shlomo was good company, but as he became more involved with the group, his time was starting to become taken by the same activities he had done during the war. Planning, arranging, and executing assignments and mission is what he excelled at. Jake was there to help as much as he could.

Among the members of the new organization was a starving teenage girl named Sara Flom. Her story struck Jake as one of the hardest he had heard during the war. She had been separated from her parents during the Sudetenland surge of the German Army. Through a combination of luck and drive, the girl had managed to escape the fatal destiny that befell her parents in the ensuing Holocaust of European Jews.

She was among a small group of ten children and three adults that had managed to stay alive by moving from place to place as quickly as they could. Sometimes they had to move eight or nine times in one day, in order to evade threats above ground. This constant state of worry and emergency had lasted for nearly the entire war. When Jake first met Sara, she was so thin that her ribs were visible through her white blouse.

When the war ended, rescuers found the squalor unbelievable. People, especially the children, were in a state of near death. Many were doomed to die while rescue groups were attempting to save them. This was the near condition of the frail body of Sara Flom when she left the horror of living underground for many months.

Many children, just like Sara, had managed to stay alive through similar means of survival, hopping from one hidden shelter to another. Every one of them was fated to be orphans when World War II concluded.

Like so many of them, Sara hoped against, all odds, that she would be able to return to her home in a small village near Chrudim.

Once there, she hoped to find her parents alive and waiting for her with open arms.

It was a dream—one that, in the darkness of night, she knew in her heart would go unfulfilled. But like Jake's dream of finding Leah, it was what the two of them needed to fill themselves with hope every time they woke in the morning.

The Germans had devastated much of the area of Bohemia and Moravia. The only information she could obtain was the general knowledge that most of the Jews had been rounded up. There was no one who had any knowledge of her parents' ultimate fate.

Sara had survived the war experience in Prague. With the war ended, she was now doing what she could to help others who had known a similar fate. But she was still weak. As they were both part of a new underground movement, Jake found himself attracted to the young woman. He did what he could to help nurse her back to health. He would slip her half of his rations. If there was an extra bit of milk remaining, she found it in her cup, not his. In time the two grew close.

Shlomo could see what was happening and let his friend know that he was happy with what he saw.

"Maybe she can draw you out of this shell. God knows that with so much loneliness and hatred and devastation around us, you could use some real companionship."

As her appetite returned and her health improved, the attraction between the two became obvious. It seemed almost preordained that these two young Jews would find each other and attempt to erase the horrors they had witnessed. Others in the underground were happy to see each of them find a renewal of life and spirit in each other's company.

To have such a deep connection develop so quickly was not anything Jake had ever thought would happen to him. There were those brief moments with Marissa, all of them under extreme wartime conditions. The thoughts of what they had shared while fighting together seemed to be a promise unfulfilled. Like the war itself, it was something that was of the moment—an experience that was meant to teach him about love and togetherness.

# SARA

For the first time since he had left Pinsk, Jake began to feel as if there was some sort of permanence in his life. The weeks spent in the arms of Sara gave him sensation of being grounded, of belonging somewhere that approached normality.

The experience was much different for him than his time with Marissa had been. The wartime coupling of two lonely soldiers had taken place under unusual circumstances. The war created such an artificial environment that in his couplings with Marissa, he had felt as if they were animals, trying to find life anywhere they could. The connection was, indeed, physical and intense. Even when they shared their thoughts and hopes for the future, what they told each other seemed to be as fragile as a glass flower in a windstorm.

Jake entered into his romance with Sara with a different perspective. His union with the orphan girl was just as strong and, in many ways, much more so than it had been with Marissa. As with so many who came together during and just after the war, their desire for each other knew no boundaries. Having lived with death so close for so long, they found life in each other's arms. In days they were spending every waking moment in the company of each other.

Sara was a strong, strong woman who had a deep sense of purpose. He loved her commitment to the ideas and love found in her Judaic heritage. For the first time in his life, he found himself wanting to speak directly about his own growing beliefs and thoughts about what it meant to be a Jew.

With the knowledge that war was no longer an ever-present threat, they each believed that it was possible to make plans for their future. It was clear that each of them found deep satisfaction with the other on a level that they had never thought could exist. Despite the fact that they had only been together only a few weeks, Jake could see himself spending a lifetime with her.

In time their discovery of each other was tempered by a growing understanding that, as well as they seemed to work together, they each had different ideas about where their lives were heading. This realization that, by their own choice, this time together may, in fact, be temporary did nothing to inhibit their ability to find so much joy and pleasure in each other's arms.

Even with so much left to discover about each other as the days slipped into weeks, it was evident they would soon have to confront the future. One night, as she lay with her arm across his chest and listening to him sigh, she told him they needed to figure out what they were doing together.

"To not do so would reduce our shared time together to a lie."

To hear her say such a thing was one of the reasons that he loved being with her so much. She was honest, she was good, and she knew who she was. Above all, she wouldn't let him lie to himself either. Like the greatest of soldiers, she was willing to give up something of her own for the greater good.

They spoke openly that night. He understood that Sara's past was to color her future in a different way than his would. She had a genuine desire to depart from Prague as soon as she was able to. It was her intention to leave the misery that she experienced in wartime Czechoslovakia behind. All she needed was the means to make this come true. Her ultimate destination would conflict with what he saw for himself.

For Jake, he was looking to move to the United States. Once there, he could leave behind the death and destruction that he had seen and lived through in Europe. In such a land with nearly endless boundaries, he would at last be able to surround himself with the wall of privacy he desires.

One afternoon, Shlomo—knowing full well of their mutual desire to escape the dark, gray skies of Prague—pulled them aside.

"As Jake will tell you, I have connections." He looked to his friend and smiled. "During the war, one of our greatest and saddest adventures was set up due to connections that my family had across the continent."

Sara asked him, "Are you speaking of the dunes in the North Baltic?"

Shlomo looked surprised. "You are, indeed, special, if he told you of our heartbreak on the shore that night."

Jake turned red and simply said, "Go on…"

Sara took his arm as they began to listen to what Shlomo had to say.

Their stocky friend told them that he had managed to acquire passports for them. The announcement was completely unexpected and left the two of them speechless.

"But that such paperwork would come at a price," he told them. "There are palms to grease. Once we have done what is needed, all three of us will travel through the Netherlands to our own chosen destinations."

"But how…?" asked Jake.

"My family has deep, deep connections that have once again grown strong with the end to the war." He paused and added, "I only ask that you never question how this was able to happen. What we need to do is concentrate on how we are going to make this happen."

Jake shook his head as Sara squeezed his arm. Fully aware that they were setting up the very means by which they would part from each other's life for good, they each nodded yes.

# JAKE THE HORSE THIEF

In time the arrangements were made. In payment, Jake had allowed a small amount of the jewels he had been carrying for five years be traded on the black market. He trusted Shlomo completely and was surprised when two of the smaller ones he had given his friend were returned to him.

"They didn't take them?" asked Jake.

"Negotiations are part of life, Jake," said Shlomo. "I would have put them on the table if the deal demanded it, but luckily, it didn't."

"Sara is covered, right?"

"Of course. Now let's find her and make arrangements, for we leave tonight."

Once they had located Sara, the three sat down and went to work, planning their move. Shlomo pulled a light yellow envelope from inside his shirt. He placed a train ticket, a boat pass, and an identification card in front of Sara and Jake. The last things he put in front of them were the papers authorizing them to travel across boundaries.

"This is where the money went. Getting these is nearly impossible. No one should be able to take them from you. Look who signed them, and memorize that name."

Both Jake and Sara were amazed to see that the documents were signed by one of the highest officials known in the United Kingdom.

Sara looked up and started to say, "Whoever your family knows—"

Shlomo put a finger to his lips. "Our agreement is, 'no questions,' right? Now, let's get to work here. Take a look at your names, and tell me if there is a problem."

With the swipe of a pen, Shlomo Levitz and Jacob Horvicz had become "Sid Levy" and "Jesse Horton."

Looking at Sara, Shlomo said, "You can go back to your real name once you get to Israel."

She smiled and said, "It would be impossible for you to know this, for I am quite sure that I have never even told Jake this. But my mother's name was Siskin. To see that name on this card and these documents tells me that there is some small meaning to all this." She brought her arms up and created a big circle. "Everything comes full circle. It is, indeed, a big world, boys."

That night the three friends left in darkness to catch a late train. After boarding, they settled in for a long ride that took them through Germany until they crossed the border into the Netherlands. As the train flew through the night, Jake and Sara snuck away from a sleeping Shlomo for some alone time.

Finding privacy in a small, unoccupied room in first class, they settled down together for the rest of the ride to Amsterdam. They passed the time just as they had lived in the last few months, with passion, love, and respect.

It wasn't until they heard the train whistle blow and the conductor walk by announcing the arrival that they realized how fast time had gone. Sara began to hug Jake so hard he could barely breathe.

All that she could bring herself to say was, "I really like your red hair. Try not to cut it too often." Her hands flew up to her mouth, and she turned red as she began to laugh. "God, that dumb…"

"After all we have been through together, you shouldn't worry about that."

"I don't," she said. "I just guess that I know that at some point in the next few days, we are going to have to say good-bye…" She grew visibly nervous.

"How about we just skip that and go to what is important?"

"What's that?"

"Instead of having to say good-bye in a few days, let's just say something now." He paused and looked at her with a smile on his face.

She hugged him again and said, "Thank you, Jesse Horton."

He flinched as she said it. It was the first time that anyone had called him by his new name. It sounded odd, especially coming from her.

"Thank you, Sara Siskin."

With that, he turned and walked out of the room. Together they moved back across a couple of cars as the train slowed down. Finally, they found Shlomo holding on to a pole by an exit door.

Seeing the two of them approaching, Shlomo asked, "Ready to go and start over, Jake?"

Rubbing a hand through his thick red hair, Jake the Horse Thief said, "My name is Jesse Horton. I don't know who this 'Jake' is, sir."

Shlomo put his hand out and said, "Sid Levy. Good to meet you, Jesse."

# SID AND JESSE IN THE NETHERLANDS

Within days of the war's end, various members of Sid Levy's family had managed to escape from Lithuania. Some had gone to other parts of Europe, but several had settled in Amsterdam. This was one of the keys to Shlomo's ability to get the paperwork required.

Together the three veterans of the war now stood on the open streets of Amsterdam. They looked at each other, unable to believe that they had made it this far. The next step was to secure passage to their ultimate destinations. Without a word, they walked the streets for an hour. After a while, they stopped in a café, took a table on the sidewalk, and ordered a coffee.

Sid's connections in Amsterdam presented avenues for converting gems into the hard cash that he and Jesse always needed. They both had talked about how it would be hard for him to get so much of what he was carrying into America. The time had come for Jesse to rid himself of the burden of carrying so much of contraband.

It was a given that there were probably buyers for Jesse's jewelries. But anyone serious about the purchase was bound to be suspicious of the provenance of the jewels. Both Sid and Jesse knew that what they had was not readily traceable to the usual sources. Legitimate merchants would undoubtedly be worried that Jesse's jewelry was stolen goods.

The contacts that Sid's family had weren't limited to just government officials. During the war, a strong and very viable black market had risen across all borders. Independent organizations such as these always seemed to develop when things seemed to become hard to find. Certain members of Sid's family may or may not have had something to do with these elements of a postwar Europe.

Through these contacts, word came back to Sid that the jewelry held by Jesse was, indeed, considered to be hot. Over the next few days, the two former members of the Jewish Partisan Group met with various buyers to see what could be done. An evaluation of some of the pieces, specifically the antique watches and rings, determined that they could easily be traced back as stolen goods.

One of the more knowledgeable prospects pointed out that several of the pieces could have been a J. Malkin creation.

The revelation that others could make a direct connection to Malkin shook Jesse to his core. While nothing on his outside demeanor could betray his shock, he would later believe that his heart had skipped a beat when the buyer had mentioned the name "Malkin."

While the others in the meeting offered suggestions as to how to best sell some of the jewelry, Jake lost touch with the conversation. As one of the men rattled on about how he would love to take a chance on the lot, Jake found one question dominated his mind: As Jesse Horton, will he be able to throw off the life of Jake and assume the mantle of someone new?

While he ruminated over the past and wondered over what the future would bring, Jesse began to feel as if there was a large part of the story missing. It wasn't so much a feeling of concern as it was that something was approaching him from somewhere unfamiliar and he didn't know what it was.

It was frustrating for him that he couldn't put his finger on what was coming over him. During his time in the Jewish Partisan Group, he and his fellow members had found that a certain intuition would develop between them as they went out on rescue missions—especially between him and Shlomo. In the field, it was as if they could anticipate each other's moves.

*That's what this is,* he thought to himself. *There is something unknown that I am anticipating. I know that it is about Jake. No matter how much I move, or if I change my name, there is something I can never change. No matter what, I am connected to my past.*

The idea of "identity" echoed across his mind for so long that it took Shlomo to bring him back to the table.

Hitting his friend on the arm, he said, "Hey, Jesse, let's take what our friend has told us and go somewhere and get a cup of coffee."

Shaking his head, Jesse responded, "Sure thing, Sh—" Catching himself, Jake finished the sentence by saying, "Sid."

Out of habit, he had begun to address Sid Levy by his old name, Shlomo. This was an amateur mistake that he couldn't let happen again. He looked over at Sid and smiled.

Ignoring the mistake, Sid shook hands with the jeweler who had taken time to appraise what Jesse had to offer and said, "My friend sometimes thinks too much!"

The jeweler gave him a wink and said, "Something we all do all too often!"

Jake followed Sid's lead by saying good-bye. With the jewels once again in their pouch, the two men left the back room of an Amsterdam shop.

Once he was sure that they were out of earshot, Sid grabbed Jesse by the shoulders and said, "You got spacy, you okay? We have to make a decision to make here."

"Yeah, just a lot of info. I think too many people are starting to see what we have. Let's get this closed. I am getting a bad feeling here."

"Me too, buddy, me too. Let's close this deal, get Sara, and all go to America."

Both were anxious to get on with their new life.

# LEON MALKIN'S UNCLE

There had been times during the war that Jesse had completely forgotten about the jewels. Every time the Jewish Partisan Group found a secure base to work out of, he had found a place to bury or hide the jewels. Over the course of over four years, they had been kept in a tree trunk, in the hollowed-out main rafter of a secluded barn, several deep crevices inside a cave, and various holes in the ground.

Only one person knew that he had the jewels. The trust between Jake (Jesse) and Shlomo (Sid) was absolute. But even Shlomo never knew exactly where they had been hid. Both men realized that if they sold some of the Malkin jewels, the action would attract attention to the group. So they had limited the number of sales to three over the course of the war.

In the second year of the group's existence, they had arranged for a small sale of two emeralds. That sale had provided enough money to buy foodstuffs for the group as well as arrange for safe transportation through the Netherlands for a small group of elderly Jews.

The second instance was when they needed money to arrange for a submarine to transport the book of the Gaon Vilna.

The third and final time that any of the jewelry had been sold was near the end when they desperately needed both fresh horses and a van in order to transport a group of children to safe haven outside of Lithuania.

Each time they had sold an item, they were careful to make sure that there were no identifying marks on the stones. In each instance, they had worked quickly and efficiently through a black market dealer that Shlomo had known prior to the war.

The dealer had tried to go behind their back and find their source. But in time, he had come to realize that the merchandise they were selling to him came from diverse sources. In the long run, he had been more than happy with the profit he was able to make from the few things they had sold to him.

There were many reasons that Jake preferred to keep the jewels away from where he was living. Naturally, there was the possibility of theft. As devoted as the group was to each other, they represented a lot of money. He also feared putting the group in jeopardy, for if any outsider had an inkling that he was carrying so much wealth at his disposal, they would surely come after him or anyone associated with him.

The last and greatest reason was that the jewels reminded him of Leah. As to what they meant to Julius Malkin, he really didn't care. The man had lost his life assaulting Jake's sister in a cruel and vile manner. To Jake, Julius Malkin had sealed his fate when he led an innocent girl down a dark alley, looking for a good time.

Sitting in a small hotel room in Amsterdam with Sid, Jesse had lain the entire collection out on the mattress before him. The two men had organized what he had as best as they could. For the first time since he had obtained the ill-gotten gains, Jesse marveled at what he saw.

On the far right, sunlight bounced off of about twenty diamonds. Some were cut; others lay there in their natural form. Either way, the way they reflected light nearly hypnotized the two men.

Just inches away from the diamonds, there were a few emeralds with three rubies as close neighbors. To see the nearly translucent green of the former next to the deep red of the later was a privilege that neither of them would ever forget. In the middle of it all, there was an assortment of small rings, each with a precious stone mounted among gold inlay. There was also an assortment of bracelets and earrings.

More than anything that lay before them, there were four rings that stood out. They looked to have been designed with the touch of an artist. Sid held one up to the light and examined it in detail.

He told Jesse, "That guy must have been a designer or, at the very least, knew one who was an artist at his work."

Julius Malkin was, indeed, a skilled designer. He was also the brother of the Butcher Malkin, a rapist with an appetite for young girls.

At the time that he and Sid were in the hotel room, Jesse didn't know this. When his name came up, Sid had said, "At least we won't have to deal with him again, nor if there is any luck in the world will we have to deal with any of the Malkins, period!"

Sid's comment was the first time that either he or Jesse had ever addressed who Julius Malkin really was. To them he was nothing less than a vile man that the universe had rewarded with its own special form of justice. What they didn't know about the man was that he was fated to live on long after his death in that alley in Minsk.

When Jesse had hurriedly left the jeweler's body in that shallow grave in Minsk, he had also left behind any concern that he could ever be connected to the man's murder. Given the atrocities that were happening on a daily basis in Central Europe during that time, it would be impossible for someone to be able to say with certainty that Malkin had died at the hands of one of the Horvicz orphans.

Jesse did consider the possibility that one day Malkin's body would be found. And, indeed, it was, for the ground that had been used to cover him was solid but shallow.

The ravages of war had left that small area of Minsk relatively untouched during the war. No one had a reason to ever venture there.

After all, it was only an alley between two meaningless buildings. No soldier ever saw a need to walk down it as it was a dead end. For the same reason, no citizen thought to hide there.

Then one day, as the war was ending, a torrential downpour unleashed a small flood that rolled between the two buildings and uncovered a curious lump of earth. It went unnoticed for days until one day, while walking home for his store, a shopkeeper absentmindedly took a turn down that way. Realizing that he was lost, he looked around and noticed that an arm was hanging out of a lump of dirt.

The hastily dug grave, its topsoil loosened by the downpour, had finally worn away.

Looking to avoid even the slightest amount of responsibility for the incident, the shopkeeper immediately notified the military authorities. The governmental detail assigned with identifying the dead in a war zone simply hauled it to the local morgue and set up an order to have it sent to an open grave the next day.

That night, a young man who was responsible for janitorial services in the building thought that he noticed something familiar in some of the clothes he was hauling away to the furnace. Inquiring of the night clerk, he found that they had belonged to a man who was scheduled to be taken away in just two hours.

Holding the man's coat and pants above a trash can, he made his case to the night clerk in charge of the mortuary.

"I think that this coat belonged to a man who had dealt with my uncle. I recognize them because my uncle was the tailor who made them," said the young man.

The clerk on duty that night was a young woman named Anissa. She was a local who was hiding a deep secret. Due to her blond hair and blue eyes, no one ever thought that she could be Jewish. When her mother had seen the Nazis coming down the street that horrible day, she had sent her daughter out the back door to stay with a sympathetic Lithuanian neighbor, who later claimed the girl as her own child. It was only through this dangerous act of kindness that she had escaped the camps.

Four years later, and now nineteen years old, she had taken a job in the local morgue, in the hope of becoming a doctor after the war was over.

With nothing better to do that night, she walked the tailor's son over to the table where the body lay. He didn't even flinch when he saw that the back of the man's skull had been caved in. His face, though spotted with deterioration, still held some observable details. In seconds he gave the unidentified body a name.

"That's Julius Malkin. I am almost certain. He would come into my dad's shop and order shirts to be exactly fitted but six months later claim that they had shrunk when, in fact, he was just getting fat!" said the nephew of the tailor. "An asshole like that tends to stick out in your memory!"

Suddenly, Anissa felt a wave of sickening memories come over her. When she was fourteen, the very same man had tried to talk to her while she was playing in the town square. The memory was crystal clear to her. As he approached her that day, she felt scared and afraid as soon as he had started speaking.

Closing her eyes, she could see the little bit of spittle falling from the corner of his mouth as well as his greasy hair spilling out from under his expensive cap. In broad daylight, he had asked her a series of questions that she had found hard to understand. When she had felt the flush of embarrassment rise in the cheeks, he had attempted to pinch one of them.

She thought of what he had said to her right before she turned to run away.

"You must come and see me in a couple of years, when you get old enough for me to really embarrass you!" With that, he winked and started laughing.

For years she had shoved the thoughts of that day deep into the back of her mind. Anissa had never told anyone, for she knew that he was a powerful man in town. She wanted nothing to stay in the way of becoming a doctor.

Reporting the man's identity to her supervisor, she was told to document the details of his death and to hold off on sending the body out pending some sort of notification for the family.

In truth there was no effort made to find a family member. Thus no one was willing to assume the responsibility and costs of taking charge of Julius Malkin's corpse. In three days, his body was sent to a mass grave.

With the insanity of the war, it wasn't unusual that Mayer Malkin wasn't aware of Julius's demise. People were dying all around him. It was only through his own money and skill as a butcher that he was able to keep his family safe during the war. Mayer Malkin was too concerned with keeping his immediate family together. His brother, the jeweler, was not high on his list of priorities.

Finally, a clerk in the postwar Belarus government authority noticed a familiar name in the books of the Morgue in Minsk. Personally dedicated to helping families find deceased members who had disappeared, he decided to clear the matter off the community's books. It was then that he instituted a search, which led to finding the Malkin family in Pinsk.

Mayer Malkin had never really been in communication with his brother. Julius was five years younger and early in life had cultivated a much more cosmopolitan image than his brother, the butcher. By his early teens, Julius regarded Pinsk as a backwater village with few opportunities for the lifestyle he envisioned. Planning ahead, he saw increased opportunities by learning several languages and combining them with a commercially viable skill.

Studying hard, he had become fluent in Russian, French, and English, while his brother had become skilled in butchering animals.

Julius had little use for the Yiddish he spoke as a child. The only time he found it useful as an adult was when dealing with the Jewish diamond merchants of Belgium and Amsterdam.

In the decade before the war, he learned the business and artistry of the jewelry trade while wandering through Central Europe. A charming vagabond, he still took time to return to Pinsk and spend a holiday with his brother and his growing family. A boisterous man, he enjoyed his nephews and in time formed a tight bond with the boy named Leon.

The other sons were clearly destined to follow their father into a butcher's lifestyle as well as the business of moneylending. To Julius's eye, only Leon stood out. He alone had the continental style and natural countenance that he himself favored. When he visited the butcher, he made sure to bring Leon certain books that would lead him to an understanding of what lay for him in the outside world.

With the start of the war, communication between the two brothers became difficult. Preoccupied with their own survival, the Malkin family in Pinsk was only dimly aware of Julius's wanderings. They had no idea that he had accumulated such wealth. A selfish man, Julius Malkin had taken great personal risks in acquiring his riches and had no intention of sharing his wealth or relating a single note of information concerning those riches.

With one exception.

On every visit, Julius had given Leon advice on life, such as, "Don't hang around Pinsk for the rest of your life, there is no future here."

Over the course of numerous conversations and only after carefully questioning his nephew's intelligence in practical matters, as well as observing his ability to think positively, Julius took him into his confidence.

"There is a war, Leon, and in case some of us don't make it, I want you to be able to profit from my life." Pulling the boy close, he whispered, "Listen to me very carefully, and remember this number I am going to tell you. If necessary, tattoo the number on the bottom of your foot so that you will never lose it. When you are positive that I am no longer among the living, and only then, travel to Forty-One von Hellern Place in Liechtenstein. There, introduce yourself to Christopher Baunhauf. Give him the number I just gave you." Pulling the young man within inches of his face, he added, "Do this only after my death."

Leon knew that his uncle was far richer than his father or brothers suspected. Until the ugliness of war began to invade his life, it was his dream to work with Julius in the jewelry field. As did his uncle, he saw himself as a step above the City of Pinsk.

"Maybe even two steps," he would tell himself while dreaming of a life on the road as a reporter for a newspaper.

As a young designer, Julius Malkin had marked many of the rings, watches, etc., that he worked on with his code. It didn't take long for his name to become a brand. Before the war, jewelry stores marketed his work as, "Designed by J. Malkin." It didn't take long for the Malkin name to spread over the jewelry business of Western Europe. In the last few years leading up to the war, Julius Malkin became a very wealthy man.

During those years leading up to the war, Julius had been very, very active in another way. The fame garnered by his skills as a jeweler had made him well known to those fleeing the Nazi onslaught. There was profit to be made by providing a quick means for those who were leaving, to turn their valuables into cold, hard cash.

At great risk, he traveled to many European capitals, each and every time making quick trades with as many desperate individuals as he could. Since he held all the power as the buyer, he could make large profits from the misery of those who wanted out before the war began. When he needed to, he was more than happy to throw cash around to government officials and higher-ranking soldiers to look the other way in order to help his business.

He used the large City of Minsk as his base of operations. There Julius Malkin evaluated the jewelry, musical instruments, and belongings he was offered. When a piece of jewelry showed special value, he would often take time to improve the design as much as he could, adding his name in the process—thereby increasing the item's resale value on the black market even more.

With the war over and his uncle confirmed as dead, Leon was free to travel and redeem his uncle's gift. In preparation for his trip, he had saved the small amount of cash necessary for his travel to Liechtenstein. When questioned why he was leaving, he gave no real details. Few would suspect what lay for him in another country. His father had expected him to work in the shop and tend to his horses for the rest of his life.

Leon knew that there was nothing to be gained by telling anyone about the true details of his reason for leaving. He respected all his uncle's wishes and never once related the story to anyone.

The fact that Liechtenstein was noted as a tax haven impressed him with his uncle's sagacity. It also pleased him that his Uncle Julius had regarded him with such trust. As he left the butcher shop behind, Leon came to understand and appreciate why his uncle wanted to separate himself from Pinsk as well as his bother Mayer Malkin's coarse ways.

Once in the bank, the meeting with Christopher Baunhauf gave Leon Malkin information and instructions regarding his uncle's reputation and considerable wealth. All of which increased his admiration for his late Uncle Julius. He also decided that since his uncle had trusted the man, he would as well.

Baunhauf advised Leon, "There will be some who will question the provenance of some of the gems your uncle acquired, but I believe his story will stand the test of time."

The official also gave Leon his opinions on the best way to deal with any others who may be looking to profit from such a wealth of gems and jewelry and money.

"There is one man in particular that you should avoid. If forced to, make sure to be careful if you deal with Sam Mandelbaum in Amsterdam. He's one of the largest dealers out there and knows almost everyone in the business. So it is inevitable that you may run into him. He bears the stamp of legitimacy and is very, very smart, but he will never serve you the way you should. There are probably a few bums left over from the black market and gem thieves of World War II, so be careful of whom you deal with. If you want, send me their names, and I will reply quickly with my take on their reputation."

Leon spoke to Baunhauf about his uncle's death.

"I have some friends with accounts here who have connections to the officials who could provide details," replied the official from the financial institution. "I will only charge you if I succeed. If I encounter any expenses in my search, I will tell you. In these kinds of operations, no one keeps a paper record."

There was something in the way that Baunhauf spoke that made Leon wonder about his uncle's death. He wanted to shake it off, but he felt as if his intuition was trying to tell him that there was something more to the story.

Looking at Baunhauf, he said, "He knew too many people and was too wealthy for him to just die at the hands of a soldier. It would be nice if we could find some better details. Maybe he had an autopsy that is hidden somewhere. Something like that would help me in my grief."

"At least we can try," replied the banker.

Shaking Baunhauf's hand, Leon said, "Good. See if you can come up with something. I will be here for at least another week. After that, I will keep you informed of my whereabouts. And thank you for serving my family so well."

The two men parted as friends. Walking back to his hotel as a man far richer than he had ever thought he would be, Leon Malkin made a promise to himself.

"I will never stop until I am sure that my uncle's death was by accident. And if it wasn't one, God help the man that put him in his grave, for I will stop at nothing to find him."

There was one other aspect to Leon's desire for vengeance. He had never forgiven little Jacob Horvicz for stealing a horse from his father and riding into the Pripet Marsh. The accident that left his brother with a crippled leg that required the constant use of crutches was something that should have never occurred.

When he did talk about Jacob, he told others that, "The kid was kind of my friend. He could have just taken the girl in the middle of the night and hopped a train. Little bastard had to get fancy."

Still, his desire for vengeance wasn't that great. He knew what it was like to feel trapped and, somewhere in heart, understood why Jake had to leave as he did. Despite the fact that he had left his brother crippled and stolen a horse, he could forgive the guy. If they ever crossed paths, they would have some words, but ultimately, Leon would just be happy to see someone who had survived the war.

That ability to forgive Jacob Horvitz would soon change.

# GOOD-BYE TO EUROPE

During the time that Leon Malkin was discovering a new life in Lichtenstein, Jesse Horton was sitting in Amsterdam and growing anxious to immigrate to the United States. As he had once lay awake dreaming of leaving Pinsk with Leah at his side, he now lay awake at night dreaming of the "promised land" across the sea.

Over the last two weeks, he and Sid had learned that it would take a considerable amount of money to unlock the key to the United States. They weren't naive about the prospect and had, in fact, expected as much.

The war may have ended, but many restrictions were still in place. It went without saying that the old demon of anti-Semitism was still rearing its ugly head when it came to some officials. Regardless, the collection of jewelry that he had concealed for over four years of war was going to finance that dream.

Shlomo did not share that dream. Over the course of many months of personal introspection, the former leader of the Jewish Partisan Group had determined that his future lay in the continued battle for freedom in Israel. He had determined that, ultimately, Israel was a better objective for him.

The decision hadn't been arrived at lightly. After the three travelers had arrived in Amsterdam, Sid had felt the pangs of nationalism and pride grow in his soul. At first he had dismissed them as panic.

"Moving to any new country would be painful," he told himself.

But as he looked around, he saw that there was a lot of work to be done in keeping the memory of the *Jews Who Were Left Behind* alive.

He didn't speak to Jesse or Sara about his decision. When the time was right, he would let them both know. In the meantime, he continued to investigate the many avenues open to Jesse and Sara for selling the jewels.

Jesse Horton did not want it to be known how he came into possession of such a fortune. In that knowledge, Sid understood contacts would have to be carefully investigated and evaluated. In postwar Amsterdam, there were legitimate tradesmen available as well as former black marketers lurking behind the scenes who were ready to haggle but pay very little in the end. It was important to Sid that he maximized everything he could for his friend.

Sid used his various black market contacts, and it was recommended that Sid contact a man named Henry Weil. It was known that the man had personal financial problems and was willing to take the risks necessary to unload such valuable and esoteric items.

He was also the son-in-law of one of the owners of J. Mandelbaum Jewelers, a very well-respected Amsterdam firm.

By coincidence, this was also the same firm that Baunhauf had warned Leon Malkin about when he had come to collect his uncle's fortune. Unfortunately there was absolutely no way that Jesse or Sid could have known about the firm's reputation for shady and dishonest deals.

Weil had become excited when, as the two sat at a small roadside café, Sid described the beautiful and hard-to-trace items. Anxious to clear debt of his own, Weil, trying to act cool, suggested a clandestine meeting.

He had told Sid, "Considering the questionable background of the lots, very delicate arrangements have to be agreed upon before proceeding."

"It goes without saying that we should both protect ourselves," said Sid in reply.

His contacts had told him of Weil's situation. He watched the man sweat nervously in the cool of a mild afternoon. Sid knew that he had to be extremely careful when dealing with the man.

Together the two men agreed that it was imperative that they meet quietly in a discrete location, examine the jewels, and bargain over agreed figures before arranging any form of payment. Since he knew that layout of the city far better than Sid, it was Weil who set the location.

"There is a large synagogue on Singel Boulevard. I'm sure you can find it easily. On Saturday, after the morning service, follow me in a car. Drive slowly, and keep many car lengths behind me until you reach 5700 Singel. There is a garage with an automatic door. Blink your car's light twice, and one of my men will let you in."

"I would prefer an open-air location, Mr. Weil," said Sid calmly.

Weil reached across the table and held his palm open in what he hoped would be perceived as a gesture of peace and trust.

"I understand that you are leery, but I need to make this buy. To steal them from you would only make them hotter." He smiled and drew back into his seat. "And to add to my problems, I would have to deal with you. Your adventures in the war precede you. I know that you are not a man to be messed with."

As he got up, Sid showed no emotion. "Look, I appreciate the acknowledgment, but still, it isn't something I am comfortable with. But what choice do I have? I trust the men who recommended you, and in turn, I trust you."

Leaving a few bills on the table to cover his coffee, he touched the brim of his cap and walked away.

Saturday came, and Sid took steps to ensure safety during the meeting. He enlisted family members to guard against any ambush along the way as he was led to the chosen destination. Prior to synagogue, he had examined the surroundings to be sure of its safety before beginning the proceedings.

As he watched Weil come out of the synagogue, he saw him get into a car with three other men. Secure in the number of his cousins that were going to discreetly follow him to the garage, he took off slowly, following Weil as he had been told.

Once inside the garage, Sid got out of the car. As he surveyed the scene, it was obvious that two of the three men with Weil were packing guns underneath their coats. He was sure that they took full notice of the pistol that he had tucked into his belt as well.

Smiling broadly, Weil said, "Relax, I am not going to do anything stupid, my friend." Gesturing toward the men with him, he continued, "They always travel with me. Please understand that we are all businessmen here."

Unaffected by Weil's comments, Sid stood by the door to his car. At first all four of the men in the garage approached him.

Sid waved a hand in the air as he spoke, "Have your friends stop there, Weil. I only have business with you. I am sure that you can understand my concern. You wouldn't do this any different."

Weil raised his hand, and the men stopped. He came over to the side of the car and asked, "What have we got, Sid? I have to get home for dinner by three. After I talk to you, I have to run any possible purchases by my own people. So let's get this going here."

Reaching into the car, Sid pulled out a small bag and then walked around to the back of the car. Spreading out a soft, dark cloth across the top of the trunk, he then opened the bag and placed a few items out for Weil to review.

Henry Weil shook his head at what he saw and smiled at Sid. "Impressive, impressive, indeed, my friend. I can see why you are nervous. May I pick up one or two?"

Sid nodded and watched as Weill held a few pieces up to the light. No matter what he picked up, his eyes kept coming back to a large ring that Sid had placed off to the side. It didn't take long for Weill to pick that up as well.

"This is definitely a unique animal. I am almost positive I can pick this up. My choice here is a bunch of small items or one big one. And this one," he said as he held the ring up for Sid to see, "is the one to take."

Without showing any reaction at all, Sid quoted a price that he thought would be a ridiculously high figure for the gem. He was surprised that he didn't have to lower the sale price very far, for it took no more than a minute for Weill to accept his price. The conditions of transfer would be harder to negotiate.

After prolonged discussion, they agreed to meet at the rear door of the Mandelbaum store in three days at five forty-five in the morning. The price was determined to be $46,000 in US cash. Weil balked when Sid said sternly that the sale would have to be paid in US cash. Adding that, "I hope that you won't be insulted that I'm going to test samples to make damn sure that none of it is freshly printed!"

"No problem, Sid. I understand. There is so much bad money floating around lately that I would easily do the same myself."

Wrapping up the jewels, Sid nodded at Weill and got back in his car. One of the men stepped over to a button on the wall and opened the door to the garage. In seconds Sid was back in daylight.

Back at the hotel, Jesse was astonished at the conditions of the transactions that Henry Weil had imposed. Sid told him that the conditions made sense.

"Business as usual," he said.

Three days later, Jesse and Sid found themselves waiting in the darkness as a large truck pulled up. Sid saw the same three men that he had seen the other day at the garage. Prior to the meeting, he had described Weill and his three friends to Jesse. It was determined that if trouble did erupt, he was supposed to shoot the two shortest ones and that Sid would take out Weill and the other one himself.

As backup, Sid had arranged for four of his cousins to be on the roofs that surrounded the store. Their instructions from Sid were simple.

"On the first shot, you rush the door and kill anyone who happens to be in the store."

All four of them nodded yes.

Sid added, "And try not to shoot Jesse or me…okay?"

Once inside, the transaction went by surprisingly quickly. The gem was again inspected by Weil and met with his satisfaction. The cash was delivered and counted with great efficiency.

Just as the meeting was about to end, Weill added a request that Sid and Jesse found somewhat odd.

"I need to pretend that we have had a physical struggle. Just tear my shirt. Tear my shirt, and bruise my cheek, you don't have to go too far, just make it look good! And then get the hell out of here!"

"You have one of your friend's take a poke at you, Weil, that isn't going to happen. Our business is done," said Sid as he closed the suitcase holding the money.

"Come on, one of you have to hit me at least once. I can't have this kind of money associated with a sale. I have to make it look like a robbery. So what do you say? I know that you guys were trying to sell these for a week or two. I am the one who helped you. So in some ways, I guess you kind of owe me. Now, don't you think that…?"

Jesse swung at the man and hit him squarely on the cheek before he could end his sentence.

Leaning in, he said, "Just to be clear, I hit you because you wouldn't' shut up, not because you asked me."

Weill touched his lip and found blood. "Oh, come on, you can do better than that, you redheaded monkey bastard."

Disgusted with himself, Jesse stood up and turned to walk away when he felt a hand on his shoulder. He turned just in time to see one of Weil's friends trying to stop him. As he had done with Weill a minute earlier, Jesse swung and landed a powerful blow on the side of the man's head, sending him to the floor of the store.

Sid pulled his pistol out and pointed it at Weil. "Come on, Weil. What's up with all this shit, huh?"

Jesse moved to stand back-to-back with his friend. With Sid's pistol pointed straight at Weil's head, they left through the same door they had entered.

Once out of the room, Sid signaled to the men on the roof that there was a problem. They then jumped into their borrowed car and took off as fast as they could without attracting attention.

As Jesse and Sid accelerated through an unlit street, they were joined at a distance by a car driven by Larry Levy, Sid's cousin. With the suitcase of cash cradled on Jesse's lap, the two men thought that they were on the way to freedom when, from around a corner, came a speeding cab.

Caught off guard, Sid found himself being pushed up along the edge of the road by the cab. Looking over, he didn't recognize the driver. All he could see was a dark-haired man with a cap pulled over his eyes. He looked to be all concentration as he never once made eye contact with the man he was clearly trying to kill.

Looking in the backseat, Sid realized why. The window was open, and the barrel of a semiautomatic was pointing right at the passenger side of the car. In a second flames burst as the air filled with the sound of repeated rounds being fired.

Sid hit the brakes as hard as he could. The sound of screeching tires now mixed with the sound of shots flying out of the back window of the cab. He could feel the car start to bounce as a round of bullets definitely hit the front right fender. In seconds the attacking cab adjusted itself, and they were now side by side once more.

"The ravine is about eight seconds away," said Jesse calmly.

"Yep," was all that Sid could say. He knew that this would mean death if he couldn't get this dark cab off of them.

As he watched the gunman in the backseat about to ready a second round of bullets into their car, he noticed that the car driven by Larry Levy was coming up quickly behind him.

His knuckles white from the effort to keep his car from crashing, Sid slammed the brakes so hard that it threw Jesse into the dashboard. The move was so unexpected that the car that had been pinning him to the side of the road jumped ahead.

Now behind the vehicle that had been chasing them, Larry hit the gas and swerved around Sid. In two seconds, he was the one now pinning the cab to the side of the road. The two cousins had managed to switch roles! Sid was now bringing up the rear, and Larry was now forcefully banging up against the cab.

Jesse righted himself just in time to watch the cab change tactics. Gunning, the gas the driver pulled in front of Larry and then, without firing another shot, took off into the night.

Sid stopped his car in the middle of the street. Larry pulled up next to him from the opposite direction.

Rolling down his window, he yelled, "Get out of here right now! The cops are on their way. I can probably take care of this, but you have to roll now!"

Without a second to waste, Sid took off just as the sound of a siren began to grow closer. Taking care to keep to the speed limit, he made it back to the hotel. There he parked the car in a dark corner of a garage and ran up to their room. Once there, they sat for a few minutes as they calmed down. Sara looked on in anguish. She had warned Jesse that she had bad feelings about the exchange, and now they had come true.

When she heard the details of the story, she said nothing but sat next to Jesse and hugged him for the next five minutes.

Back at the scene of the chase, Larry Levy had met with the police. It took a few dollars, but the details of the chase were amended to say that Larry had been attacked by a dark sedan in an attempted mugging. He knew both of the officers and asked that they let him know if they ran across the cab that had caused the incident.

# THE QUIET IN THE DETAILS

As they sat in the hotel room, Sara, Sid, and Jesse examined what lay ahead. The plan was to leave at eleven that night on a plane for America. It was to be an undocumented flight, designed to carry about twenty refugees to freedom. It was scheduled for an eleven-hour stopover in Greenland, where they were to pick up several other passengers.

Sid took a deep breath and was just about to tell Jesse about his plans for Israel when there was a knock at the door. Shoving the money into a closet, Jake got up to answer the door. It was Larry Levy.

"Look, I got some weird news, guys. It seems that they found the cab abandoned by the side of the road about three miles from where we were chased. It was pretty beat up. The paint on the side was fake. It wasn't even a real cab. It was a junker in disguise."

"Figures," said Sid. "I never trusted Weil, he was trying to get his money back."

"No!" said Larry. "This is where it gets weird, I thought the same thing. But the guys I know on the Dutch Police Force told me, on the driver's steering wheel, there was a note taped to it that said, 'We will get you Jake!'"

The room fell silent. Sid looked to Jesse. Neither man said a word.

Larry took a place against the wall and said nothing.

It was Sara who finally spoke, "I don't get it…"

"I do," said Jake. Moving to the closet, he pulled out five hundred dollars and handed it to Larry. "This is enough to make the note disappear and fix your car?"

"More than enough, Jesse." Pulling two of the bills off the five he had been handed, he tried to hand them back to Jesse. "I only need three to keep the cops quiet. I can fix my own car. I owe Sid for too much in this lifetime."

Jesse pushed the offering back to Larry. He refused the offering again. Then he told Jesse and Sid why.

"No, I owe all of you. I don't think Sid ever told you this, but you guys got my mother-in-law out in 1942. My old lady has been thankful as hell ever since." He held the money out for Jesse to take.

Sid stood up and took his cousin by the arm. "Look, you owe nobody anything. We did what every one of us would in that situation. Besides, you set most of this up." Moving him toward the door, Sid finished by saying, "And we really have to get going. We are falling behind. I got planes to meet and people to talk to."

Jesse stood up and shook Larry's hand.

"Thanks for your help today. Probably won't see you again, so good luck. Use the money to buy your mother-in-law a new dress."

As Larry waved good-bye to everyone in the room, he said, "I'll be able to get her a hundred with this!" Pocketing the money, he finished by saying, "Thanks to all of you. Have a safe trip."

Shutting the door behind him, Sid went over to Jesse and asked, "You know what the note meant?"

Yeah," said Jake, "I know."

He placed the case with the money on the bed and began to divide it up.

Sid coughed nervously and began to speak, "Look, Jesse, I got something to tell you."

"Yeah, you're going to Israel," said Jesse.

"Am I that easy to read, buddy?"

"No, but you can't spend four years fighting side by side with a man and not know how his mind works."

As he spoke, Jesse piled up $25,000 of the money and split it into two. He pushed half toward where Sid was standing, and half, toward Sara.

She winced as if she knew what was coming

"Jake…" she said.

They looked at each other for a long minute.

Sid stood and said, "Cover the money. I am going down to the café, and I'll bring back a couple of sandwiches." He was shutting the door before he finished the sentence.

With Sid gone, the two lovers continued to look at each other. Nothing was being said, but they both knew what the silence meant. It was time to go their own separate ways.

The thought of having to leave Sara became unbearable. But the note on the steering of the abandoned car had changed everything. It was clear that he couldn't subject Sara, who was already subject to recurring nightmares of her wartime ordeal, to a life of uncertainty with him.

The only option was a better life in the Jewish land of beautiful Israel. She was going to either have to return to Lithuania, which he doubted she would do, or go with Sid to Israel. All he wanted to do was ease the horrors she had bitterly known. To subject her to a life of being chased would be selfish and unforgivable on his part.

Sara's heart was breaking, but she knew that whatever he decided would be the right thing for them both. She thought back to just a few months ago, when she had first found safety and warmth in Jesse's arms. He was the one who had nursed her back to life. It was in his arms that she had first discovered deep emotional stirrings.

It was excruciating for Jesse to reach the necessity of ending his life with Sara. Falling back on his own inner strength, he steeled himself against any emotional display. The wall of privacy that had always protected his inner self did not crack.

"It's the note, isn't it, Jess?" she asked.

"Yes, honey. I am doomed to be followed for the rest of my life. We would always be hounded. I have to let you go now, for I can't guarantee your life against the demons who are my mortal enemies! If we stayed together, that is how you will die. I have seen too many loved ones die to risk another."

Standing, she slapped him and screamed, "You selfish bastard. We have all seen loved ones die! You don't get to make decisions for me! I don't care who is chasing you! I want to spend my life at your side..." She threw her arms around him and began crying. "It's just wrong," she muttered. "It's just wrong."

Smarting from the unexpected slap, Jesse embraced her. He spoke gently to her as he caressed her hair, "A few more minutes together. That will carry us into the future, Sara."

Pulling him tight, she said, "You're right, I know it. Our children would be chased as well as us. I don't know what is chasing you, but I hope you can outrun it."

For the next ten minutes, they lay side by side, holding each other as close as two people ever could. Soon, a knock came, and they pulled apart. Sara rose to wash her face. Sid entered with a paper bag and a couple of bottles of soda.

"Sandwiches, folks. Let's eat, for we have to meet the contact in half an hour." He looked to Jesse and said, "Our man is downstairs eating. He told me the flight is pushed up. We meet him in thirty minutes, and you are going straight to the airport."

As they ate, Jesse pushed a small pile of money at each of them. "That's $12,500 each. When you get there, I will find you through contacts and send you what I can over time."

Sid took the pile and put it in his pocket. He looked at Sara and said, "Our flight to Israel leaves in four hours."

Jesse looked surprised, "How did you know she was going with you?"

"Not thirty minutes ago, a man told me, 'You can't spend four years fighting side by side with a man and not know how his mind works.' So you have any more questions?"

As sad as she was, Sara knew that what had happened in the last half hour would be best for them. Her appetite had disappeared, so she put her sandwich into a small bag that she always carried.

As she did, Jesse pocketed what remained of the proceeds from the sale of the ring.

Jesse and Sid finished their sandwiches as she said nothing. The news of the note in the discarded cab had changed everything.

After ten minutes, Sid said to Jesse, "I will be downstairs at the last table in the right corner. See you there." He looked to Sara and followed saying, "I'll come up for you when we are done. Try to get some sleep if you can."

She nodded yes as she watched him leave.

Alone for possibly the last time in their lives, the two lovers embraced each other tightly.

"Thank you, Jake, I'll always love you!" was all she could think to say.

Even though it had been less than a week since he had officially changed his name, he found it odd to hear his original name being used. He kissed her on the top of her head, as he had a hundred times on the last two weeks.

Pulling away from her, he looked her in the eyes and whispered, "Thank you for sharing your life with me."

He stood and walked to the door. She began to cry, and as she did, Jesse found that wall he had built around himself started to crumble. Unable to say anything else, they left without either of them saying good-bye.

## ROBERT STEINBERG

As he moved toward the staircase to meet Sid and the agent in the café, he found himself having to stop and grab on the rail of the staircase in order to keep from falling to his knees in tears.

The embrace would remain with the two lovers forever.

# LIFE OF THE JEWEL

Sam Mandelbaum pivoted from where he was standing behind the counter and continued his sharp tirade at his son-in-law, "You goddamn idiot! You could be ruining the reputation Mandelbaum Jewelers has built over 150 years! I don't give a shit that you recognized a bargain! How in hell can we prove the provenance of this piece?"

With that, he pushed the ring that was resting on a small piece of velvet cloth toward Weil. He had spoken with so much venom that it left his son-in-law quaking where he stood!

However, he was a professional and a man who understood how hard it can be to resist a good, safe bargain. In a minute, as Weill stood mute, fearing another outbreak from the man, Mandelbaum calmed himself and looked again at the very unique ring. Seeing the ring a second time, its image brought forth the memory of a customer who had unloaded something similar not a few months earlier.

Immediately, after the end of World War II, a man he had never met before had approached him using another dealer as reference. The man was tall, thin, and spoke with the slightest hint of a German accent.

While he had conducted himself as someone who knew the jewelry industry, it didn't take long for Mandelbaum to figure out that the guy was a self-important rube, who had no idea as to what he actually possessed. He had conducted himself with the air of a man who had once been important and was now trying to mask his arrogance and conceit in an overly polite manner.

When the ring the man was selling was laid out before him, he had noticed that it bore an inscription that led Mandelbaum to believe that it was a Malkin creation. Unless the rube was going to tell him it was a Malkin, he certainly wasn't going to say anything.

After the man left with cash in his pocket, Mandelbaum had taken a week to conduct a full investigation on the history of the highly unique ring. When he discovered the jewel's history and significance, he was stunned. The arrogant rube had sold him one of the legendary "Five Sisters' Rings"!

Now, without knowing the consequences, nor the importance of the ring, Sam's "idiot son-in-law" had purchased another treasure of inestimable value. This meant that Mandelbaum now controlled two of a set of five. He was, indeed, sitting in the catbird seat! A single ring in the series was something to have. But to own two of the set put him in an enviable position. He could virtually name his own price if he were to sell these as a pair.

Motioning for his son-in-law to sit down, he asked the boy if he knew exactly what he had bought.

Henry Weil nervously shook his head no.

"Let me tell you what we have here, Henry," said Mandelbaum as he settled in. He then proceeded to tell the father of his grandchildren exactly what they had before them.

"As the tale was told through the ages, and I learned of it last year, it all started with a French nobleman of the late eighteenth century. Looking to appear magnanimous and equal in his love for each daughter, he commissioned an artist of the court to craft a beautiful ring for each of his five daughters. They were to look similar but differ in small, minute ways.

"When finished, they were immediately noted for their exquisite design as well as for the amount of jewels they contained. In the center was a small diamond surrounded by emeralds. On one side was an exquisite chip of a pearl. On the opposite side, the initials of each daughter w spelled out in silver.

"Sadly, as multiple siblings are wont to do, the young women criticized each other and argued viciously over the rings. Finally, the old man became disgusted at their petulant displays of pettiness and removed the rings from the presence of the spoiled females."

That was all that he knew of the history of the rings. There was more to the story. The details of which were to directly affect the life of the man once known as Jake the Horse Thief.

After taking the rings from his daughters, the nobleman then made the Five Sisters' Rings part of his personal collection of valuables. There they remained, in royal vaults, until the war clouds of the 1930s frightened the impoverished scion of the eighteenth-century nobleman. Fearful of the growing power of Germany, the possibility of finding haven in French Canada loomed large for the aging alcoholic. In order to slip away from tumbling empire, he would need cash for life in America.

And he would need it quickly.

Digging into his collection, he realized that the Five Sisters' Rings were the solution to his problem. At that very moment, Julius Malkin was enriching himself by solving just such a problem for both the rich and the poor. If something needed to be sold quickly and someone had the money, it was just a matter of who. All Julius Malkin needed to do was get them to agree to his price.

His first bid was extremely low. But the man was desperate to leave for French Canada. The price that Malkin offered to the last heir of the eighteenth century fortune appeared to be, in the words of the man when he was handed the cash, "this is, indeed, a godsend."

Walking away from the sale that day, Julius Malkin knew he made the greatest bargain of his career. All five of these truly legendary rings were now in his passion. He could care less for the rings as object themselves. He considered the work shoddy and almost amateurish in both their design and construction. But he loved having been part of the history of the rings. He was now in the middle of their loss and eventual recovery.

Now, not even a decade after Malkin had made such an incredible buy on the set of all five rings, Sam Mandelbaum found that he possessed two of the legendary Five Sisters' Rings. His research into the provenance of the two rings he now possessed had made him very happy. All he had to do was, somehow, to make sure that any sale looked—at least to anyone on the outside—legal.

Weil wasn't as dumb as his father-in-law believed him to be. The reason that he had set up the fight with Sid and Jesse was so he could set up a protective cover story. There had been a camera on the premises. It was set up to take pictures when it detected movement in the store. It was also set up at a specific angle—one to keep certain people and activities out of the picture. He now told his father-in-law about the camera.

Mandelbaum decided to jump into action.

"Let's get them before they get us, sonny!" he said to Weil. "Now, go get some of those pictures that were taken that night and see what we can come up with."

Calling the newspaper, he told the reporter there had been a robbery. They gave the reporter the best pictures possible, ones that left them in the clear.

This story now created the impression that the jewels had been in his custody for years. In the article, Mandelbaum falsely claimed that he had bought two of the rings straight from the felling relative of the French nobleman.

The next day, the headline screamed, "Courageous Employee Saves Jewels!"

The article stated that, "Early yesterday, an intruder had forced his way into Mandelbaum Jewelers just as Henry Weil opened the store. The burglar attempted to steal a tray of expensive rings. Mr. Weil fought off the intruder after a ferocious struggle and saved the jewelry."

There was even a picture on the front page as well as a smaller headline that said, "The store's security camera had managed to film a picture of the potential thief!"

The newspaper had a partial photo of a man described as "a red-haired individual who was fleeing before the police arrived."

In addition to the evidence, it mentioned that two of the rings saved were among the historic Five Sisters' Grouping. The publicity erased the fact of a "black market purchase." The story and a few well-placed bribes were all that were needed—at least, as far as the authorities were concerned.

Like any subculture, jewelry merchants are a tight-knit group. The news about the heroism of Henry Weil of the J. Mandelbaum Company spread throughout that community.

Leon Malkin was one of the first to know about the incident. He had become the conservator of the late Julius Malkin's estate and had quickly become an expert in the evaluation of jewelry. His studies as well as conversations with jewelers who knew his uncle personally had taught him the history of the Five Sisters' Rings and his uncle.

On one visit, his uncle had bragged to Leon in private that he had, in fact, secured the rings. With that knowledge, Leon knew that Mandelbaum's story was, indeed, fiction, for the rings had been stolen from his uncle! Now, all that mattered was to figure out how Mandelbaum had really come to find the rings.

Once he was sure that what he thought to be true was, indeed, true, he rushed back to Pinsk with the article. When Mayer Malkin saw the photograph that accompanied the article, he immediately saw the red hair of the man fleeing the scene.

He yelled out for anyone within half a mile to hear, "That looks exactly like Jake the Horse Thief!"

The old man was convinced that he had found the young boy whom he had once chased into the Pripet Marshes not too many years earlier.

The photo taken by the security camera in the store was, indeed, hazy as well as lacking in any form of real detail, but in the mind of the old man, it was enough to set off a smoldering memory of arrogance, theft, deceit, and defeat in the Pripet Marsh.

It had occurred to Leon, when he saw the photo, that it might be a grown-up Jake. But the possibility seemed so far out of reality that he wrote it off. Then he began to think.

The day before the story of the robbery had broken across the continent, Leon had received a note from the Banker Baunhauf. Through his sources, he had located the coroner's report on Julius Malkin. The evidence told of how one side of his skull had been caved in. In addition, his body had been kicked repeatedly and beaten in manner that is consistent with assault.

An accompanying notes mentioned that, "If I was working this case in your town, I would consider this the body of a murder victim."

Then, on a second page, he read, "The clothing held a note inside a pocket. It was a list of jewels that he had taken with him for sale. Various names were on that list. Please find that list included."

Reading on, Leon saw that the list held a good number of loose diamonds, emeralds, watches, and a few other abbreviations for stones that he recognized from his studies. At the very bottom, in his uncle's own easy-to-recognize script, were the words, "Five Sisters' Rings: B. in Lichtenstein."

Leon put the note down and pursed his lips together. His uncle was on his way to deposit the rings in a safe place. The little stones were to be used as bribes as he crossed the border! If he had reached Lichtenstein safely to make the deposit, he would be alive today!

Then he looked hard at the picture in the paper. He was now sure that it was a fully grown Jacob Horvicz. He had spent too much time with the boy hanging out at his father's corral to not know the boy's physical characteristics.

One thing he knew was that Jake, while he did take a horse, hadn't become a real thief. It wasn't in his makeup. Leon knew the kid really well. He had a deep sense of honor. After all, he hadn't picked a fight that night when his sister went charging out into the night. The kid knew the law.

Leon looked at the article again and realized that the jeweler who now had the rings had the same name as the jeweler whom the banker in Lichtenstein had warned him was the most dishonest man in the black market.

A light went off in the head of Leon Malkin. The story was a plant to establish a legitimate provenance for the rings! That wasn't a robbery; it was a sale. Jake was selling Mandelbaum the rings because the jeweler was the only man who would buy such hot and valuable material.

Leon said it out loud, "Jake was in that store to sell the rings!"

The truth rose over Leon's body as heat rises from the ground to the air.

"Jake had the rings, which meant he either killed my uncle or knows who did." Sure, it happened during a war, but Jake was in the middle of his uncle's death!

This was too much for Leon. He had already forgiven the orphan Horvicz once for making his brother a cripple. To forgive him for being part of the murder of his uncle was too much for him to do!

He knew that in some way, Jake was responsible for his uncle's murder. He explained his theory to his father and backed it up with facts.

Clenching his fists, the butcher's anger was so close to the surface that he could barely control himself.

"If Jake the Horse Thief is still alive, I will hunt him down and kill him!" said Mayer Malkin.

Taking up the idea, Leon Malkin vowed to use every resource he had, including what he had gained from Uncle Julius's estate, to find Jake the Horse Thief and exact revenge for what had happened so long ago.

It was a desire for revenge that would drive the Malkin family for a full generation.

At the time he was flying to America, Jesse Horton had no idea that he was facing an unbending threat from the Malkins. He had an idea that something was wrong. But he felt that a new name and a move to America would clean up a lot.

The situation was so fraught with mortal danger that he definitely had to send Sara away. On his own, he could stay low and avoid the Malkins. With a wife and the inevitable children that would surely follow, he could never find a moments peace with the thought that a Malkin holding a gun would be around the next corner.

For Jesse, getting to America was far more important than obsessing over rumors and possibilities. There was one undeniable fact: he had three of the other Five Sisters' Rings, and secondly, they must be worth a fortune.

The photo in the newspaper showing a person fleeing from Mandelbaum Jewelers right after the robbery was hazy. But the feature did show his red hair. And it clearly matched his height.

Before he even thought of boarding a flight to the United States, Jesse removed his bright red beard and went the extra step of shaving his head as well. If he was going to travel like this, he was going to be comfortable.

Most importantly, he would be able to move safely without the fear of being recognized. When the hair would grow back in, he would dye it another color. Today he was traveling as a man free from all worries.

# UNITED STATES—FINI: JAKE THE HORSE THIEF

That, as far as I can tell, is as much of the story of Jake the Horse Thief's early years as I could find. Much of what you just read was taken from the prayer book that I had worked so hard to find. The details were filled in by my many conversations with the man over the years.

I guess I've always been in the right place at the right time. It wasn't an impossibility that Jake the Horse Thief found his way to my doorstep!

When I finally met him, Jake was known as Jesse Horton. He was looking for "landsmen from Kovno Caberna" with the last name of Horvicz, or something close to that.

Me? I'm a cash contributor to an organization dedicated to the history and immigration of Jews from Eastern Europe. I also write on the subject in a variety of publications and speak to organizations around the country as well. The main office for the organization office is in New York.

The story of Jake came to my attention when one day, out of the blue, the main office called me at my home in Baltimore.

"Bob Hurwitz?" asked an unknown voice on the other end of the line.

I confirmed that it was me he was calling speaking with.

"This is Jack Sobel of the Associated Jewish Charities in New York calling. We met briefly after a talk that you gave at an Associated Convention in Baltimore a few months ago. You made some very significant points about the *Jews Who Were Left Behind*. My colleagues and I were impressed."

Naturally, I was flattered. I told him, "Many, many thanks. It was a good convention, and I was honored to speak. Is there something I can do for you today? Can I help you in some way?"

"I have a young man in my office who just arrived in America. He is anxious to talk to someone who knows and understands the experiences of Lithuanian Jews during World War II. As soon as I met him, I thought of you and your talk on that very subject. It occurred to me that you might want to meet him. His name is Jesse Horton, and this is only his second day in America. He is a bit different than the usual immigrant. It is really clear that he has given a great deal of thought on coming to America."

"How so?" I queried

"Yesterday Jesse Horton cleared customs in LaGuardia Airport. The first thing he did after that was to look for a familiar name, something that he could recognize. You know, he's in New York for the first time and a bit overwhelmed by all that he sees, but he needs to find a hotel. Unfamiliar with the city, he looks for something with a Yiddish or Jewish-sounding name. As these things happen, he saw the Jewish National Fund in bold letters. At first, they really didn't understand what he was looking for. As soon as they understood what he needed, they called our office."

I listened as he hesitated for a second, as if he was trying to figure out what had happened and explain it in the shortest possible way.

Then he went on, "It didn't take long for me to understand that Jesse had been preparing for his arrival in America for a long time. He wanted to find a Jewish organization that would understand his background. He was looking for a group of people or an organization that would help him acclimate to his new surroundings. I couldn't help but think of you."

"Makes sense to me. When can I talk to him?" I asked.

Sobel told me that Horton was standing right there with him. Figuring that there is no time better than the present, I said, "Put him on!"

After a polite greeting, it quickly became clear that Jesse had, indeed, been studying hard in preparation for his move to America. While he spoke haltingly, his English was pretty good for a man who had never much occasion to speak the language in actual conversations. It was easy to tell that he was somewhat flustered by what he was dealing with during his arrival in America. It's only natural. To come over from Europe and see the nonstop activity in New York would shock anyone.

Looking to give him a sense of comfort and familiarity, I got the idea to speak to him in Yiddish. I hoped that it would serve as a bridge between us and help him to feel free to converse. As I began to speak his native language, I could feel a sense of relief come over him almost immediately. From that moment on, he seemed to be breathing a bit easier.

Speaking in Yiddish, he told me, "I was born Jacob Horvicz in Pinsk in what is now known as Belarus."

My own studies had made me very familiar with the region. I was definitely intrigued in what he was going to say. Over the years as a researcher, I had found that some of the best stories start in a very specific place.

He went on, "I ask that you listen to my story about Lithuania. Then I hope you will understand why I changed my name to Jesse Horton and what I hope to do in this new country."

"I'll be glad to hear your story," I told him. "After all, I'm also a Litvak!"

"Wonderful!" he said. "Then we will be starting on the same page when we talk."

Pressing on with the details, I asked, "How about we meet tomorrow in Baltimore? You can tell me all about yourself. If that is okay with you, I will make arrangements for you to come on down."

He seemed thrilled at the offer. I explained how this would work, and then I asked to speak to Sobel again. Jack Sobel generously offered to make the travel arrangements for Jesse. He told me to expect a phone call from his secretary with the details in about an hour or so.

The next day I met Jesse at the BWI Airport. I had expected to see a nervous and much older gentleman. Instead, I was greeted by a man not much younger than myself with a clean-shaven bald head. He was tall and lean. When he put his hand out for me to shake, I took it and found that the energy I was feeling from his presence came through in his grip. This was a man who had a purpose in life.

As we had on the phone, we spoke in Yiddish. I told him that we would work into speaking English over time. But for now, it might be best if we stayed with what we know best.

We were friends within minutes.

On the ride home to my condominium on Slade Avenue, we each had to struggle to get a word in. When we passed a policeman sitting at the side of the road on Slade, he asked me why the man wasn't out trying to stop a crime. I explained to Jesse that he was, in fact, stopping a crime. The cop was sitting there looking for speeders so he could give them a ticket, which would involve a fee as a penalty.

"Then I will never speed on Slade Avenue, for I do not want to give my money away for free!"

"Wise choice," said I.

He was anxious to tell his story, and I wanted to make sure that I wrote down every word he had to say. When we pulled up, he seemed to be particularly impressed at the doorman of my building as well as the valet parking.

"I lived in caves and bombed-out buildings for nearly five years. So forgive me if I seem to be a bit overwhelmed with it all," said Jesse with his eyes wide open as he looked at every inch of the street and building.

"To see the massive skyscrapers of New York and now this, it is like watching beautiful bombs going off in my brain. It is just unbelievable!"

Once we were in my condo, we shed our coats and sat down. As soon as we settled in, Jesse began to ask questions.

"I already know enough about America to know that this must be a wealthy neighborhood. Isn't that true?"

"Not everyone in Baltimore is this wealthy," I assured him with a laugh.

With that, he sighed and broke into a big smile. The fact that I can understand some Yiddish created a strong bond from the start. I was anxious to ask him questions, but he wanted to know more about me and my neighborhood before he opened his story.

"Is this a Jewish neighborhood?" Jesse asked.

"In the blocks surrounding this building, 75 percent of the people are probably Jewish. But most of the Jews in Baltimore are solid middle-class people that you will enjoy meeting."

I stood and asked him if he wanted a drink. He nodded yes, and I made a motion for him to follow me. In a minute we were standing at a small bar I keep near the window. He showed he was no greenhorn when he pointed straight at the J&B Scotch. Pouring a couple of glasses, I handed him one. He took it and then indicated that he wanted to begin his story.

Jesse Horton hadn't been in America more than two days, and all he wanted to do was talk about the *Jews Who Were Left Behind*. I was impressed by his dedication to the subject. He was looking for any Baltimore or United States connections. At this point, he had yet to mention or discuss intimate details about himself or his old identity as Jake the Horse Thief.

When I mentioned Kovno Caberna and Baltimore in the same sentence, I received a broad smile of recognition from Jesse. I knew that it seems as if half the Jews in Baltimore had kinfolk that came from the area of Kovno Caberna.

Those who departed from the region before World War II were the very fortunate. The Nazis sealed the Kovno ghetto August 15, 1941 with twenty-nine thousand people impounded. As far as I know, almost all of them perished. After I gave him some basic details about the area, he told me his story as part of the Jewish underground at that time.

I stood in awe of the man who was now in my house. Never in a million years would I have ever thought that someone who had done so much to help the Lithuanian Jews of the region would be drinking Scotch at my bar. He immediately became a hero to me for his group's efforts in saving the Lithuanian Jews.

I told him that there are many Jews in Baltimore with the surname of Horowitz, or Horwitz, or something close with a similar spelling. We agreed that it was possible that Jesse's surname of Horvicz could have even undergone the change in immigration procedures to become Hurwitz, which is my name!

So the thread of being a "landsman" became even stronger. We started opening up to each other. He began telling me this amazing story. I took notes like a madman as he talked of the years. Every part of his tale could be gleaned from the notes written on the borders of the prayer book that he carried with him for more than thirty years.

Before elaborating on my friendship with Jesse Horton—or, as I like to remember him, Jake the Horse Thief—a few words about me are due.

My name is Robert Hurwitz, and as I write this, I am forty-eight years old. Twelve years ago, my wife died in an automobile accident. We had one child, a son. He now attends MIT. Five years ago, I sold my computer supply business at the top of the market—a smart move, which benefited from good timing. As a result, I now have what can be described as moderate wealth. As a result, I enjoy almost complete freedom from everyday obligations.

With our glasses refilled, I told him, "Jesse, I'll guarantee complete secrecy for anything you tell me, please continue."

Jesse then began the unforgettable tale of his life. He took a deep breath and began.

"I was an orphan. As a six-year-old, I quickly realized what that meant. Rabbi Vilnish became my foster father because no one else in Pinsk wanted me. I was a solitary boy. The few Jewish boys in Pinsk were foreign to me. Other than Reb Vilnish, there was only one person to love and be loved, and that was my sister, Leah."

I have never heard a flatter, more even-toned voice ever tell a story in my life. It was filled with heartbreak and loss, yet I never heard a bit of emotion in what was said. It was as if he was in complete control of what he felt.

When he paused, I nodded my head, and Jesse continued, "I was never a teenager. There was no time for that episode. I had to become a man and rescue my sister and save her from the hell that was Pinsk and the Malkins."

Jesse slumped in his chair, and I believe, as he opened up, he reverted to himself as Jake. I listened in amazement as he led to the reason that Mayer Malkin called him Jake the Horse Thief. As his tale emerged, it became apparent that the escape that he and his sister made through the Pripet Marshes had set the tone for his life. Young Jacob Horvicz would always be fleeing demons!

The bitter, bloody struggle that he and Leah experienced with the stranger on the road to Minsk stamped Jake with an emotional scar that is permanently seared into his being! It was inevitable that Jake/Jesse would attempt to construct a wall of privacy that would remain with him forever. When Jesse reached a point where he had to divorce himself from the demons brought on by his years in Europe, a crack in that wall appeared.

That afternoon, I became the recipient of his trust and his need to unburden himself about life as Jake. Listening to his story of Julius Malkin, I was stunned to hear that he spoke so openly of what he had been carrying for all these years, both physically and spiritually. He began the tale slowly, with a surprising revelation.

"Robert," he said plainly, "I have a difficult problem. I have been wearing a pouch of jewelry almost as a second skin. It has reached a point where something must be done about its contents."

When Jesse (or was he Jake now—for at times, as he spoke, I felt as if two people were telling the story…) said this, I gasped at this intimate tale.

He continued, "From the time I was a boy, I wanted to be the protector of my sister, Leah. I aimed to rescue her from the hell that was the Malkin household. On our trail to Minsk, I was proud of myself until my careless actions caused her permanent grief. I was caught stealing fruit by a farmer, and before I could escape, I suffered a serious wound."

Again I was startled at what I heard. I murmured, "Please don't stop."

Jake was nervous, but he continued, "We were in a desperate situation. The knife wound was infected. I needed medical attention. We had a little money, and we were hungry. Two kids in trouble, and we had no one to turn to!

"While I sought medical attention, Leah, feeling that she wasn't carrying her weight in our travels, made the decision to start begging for help. She confronted several people, one or two did help, but it was only amounted to a few coins. Then she saw what appeared to be a prosperous merchant, and she made a desperate plea for help."

Jake had to take a deep breath before he could continue with this harrowing tale.

"The merchant, with a quick glance at the trembling Leah, made this harsh proposal, 'Let's have some fast oral sex!' My shaken sister was an innocent young woman and barely understood his command. When she shook her head and sputtered, 'No'…"

Telling the tale out loud upset him so much that he was growing nervous. I waited for Jake to catch his breath, and after he did, he went on.

"The merchant grabbed Leah's hair and pulled her head down to his now-opened fly and shouted, 'Now you can earn fifty US dollars, bitch!'

"Feeling that she was in a hopeless situation, she pretended to acquiesced to his demand. Suddenly, filled with anger and desperation, she took action. Bringing a rock up from the ground, she slammed it into his crotch. Again and again, she struck back at the vile pervert.

"As he fought back, he bloodied her face. But surprise was on her side, and in a short time, she quickly dispatched Julius Malkin to his death."

He looked away in shame.

Not exactly sure of what he was telling me, I said quickly, "Oh my god, what happened?"

At this moment, Jake shook his head and sobbed. I could only guess the effort of trying to hold so much inside; the man had finally broken through.

When he regained his composure, I asked him again, "What happened next?"

As he went into detail, he occasionally repeated what he had just told me. But it certainly wasn't any less shocking.

## JAKE THE HORSE THIEF

"In desperation, she somehow regained her feet and retaliated, smashing his skull with a large stone and causing his death. In the battle, the owner of the pouch tried to beat my sister without mercy for refusing to perform such an act. Leah's beautiful face was bloodied. Her shirt was ripped away when he cast her to the ground."

Jesse was very distraught while relating the tragic event. I was shocked that Jesse was telling such an intimate tale.

He stated the result plainly and simply, "She clubbed him to death with the stone. He got a few blows in, but she killed him outright."

My guest related, "At that time, the Nazis were attacking the Minsk area in full force. They had planes, tanks, infantry, and everything at their disposal. Everyone not in the battle was on the move, gathering belongings and fleeing for their lives!"

Jesse began to grow excited as he went on, "I had suffered a disabling injury while my sister, Leah, was fighting for her life! We didn't have more than a moment to go through the attacker's belongings to discover this pouch of jewels and then to flee the German onslaught!"

Jake the Horse Thief, a man of proved courage and manliness, cried bitterly when he related this sad tale. I poured a stiff drink for both of us and calmed my new friend.

He then regrouped his emotions and then, in fragments, he continued.

"I retained most of the jewels in the pouch and attached it to my body and then had some jewels sewn into garments that Leah wore at all times," Jesse continued the sad tale.

"After she dressed my wounded arm, we spent several months crossing what is now Belarus, until we found Vilna, Lithuania, where we were apprehended by collaborationists. After a brief struggle, we were overcome by the Lithuanian collaborationists. They soon recognized that they had a desperate female on their hands. I could see the damn Litho guards stripping off her clothing while she fought and screamed to no avail. We were separated forever."

Jesse continued crying before being able to continue.

Once he had regained his composure, he said, "The last I ever saw of my dear sister was Leah being thrown into a German Army van."

His efforts to find Leah alive would be another one of the million-plus stories of the Holocaust.

When he ended his story, I could think of nothing but to offer dinner. It took a few minutes for Jesse to regain his composure and smile at my hospitality.

During the small dinner in my apartment, Jesse began to exhibit a hesitant but increasing comfort in our friendship. Somehow, I had accomplished something that those who had preceded in meeting Jesse had not done before. I was able to crack the shell of privacy that Jake the Horse Thief had constructed around himself.

As others had told me over the years, the profitability that I had in business was due to my ability to be a good listener. Today that skill paid off in a way that I would have never imagined.

He then opened his mind and admitted that the possession of the pouch of jewels had become a mental burden.

Jake continued, "After the war ended, with the aid of my friend Sid Levy (formerly Shlomo Levitz), I sold some of the gems. At that time, I developed an understanding that the remaining jewels are extremely valuable."

After a solemn pause, Jake continued, "I fervently wish to help three people who were with me during the darkest days of my life!"

His mouth quivered, and he seemed on the verge of breaking down in tears, before he stopped and uttered with quiet but deep emotion, "They are in Eretz Yisroel. I'm certain that they may have arrived there with little more than the clothes on their backs! Additionally, I would like to see a shul (synagogue) constructed for the remaining Jews left in Kovno and, if possible, build a second one in Vilna."

He said all this without losing a breath. It was evident that sending these dispensations would be very important to this soldier for Jewish freedom!

I replied, "I will attempt to make your wish a reality. But first, get your breath back, and then we will talk about your jewels. Let's take a break. You can rest in my guest room."

I led him to the second room that my son uses when he returns to visit. Jesse stared at the pictures on the wall. My son had always hung diagrams and images of science as opposed to what other kids put on their walls.

"What a place to grow up in!" he said excitedly. "Needless to say, I can't help but to think of my small cot in the corner of the rabbi's kitchen. It was small, but it was home!"

There was nothing small or petty to be found in Jesse's comment. I could see that he was truly amazed at my apartment. Jesse's head began to droop, and it was evident he needed rest.

After telling him to sleep as long as he wished, he said, "Wake me in an hour, that's all I'll need, I'm on a different clock."

An hour later, I knocked on the door and asked him if he needed anything. He told me that he would be with me in a minute. Sitting at the dining room table, I watched as he walked out completely refreshed.

He informed me, "Even as a kid, I could get by with a minimal amount of sleep."

I asked if he wanted anything before we started to talk about the details. Jesse told me that he was fine.

Then he said, "I feel that I can trust you, so please, let's continue."

I started by saying, "Before we go about assessing the value of these gems, let's make it clear that you definitely want to retain considerable privacy about every aspect of this matter?"

Jake thought for a long minute before answering, "How difficult will it be to assess the values without it becoming common knowledge? Then I need to know if it would it be possible to sell the jewelry privately."

Before answering, I had to ask him, "How dangerous to you, and to anyone else, would knowledge of the sale be? And could you be facing criminal charges?"

I could see him thinking about how to answer the question. There were a number of ideas to consider when it came to their sale.

What evidence existed of the death of the man that Leah killed? How culpable was Leah of the crime of murder? How culpable would he be as, what can only be called, her accomplice?

German troops were flooding around the area of Minsk where the deadly incident occurred. There was no civil authority present. Should Leah and/or Jesse have reported the incident at that time? Or even at any time in the following years? And if so, to whom?

Was his claim to the jewels even ethical? Did he have a legal right to the lot?

Jesse then disturbed my thoughts and exclaimed, "Shall I no longer be Jake as we attempt to sell the jewels? Should I now be my new identity, Jesse Horton? Should I attempt to find the relatives of the deceased?"

I could not answer Jesse Horton's questions. All I could ask was, "Who am I to answer these questions?"

There was another moral dimension to all this. Should Jake attempt to find the heirs?

After some time of considering his responsibility in the matter, Jake spoke, "I do not feel any great measure of guilt from anything that happened. That said, with any surplus value from the sale of gems, I wish to make the bequests I've just mentioned."

He continued, "I do not wish to endanger you financially or physically. If you do choose to advise me, I will do everything I can to make sure that all arrangements are free of your involvement. From now on, I also think that it will be best for you to address me by the name I've legally assumed, Jesse Horton."

After I had heard the entire tale, I had to take a moment to consider what had just happened. Jesse Horton had given me a part of himself. This was something I would treasure for the remainder of my life. I correctly sensed that what I had received from him was unique, and I was the sole recipient.

It was, indeed, overwhelming. Before continuing, I suggested we have a snack that I had prepared. Jesse was unexpectedly pleased to have a break in what had become an emotional aspect in our meeting. Jesse wasn't familiar with the corned beef sandwiches and potato salad, but he was happy with what he titled "a great new experience in food."

The hour was growing late, and I asked him, "Where are you staying tonight?"

When I realized he was thinking of a nearby motel, I saw the opportunity I wanted.

"I have that second room here, and it will be ideal for you, please don't refuse!"

Jesse attempted to say something, but I had already carried his coat into the room that had once belonged to my son. I suggested that we talk about practical living arrangements for Jesse that night, and he could make the plans he discussed about the jewels the next morning.

Jesse was most anxious to talk about a topic that surprised me.

"I'd like to own an automobile like yours. Where can I buy one?"

"You are barely in the United States. I can see you have much on your mind. I'll try to help you get settled—"

Cutting me off before I could finish, he exclaimed, "I have the necessary funds to buy an auto!"

Smiling at his enthusiasm, I pointed out, "First you will have to obtain a license to drive a car! Also, we have to consider steps to your citizenship. Are you going to be living in the United States? I can help you arrange those important things."

He had a reservation at a motel in Pikesville, but he wanted a place to live in, like mine, only smaller and not so fancy.

"I don't need a doorman or a valet to park my car."

I suggested that he inquire at the apartment buildings on Park Heights Avenue, which are not far from my condo on Slade Avenue. (Guess what! He would wind up in a building with a doorman!) We talked about a few other things retail over a good night highball.

The next morning, I gave considerable thought of what he had told me the previous night. Ultimately, it seemed clear what had to be done.

I recommended that he visit a retail jeweler in Baltimore that I respected. For a customary small fee, the jeweler evaluated what Jesse had with him that day.

My jeweler friend was amazed to see such a high-quality display of jewels. He told us that the real money was in the three very unique and individualistic rings.

"What you have here would bring the best return at private auction, especially if they were sold as a single unit. You know, keep the three together."

I agreed and said that I found his advice sound.

Jesse knew that the three unique rings were related to the ring that he sold, at less-than-legal standard, to Henry Weil at J. Mandelbaum Jewelers of Amsterdam, the Netherlands. He wondered aloud if that would cause a problem.

The jeweler speculated that knowledge of where the other rings in the set were could only enhance the value of what Jesse possessed. Knowing the details as I do, I had to agree.

Before making any additional commitments concerning the sale of the jewelry, I told Jesse, "You have mentioned that you sold a ring at less-than-legal standards to Henry Weil at J. Mandelbaum Jewelers of Amsterdam. This may put a cloud on the provenance of the jewelry, making them difficult to sell at any reputable buyer."

"What do you recommend I do?"

I answered, "First I want to thank you for the confidence you have shown me in such important matters. Then you must have a good story to affirm the provenance of your pieces, but that's not all."

Jesse asked us, "What should I do next?"

"It is going to be just as important that Mandelbaum in Amsterdam has as good a story as you do. It may be best to contact Mandelbaum on a secure phone line and establish some understanding with them before going any further."

I added, "Be careful, from what you have told me, you will be dealing with a very wise old bird, who will not give an inch in any proceedings. Also, you should contact a lawyer to advise you of exactly what to say when you call Mandelbaum. My friend and lodge member Ben Bernstein is a retired attorney. Can I set up a meeting between the two of you? There you could talk to him, before taking any additional steps."

The next morning, Jesse, Ben Bernstein, and I had a breakfast meeting at a small restaurant on Reisterstown Road. Jesse was forthcoming and direct in the details, which immediately earned Ben's trust.

"I am too old to waste my time with falsehoods. I thank you, Jesse, for telling straight up what I am dealing with here."

With that, he used the clear side of the placemat and created a series of steps we should take in order to protect ourselves. Ben also suggested that I assist Jesse in contacting Mandelbaum on a secure line.

It took two additional days for us to work out the details, but finally, Jesse was able to make the call. We used my condo as a base. The phone call was made, and I hit "record." This is exactly what I heard that day.

"Mr. Mandelbaum, this is Jesse Horton calling from Baltimore, Maryland. I hope I find you well?"

Mandelbaum answered, "I'm okay, but this call must be costing you a bundle, so it's best you explain who you are and why in the hell you're calling!"

"I'm the knave mentioned in the newspaper article that made your son-in-law look like a hero. You must remember that story, the one where he was defending the store against a thief?"

Mandelbaum sounded nonplussed as he said, "So?"

Jesse told him point-blank, "I'm the one that sold a very valuable ring to Henry Weil!"

Mandelbaum, in a loud voice, shot back, "Is this some kind of scam? You better watch out if it is, for I hate to have my time wasted. I wasn't born yesterday! I've heard them all!"

"Hold it, sir. I know that you hold two of the Five Sisters' Rings…"

Mandelbaum interrupted, "So what? I possess them legally, and what do you say your name is?"

"My name is Jesse Horton, and I own the other three of the set known as the Five Sisters' Rings."

It dawned on Mandelbaum that he wasn't dealing with a fool or a blackmailer. Using a more quiet voice, he said, "I thought they were lost forever. Where in the hell did you get them?"

"I believe that I have adequate provenance. I believe it will be very advantageous for us to meet in a mutually rewarding setting, do you agree?"

He answered, "I'm getting your drift, I think you believe that to combine them in a sale, they'd be worth a fortune, isn't that so?"

"You understand my thoughts completely. Now, where do you suggest we meet?"

Sam Mandelbaum, sensing the possibility of the biggest payday of his life, hesitated for a good long while.

Then he spoke quietly, "I wouldn't want anyone to know about the meeting and where it is, before we actually hold it. If you can travel, an ideal place could be in Iceland. Airfare is cheap from here. I know of a good hotel in Reykjavik. It would be neutral ground, and I think it would be as secure as we can find."

"I'll think about Iceland from this end and get back to you tomorrow. If your proposal turns out to be doable, how about agreeing to a tentative meeting within fifteen days?"

With that, they exchanged good-byes and ended the call.

Working separately, Mandelbaum and Jesse made their own travel and security arrangements to meet in Reykjavik. The exact location, place, and time were secret.

Jesse asked who could serve as his legal counsel, and I suggested Ben Bernstein.

"He is a top-notch lawyer who is excellent at contract negotiations."

Jesse agreed.

I also thought that Phil Waltman, the jeweler who had previously advised Jesse, be part of his team. Jesse thought this was wise also.

Eight days later, our team of four set out for Iceland. In no time, we landed at Keflavik Airport, Iceland.

We were met there by Sam Mandelbaum and a small contingent of his advisers. He had arrived two hours earlier from Heathrow Airport, England.

The two groups met at 10:00 p.m. in a private room of the Regal Hotel in Keyjkavlik. With the sun still shining in Iceland, we had to close the drapes before proceeding. Sam Mandelbaum and

Jesse Horton each had their own priorities when it came to the meeting. The idea would be to get both on the same page.

When Mandelbaum had acquired the two rings, he had prayed that the three remaining rings had survived the war. To have all five rings in one place would make the lot worth an unimaginable fortune to anyone who had them.

However, it was the tale of how his son-in-law acquired the ring from Jesse that made Mandelbaum reluctant to meet Jesse, without complete security. Way back in a dark corner of his mind, he wondered how he could be certain that this wasn't some wild nefarious scheme cooked up by his son-in-law, the decidedly unintelligent Henry Weil.

Jesse had his own measure of reluctance. Remembering how he had acquired the rings, Jesse worried about arrest and possibly being sent to jail as a thief.

When the two groups finally met, both parties stood in awe at what they saw laid out on the table before them. The artistic excellence of the rings notwithstanding, the excitement of seeing the five rings together was overwhelming to them. The presence of the rings in one place changed the tenor of the meeting.

After a minute and close inspections of the jewels was conducted by a representative of each side, it was agreed among everyone in attendance: the collection of Five Sisters' Rings were, indeed, a reality. The history of the rings was acknowledged and verified.

Before arranging a joint sale or a public auction of the Five Sisters' Rings, there remained some important legal considerations to resolve.

Ben Bernstein had done his homework in international law and was ready to assist Jesse in all the legal ramifications.

Sam Mandelbaum retained a lawyer who was a member of his family, Levi Wolfe. Both lawyers spoke Yiddish and English, so it was hoped that negotiations would go smoothly and efficiently.

Naturally, being lawyers, that idea went out the window. After much time was spent arguing details back and forth, it was agreed that both parties would observe the following rules of sale.

First would be the division of profit of sale minus expenses. This brought prolonged discussion by both parties.

Ben Bernstein, for Jesse Horton, argued, "Mr. Horton is furnishing three of the Five Sisters' Rings in the grouping. Additionally, many years ago, he sold another ring to Amsterdam Jewelers under less-than-legal standards. It was Jesse Horton who, at one time as Jacob Horvicz, had found all five of the rings."

At this moment, Levi Wolfe, speaking for Mandelbaum, interrupted and said, "You are referring to his wartime activities?"

Mr. Bernstein then countered, "Let's not fight World War II all over again. Mr. Horton saved thousands of our fellow Jews during this time. He's a hero, and I suggest you try not to attack him, lest you look like a fool among our community. Also, what he did has a few of the losers out there, looking for him as a matter of revenge. Considering that Horton is providing the majority of the rings and the best history, he should receive 75 percent of the profits."

Levi Wolfe promptly asserted, "Mr. Mandelbaum brings many years reputation to be considered in arriving at how much any party would bid on the grouping. Mandelbaum must get 50 percent!"

After a long discussion with their clients, a compromise was reached. Jesse Horton would get 58 percent of the profits, and J. Mandelbaum Jewelers would get 42 percent of the proceeds. Both amounts were to be tallied only after all expenses were met. After that point was settled, there remained other important agreements to be discussed.

Levi Wolf started by saying, "Our client's reputation is at stake. What we present to the auctioneer must have excellent provenance as to its legitimacy."

"I'm familiar with the laws of provenance," said Bernstein. "We must cooperate and agree jointly on every detail."

When Jesse heard this dialogue between the lawyers, the image of Leah standing over the dead body of Julius Malkin flashed through his mind. He knew he would have to relate some part of this mortal fact carefully to his lawyer.

Slowly, Jesse began to tell the group, "I found a pouch containing jewelry in an alleyway. I was hiding there with my sister, trying to avoid detection, as the invading warlike forces rushed in. It was mid-1940, and people and soldiers were moving about rapidly to escape the Nazi threat of conquest that everyone believed was imminent."

Bernstein questioned Jesse, as if he was on a courtroom stand, "Did you see an individual being killed for the jewelry?"

It was a question that Jesse could answer honestly, "No, anyone around the pouch was dead, long before I spotted it."

His lawyer continued the investigation, "What were the general conditions in Minsk that day?"

"Everyone was frightened and on the move," answered Jesse. "There were thousands of Jews leaving as fast as they could. As to the bag, I had hoped to find some food or a few kopecks in order to buy something to eat."

"Did you throw away a bill of sale or any paperwork involved with a sale at all?"

"No," was all Jesse needed to say.

Unless someone was to challenge the sale, when it went to auction, the jewels were clearly found.

With that, the discussion of provenance was closed. No one could possibly challenge the find—especially with the former owner's own admission on record that he had sold the jewels on the black market in order to flee France. Anyone could have found the jewels. Unless someone wanted to come forward and produce paperwork to that sale, the jewels had a clear record of each step of ownership.

Later, as we sat around the dinner table, Bernstein related to me that the Nazis slaughtered almost the entire Jewish population of over twenty-nine thousand in Minsk—a fact I fully understood as real. No wonder the Jews in Lithuania were trying so hard to leave that day in 1940!

The discussion concerning provenance continued as Levi Wolfe spoke for Sam Mandelbaum.

"The war was over for some time when those who had been embroiled in it began to arrive at my client's store. They openly displayed a wide range of jewelry they wanted to sell and, in some sad cases, to pawn. When it was possible, Mandelbaum Jewelers made sure to alert authorities of any jewels that they knew had been confiscated by the Nazis."

Jesse interrupted by asking, "How about the two pieces that you have from the Five Sisters' set?"

"We used all available means to establish provenance," said Mandelbaum, a touch defensively. "It was difficult to discern any value when we purchased each piece separately, especially with a large space of time between the two sales. To this day we have never discovered anyone who had claimed these pieces were stolen or lost."

His attorney then added, "We are positive that our two Five Sisters' Rings have satisfactory provenance."

The main details addressed, Jesse and I retired to get a drink. This gave Ben the chance to reach an agreement with Levi Wolfe on how the provenances of all the Five Sisters' Rings would be presented to the auctioneer.

In half an hour, we were called back to the meeting. After these important preliminary discussions, Jesse and Mandelbaum made one more decision.

They both agreed to a stipulation that a national museum would be the best possible owner of the grouping. It was important to them that the rings be available for the public to view. A private buyer might pay a bit more, but Jesse and Mandelbaum felt that the heritage of the rings and what they represented was far too important to lay hiding for decades in a rich man's vault.

The lawyers knew of the international reputation held by the respected British auctioneer Malmby. It was only logical that they would be selected as the auction house that would list the Five Sisters' Rings.

When the details were completed, it was four in the morning Reykjavik time, and it was still daylight.

In the next few weeks, a single secretary from the auction house Malmby kept each side appraised of the steps to hold the auction. Quietly, museum directors of five nations were invited to bid. The participants, the bidding, and the final price were kept a secret. Hopefully, it always will be.

The initial listing caused quite a stir among the directors for museums located in Paris, Brussels, Antwerp, Rome, and London when they received personal invitations to bid on jewelry at Malmby's London Gallery.

The directors all knew that Malmby's was never one to waste anyone's time or energy on examining insignificant works. The auction house arranged accommodations for the staff of the museums, who were to function as the bidders, to be welcomed at hotels in the Greater London area.

It isn't often that such historically important jewelry was the object of a major art auction. Each of the museum directors brought their own curators to the auction. The curators of the potential bidders were given only enough information to create a great sense of anticipation. They all knew that in the aftermath of World War II, many famed pieces of jewelry were unaccounted.

When they learned what the auction contained, they were surprised that an item thought to be irretrievably lost was there in front of them to be auctioned!

The provenance of the rings was questioned at great length by the bidders. During World War II, the Five Sisters' Rings appeared to have disappeared as did many other valuable possessions of the famous and the nobility.

The last known owner of the Five Sisters' Rings was the alcoholic son of a French nobleman. He had once given an interview, where he stated as fact that he had sold the jewels on the black market in order to buy his way out of France during the war.

As to what had happened to them next was the subject of much speculation. All that was confirmable was that the jewels had been sold to a stranger for quick cash. The old French nobleman had lost them in the coming war. No recording of the transaction was ever made. The money was exchanged, and the new owner walked away with the rings.

In all this time, no one else had ever presented any note involving previous ownership of the rings. It was agreed among them that the successful bidder at the auction would possess adequate provenance of the rings and be considered the sole owner.

The auction began after each bidder was given an opportunity to examine each ring for imperfections and artistic value. The time limit was exactly one hour.

Each of the five rings was considered to be a flawless example of perfect beauty. Their value was greatly enhanced by the history of how and why the Five Sisters' Rings were created. The combination of both factors drove the price of the five gems to great heights.

Once the pieces were individually evaluated, each of the museum directors presented their bids with enthusiasm. Every one of them felt that they had the greatest backing and the best chance to win the lot. But as positive as they all were, only one of them could leave with the jewels in their possession.

In minutes it became apparent that nothing offered by any of the other museums could top the bid made by France. The country had such an emotional attachment to the origins of the Five Sisters' Rings that they believed no expense must be spared, for they only could have one home. A permanent exhibition in the Louvre!

Jesse Horton and Sam Mandelbaum had agreed on differing shares of the proceeds of the sale of the Five Sisters' Rings. Mandelbaum, from previous experiences, had an idea of the riches the auction would generate. But Jesse Horton was overwhelmed by the stunning amount of wealth he had acquired through the auction!

With his share of the proceeds, Jesse paid for the restorations of small synagogues in both Kovno and Vilna, Lithuania. He then arranged for the purchase of apartments in Tel Aviv, Israel, for his old friends Sid Levy and Sara Flom.

Oddly, when he completed these dispensations, Jesse did not experience any sense of accomplishment.

Jesse regarded the donations to the two synagogues in Lithuania as a duty, but the gifts to Sid and Sara were an apology. He had been quietly tormented by the realization that he had abandoned two of the most cherished people he had ever met. The gifts were a thank-you to them for being in his world.

He could not fathom the depths of his being. A conflict grew inside his soul. The question never left him. Is there any difference between Jesse Horton and Jake the Horse Thief?

As to what I thought, I can't say that I was surprised at the nature of Jesse's mental state. I had become what I believed to be a true friend, but I would never be quite sure of just who Jake the Horse Thief was.

I was surprised to learn that Jesse had eventually given much thought concerning the great riches he acquired from his share of the sale of the Five Sisters' Rings. I must admit that I was shocked when he insisted on a gift to me of a new Cadillac Sedan, soon after we returned from Iceland.

Much later, after I presumed that he had died, I would discover that in addition to one private bank account in Baltimore, he had opened many similar accounts, with banks in widely different parts of the United States. The total in these accounts amounted to over several million dollars! Jesse Horton, or Jake Horvicz, was a man with an inborn shell of privacy that even I, a very trusted personal friend, did not completely crack. The instructions for finding these accounts were hidden in the safe deposit box of a Baltimore bank. They only became known after his death.

There was no trouble with Jesse's relationships with women. Females were attracted to Jesse almost as soon as they met him. The older members of my family found him interesting and a polite conversationalist. I couldn't help noticing that women from seventeen to fifty-seven regarded him with sexual overtones.

Mutual sexual attraction was to trigger a deep change in his life.

Jesse's life did not change when the Five Sisters' Rings were sold. He still enjoyed the simple things and never moved from the condo that he had bought when we first met.

In a rare moment of unity, the art world agreed that the Paris museum was the historical as well as the perfect home for the grouping. The Five Sisters' received a prominent and beautiful position in the Louvre.

This did not escape the attention of one special visitor to the gallery, Leon Malkin.

When the news of the supposed criminal action at J. Mandelbaum Jewelry that had netted them the second ring was published, Leon Malkin recognized the redheaded figure in the picture.

The appearance of the rings at the Louvre set off a fire storm of litigation in Paris. The Malkins claimed that a thief had stolen the gems from the late Julius Malkin. World War II, and its aftermath, caused an interruption in the proceeding due to an interruption of proof of ownership between the eighteenth-century noblemen to the present day.

In his interview, the last person to own the rings had never stated to whom he had sold the rings. It was impossible for the Malkins to show any legitimacy to their claim. The litigation brought forth by the Malkins has never completely died and will apparently drag on forever.

This inability of the court system to find that Julius Malkin was the true owner of the rings was maddening to Leon Malkin.

The Leon Malkin who rained lawsuit after lawsuit down on the Louvre was a much different person than the friendly young fellow whom Jesse knew when he was back in Pinsk. In the intervening years, Leon had followed his Uncle Julius's advice and left Pinsk to increase his education and divorce himself from the gross attitude of his father and the farm life of Pinsk.

Leon had once been a friend to the very young, red-haired Jake, but now he had become a mortal enemy of Jake the Horse Thief!

Since the war, Leon Malkin had paid investigators great sums to look for what had caused his uncle's death. In that time, he had unearthed enough information to lead him to believe that Jake Horvicz had stolen the Five Sisters' Rings directly from his uncle.

In the course of these investigations, he had also unearthed enough information that gave a good amount of weight to his personal belief that it was Jake that had killed his uncle. It was determined by one investigator that Jake and his sister were seen by a young couple on the side of the road that day in Minsk.

When interviewed by the investigator, they claimed that they had given half a loaf of bread to two children who looked just like Jake and his sister.

The investigator had gotten the information by pretending to be the older brother of the two orphans. Such is the way of investigators.

For Leon, this placed them in the same city as his uncle, on the exact same day. It was now confirmed in his heart that Jake had undoubtedly murdered his uncle.

When he stared at the display, which held the Five Sisters' Rings inside the Louvre, Leon seethed with impotency and frustration. He vowed to gain revenge and bring Jake to justice for the theft of jewelry, as well as the death of Julius Malkin.

Seething with rage as he stood there, he said to anyone within earshot, "Once more, let us remember my father's cry! Find Jake the Horse Thief!"

From that day forward, Leon Malkin would never let up in his quest for revenge of his uncle's murder.

The rings were not the only jewels that Jesse owned. The remainder of Julius's estate was considerable. Leon was determined to discover the best opportunities possible in order to increase the wealth he was holding.

When World War II ended, the Communist Regime of the USSR dominated the lands of Eastern and Central Europe. Leon had taken great care to make lasting friendships with certain Russian authorities. Favors, bribes, and cash had enabled his family to hold on to their homes and businesses in Pinsk.

However, no one knew that Leon had much larger plans. When Soviet Socialism was supplanted with a more capitalistic system, Leon began purchasing land around devastated Minsk. With the USSR regime a distant memory, Minsk grew rapidly to a city of over two million residents. Leon Malkin was in a perfect position to benefit from the growth of his holdings in and around Minsk.

Malkin used his increased wealth to keep up the hunt for Jake the Horse Thief. Detectives were employed to discover Jake's whereabouts and who his friends were. This desire to find Jake the Horse Thief grew to become an obsession with Leon Malkin. To anyone who would listen, he became fond of roaring, "I want Jake the Horse Thief, dead or alive!"

# MONEY IS ONLY A TOOL

Jesse had long worried over the consequences concerning the death of the man his sister had killed. Despite the care of all his efforts, Jesse was not positive that the stranger was Julius Malkin. The stranger she had killed just did not fit the description of the Malkins that Jesse could remember.

In my living room, Jesse sadly shook his head and slumped in his chair.

He murmured, "I'll never forget the picture in my mind of Leah and the stranger and the dead body."

I wasn't aware of the tragedies that Jesse experienced before we met. It soon became obvious to me that he would have to live with these tragedies forever.

Doing as much as I could, I helped Jesse retain as much privacy as possible after the auction had taken place. The coverage in the media had been global. It wasn't easy keeping him out of the papers.

The remaining items in his care were quietly turned into cash. He then turned his attention to the charitable bequests he favored.

Jesse was faced with the problems that most philanthropists must endure. Anonymity is difficult to maintain, in direct proportion to the amount of the gifts. Give to one worthwhile organization today, and another will pop up on your doorstep three hours later. Though he tried to remain anonymous, Jesse Horton's charitable gifts were too large to escape notice, and eventually, they attracted attention from unwelcome sources.

While arranging for the restoration of the synagogues in Lithuania, it was necessary to meet with the executive secretary of the Associated Jewish Charities of Baltimore.

Sylvia Glaser was not only very efficient but a charming thirty-five-year-old divorcee, brunette, with sparkling gray eyes and a keen intellect.

After completing the necessary paperwork, Sylvia plunged into discovering exactly who could be so generous in such a wonderful cause.

She struck up a conversation with Jesse as they sat together to sign the final paperwork for the transfer of the money. Sitting there as she spoke, a beaming Jesse was flattered by the attention of this attractive woman, who only ten minutes ago had not known him.

In her responsible position with the Associated, Sylvia met men and women with varied educational and experienced backgrounds. There were people who had known the horrors of the Holocaust, men who were CEOs of corporations and professors and schoolteachers. Compared to what she had heard that day with Jesse, they all paled. None that she had ever met before held such a story as Jesse did. She was sure of one thing: she wanted very much to get to know him much better.

At their initial meeting, she attempted to put Jesse at ease by having her clerk serve coffee in her inner office. Its intimacy was a ploy that she had utilized on many occasions. It had rules. But this time it was different.

Sylvia usually sat at a desk. After meeting Jesse initially, she had chosen a more informal place on the couch in her office, almost side by side with Jesse. Accustomed to putting people at ease, she soon had Jesse talking more about himself than he realized. In the course of the conversation, she did not completely stray from the topic of

Jesse's visit to her office, but she exuded an aura of femininity that she wanted Jesse to appreciate.

In her past, Sylvia had been briefly married. The relationship ended on an amicable and civil note. There had been other men over the years. None of them had ever held her attention the way that she was experiencing after less than thirty-five minutes in her office with Jesse. She found an excuse for another meeting with him the following week. She had chosen to use his reluctance regarding his name appearing on the buildings of the synagogues in Lithuania as a reason for another meeting.

This was not difficult to arrange. Jesse was as anxious as she was to meet again. Sylvia was a vastly different female than any he had ever known—vibrant, witty, clothed in an elegant aura that was beautiful while being unstated.

Sylvia knew that there were sexual overtones in their second meeting but recognized she needed a careful examination of their personality differences.

There was a vast chasm in their backgrounds. Jesse Horton had acquired very little formal education, but necessity made him absorb a working familiarity of several languages. Jesse had retained vestiges of the Yiddish accent of his birth, which to his ear, he found a touch embarrassing.

He constructed a wall of privacy to protect himself from problems, imaginary and real. With Marissa Volnick and Sara Flom, this wall of privacy had not been necessary; but with Sylvia Glaser, there was a vast difference.

When I saw them together for the first time, it was apparent that Sylvia realized that she could be a buffer in social interactions that could create inferiority attitudes in Jesse's mind.

Jesse flourished in the small intimate gatherings that Sylvia composed without any fanfare.

My own discerning eye did note the growing evidence of the physical attraction building between my friend Jesse and the alluring Sylvia Glazer. She presented the cool, sophisticated demeanor of the world that she had known her entire life, but there was a smoldering sexual fire ablaze when she was near Jesse.

The only hurdle to their mutuality, I could envision, was the wall of privacy that Jesse wanted to construct around his world. This wall had existed from his early childhood and could not be erased. Jesse had tried to banish forever the venom that remained in his memory of several decades past. These memories were undoubtedly part of his desire for privacy. The thought of the rape of his sister by Mayer Malkin would always remain. Equally hard to erase was the sight of the body of Julius Malkin, slain by Leah and their need to flee from the terrible scene.

# LEON MALKIN SMOLDERS

Julius Malkin had seen in his nephew Leon the nearest image of himself, among all the others in the remainder of the Malkin clan. He had a gift spotting the one relative who would honor and respect him after his death.

Leon examined the few facts that were available after Julius's corpse was discovered. World War II had torn apart the area of greater Minsk, and there had been little possibility to unearth finite clues. He had his suspicions but demanded that he find clear proof of what Jake the Horse thief had done before he could move on him.

The wealth of Julius Malkin's considerable estate greatly aided Leon in his quest to unearth the mysteries of his uncle's death. Once it had been discovered, the will gave considerable latitude to Leon in disbursement of funds. He diligently employed those funds in locating the individuals guilty of the murder. Julius Malkin's wealth had grown by the acquisition of jewelry and other works of art that had been easily transportable.

It was an extremely dangerous and often illegal scheme. As he worked, he was aware of the perils that such questionable activities involved.

But consequences be damned. He firmly believed that it was all worth the rewards.

For Leon, the idea that Julius took such risks raised the possibility that someone had murdered him to wrest the valuables he would often be carrying on his person.

The announcement that the Five Sisters' Rings were being displayed at the Louvre was big news in the jewelry art world. Since his wealth had come from being a member of that world, the news did not escape Leon's detection. The grouping of the entire set of Five Sisters' Rings Grouping attracted great attention among art lovers. The story of an eighteenth-century French nobleman creating the rings for his petulant daughters added to the interest of the general public. This notable event in both the art world as well as among the public was duly noted by Leon Malkin.

There had been strict efforts to keep secret the identity of the individuals who brought the Five Sisters' to auction. However, news that J. Mandelbaum was involved had become public knowledge. The Mandelbaum name is too well known, and Sam Mandelbaum himself had been seen in London at the time of the auction.

In the press, there was much talk about another party's involvement in the auction. It took several bribes, but Jesse's name stayed out of the picture.

As an interested observer, it appeared to me that Sylvia Glaser was exerting a growing and profound difference in Jesse's look on life. I could see that she had partially dispelled the wall of privacy that had engulfed him. To see him finally open up in such a way did my heart good. The man, my friend, deserved happiness after all that he had experienced in his life.

Over time, Jesse and Sylvia became noted at the art exhibits and the symphony as a couple. But that acknowledgment couldn't quench his necessity for being a part of life and not a mere observer.

In her position at the Associated Jewish Charities, Sylvia facilitated donations as well as frequently arranged for fetes to acknowledge contributors.

Her charm was unquestionable. Her arguments with Jake that he attend more events were unassailable.

"It would increase interest for your quest for donations if you attend a gala Sunday night with me. You will meet interesting and wealthy people, can I count on you, my dear?"

He would squirm and look for a way out of the commitment. "Sylvia, I'm so sorry, I'm not comfortable in crowds, but I do want to see more of you."

She would counter, "Well then, there are a few people I would like you to meet. I could arrange a cocktail party in my apartment. After all, I'm counting on you!"

For this particular party, I had heard from Sylvia. It was thought that my work in locating Lithuanian refugees and others might prove to be interesting.

She had also invited two couples, who were leaders in the Jewish Community.

As she told me, "They were fascinated by the tales of Jesse's experiences with the Jewish Partisan Group in Lithuania. Before the guests left, I made him promise that he would help me straighten up after they left."

This was obviously a plot for her to get Jesse alone.

She confided in me, "I know there is a physical attraction, so I made the most of it, and I suggested that the hour was late and he should spend the night with me. Somehow, he got the message. Well, I'm sure you can figure out what happened!" She smiled at the memory.

In his past life, as Jake, he had only known fleeting relationships with women. His love with the ill-fated Marissa in their first encounter came together intense, demanding on both, and mirrored the violence that surrounded them. To Jake Horvicz, Sara Flom was too much on the idea of capture or, even worse, of death that had hung over both, and their lovemaking was more of tenderness than sexuality.

Sylvia Glaser managed to find a crack in the wall of privacy that Jesse Horton constructed so carefully.

When the crack came, he wanted to bury himself into Sylvia, enjoying every part of her. She too was barely able to control this passion when they met.

I was astounded when I heard the sophisticated Sylvia murmur, "Oh, wow," when Jesse entered a room. I realized that whatever spark that existed between those two had become a raging inferno!

However, when the subject of money came up, he did his best to distance himself. That changed when Sylvia remarked on Jesse's support of the restoration of synagogues in Lithuania. She encouraged him to speak on the plight of Jews who had been left behind in Europe after the conclusion of World War II.

"There are many audiences in Baltimore who will thrill to hear of your part in rescuing Lithuanian Jews in the darkest days of the war. You must let others know of your barely suppressed tears when you guided these elderly Jews to freedom!"

Impulsively and fueled by what she felt was the validity of her vision, she grabbed Jesse's shoulders and said, "It's your duty to remind everyone of the *Jews Who Were Left Behind*!"

He agreed to speak only once. At that event, Jesse's tale of the underground in Lithuania during World War II enthralled the audiences. His tale of escaping captivity through the sewers of Vilna and joining the Partisan Group sparked quickening interest. The story of successfully moving the work of the Vilna Gaon out of Lithuania, by way of a submarine, brought nods of approval and cheers from every member of the audience.

When he concluded, his tale was met with standing ovations, as well as monetary pledges of support for his cause. As a personal note,

I can only say, that praise is due to Sylvia for her influence on Jesse's change of personality.

Jesse Horton became a sought-after speaker throughout the Jewish population of Baltimore and Washington. He concentrated on the topic he knew personally, the *Jews Who Were Left Behind*! Every time she listened to him speak, Sylvia glowed with happiness at the changes she recognized in Jesse.

I took it upon myself to insert a note of caution into Sylvia's happiness when I reminded her of the possible demons in Jake the Horse Thief's past. No matter what I said, no warning about what might happen, if others were to find him, was able to stifle her enthusiasm for what she had done.

After all we had done to keep Jesse's name out of the press during the auction, the greatest achievement of his life was going to betray him. It was his burning desire to help the *Jews Who Were Left Behind* that would lead to the Malkin family finally locating him in America.

When the inevitable happened, I was in Las Vegas at a stockholders' convention. It was the headline on a two-day old newspaper, which was sitting on the end table in the hotel lobby, that got my attention. What I read staggered me. Without even reading the story, I knew immediately what it was about.

"ASSAILANT KILLS WOMAN AT CHARITY FUNCTION—COMPANION CRITICAL!"

The brief paragraph that followed the headline told me everything that I needed to know:

> An assassin attacked two people leaving Baltimore Hyatt—Sylvia Glaser, slain, and companion, Jesse Horton, in serious condition. Gunman killed by Baltimore Police after gun battle.

Their identities were confirmed in the body of the story.

> Ms. Glaser was executive director of Maryland Associated Jewish Charities. Mr. Horton has been active in local charitable causes. The assailant was a twenty-three-year-old foreign transfer student, Joshua Malkin, a citizen of Minsk, Belarus.
>
> Police report the assailant moved quickly from between parked cars on Howard Street in front of Hyatt Hotel and fired five shots at the victims. Two Baltimore policemen cornered the gunman, and after a brief gun battle, Malkin was slain.

When I finished reading the story, I collapsed into wracking sobs.

# THE DETAILS OF THE ACT

When Jesse and Sylvia Glaser left the Downtown Hyatt Hotel, a gunman had jumped from behind a parked car and fired five shots at them. One shot tore through Sylvia's midsection, killing her instantly. Three more bullets struck Jesse Horton, leaving him critically wounded.

Two Baltimore policemen quickly cornered the gunman, and after a brief gun battle, the assailant was slain. The assassin was identified as a foreign transfer student, Joshua Malkin, twenty-three years old. His home was listed as Minsk, Belarus.

Contact was made with Leon Malkin of Minsk, Belarus, who immediately flew to Baltimore. Once there, he confirmed that the assassin's body was, indeed, his son Josh.

In a move that caused many to question the motive behind his son's action, Mr. Malkin did not offer condolences to the family of Sylvia Glaser. Despite numerous requests, he refused to be interviewed by the Baltimore or national media.

When Leon Malkin returned to Belarus with his son's body, he was deluged with questions by the media in Minsk. Unlike his experience in Baltimore, he chose to address their inquiries.

Despite the specificity of the questions, the answers he gave were cryptic and brusque. In the middle of all that he said, there was one statement that puzzled the television and newspaper viewers.

Out of the blue, he had said without prompting, "I'm getting revenge for you, Julius!"

The media went crazy with speculation.

It was only after an intrepid and driven reporter dug deep into the old files kept by newspapers that served both Pinsk and Minsk that a theory began to emerge. It was based on files that told of the strange mystery of the killing of Julius Malkin, many decades earlier.

Back in the States, the murder had moved into a hot spotlight driven by ratings and public demand. Every person involved in the murders found their lives under the microscope of media attention.

The *Wall Street Journal* ran a lengthy article, making the connection that the Julius Malkin Investment fund of Liechtenstein was reported to be the financing source of the Malkin Construction Corporation of Belarus, which has been one of the leaders in the restoration and reconstruction of Greater Minsk.

The public followed Jesse's condition obsessively. The *Baltimore Sun* reported that the emergency staff at Johns Hopkins Hospital had managed to contain the damage to Jesse Horton's bodily functions. However, the distinct possibility of brain damage made it necessary to place him in an induced coma.

The neurological team at Hopkins insisted that through it all, Jesse should remain at the hospital for intensive treatment and observation. Finally, after what seemed an eternity, he was removed from the induced coma, and Jesse began talking.

At first it was confusing. Always caught in the idea of a dual identity, it was hard to figure out who was actually talking. Was it Jesse, or was it Jake? Or was it Jake talking to Jesse? The team of neurologists knew very little of Jesse's life story. That he had legally adopted the name Jesse Horton, after answering to Jacob Horvicz for his formative years, was no longer a mystery.

Even though the neurologists were not yet aware of the extent of damage to his brain, they tried to assure me that there is no possibility of a "Jekyll and Hyde" condition in Jesse's future.

After some testing, it was determined that it was time to inform Jesse of Sylvia's death. When he was given the news, the attending physician was met with only a blank stare that lay across the face of his patient.

Who was he? Was he Jesse who acquired a fortune by dubious means and used the fortune to become an American?

Was he Jesse, the lover of a woman named Sylvia?

Or was he Jake Horvicz, who rescued his sister from hell?

Was he Jake, who risked his life to save Lithuanian Jews during World War II?

There was even greater confusion when he was told that Sylvia was killed in the attack that almost killed him. I could not tell if my friend was Jesse Horton or Jake the Horse Thief.

Two weeks after he had been taken out of the coma, his health took a swing for the better. The crisis had seemed to pass. I was finally able to briefly visit Jesse in his room.

The image of such a strong man, lain so low, nearly drove me to tears. I believe there was some recognition in his eyes when he saw me, but he couldn't respond verbally.

In time it was the fact that he had always kept himself in good physical condition that led to a partial recovery. I must use the word *partial*, for there was damage to his brain—the degree of which made a complete recovery uncertain.

When Jesse had visited Baltimore for the first time, he had told me his story. Almost immediately, we had developed a deep friendship, as if we were fated to meet.

After several congenial meetings, he had said, "I am an orphan with no known relatives. There are things that demand attention. I'm asking you to assist me in all vital consequences and papers."

Struck by his trust in me, I felt privileged to be even considered as such by a man who had risked life and limb to save Jews in war-torn Lithuania. Without even thinking about his request, I agreed to it. Ben Bernstein had been the right choice to serve as Jesse's lawyer. He expertly handled all details concerning a will as well as the advanced directives that accommodate his wishes in the unlikely event that end-of-life conditions arise.

In response to his request, I—Robert Hurwitz—had become Jesse Horton's legal protector. It was no problem for me to hold a clear conscience of that title's responsibilities.

I could have never anticipated what I would be faced with, following the shooting.

Other than his confused mental state, Jesse had made excellent physical progress. The doctors were not contemplating a brain operation until he had undergone extensive observation at Hopkins world-famous facility.

However, now that he was conscious, Jesse was giving no thought to the doctor's orders that he spend any more days at Hopkins! Just forty-five days after he had emerged from the coma, he was found alone on Aisquith and Orleans Streets, two blocks from Johns Hopkins Hospital, before the attendants were able to return him to the hospital!

With some trepidation and noting the difficulty in controlling him, the doctors dismissed him after another forty-five days. When he returned to his apartment on Park Heights Avenue, located on Baltimore's northwest side, I hired a male nurse to watch him and to attend to his needs.

Within thirty-six hours of returning home, he managed to evade detection and escaped down a back stairwell to a parking lot, where his small Chevrolet was parked. Jesse had previously hidden a spare key somewhere in the steel body of the car.

Within minutes, Jesse was gone!

There was great consternation when the dozing caregiver alerted me. I immediately rushed to Jesse's apartment. In the frantic moments after I arrived, I discovered that Jesse had taken only a few objects. They had apparently been packed in a duffel bag that was also missing from his apartment.

After I did an extensive search of his apartment, I discovered that there were only three items that were missing. He had taken the old, weather-beaten prayer book that Rabbi Vilnish gave to him, the pouch that originally belonged to the stranger on the road to Minsk, and a small address book.

Those were the only definite objects missing.

# THE CONCLUSION

For the next twelve months, I engaged in what ultimately proved to be a fruitless quest. Finally, I had to admit to myself that Jesse had perished or, at the very least, had somehow disappeared. I would never see my dear friend again, but it wasn't for lack of trying.

Did he plan his escape? I can't truly tell if he did. As Jake, he had extensive experience in varying environments. He knew the empty road as well as the metropolis. That said, what were the reasons for removing himself from everything that was familiar and loved?

Was guilt the reason? As Jesse Horton, he stated that he did not feel any guilt when Leah killed the stranger. The wealth that Jesse Horton realized after Leah's action was considerable. Has the brain injury he incurred upon the attempted assassination in Baltimore thrust him back into Jake the Horse Thief's cognition?

His life had become vastly different when his sister had bashed in the brains of Julius Malkin.

Did Jake believe that he was the cause of tragedy in the women he had known? There were bitter tears when he parted with Sara Flom. The State of Israel promised her the secure future Jesse Horton wasn't ready to provide. Leah and Marissa and finally, Sylvia met tragic deaths by being part of his intimate world.

Does he know exactly who he is?

Was it fear?

Jake had known since those fateful days on the road to Minsk that there were those who held decades-long motives for revenge.

Those motives had come true as they assassinated Sylvia Glaser and almost killed him.

Was it retribution?

Was Jake on the road, exacting a war of revenge? If so, where was he, and with what persons? Would his own revenge ultimately satisfy something within himself?

Was it possible that his brain had been altered by the assassin's bullets? Hopkins doctors had been unable to give anyone a definitive answer. All they had was that chilling blank stare on Jesse Horton's face when he was awakened from the induced coma.

I couldn't answer these questions, and I don't believe anyone else could.

Every effort was made to find Jesse, through legal channels and personal investigation. After a year, I gave up. There was never any finding of his death, and rightly or wrongly, why should I interfere with his wish not to be found? Prior to his escape, he had often expressed a wish for privacy, and I believed it was time to respect his wish.

Twenty years after Jesse's disappearance, my life had gone on. I still thought of him every day, and Sylvia as well.

Out of the blue, one day there was an unusual occurrence that I couldn't quite understand. It was at place that I have been a member for many years, Temple Abraham.

It happened at the bar mitzvah of a friend's son. The temple administrator, Morris Berman, pulled me aside and told me something I had never heard before.

He began, "Each year, on a particular date, the temple receives a generous cashier's check on the anniversary of the death of someone named in the letter as Leah Horvicz. I took it for granted for a few years, assuming that she was someone who had preceded my time as a leader. Then one day, I became curious. Getting such a generous check every year was very puzzling. So one day, I examined temple records going back over fifty years and could find no record of such a person!"

He lifted his hands and shrugged his shoulders as if to say, "What the heck does this all mean?"

Continuing, he said, "The money was always given anonymously, and there was no one to acknowledge."

After hearing this peculiar news, I knew without question that there was only one person who could be the anonymous donor. The most interesting man I have ever known may be still alive, and I must find what has happened to him!

As was his habit, Morris Berman photocopied the front of every check the temple received. The cashier's checks for the Leah Horvicz memorial held no clue other than the name of the various banks that issued the cashier's checks.

With only this meager evidence, I determined that after a twenty-year break, I would attempt to find Jesse Horton, also known to some as Jake the Horse Thief.

Why did I decide to embark on such an endeavor?

My friends think I'm crazy. One teased me by saying that I have an "ego-driven mentality." Another suggested, "Hey, Bob, go look for the lost ark!"

I laughed off these jibes and considered what is paramount in my life at this moment.

The thought of the most interesting man I've ever known crowded my brain. Jesse and I were such good friends that he had me appointed as executor of his estate, and as such, I had already exhausted every possibility in a vain effort to find him. Or even his corpse.

It was time again to think of how much I knew Jesse, as well as how much I knew Sylvia Glaser.

# JAKE THE HORSE THIEF

I believe that, in his lifetime, I knew Jesse Horton better than anyone. Shlomo Levitz, aka Sid Levy, was a great comrade for Jake Horvicz, the warrior for Jewish freedom. I only have stories regarding the Jake of those days. He led a different life before he came to America and landed in my apartment as Jesse Horton. Here he related to me the most important events of his life.

Jesse attempted to settle very intimate policies and regards concerning his present and future life and death. I have said enough about that already. Sylvia requires much more to be said.

In the few years that they knew each other, I am positive that Sylvia made a lifelong impression on Jesse Horton. Sexually, Jesse never knew anyone like her. I could only sense the physical nature of this. As a red-blooded male, I could see a hunger that any man would envy when Sylvia saw Jesse.

Sylvia too was the only woman who apparently was ever able to crack the wall of privacy he had constructed around himself. She recognized that Jesse worried about his foreign accent. It was not Yiddish; it wasn't Russian; and it couldn't' be identified as Czech. It was an amalgam of the lands of much of Eastern Europe. He desperately wanted to speak proper and good English. She pursued the effort to help Jesse while not making him too conscious of her efforts.

Perhaps it is not exceptional that Sylvia appears to resemble the description of Leah Horvicz that Jake had given to me. Sylvia was approximately five foot eight. She had long dark hair and beautiful dark eyes. Her figure was definitely the type that males give a second look. Together with Jesse's six-foot-one build and curly red hair, they made a striking couple. The vision of Jake and Sylvia together, before the assassin's bullets struck them down, brings tears and sobs every time I think of them.

Reluctantly, I've had Jesse Horton declared deceased. But after all this time, how can I neglect pursuing any avenue of discovering what has happened to my friend?

In searching for my friend, the first thought that crossed my mind was, whether I was trying to find Jesse Horton, the handsome middle-aged man who charmed audiences with tales of his past in Europe, or has he reverted to Jake the Horse Thief?

When the emergency vehicle left the scene of the attempted assassination on the Baltimore Street, I knew without a doubt that *Jesse Horton was struggling to stay alive!* The close proximity of the great Johns Hopkins Medical Center to the place where he was shot proved to be vital in those crucial moments. A bullet had passed through the side of Jesse's brain, and a bullet fragment was removed in the emergency room. It could never be certain to what degree this injury had affected Jesse's thoughts or personality.

The fact that Jesse sent checks on the exact day commemorating Leah's death was a reminder to Jesse of the love that his sister and he had together as children and would treasure forever. Also, the checks would seem to indicate that he had a great facility on that part of his brain, but it left vexing questions of what he did in the years that followed and what he did or did not do.

Perhaps my ego bothered me. After all, wasn't I his great friend and confidant? He had, in great haste, left almost everything to me connecting himself in what appears to be Jesse Horton's life. In attempting to find him, should I search for clues in his actions and behavior as Jake the Horse Thief or as Jesse Horton?

When Jesse Horton hurriedly left his apartment in Baltimore, it was obvious that he had no wish to be found! It is nothing more than a guess what his injured brain had done to his ability to behave insidiously.

I immediately thought, *As Jake the Partisan Fighter in Lithuania, he had exhibited his ability to behave rationally.*

I questioned, "Have the instincts he has acquired since his flight from Pinsk made Jake extremely difficult to follow?"

It is evident that I was going to have a difficult time finding my friend. It is only due to the knowledge that he has suffered a serious injury, and one that he may not even realize its full extent, that I am determined to find him.

Having knowledge of the origins of the cashier's check sent to Temple Abraham, I had the barest of clues to follow. Not discouraged, I made plans. I bribed girlfriends by taking them with me and stopping at fun resorts on my fruitless efforts to find my friend. I was accompanied to Nashville, New Orleans, Hot Springs, Arkansas, and Denver, with charming companions, until Santa Fe, New Mexico.

My money didn't run out. But in each place we visited, my obsession ceased to be fun for Cynthia, Barbara, Lois, and ultimately, Mae. At each stop, I spent hours investigating possible sightings of Jesse.

After visiting the banks that had issued cashier's checks to Jesse Horton, I realized that most stops would only be hunches. From the ancient clues, there appeared to be a close time element between Santa Fe to Phoenix on the dates listed on the cashier's checks. When I dug through the decades-old dusty files in Phoenix, I uncovered a sheriff's report that someone had attempted to steal belongings from a man with distinctive red hair, bushy red beard, and a slight accent.

That individual overpowered the unlucky thief at the bus stop in Phoenix. In the deputy's charging document, the redhead gave his name as Jake H…The last name was not decipherable on the years-old document. It was notable that the man who had been attacked had refused to bring charges. After thanking the sheriff's deputy, this rock-ribbed guy had climbed aboard the next bus going westward.

This was the final clue of my quest. I took a chance and drove westward on Route 10. At Tonopah, the trail—such as it was—appeared to have ended. There was one event that the old-timers in Tonopah were anxious to still want to talk about. They related that a silver mining company in the nearby White Flat Mountains suffered a huge explosion eight years ago. The mine operators seemed to have been in a great hurry to abandon the disaster. They did leave one sad memory of the men who had worked the mine.

One-half mile from the site of the explosion, there was an area of hastily dug grave sites. Earthen mounds with slabs of wood marked the final resting places of the unfortunate men who had perished in the disaster. I was astonished when I saw, scrawled on a slab of wood, a Jewish Star and the barely decipherable name "Jesse Horton."

What had happened in Phoenix eight years ago went a long way to finding Jesse's last resting place. Tonopah was the first bus stop on Route 10 going westward eight years ago. When I described Jesse, no one could remember anyone that fit the description; it was too long ago.

The big event of eight years past was the mine disaster. I had been on the trail of Jesse Horvicz for so much time that I wasn't going to pass up this possibility, so I looked real hard at what had occurred at the mine explosion in the White Flat Mountains eight years ago, and I had succeeded in my quest.

I had found Jake the Horse Thief, and I cried.

# JESSE'S LAST WORDS

When I stopped crying, I thought about something Old Ike Parker said about a strange occurrence a few days before the silver mine blew in the White Tank Mountains.

"Two men in a brand-new Chevy truck stopped for gas here, in Tonopah, and had looked at a map in the store."

I figured I had come this far in my quest for Jake the Horse Thief, so I looked into the ancient county records to locate the county sheriff of that time.

According to the sheriff, the men and the truck completely disappeared. This was unusual in these parts, so I tried to locate the sheriff. He had died two years ago, but his widow was willing to talk to me after a little bit of sweet-talking.

"Pa said that when the mine blew, there was a helluva mess. He was suspicious that the two men who stopped in Tonopah in a brand-new truck could have had something to do with the mine disaster."

She had begun to shake as she tried to remember more details. Knowing that I was close, I urged her to continue.

After a minute of reflection, she continued, "Pa never found a connection to the mine disaster, and the Chevy truck completely disappeared. But after the federal mine examiners left, Pa later found something they missed."

I grew excited, so I urged her to tell me more, and she said, "Years later, in what must have been a garbage dump at the mine, he found this sack with a little notebook inside, so he saved it."

Before I could say another word, the widow sternly said, "Now, mind yourself, I keep a clean household, so I cleaned all the garbage off the sack and got rid of the garbage odor!"

She let me look at the sack, which was made of what was once a sturdy material. Inside was a small notebook that looked familiar, in spite of its age.

I immediately offered to buy the sack and the little notebook, but the widow stopped me and said, "I don't want this ancient bit of trash, but I'd appreciate it if you could give me a lift to the general store."

I was very happy to give her a lift and wait until she made a few purchases. When she was done, I drove her back home. The entire time, I couldn't wait to get back in my car and look at the notebook. I recognized that it wasn't a notebook. It was a siddur, a Jewish prayer book!

The notebook was written in the same cryptic style that Jake the Horse Thief had employed in the little siddur (prayer book) that he carried with him for the remainder of his life!

My heart skipped a beat.

In several parts of the notebook, the pages were stuck together with time and moisture. Fearing that I would damage the small book, I stopped trying to break them apart until I could return to my home in Baltimore.

Once home, I found a professional who worked with damaged books, who I knew could separate the pages. I was close to finding the most interesting person I have ever known. The fact that he had written this after disappearing made me doubly anxious to absorb it.

There was a minor problem in translating what Jesse had written. He scribbled all the information in Hebrew and Yiddish. With the aid of a rabbi, we were able to develop an effective and what we believed to be accurate translation.

When Jesse Horton left us, it was with nothing but the best of memories he had for Baltimore and for me, Bob Hurwitz. Jesse and I had formed a bond that would never be broken. I felt a deep sickness in my stomach when I discovered he was gone.

However, he wanted to put some distance between himself and those he had grown to know in Baltimore. Jesse did not want anyone else to pay the penalty of the wrath of the Malkins.

This warrior of battles in Lithuania in World War II was not afraid of facing the Malkins.

It was the memory of Sylvia Glaser meeting her death because she was with him that could not be erased.

Jesse, and as Jacob Horvicz, had always wanted a wall of privacy. Apparently, as much as he loved our friendship, he believed he had to separate himself from all that he had known. To me, Bob Hurwitz, this was a bitter pill to swallow.

The small notebook had much to say. Much of what could be translated was in the form of places he had visited and money he spent at each location. Jesse endeavored to visit, at his own solitary pace, the America he dreamed about when he was a member of the Jewish Partisan Group in Lithuania.

One of the first experiences noted in Jesse's little book began in West Virginia. He was dismayed by the poor living conditions of the miners who worked the coal mines. He was particularly disturbed by the poor educational facilities for the coal miners' children. He made an anonymous contribution to the miners' union to improve the education of the school miners' children.

As he traveled, Jesse made similar donations in Erie, Pennsylvania; Tulsa, Oklahoma; Boulder, Colorado; and other rural environments in order to aid the family of miners. As to his motivation for helping them, the only reason I could find was that American miners apparently fit the same pattern of life to Jesse, as those who were left behind in Lithuania. Even among the miners, he did not appear to have left any permanent relationships.

However, there were a few notations that gave a hint that he did not become asexual in his curious travels.

On one page, he noted, "Pitts. 50 motel Laura, 2n."

Did this mean that he met Laura and spent two nights with her? Another notation, "Den. 92 Mindy hot."

Could this possibly have meant that he spent ninety-two dollars with Mindy in a hotel, or was Mindy a "hot number"? Over the years, there were frequent other cryptic notes similar to the above.

Of course, it must be said that Jesse did not expect anyone else would see the little spiral notebook. The question is, Why did he, who so valued privacy, carry and make any record of his travels in the little book?

Since leaving Baltimore, Jesse had gone to great lengths to become invisible to anyone in his world. He practiced any artifice he had learned in Europe to avoid personal notice and to protect those he treasured. His travels in America were carefully planned, but to no avail.

Jesse's wandering through America was upset one night outside a motel near El Paso, Texas. He wrote these words in his small notebook.

"A rapidly approaching black pickup truck slowed momentarily and fired a gun burst at me as I unloaded my rental car. One bullet tore through the duffel bag I was carrying, narrowly missing me. The black pickup truck did not hesitate to assess damage but rapidly vanished into the darkness. By the time police arrived at the scene, I hid the only evidence of gun play. I didn't want any mention of the incident in the media."

Obviously, Jesse wanted to maintain his privacy, and he knew this was not a random occurrence. It was another example of the Malkins' never-ending desire for revenge.

As he always did, Jesse believed he must face the problem alone.

The last contact in the small notebook was indicative of the other forces that drove Jesse.

A small silver mining operation had been organized in the mountains just north of Tonopah. Jesse had learned that the mine employed many young Native Americans. Word spread that the pay was low and conditions poor and unsafe. For many years, Jesse had been a champion protecting miners' families, so he began quietly investigating the silver mine operation in the White Tank Mountains.

No one could remember seeing anyone fitting the description of Jesse Horton passing through Tonopah, but the records of the mine operators indicate that he visited the mine. His notebook confirmed that he intended to investigate the treatment of the miners. That was the last legible notation in his little book.

When the silver mine blew, its explosion could be heard and felt in distant Tonopah. Not all the dead bodies were recognizable when the mine blew in the White Tank Mountain's disaster.

Jesse Horton had been wearing a neckpiece with a Jewish Star emblem that made his body easy to identify. Several of the Native American boys had tattoo marks of their tribe, enabling relatives to claim their bodies for burial in Native American soil. However, there were several bodies that were never identified or claimed.

There were two bodies that were not claimed and were puzzling. Those corpses were not wearing miners' clothing. I've drawn a mental picture that those two bodies were from the Malkin clan, hunting Jesse.

The mysterious disappearance of the black pickup truck with two men was never solved. The truck, with two men inside, was last seen heading in the direction of the silver mine. Maybe the sad bloody tale of the mortal enmity of the Malkins and Jake the Horse Thief ended in the explosion that rocked the mountains of Arizona.

## ROBERT STEINBERG

A life that had begun in Byelorussia seventy-five years ago for Jacob Horvicz ended in a shallow grave for Jesse Horton on a mountaintop in Arizona.

Call him Jesse Horton.

Or call him Jake the Horse Thief, the defender of *Jews Who Were Left Behind*.

But I will never forget him.

# EPILOGUE

My name is Robert Hurwitz, and I have been the narrator for the latter part of the life story of Jake the Horse Thief. I have known him as Jesse Horton during the years after he arrived in the United States.

Before that, I only knew him as he portrayed himself to me, or from information that could be gleaned from verifiable historic sources.

The following opinions and observations are a result of my own construction. For brevity, I will only call him Jake in the following paragraphs.

That Jake was a hero on several occasions, I have no doubt. He did not ask for praise at any time, except when he was importuned to do so to raise funds for a worthy cause. That singular occasion attracted a clan that wished to avenge the murder of a family member. The murder was committed by Jake's sister, Leah. Therein lies the question of Jake's character.

Jake never reported any facts of the murder. That he believed the murder was warranted, he left no doubt. Regardless, Jake did not leave any information concerning the location or disposition of the victim's body. There is one indisputable fact of the murder; it eventually made Jake Horvicz a very wealthy man.

There is some evidence that at moments after the murder, Jake had some thoughts about the occasion. However, those moments were colored by the thought of the grief being felt by his sister, Leah, after the murder occurred.

Jake constructed a wall of privacy around his person. It is impossible to know what thoughts of the murder were seared in Jake's mind. However, the wealth that he accumulated was incontrovertible.

He left many charitable gifts anonymously during his lifetimes. To this day, there are many miners' families or unions that are unaware of his charity. It is tragic that on the one occasion in Baltimore when he publicly talked of his charity, it led to his lover's death and his retreating into anonymity.

Should his body be disinterred and memorialized somewhere else, or should the remains of Jake, aka Jesse Horton, be left on a dusty hillside in Arizona?

THE END

# ABOUT THE AUTHOR

Robert Steinberg was six months into writing *Jake the Horse Thief* before he realized that he was being inspired by his maternal grandparents. It was his grandparents' good fortune to leave Lithuania before Nazi Germany overran Mid-Europe. His grandfather could have been just like Jake. His grandmother got a job in a cigar manufacturing plant in Baltimore. A matchmaker suggested a beau to her. She refused because the prospect looked too old to her. However, the picture of a younger brother excited interest, and it didn't take long before his grandfather won her affection. They were married in 1892. They happily came to Baltimore and had seven children, all raised as orthodox Jews. One of the grandchildren of their brood is the author, Robert Steinberg.